PASSIONATE BARGAIN

Pierce St. James lay back on one elbow on the divan, staring at Gabrielle. "You propose to purchase my services as a lover, for money?"

"Not as an *actual* lover. As a lover in name only," she clarified, adding, "And only for a few weeks."

The notion captured his jaded fancy, insinuating itself into his highly developed sense of the absurd. *In name only.* The term applied to marriages, not affairs. And it was that very fact—the perfect irony of pretending to sin—that appealed to the social scapegrace in him. What a delicious game that could be. And how very interesting of her to propose such a thing.

He slid his gaze over her curvaceous form and lush, intriguing mouth . . . which just now was set with concentration.

"Agreed," he told her. "But I think a bargain as unique as this should be sealed with something more befitting than a clasp of hands."

Before Gabrielle realized what he intended, he had pulled her into his arms and was lowering his mouth to hers. . . .

Bantam Books by Betina Krahn

The Last Bachelor

The Perfect Mistress

Betina Krahn

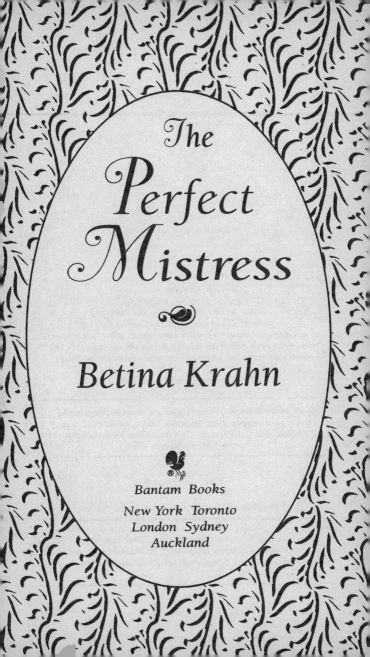

Bantam Books

New York Toronto
London Sydney
Auckland

THE PERFECT MISTRESS

A Bantam Book / October 1995

ISBN 0-553-56523-0

Published simultaneously in the United States and Canada

Bantam Books are published by Bantam Books, a division of Bantam Doubleday Dell
Publishing Group, Inc. Its trademark, consisting of the words "Bantam Books" and the
portrayal of a rooster, is Registered in U.S. Patent and Trademark Office and in other
countries. Marca Registrada. Bantam Books, 1540 Broadway, New York, New York
10036.

PRINTED IN THE UNITED STATES OF AMERICA

RAD 0 9 8 7 6 5 4 3 2 1

For those special people
whose generous help and friendship
have made this book possible:

WENDY MCCURDY
RUTH COHEN
and SHARON STONE

With love and gratitude.

The Perfect Mistress

1

London / April, 1883

"You're in for it now, my girl."

The majordomo's whisper resonated in the quiet hallway as he reached for the polished door handle.

One of the massive double doors swung back, and the low drone of voices and the scent of perfume rolled from the opening. Gabrielle LeCoeur stiffened and cast a dread-filled look at the stone-faced houseman. He narrowed his eyes and gave her a nudge that propelled her through the opening into her mother's boudoir. The latch clicked softly

behind her and she was left alone to face her fate . . .
Gabrielle in the lioness's den.

The large chamber was filled with the soft glow of evening light, grandly baroque furnishings, and the pervasive aura of woman at her most sensory and elemental. Every curve of the polished mahogany and drape of silk damascene . . . every hue, from delicate mauve to rich burgundy . . . and every texture, from lush velvet to glittering gilt, was contrived to recall the chamber's owner and prime occupant, Rosalind LeCoeur. The lighting and furnishings were carefully arranged to direct every eye, from every possible perspective, to her. Gabrielle's gaze traveled along one of those cannily composed lines of sight toward her mother. She groaned silently.

There sat Rosalind on a round silk divan flanked by sprays of imported spring flowers. She was surrounded by three other women, each attired in a floral silk dress with an elaborate bustle and an extravagant "picture" hat.

"I take it you have recovered from your little 'upset,'"
her mother said, waving her into a chair with a superbly manicured hand. The remark was more an order than an observation.

As Gabrielle complied, four pairs of experienced feminine eyes scrutinized every drape and furl of her gown and every curve and line of her body beneath it. She perched stiffly on the edge of the high-backed parlor chair placed strategically before them. She hadn't known *they* would be here: her mother's bosom friends. It boded ill.

"Really, Gabrielle, getting sick in front of him . . .
very nearly *on* him!" Her mother rose and stared at her with consternation. "How could you behave so toward a gentleman who has come to seek your hand?"

It wasn't the sort of question that required an answer. Gabrielle bit her tongue to keep from declaring that her hand had not been mentioned—though a number of her other parts had been quite thoroughly discussed. It wasn't her fault she had gotten sick, she thought mutinously; the overheated wretch had smelled of garlic and that putrid ambergris. And if he had kept his tongue to himself during that interminable kiss, she might have managed without almost giving up her din—

"You not only failed to captivate the count, you may have put him off altogether," her mother said, pacing back and forth, turning so quickly that her tea gown billowed about her. "A man of his station would never find such a green and unpredictable girl appealing. And after all my efforts on your behalf—that expensive schooling and travel, those endless lessons and countless brushes of culture. What good are they if you do not display them to advantage? . . . What have you to say for yourself, young lady?"

What *did* she have to say? She hadn't wanted to believe that it truly would come to this: her education, her experiences, her talents, and even her very body were to be employed for the sole purpose of enticing and pleasuring a man. But it *had* come to this. It was now or never, she realized. Squaring her shoulders, she took a deep breath and met her mother's narrowed eyes.

"I didn't like him," she said.

"Didn't *like* him?" Roses bloomed in Rosalind's fashionably pale cheeks as she exchanged looks of astonishment with her lady friends. "See here, Gabrielle . . . he is by far your best prospect." She stalked closer, visually probing Gabrielle's person. "Like it or not, we must get on with settling your future. You are nearly nineteen years old. You cannot go on wearing hair bows and white voile forever!"

White voile. Gabrielle looked down at the frothy white confection of a gown that was fashioned in a sly but unmistakable parody of a young girl's schoolroom pinafore: ruffles over the shoulders and an apronlike front that darted in snugly at the waist to reveal attributes that declared the wearer to be beyond schoolroom days. When she glanced up, the others were staring with discernment at those same ruffles and darts and at the waist and bosom they both concealed and displayed.

"You have quite lost the 'baby fat,' *ma petite*," one of her mother's friends crooned in French accents. "Not that you have not blossomed well. . . ."

"No offense, my dear, but you're on the brink of outgrowing your virginal appeal," a second declared with a look down a patrician nose. "And one must never outgrow one's virginal appeal before one disposes advantageously of one's virginity."

"Take it from me, lovey," the third advised in countrified tones, "there ain't nothin' men find more tiresome than a stringy *old* virgin."

Gabrielle's skin caught fire at their assessment of her perishable value as an object of desire. She squeezed her hands together in her lap as she struggled to control her rising anger. "Perhaps . . . I'm not ready."

"Not ready?" Rosalind began to perceive the hostility beneath Gabrielle's embarrassment, and she straightened with alarm. "What an absurd notion. You are well educated, suitably accomplished, impeccably well mannered, and certainly of the right *age*. It is your destiny, my dear, and you must reconcile yourself to it."

"Reconcile herself? *Mon Dieu*—she should fall to her knees in gratitude!"

"Not every young miss gets such a fine chance!"

"She should be preparing for the singular and incomparable joy of a woman's life . . . *a man!*"

"And a splendid destiny it is." Rosalind resumed her discourse, adopting a pose of subtle drama, her arms open wide. "The swell of grand passion . . . the searing delight of being in love . . . the thrill of being desired . . . the absorbing intricacy of romance . . . the rapture of being crowned queen of a man's heart and made the center of his life . . . Nothing on earth can surpass the pleasures of spending sweet, stolen hours in the arms of your one true love."

"Not to mention the lovely gifts."

"Th' clothes."

"The stock portfolio."

"This is a matter of the utmost importance, Gabrielle." Her mother pinned her with a look that fairly crackled with imperative. "The count is admirably suited . . . a man with a thorough knowledge of the world, a generous nature, and an enormous bank balance." Then she hastily added: "And he is so gentlemanly and well favored. Just the sort to steal a girl's heart and keep her madly enthralled for years to come."

"So delightfully bowlegged and bulbous-nosed," Gabrielle muttered before she could stop herself. "And with the way he spits and sprays when he speaks, I should certainly never want for something to water my pot plants."

"Water your—" With a furious motion, Rosalind drew a handkerchief from the bosom of her gown and began to dab at her reddening face. "It is clear that you have no notion of the pitfalls that lie in wait for a headstrong, disobedient young girl who faces the world alone. You must submit to the guidance of your elders—we who have your interests at heart and know what sort of choices must be made. A young girl cannot possibly know her own mind in such intricate matters."

Every word struck a nerve in Gabrielle as she struggled to keep silent. How could they possibly have any idea what she knew or wanted or cared about? She had been back in London, in her mother's house, for only three months. Three months out of the last twelve years. And now her mother could not wait to be rid of her . . . again.

"Well, I cannot speak for other young women," she

said, curling her hands into icy fists around the white ruffles on her lap. "But I certainly know my own mind. I *am* nineteen—old enough to know what I want. And it certainly is not the count!"

Rosalind blinked, alarmed at her daughter's unprecedented display of defiance. "If you find the wealthy and generous count so objectionable—dearest heaven, Gabrielle —just what sort of man *do* you want?"

"A man who saves his money and doesn't gamble, hunt, or drink to excess. A man who is dignified and presentable in public and will have the decency not to burden me overmuch with his presence in private," Gabrielle proclaimed, watching her mother flinch as the words struck. "I want a man who belongs to the Athenaeum and Liberal clubs and spends every evening there, engrossed in Voltaire or politics or the price of pork. I want a man who tends his own business and doesn't bother me with it . . . or with his innermost thoughts and longings."

Rosalind drained of color and stumbled back a step. "Dearest heaven, Gabrielle, that sounds like . . . a . . . a *husband*."

Gabrielle met her mother's horrified gaze and braced.

"Precisely." She swallowed hard then came straight out with it: "I don't want a grand romance, a thrilling passion, or a life of intoxicating love. I want to be *married*."

She had finally said it. After three interminable months of being groomed to take her place in her mother's world, it was in the open at last. She didn't want the kind of life her mother had. She didn't want to be a *mistress*; she wanted to be a *wife*.

Her declaration was met with stunned silence.

"I am sorry if my desire to marry disappoints you," she said, summoning every last spark of her courage. "But, I simply am not constituted for life as a great courtesan, like you." She glanced determinedly at the others before turning back to her mother to announce: "I . . . don't have the juices for it."

Rosalind blanched, couldn't seem to expel her breath, and after a moment, crumpled gracefully onto the lush brocade of the divan. One lady friend rushed to her side and patted her cheek, another hurried to ring the bell, and the third flew to search the dressing table for smelling salts and toilet water.

"Wicked girl—how could ye speak such to yer mother? Marriage, o' all things!"

"A vile affront to *l'amour*."

"A cold, filthy bargain . . . a veritable desert of duty and dullness."

They fanned Rosalind with a silk pillow, waved a small blue bottle under her nose, and wetted a handkerchief with cooling toilet water to dab on her temples. She soon revived, and once assured that her condition was not serious, the trio of experienced courtesans turned their attentions to Gabrielle, determined to set her straight on the nature of marriage.

"You have not the slightest notion what wives must endure, *ma petite*." The Frenchwoman, Genevieve, shook a finger at her. "They must bear both the weight of a man's name, as well as the hideous rules of society."

"Wives mus' bear with th' evil tongues of gossips and jealous rivals and well-meanin' friends," the country girl, Clementine, declared. "They get saddled with bawlin' kids an' cantankerous relations at holidays and old bores at parties . . . an' have to sit through charity meetin's an' church—"

"A man's devotion"—aristocratic Ariadne took it up with a vengeance—"his passion, his generosity—is always directed at the source of his pleasure and happiness . . . his *mistress*, not his wife!"

Rosalind struggled up onto her elbows and then, with

the others' help, got to her feet and stood trembling before Gabrielle.

"The women of our family have been mistresses and courtesans for at least four generations. Your great grandmother was the enduring passion of two different earls of Brentwick and your great aunt, Theodora, who left you such a tidy sum in her will, died at seventy with the distinction of never having been loved by less than a duke of the realm." She paused for a moment, narrowing her gaze on Gabrielle. "You were born of a grand passion, and that is your destiny. You were meant for love and romance . . . to be the hunger in a man's eyes and the fire in his soul. You were meant to be the *desire* in a man's life, not the *duty*. You were born to be a great mistress, like your mother!"

Gabrielle lurched from her seat, whirled, and gripped the back of the chair with whitened fingers. "And what if I don't want to be anyone's grand passion? What if all I want is a *husband* . . . a dull, respectable sort of a fellow who will depart each morning at nine and arrive promptly back on the doorstep at eight, ready for slippers and a book by the fire?" The way Rosalind swayed and emitted a choked sound from behind the hand she had pressed to her mouth only spurred Gabrielle's determination.

"What if I want cottage pie, tea at four o'clock, and Sunday mass at St. Paul's—instead of chateaubriand for two, champagne at midnight, and a risqué revue at the Grecian Saloon? What if I want a house full of children stringing popcorn for a Christmas tree and calling cards that have 'Mrs. Somebody-or-other' printed on—"

"Gabrielle, *non!*" Genevieve cried, anxiously patting Rosalind's limp hand.

"Mother Mercy—listen to ye, girl!" Clementine declared, horrified.

"How could you be so heartless?" Ariadne demanded. "So reprehensibly willful and *modern*?"

"It is just my insensitive and 'modern' nature, I suppose," she replied, with the turbulence of her heart flooding into her voice. "Proof that I am not suited for anything so exalted as being the great passion of an important man's life."

For a moment they were struck dumb. The possibility of her truly rejecting a life of comfort and ease, of passion and pleasure, was simply beyond them.

"Enough!" Rosalind threw up her hands in maternal frustration. "Take yourself back to your rooms this instant, young lady, and prepare yourself to fall in love. I intend to see you settled with the great love of your life within the next two months . . . with the count or with another suitable nobleman."

"I—but I *cannot*—" Anger, fear, and desperation rose within Gabrielle in dark successive waves. Struggling to stay above that rising tide of despair, she held her head high, snatched up handfuls of her skirts, and strode furiously for the door.

The wall vibrated as the door slammed behind her, and not an eye blinked nor a muscle moved in the chamber until the last echo of her departure died away. Rosalind was the first to move. She clasped a hand above her pounding heart, teetered to the divan, and sat down on it with an uncharacteristic "plop."

"Where did I go wrong?" she said incredulously. "I gave her every luxury, every advantage, and this is how she repays me . . . by demanding a *hus-band!*" Her voice cracked over the last word and she choked out: "Marriage . . . of all things!"

She fumbled among the silken pillows, searching for her missing handkerchief, and was handed a substitute out of Genevieve's bodice. Dabbing her heated face, she looked up into her friends' stunned faces. "I . . . I have waited too long . . . I see that now. I should have brought her home from France earlier. But I thought it would be good to give her a bit of travel first. Gentlemen so like to speak of their travels in intimate conversation, and I assumed she would . . ."

She halted, realizing that she had assumed far too much with regard to her only child. Worse—she had ignored recent hints of trouble in Gabrielle's lack of interest in acquiring a new wardrobe, her refusal of milk baths and massages, her spiritless attempts at music and conversation, and the increasing frequency of her megrims and womanly indispositions. How had things come to such a pass?

Staring into the distance and into the past, she looked for an explanation in the way Gabrielle had spent the years she was cloistered behind the walls of L'Academie Marchand, just outside Paris. She had sent Gabrielle to the exclusive school for a thorough and genteel education: lessons of all kinds, from art and music to dancing and horsemanship, and improving lectures on literature, art, history, philosophy, and the natural sciences. Regular reports from Gabrielle's headmistress had painted a glowing picture of her development: she had an excellent mind, natural artistic talent, an angelic singing voice, and stunning skill at the pianoforte. She was a great favorite amongst the other girls, as well. . . . Rosalind froze, with her eyes widening at what she glimpsed now in perfect hindsight.

"It was that wretched school!" she announced, her horror deepening. "The other girls! Dear God—she was thrown in with all those blue-blooded daughters being groomed for a life as society's proper brood mares. Marriage." She made a face as if the word itself left a foul taste in her mouth. "That *has* to be where she got the notion."

"A fancy French lady school . . . o'course they'd fill 'er head with 'respectable' nonsense," Clementine said, leveling an accusing look on Rosalind. "All that talk of 'proper this' and 'decent that' . . . it'd be enough to dry up any-body's juices."

Rosalind flinched. She hadn't thought about the social milieu her daughter inhabited, only about the fact that she was being well educated . . . well out of the way.

"Her juices are *not* dried up! My Gabrielle has as many 'juices' as anyone in this room!" She straightened regally. "She is *my* daughter, after all . . . an uncommon beauty . . . a creature of quixotic spirit, of deep but unawakened passion." Rising, she began to pace with a smoldering drama that had held a duke of the realm spell-bound for more than a score of years. "And a *wife*—merciful heaven! She's far too beautiful, educated, and refined for any but the highest nobility. Surely she knows that the circumstances of her birth would make such a match im-possible for her. Who on earth does she think she would marry?" She paused and glared into the distance and the future, as if by sheer force of will she could direct it. "No, she is meant to be a *lover.* She'll make a splendid courtesan —the perfect mistress! She'll have a famous and fabulously romantic liaison, or my name isn't Rosalind LeCoeur!"

New determination filled her. "I want her settled and this entire business out of the way before the duke returns from his safari. Genevieve, can you call on the count and try to persuade him to see her again?" The Frenchwoman sighed and nodded with a pained expression that indicated she held little hope for an affirmative response. Her doubt caused Rosalind to frown and tap her chin with a calculat-ing finger. "Still . . . to be safe, I ought to send for my cousin, Bertie. He has access to all the best clubs. I'll have him search for another prospect—a young lord—an earl at least—with deep pockets, an eye for beauty, and a weak-ness for unapproved pleasure."

She sailed out the doors, and the others followed her to

her daughter's suite in the east wing, where she threw open the doors of Gabrielle's apartments and charged inside.

"Gabrielle Augustine LeCoeur . . . show yourself!" Rosalind demanded, stalking across the thick carpets of the brocade-clad boudoir and pushing back the door of the gilded bedchamber. "I have a few things to say to you, young lady!"

It was empty.

Moments later, Rosalind stormed from Gabrielle's chambers with her complexion mottled and her eyes glowing blue fire. "Gunther!" she called furiously for her major-domo, who appeared instantly at the end of the hall. "Where is she—where is Gabrielle?"

The houseman winced as he reported: "Miss LeCoeur left the house some minutes ago, madam. In something of a state."

Gunther, as it happened, possessed something of a genius for understatement.

Moments before, Gabrielle had gone storming down the staircase and had nearly bowled over the sizable houseman as she blew past him and out the front doors. Hatless, gloveless, without a proper escort or even a sensible wrap, she had fled down the steps, into the street and into the oncoming night. Through a haze of turmoil and humiliation, she made her way past the imposing residences of the fashionable Eaton Square and darted down the alley that led to the mews behind it. The modest lane was bustling with the activity of servants and tradesmen: last-minute deliveries for dinner and teams being ferried to carriage houses in preparation for the evening's social engagements.

In the last three months, when she could no longer bear the excesses of her mother's house, she had slipped out through the servant entrance to walk the service lane behind the house. The sights and sounds of honest work and ordinary, spontaneous interactions always acted as a balm on her overstuffed senses. But just now, they provided no such relief. With her head down and her vision blurred, she bumped into uniformed servants, was jostled by children, stepped square into the middle of a horse pile, and narrowly missed being trampled by a brace of horses in the hands of an inexperienced groom. By the time she reached Belgrave Street, streaming tears made it difficult for her to see her own feet, much less the stares of the people she passed.

Born of a grand passion . . . your destiny . . . meant for love and romance . . . Her mother's words kept turning over and over in her head, proclaiming her fate and then demanding her assent. She had been born of a searing and illicit passion and was predestined by her birth to plunge into the same steaming hedonism from which she had sprung. Her mother believed it. Her mother's cadre of aging courtesans believed it. And together they had planned her future accordingly. Whether she liked it or not, she was ordained to be "the hunger in a man's eyes and the fire in his soul."

She gritted her teeth in frustration and swiped at her wet cheeks.

She didn't want to be a hunger or a fire or an itch or an ache . . . or anything else connected with tumultuous passions and transporting emotions! She wasn't anything like the fabled Rosalind LeCoeur, the stellar beauty whose charm had so captured the desires of the duke of Carlisle that he had refused to remarry after his wife died and had made his mistress his consort.

Gabrielle LeCoeur had no romantic proclivities at all. None whatsoever. No soaring desires, no scintillating allure, no exquisitely turned sensitivities. In point of fact, she had never felt the slightest carnal stirring or curiosity. When the other girls at Marchand had sighed and scrambled to the windows for a glimpse of the local count's handsome son riding past the school gates, she hadn't been troubled by the slightest twinge of excitement. And she had made it through an abbreviated grand tour of the continent and three interminable months of sensual bombardment in her mother's house without so much as a flicker of amorous interest.

And she was perfectly content without it. Passion, she had learned in the village of d'Arcy, was nothing but a passage to infamy and heartbreak for a woman. She had seen its devastating effects over and over in the faces of the wretched women who came from Paris to deliver their illegitimate and unwanted children into the hands of the sisters who operated a foundling hospital there. And she had seen it in the haunting faces of the little children who crowded around her and clung to her skirts when she and her schoolmates went to the hospital to do charity work. Faces among which, but for an accident of birth, might have been her own.

A woman had but two options in the world, those experiences had taught her. She could be either a wife or a mistress, and the thing that separated the two was passion. Somewhere along the way, a woman had to choose.

Gabrielle had come home to her mother's house, hoping to convince her mother to allow her to make that choice for herself. But from the moment she arrived, Rosalind had endeavored to make *her* into a *haute courtisane* . . . a pampered denizen of the high demimonde. Increasingly repelled by her mother's designs on her future, she had resisted with quiet desperation . . . until tonight.

If only she could go back to those fateful moments just now in her mother's boudoir . . . declare herself more forcefully and insist that she be allowed a different kind of life.

"I want to wear plain flannel nightgowns . . . and

shoes made of leather." Glimpsing the horse residue that clung to one of her delicate satin slippers, she hissed and tried to wipe it off on the curb. "I want to play the piano again without worrying if it is too andante or too largo to excite a man. I want to read something besides romantic plays and suggestive poetry. I want to eat food that's not flambéed!" She gave up on the slipper and strode on, her eyes glowing with outrage.

"I want to take baths in plain water . . . hang chintz curtains . . . have a vicar to dinner. And I want a name to write in till-death-do-us-part strokes in a parish register . . . a real name, not some flowery, made-up bit of French nonsense my mother took as a *nom de plaisir*. Just an ordinary man and an ordinary name! Is that too bloody much to ask?" she demanded furiously, startling a gentleman who was passing her on the street. Embarrassed, she lowered her eyes and hurried on.

A lamppost loomed abruptly out of the darkness, and she stepped around it, continuing through the deepening gloom. The air swirled around her, tugging ominously at the delicate ruffles and flounces of her gown, but she scarcely noticed. Each step she took away from Eaton Square bolstered her determination to defy her mother's plans.

That afternoon, with the count, she had gotten a glimpse of what horrors lay in store for her. Marriage, she realized, was the only solution to her problems. Somehow, she would have to find a husband . . . quickly. And how on earth would she go about finding one?

As the deepening chill of the evening cooled the heat of her frustration, she tucked her arms about her waist and glanced up to find herself beside a huge iron railing. The last of the streetlamps were being lighted, and in their yellow glow she made out the drivers of passing cabs, hunched over their reins with their hats pulled low, and caught sight of crumpled newspapers and bits of debris tumbling down the street.

A cold, fat raindrop struck, and a shiver went through her as she realized that just now she had more to worry about than her mother's determination to make her into the perfect mistress. She was caught in a breaking storm, miles from home with no money and no chaperon. What had happened to her good sense? A woman alone on the street at night was in considerable danger.

Hugging herself, she hurried on and tried to think. The wind gusts grew steadily stronger, pulling at her until the pins in her carefully crafted fall of curls gave and her hair blew free. She ducked around a nearby corner and tried to right her hair as she huddled against the side of a building and surveyed the empty street. She wasn't on Piccadilly anymore. She squinted to make out the lettering on a sign-post under a streetlamp nearby. "St. James's Street." Where was that?

With mounting alarm, she looked up and down the broad thoroughfare, noting several imposing houses and buildings that had an official look about them. Despite her disheveled state, she decided that her only option was to inquire at one of those establishments for assistance. They might think her a creature of the night and send her pack-ing, but she had no other choice. Shivering from both cold and growing trepidation, she struck off for one of the build-ings on the cross street, where the intersecting sign read Jermyn Street.

Just as she approached one ornate door, a carriage stopped on the street behind her and a pair of handsomely dressed gentlemen descended. When they saw her, with her hair in disarray and her damp voile clinging to her skin, their aristocratic faces lighted with interest and they ap-proached her. Looming large, their dark cloaks billowing and their eyes glowing, they suggested she accompany them to a "party" in a nearby hotel. Terrified, she jerked back just in time to avoid one man's grasp. She wheeled and bolted down the street. She didn't slow until their mocking laughter faded behind her.

Now tensely aware of her vulnerability, she blew with the wind from block to block. Her anxiety grew as the tempo of the raindrops gradually increased and as she watched carriages delivering gentlemen to fine buildings that sheltered lively establishments inside. *St. James's.* She remembered now that it wasn't just a street; it was an entire district . . . one that housed most of the gentlemen's clubs of London.

More than once, a carriage slowed beside her and male voices hailed her with insulting comments and offers of a night's employment. She shrank as far from the curb as she could and kept moving, her heart beating wildly. Of all the wretched precincts of London, she had had to wander into the one where men of appetite and privilege congregated! She had to find a way out of here, or there wouldn't be enough of her virtue left to seek a marriage.

Then, within the space of a block or so, the district changed. Here the buildings were shabbier, she realized, and the establishments had become more trade and tavern than club and coffeehouse. The people were the sort who plied their dubious trades in the streets regardless of the weather. Over her head, signs touted the varied establishments and entertainments of Haymarket Road.

The men with their tattered hats pulled low and the women with their frizzed hair and painted faces, all watched her with sullen speculation as she veered around them, holding her breath and praying that they wouldn't follow. But the wind at her back carried the sound of footsteps to her—big, ominous sounds of leather meeting pavement. She burst into a run. The footsteps came after her, growing steadily louder.

Panic swelled in her chest. It was difficult to breathe as she fled before the double threat of the oncoming storm and an impending attack. Closer and closer . . . she could hear her pursuer gaining on her with every step. Suddenly, a hail of cold drops came crashing out of the darkness, and moments later, the sky opened up and rain poured down like a river unleashed.

Raindrops as large as pennies pelted her skin, stung her eyes, pounded through the thin fabric of her dress. The roar of the wind-driven rain obliterated every other sound, so that she could no longer hear whether her pursuer was still behind her. Guided only by the eerie, blurred glow of the streetlamps, she kept going, directionless, scarcely able to breathe in the choking downpour. Fatigue and the dragging weight of her sopping clothes gradually overwhelmed her. Desperate to escape the driving torrent, she stumbled into a doorway and huddled back against a set of weathered wooden panels. Her eyes and lungs burned, her body quaked, and her limbs felt as if they had turned to rubber.

How long she was there, dazed and chilled, trying to recover, she had no way of knowing, but it was at least long enough to regret every headstrong and "modern" impulse she had ever harbored. Now what was she going to do? As she caught her breath and the rain began to slacken, she pushed dripping strands of hair back from her face and looked around her.

"Take a g-good look, Gabby," she muttered, shivering and glancing from her own garments to the ramshackle doorway. "This could be your life if you refuse to cooperate and Mama turns you out on the streets."

Darkness burst across her vision as something loomed between her and the rain-blurred gaslight. She gasped as it took shape—a huge greatcoated figure swooping down on her out of the watery gloom . . .

2

She was seized by the arms, hauled out of the doorway, and thrust into a carriage waiting just beyond the glare of the streetlamp. She wrestled and screamed, but she was no match for her abductor's strength. The carriage lurched into motion an instant later, and she was thrown back against the rear seat. Scrambling, she righted herself. After a pause to take her bearings, she lunged for the door and was caught, halfway there, in her abductor's steely grip.

"Help! Someone, help!" she shouted, straining toward the door and praying she could be heard in the street outside. But her frayed voice drowned in the rumble of the carriage wheels. She began to twist and shove, trying to put as much distance as possible between her and her captor. "Let me go! You have no right—"

"I have every right—every obligation to rescue you from these foul streets," the man said gruffly, wrestling with her wrists, "and to set your feet upon a higher path. Be still —I won't harm you."

Something in the calm, serious tenor of his voice made Gabrielle look at him. Rescue her? Her abductor was not one of the gentleman swells or the street toughs she'd seen earlier; he was an older man dressed in solemn black, wearing an expensive-looking top hat and a gravely serious expression. In the dim carriage light, his craggy features seemed both aged and ageless, and his dark eyes shone with an unsettling light. He apparently took her stillness for surrender and released one of her arms, settling back in the seat beside her. She wrenched her other wrist free and scooted as far from him as she could get on the seat.

"You won't get away with this," she declared, shivering.

He gave her bedraggled hair and thin, wet gown a look, and wagged his head in a way that said "poor, wretched creature" as surely as if he'd spoken it aloud. Then he leaned across the footwell to lift the seat opposite him and pull a blanket from the stowage beneath it.

"Here. Do wrap yourself and avoid a chill." He handed her the lap robe. "We shall be there soon."

Confused by what seemed an act of consideration, she hesitated, eyeing both him and the blanket with suspicion. But her cold, rain-soaked clothing made her desperate for a bit of warmth, and she took the blanket and wrapped it around her.

"Where—where are you taking me?" she demanded with as much authority as her chattering teeth allowed. When he didn't answer right away, she glanced furtively about the carriage for some clue to her captor and his intentions. The coach's interior was solidly, if not luxuriously, appointed, with polished mahogany panels, tufted leather seats, and polished brass fittings. If he was one of the high-living gentlemen of St. James, his coach and his demeanor did not show it.

"Someplace dry and safe . . . where they won't find you, my girl," he finally said, looking at her out of the corner of his eye, then staring into the darkness. "You needn't be afraid. I won't let them take you back, if you don't want to go."

Where they won't find you? A pulse of alarm went through her. Then the second half of his statement registered, and she looked at him in surprise. *He wouldn't let them take her back?* Had he been sent by Rosalind to search the streets for her?

"You know my mother, then?" she asked.

"Your mother? So it was your mother who sold you into this mean estate." He rubbed a gnarled hand over his eyes. "I know a thousand of your mother, my girl. Yours is a story all too common on these accursed streets."

Before she could pursue those cryptic remarks, the carriage stopped and the door swung open. Her abductor helped her from the carriage in a narrow, rain-drenched alley. She tried to bolt, but succeeded only in sinking into a cold puddle up to her ankles. At her cry of distress, her captor swung back to wrap an arm around her and bundle her through a nearby doorway.

"Take your hands off me!" He easily overcame her resistance, pulling her through a second doorway into a large kitchen with warm brick walls, large ovens and stoves, tidy worktables, and racks of hanging pots and utensils. At one end of the long room was a huge, old-fashioned cooking hearth topped by a massive stone mantel in which old-fashioned iron pivots for cooking arms still hung. In the fireplace a small, tidy blaze burned, warming and illuminating a servant's dining table sitting on an old parlor rug. She stood staring, momentarily stunned. It seemed the unlikeliest place in the world for a ravishment.

"Over here . . . where you can warm yourself," he commanded, propelling her ahead of him toward the glowing hearth.

An aged butler appeared and seemed taken aback to find his master home . . . with such a guest. He gave her a dour look as he removed his master's coat and received instructions, then ambled off to what she presumed must be the pantries at the far end of the kitchen.

"Where are we?" she asked. She hadn't much experience with depraved and debauched males, but the strength of his features had a certain nobility about it, and the white of his hair and the intensity of his dark, almost melancholy eyes somehow didn't inspire a proper terror in her. "You cannot keep me here. I warn you: my mother has very high connections!"

"Of course she does," he said with a twist to his mouth that said what he thought of her claims.

"I shall be missed if I don't return shortly," she insisted.

He studied her, then sat down on the bench across the table from her.

"No doubt a girl as *valuable* as you would indeed be missed." He wagged his head. "This is my home, young woman. And I have brought you here to give you a chance to think upon your sad and immoral mode of living. And, with the proper guidance, to help you see the error of your ways."

"Sad and immoral?" She scowled at him and crossed her arms. Her life wasn't immoral . . . not *yet*, anyway. "I've done nothing wrong."

Again, those world-weary eyes probed for the truthfulness of her answer. "There is no need to lie about your profession with me. Your clothes and the fact that you are abroad in the streets on such a night, fairly shout your trade. Confession is a necessary first step toward redemption . . . a purgative for the soul, which will allow you to get on with the reforming of your wayward and misdirected life."

"I am not the least bit 'wayward' or 'misdirected'!"

"Come, come, my girl. You are scarcely believable as an outraged innocent." He expelled a heavy breath, as if glimpsing a long road ahead, and got to his feet. "Your age places you quite beyond the limits of the loathsome 'maiden trade.' Why, you must be at least *eighteen*. No man in his right mind would believe you to be a virgin, lost and defenseless in the streets."

"How dare you, sir. I am a decent and virtuous young woman." But even as the words left her lips, his expression made her realize that she looked anything but decent with her hair wrecked and her wet clothes clinging to every aspect of her person.

"I dare because I am concerned for your safety, my girl. And for the well-being of your soul." He moved around the table, sending her lurching back a step. "The constables are out in numbers tonight, taking all unescorted women in the streets into custody. You know, of course, what that means."

She, of course, had no idea what it meant.

"A trip to the gaol and a medical examination." He said it as if he expected it to strike fear and trembling into her heart. When it didn't, he frowned and crossed his arms, deciding to be a bit more explicit. "You'll be arrested, plundered by their filthy quacks, then taken before a magistrate and sentenced on the spot for unauthorized prostitution."

Prostitution. The word rattled her to her very core. She sat down abruptly on one end of the bench. "I am *not* one of those poor, wretched women."

Her denial hung on the air, thinning, seeming less

plausible and substantial with each minute that passed. In that instant, she understood for the very first time how fragile the truth could be.

"In my experience, few women of the streets think of themselves as members of that degrading profession." He gave her a bitter smile and shook his head. "They think of themselves as 'just givin' a bloke a tumble' to help the family out with 'a quid or a fast fiver.' But it is all one in the same, my girl. A woman who hires her body out to a man for money is a prostitute, regardless of her pretenses or motivations . . . or her status in life." He came to stand over her, examining her with a worrisome fire in his eyes.

"You're probably quite a fetching little thing, when you're all done up. Yes, quite. Fresh skin, uncommonly fine eyes . . ." He cleared his throat. "Your manner and speech surpass the common. I imagine the gentlemen of St. James must treat you well . . . take you to exciting places, make you thrilling promises. But their attentions will not last. The days will turn to months and then to years, and, in the way of all corrupted flesh, your charms will fade. What will you have then, my girl? Broken in health and bereft of spirit, what will become of you?"

What would become of her? The question reverberated in her head. Too clearly she saw her mother's life—*the life her mother wanted for her*—linked to that of the poor, wretched women of the streets. Until now, she had thought of her mother's choice, however flawed, in terms of love, romance, and passion. But in pressing the count's case, her mother had emphasized his wealth and the luxury and material riches . . . right down to the stock portfolios. Was there really any difference between selling your body for a "fast fiver" or for an elegant house on Eaton Square?

The butler returned just then from the far end of the kitchen, carrying a tray laden with a china pot and cups, and a plate of shortbread and chocolate-dipped biscuits.

Her abductor dismissed the servant and took charge of the tray himself. Before her incredulous eyes, he poured cups of warm cocoa and thrust three-penny sweets into her hands. When she shivered, he shoved the bench closer to the fire and, over her protests, peeled the blanket from her so that she could warm herself and dry her dress. Then, to her astonishment, he got down on one creaking knee to remove her sodden, filthy slippers and lay them near the fire for drying.

"The vile rutting and couplings you must endure are not what you were created for, my child." His voice began to vibrate with urgency. "You were not born to be a slave to the tempests of the flesh, but to be a temple to the eternal, a vessel that is clean and holy and virtuous." He looked up at her, reddened, and held his breath as he pushed to his feet. "I can see in your eyes and sense in your spirit, the desire for better! Don't be afraid, child . . . others have made the daunting journey to righteousness ahead of you, and now live lives of dignity and purity and service . . ."

Gabrielle sat with a fistful of untouched biscuits in each hand, wide-eyed as her kidnapper towered above her and ranted about the rewards of abandoning her life of sin and the dire consequences of clinging to her immoral ways.

She had been kidnapped by a *reformer,* a self-styled rescuer of fallen women! Of all the predatory males who prowled the darkened streets of London, she'd had the luck to be kidnapped by the one man bent on rescuing women from the clutches of immorality. And of all the women in need of moral reform who walked the sordid streets, he'd chosen to "rescue" the one female who was still a virgin and struggling to stay that way. She bit her lip, trying to prevent a smile of relief. For the first time in two hours she felt a glimmer of hope. Perhaps she could convince him to send her home. . . .

"And to think"—he impulsively caught her face

between his hands and bent toward her—"you were sold into the clutches of a lust-maddened beast by your own mother. It sears the heart, just to think of it."

His words struck her forcefully, missing the truth of her situation by the narrowest of margins . . . the tense of a verb. "But, my child, you must not let that foul betrayal blight the rest of your life. You must not give in to the enslaving notion that her penchant for sin must necessarily taint your blood as well. You have free will—can choose a different life. You need not become the sad and debauched creature that your mother is!"

She choked on a sharply inhaled breath, and he, thinking her overcome by the shame of her situation, released her. She swayed on the bench, sloshing cocoa on her white voile and watching numbly as he rescued the cup from her. *She didn't have to follow in her mother's hedonistic footsteps. She could choose.* Gooseflesh rose on her skin.

"You are wrong about me," she said in a whisper. "I *am* a virtuous young woman. Tonight I fled into the streets to escape . . ." She looked up at him, needing to hear it make sense somewhere besides her own head. "My mother is a grand mistress, and she insists that I take a nobleman, without benefit of vows, just as she did years ago. And I . . . I don't want . . ."

"She would make you a rich man's mistress," her captor concluded, reading the confirmation of it in her darkening eyes. "And you don't want to be one."

He straightened, hung his hands on the lapels of his coat, and seemed to grow in both satisfaction and outrage, as if sensing that here at last was a creature not yet beyond his powers of salvation . . . a true rescue.

Suddenly, it was as if another being had taken him over from the inside; he began to pace and gesture wildly. "Harlotry is a loathsome and reprehensible thing to inflict upon one's own child, one's very own flesh and blood!

How low can a woman sink? This so-called demimonde is nothing more than degrading prostitution wrapped in a layer of luxury that temporarily smothers the conscience. A cold exchange of ill-gotten pleasures for money . . . with the souls of unfortunate women forfeit in the bargain." His eyes burned as he shoved his face down into hers and demanded, "Tell me your mother's name, my girl. And I shall see her brought up on charges—taken to the law and held up to the scorn she deserves!"

Gabrielle snapped backward so quickly that she nearly toppled from the bench. The explosion of his anger jarred her back to reality and set her mind scrambling. Arrest her mother for peddling flesh? Bring her up before the courts? The duke would be exposed to ridicule, made a public spectacle. And with the secret of her origins decried as a humiliating example of degradation, not even the most modest of tradesmen would want her to wife. Panic shuddered through her.

This was no rescue. His self-righteous zeal for retribution would bring her entire future down around her ears!

"Come, come—don't be afraid, my girl," he demanded, seizing her shoulders in a viselike grip. "I shall see you are protected from her and her unsavory associates. And I shall help you to make a new start as . . . a maid in a respectable house or a matron in a charity house or perhaps a clerk in a millinery shop. I shall find you good, honest work that will redeem your wayward pride and in the end, save your soul." His eyes gleamed with what could only be called excitement. "Give me the name of that heartless Jezebel and I shall see her roundly punished. I have a few 'connections' in the government myself—"

"William?" A female voice, artificially high and quivering with compressed tension, rang out across the kitchen. Gabrielle's captor released her abruptly and whirled to face the doorway that led to the rest of the house. There stood a delicate, gently aged woman wearing fine black silk, a fragile lace cap, and an expression that contained both surprise and distress. Her mouth dropped open as her gaze settled on Gabrielle. "What are you doing, William? Who is that creature?"

"Catherine!" William rushed to the woman's side and quickly ushered her back into the corridor. "Dear wife . . . nothing for you to be concerned about. . . ."

But "Catherine" apparently had other ideas, for she refused to be moved until she had an explanation. Tension pushed her voice higher as William tried to explain and pacify her in calm, reassuring tones. He quickly led her back along the corridor, out of sight. From the fading of their voices, Gabrielle concluded that William was succeeding in removing Catherine to another part of the house . . . leaving *her* alone in the kitchen.

Alone. Seizing the moment, she emptied her hands of half-crumbled biscuits and frantically wrestled her feet into slippers that had shrunk as they began to dry. With her heart beating furiously, she raced toward the street, half expecting a shout of discovery or a heavy hand to descend on her shoulder and halt her. But the only sound was hinges creaking as the door swung open. With a furtive look back, she dashed out into the alley.

"Rain again." She groaned as the rivulets of water trickling down her face made it difficult to see. But at least she was free. When she had put some distance between her and the house, she stopped and shielded her eyes to look around. She was in an alley between what appeared to be substantial buildings. Glimpsing the dim glow of streetlamps at one end of the lane, she gathered up her skirts and ran toward them.

Her earlier dilemma now returned in the rain and gloom of the night. And who knew what her erstwhile rescuer would do when he discovered her missing? She had to get out of this plaguing downpour and find a way back to her mother's house. There was only one solution to both her needs: a horsecab. And where would she find one at this hour?

Cupping her hand over her eyes, she searched the blurry lights in the distance. The street was deserted except for a carriage parked under a sputtering streetlamp a little more than a block away. The creak of iron hinges and the sharp clap of wood behind her spurred her into motion. Desperately, she snatched up her drooping skirts and dashed off the curb into the puddled street.

The driver of that carriage suddenly came to life, slapping reins, and the carriage was in motion. She gasped as it hurtled toward her. The door flew open and a large, shadowy figure leaned out of the opening. In the blink of an eye, she was being scooped up off the street and hauled inside the moving carriage.

The force that had plucked her from the street abandoned her momentarily, to pull the door shut, but an instant later loomed over her again. Dressed in flowing black and outlined in the yellow glow of the interior lantern, her new captor appeared like an apparition out of Dante's *Inferno*. When she gasped, a hand came down over her mouth, trapping her scream inside.

"I don't care what else you do, just don't scream," came a deep, cultured voice. "God, I do hate it when females scream."

After sufficient time for his words to sink in, he removed his hand, paused, then sat back across the carriage. She lay crumpled in the footwell for a moment, catching her breath. Then she scrambled up onto the edge of the seat. The coach was sumptuously appointed; lined with silver gray brocade, upholstered in gray silk plush trimmed with silk cording and tassels, and fitted with a sterling carriage lamp and brazier. And it was moving at a fast clip. Eyeing the door, she made a hasty calculation of the damage she would suffer if she managed to fling herself from the vehicle at that speed. . . .

"It isn't worth it," her new captor declared, as if he had read her thoughts.

She snapped a glance at him from her tensely cocked posture and froze as she found herself staring at a face that was somehow both dissolute and divine. Beneath a black silk top hat, a set of finely carved features were framed in a large, handsomely proportioned oval—dark eyes, a slightly aquiline nose, broad, high cheekbones, a wide, sensual arc of a mouth that just now was canted at an unsettling angle. It was an intriguing dark masterpiece of a face; for a moment it robbed her of speech.

He made a sound, deep in his throat, that might have been a laugh. "Well, well . . . You are a prize. I had no idea the old boy had sunk to such levels."

The mention of the old man made her wonder if "William" might have sent him after her. But some nuance in the way he spoke discredited that possibility. She clamped her arms around her waist and tried to quell her growing fear.

"Stop this carriage at once, and let me out."

"I don't intend to hurt you," he said in businesslike tones. "On the contrary, if you cooperate, you will leave this coach a richer woman." Out of the folds of his black evening cloak, he produced a five-pound banknote and held it up between two finely gloved fingers.

She stiffened. *Cooperate?* Her face flamed. For the second time tonight she had been mistaken for a tart and abducted! Was every man in London out tonight in a carriage, dragging women off the streets for a bit of illicit pleasure?

"A fiver," he said, watching her carefully, amusement

playing at the corners of his mouth. "Better than your usual rates, I would think."

"I don't have 'rates' . . . usual or otherwise," she declared. "And who are you to be dragging women off the streets and taking indecent liberties?"

"I don't want your 'liberties,' sweetheart, I just want a bit of talk. I'll match whatever your last customer gave you."

"I don't have a 'last customer,' either." Her teeth were beginning to chatter. "However it may ap-pear, I am not in that unenviable trade."

"No?" He smiled coolly. "You just spent the better part of the last hour in the company of a certain old man. I know because I saw him drag you into his carriage, then into his house." He leaned forward sharply, and she tried to slide to one side to avoid him. But her sodden skirts were stuck to the velvet of the tufted seat and held her bottom fast.

"This is yours," he said in deep tones, waving the banknote suggestively, "if you tell me, in explicit detail, everything the old bugger did to you."

The sound of the rain pounding on the carriage roof intruded, reminding her of the cold, relentless peril of the streets. Her body began to quake with a chill as she stared at the banknote and wondered desperately if it was enough to hire a hansom cab.

He watched her eyeing the money. "Holding out for more, eh? Very well, I'll match whatever the old cod gave you. What was it—a 'tenner'? I can't imagine him going any higher than that . . . what with his passion for thrift, strong currency, and a balanced budget." He gave a "*tsk*" of annoyance. "Was it *twenty*?"

"It was warm cocoa and biscuits," she said irritably, bracing for his response.

Surprised, he studied her response for a moment, then

gave a wickedly sardonic laugh. "Of course. He picked you up off the streets, carried you to his house, and fed you warm cocoa and biscuits."

"*Fancy* biscuits, dipped in chocolate," she insisted, pausing to fortify herself with a breath. "And if you want to know the rest, you'll have to agree to take me home."

"Home?" He leveled an incredulous look on her. "To some windowless room in Whitechapel?"

"To my home in"—she suddenly thought better of mentioning exactly where until he agreed to the bargain—"in the West End."

He raked a calculating look down her disheveled form, deciding. "Very well. Tell me what I want to know and I'll take you home."

Having ventured that much, she dared more . . . reaching down to drag the brazier closer and propping her feet atop it. As the rising heat invaded her icy limbs, she jerked her sluggish wits back to the perils at hand.

"Well . . . he took me into his house and sat me down and went on and on about the evils of the flesh and reforming my ways," she began. "And about how the road to purity and holiness is difficult, but that if I apply myself to it I can become a veritable temple of . . . eternal something-or-other." She tilted her chin up, refusing to look directly at him, but catching, at the periphery of her vision, the way his eyes narrowed. "It's true! And he offered to help me make a new start, as a housemaid or a charity house matron . . . or a shopgirl in a hat shop."

His mouth clamped into a quivering line. "A charity house matron? How uncharacteristically *inventive* of him." He leaned back and lowered his chin, so that the brim of his hat put his eyes in shadow. "The 'housemaid' and 'shopgirl' gambits are certainly familiar. They're favorites of a number of the gentlemen of St. James. But a 'charity house matron.' Ranks as something of a quirk, I would say.

And what part did he intend to play? The birch-wielding chairman of the board? A heavy-breathing contributor, perhaps?"

She scowled.

"All I know is: an old man dragged me into his kitchen, made me sit by the fire, shoved biscuits into my hands, and preached at me about my supposedly vile and immoral life. Then his wife came—at least he called her 'dear wife'—and when he trundled her out of the kitchen, I seized the chance to escape." She drew herself up with as much dignity as her chilled blue blood could muster. "Now . . . please take me home."

He paused, stroking his chin with a gloved hand as he studied her.

"You don't know who he is, do you?" he demanded, folding his arms.

"I don't care who he is," she answered crossly. When he continued to stare at her, she added: "Obviously a wild-eyed reformer, devoted to the notion of purging the streets of loose women." She narrowed her eyes at him. "I don't know who *you* are either."

A laugh vibrated his shoulders, a deep, husky sound that made her want to reach for the door handle. He leaned forward, sending her smacking into the back of the seat as she recoiled from both him and the peculiar tension he created in her with the slightest movement.

"You just spent the better part of an hour, if not in the arms, at least in the clutches of the prime minister of Britain. That was none other than the Grand Old Man himself, William Gladstone." His face lighted with a taut, annoying smile. "Now that you know the exalted nature of the company you've just . . . *kept* . . . wouldn't you like to change your story a bit?"

Her eyes widened, then narrowed in confusion. Old William was the prime minister of Britain? She had just been abducted, dried out, and preached at by the queen of England's first minister? It was too absurd to credit.

"I don't believe you," she said refolding her arms protectively over her breasts.

"That makes us even," he said almost genially. "I don't believe you either."

"He couldn't have been the prime minister of Britain."

"Oh, but he was," he said. "You see, William Gladstone —that scrupulously upstanding member of society, that devout thinker, social philosopher, and diabolically canny politician—has a penchant for ladies of the night. He prowls the streets after dark, looking for prostitutes and accosting them, under the pretext of doing 'rescue work.' He drags his poor victims into some vacant hallway or alley or doorway—sometimes even into his official residence on Downing Street—and takes his grim satisfactions, before callously turning them back onto the streets." His dark gaze drilled into her. "Now, are you ready to tell me more?"

Gabrielle didn't know what to think. The prime minister taking advantage of fallen women under the guise of rescuing them? She tried to recall what Gladstone had looked like in the London newspapers they had occasionally received at Marchand. The likenesses had varied widely and more often than not were hideous caricatures. This man seemed so much older that she honestly couldn't say if there was a similarity.

"There isn't anything else to tell. He took me to his house, tried to get me to confess my wickedness and depravity, and pleaded with me to reform my shamefully debauched ways."

"And did you? Confess your wickedness and debauchery? Renounce all your fleshly depravity?"

"Of course not. I am not depraved."

"Of course not," he echoed, smiling.

Pierce St. James, earl of Sandbourne, relaxed back

against the plush seat, abandoning for the moment his dogged pursuit of William Gladstone's sexual indiscretions, though he was far from convinced that he had the truth of the matter. He had just spent the entire evening in a miserably cold and damp carriage, trailing the prime minister through a howling storm, in hopes of gathering evidence of a scandal that would prove grounds for a crown inquiry and might topple the old man's creaking government. And he had nothing to show for it but a bone-deep chill and a cock-and-bull story of hot cocoa and biscuits.

But Pierce St. James was a very patient man. He had long ago learned the truth of the saying that all things come to those who wait. He had adopted and practiced that wisdom as a central tenet of his existence. The night was young yet, he told himself, and he still had Gladstone's haughty little piece in hand. He might yet wring something useful from her . . . if he could get her to let her guard down. He smiled. That shouldn't be a problem. Pierce St. James was nothing if not an expert at getting women to lower their guard.

Banishing the self-righteous visage of William Gladstone from his mind, he focused his attention instead on the girl huddled on the seat opposite him. She was young and fresh and surprisingly self-possessed; a far cry from the worn and filthy creatures who usually plied their trade in the Haymarket on such a night. But then, William Gladstone was known to be selective in his efforts to recruit fallen women into the ranks of the reformed. He chose his candidates for "rescue" with a connoisseur's eye for the combination of beauty and licentiousness in a woman.

Pierce slid his gaze over her flimsy gown, noting the firm young curves it clung to like a second skin. She had large blue eyes and hair that was probably quite light when it wasn't a mass of wet tangles. As his attention came to rest on her face, he felt an unexpected curl of carnal curiosity winding through him. Her face was square, framed by a high forehead, prominent cheekbones, and a surprisingly strong jaw. Her nose was straight and slender, her brows finely arched, and her mouth . . .

His gaze settled on her cold-blushed lips. They were generously curved and held with just enough stubbornness to give them a bit of a pout. It was the kind of mouth a man could feel just by closing his eyes. The kind of mouth that made a man wonder if there weren't still a few oral pleasures yet to be discovered. It was a moment before he realized that those lips had moved, and he had to reconstruct her words in his mind.

"I've told you what you wanted to know," she had said, looking perfectly indignant. "Now take me home, as you agreed."

"You most certainly have *not* told me what I want to know," he countered, eyeing her speculatively. He sensed that there was more to the story than she had yet revealed. "Nor, I think, have you told me the entire truth. And until you do, I'm afraid I cannot let you out of my sight."

"The *truth* is that I am a decent young woman who was caught in a rainstorm and accosted and assaulted by two insufferable"—she thought better of the term she intended and substituted—"*men*. And I insist you honor your word."

"Oh, a *decent* young woman." His eyes widened in belated understanding. That was undoubtedly her hook, the gambit she used to interest and involve her gentlemanly patrons. And he had to credit her; it was damned convincing. With her fresh face and artful indignation it probably worked like a charm. "I'm sure you're a regular 'rosebud.' "

Heat bloomed in her cheeks, and she abandoned her huddled posture to draw herself up straight. "You want the truth? Fine. The truth is, my father is a wealthy and influential man." Then on impulse she added: "In fact he is a titled man. And I am going to be married . . . to a respected gentleman."

"You are betrothed?" He searched the lines of her face. She was nothing if not an imaginative chit, inventing at the drop of a hat, a maidenhood, virtue, a wealthy father—a *titled* man, no less—and now a respectable betrothed. "To whom? Give me the benighted fellow's name and address, and I'll send for him to collect you."

"Well, I . . ." She halted, tripped up by his challenge. "Well, I haven't decided who he is, yet. I need to be absolutely sure of the right match. But I assure you, I am to be married before . . ." In a telling pause, her eyes flitted over some internal scene. "Before the autumn season begins. My mother has her heart quite set upon seeing me settled by then."

She lifted her chin a notch, assuming a beleaguered dignity, and he laughed out loud. She obviously had no concept of just how absurd she sounded. Nor, he was beginning to think, was she fully aware of just how tempting she looked in her ruined dress with its sodden ruffles that draped in sulky invitation over her shoulders. There was something appealingly self-conscious in the pains she took to hide her body from him. But his burgeoning qualms evaporated when his gaze slid down her nearly transparent gown—following it closely along the curve of her hips, where it flared into layers of wet flounces that clung and revealed the promising curve and taper of her legs.

She was all white and pink and smooth. And wet. In his mind he could see the way her eyes would darken as he peeled away those clinging layers of ruffles and exposed the sweetly voluptuous body beneath. Phantom sensations of how her cool, damp skin would feel trickled through his fingertips, and he could just imagine the scent of her hair.

Unconsciously, he breathed in and found his head filled with the smell of . . . horse manure.

"Good God." He snapped forward in his seat, startling her. "Where is that intolerable smell coming from?" He glanced down and spotted her dirty slippers on the brazier . . . drying . . . emitting that unmistakable aroma of the streets. "*Ugh*."

He seized her feet and, despite her protests, yanked off the offending slippers and flung them out the carriage window. While she was sputtering, he leaned his head out and shouted an order to his driver. She demanded to know where he was taking her. He settled back in his seat as the driver whipped the reins and the carriage lurched faster, and he smiled.

"To Le Ciel, sweetheart. Le Ciel."

Gabrielle stiffened with alarm. Twelve years of living in a French village made it impossible to mistake the name. He was taking her to "heaven" . . . whether or not she wanted to go.

3

*H*eaven, as it happened, was located in a large brick building with its main entrance in an alley. At least that was Gabrielle's impression, from the little she was permitted to glimpse as she was being pulled from the coach, caught up in her captor's arms, and carried through a set of double doors. Attendants in livery greeted them and led them up a carved stairway and through a maze of hallways furnished with an assortment of thick Persian carpets, Queen Anne hall tables, and hunt scenes in elaborate gilt frames. The fact that the servants seemed to know her captor and do his bidding stoked her anxiety a bit higher. Clearly, she could expect no sympathy or assistance from them.

Desperately, she tried to memorize the turns they made, but by the time they passed through a set of doors and entered a spacious, candlelit chamber, she was in a quiet panic. *Left, right, left, up a half flight of stairs, then left again . . .* or was that *right?*

"This will do nicely. Send up some Perrier-Jouet . . . and someone to build up the fire. The lady needs a bit of warming," he said with a dismissing nod. The head servant bowed and withdrew, closing the doors with a discreet clack that left no doubt that they were being given complete privacy.

He did not so much set her down as let her slide down his body to reach the floor. The contact was prolonged, direct, and so suggestive as to make the prime minister's supposed indiscretions pale by comparison.

As soon as her feet were solidly on the floor, she stumbled back, clutching her shoulders and looking with dread about the luxurious chamber.

"Where have you brought me? What is this place?"

Every visible surface seemed to be gilded, polished, or swathed in a heavy red velvet. From floor to ceiling, the place invited tactile appreciation—fairly begged to be touched. Light was provided by ornate candelabra, one of which sat on a table laid with rich linen, china, and silver. In the center of one wall was a grandiose white marble fireplace with a polished brass grate, and nearby was a massive velvet-clad divan that resembled uncannily the rounded sofa in her mother's boudoir. She knew before he spoke what sort of place this was.

"A restaurant . . . of sorts," he said, watching her reaction. "A private establishment, where one can entertain a friend . . . out of the public eye."

"I am not hungry."

"I expect not, after all that *cocoa and biscuits,*" he said with a sardonic smile.

"If you don't take me home now"—she made a step toward the door—"I shall go on my own."

"What? On foot? Without shoes?" He feigned gentlemanly horror. "I could never be so ungallant as to allow that." He sauntered toward her, sending her back an equal number of steps, where she bumped into the andirons on the hearth and just saved them from clattering onto the floor. She righted them and turned to face him defiantly.

He was taller than she had guessed, a full head taller than she, and his shoulders gave the impression of substantial strength. He was dressed in evening clothes: a black swallowtail coat and slim-fitting trousers with satin piping, an ivory satin vest, a tucked-front shirt, and ivory shot-silk cravat held by a tasteful diamond stickpin. His clothing echoed his coloring: dark hair that just now bore a faint golden sheen from the candlelight, a smooth, medium complexion that darkened noticeably around his angular jaw and square chin, and those dark eyes that reflected candlelight like shimmering pools.

"Who are you?" she demanded, as her mouth went dry. "And what do you want of me?" Ignoring her own better sense, she met his dark gaze and felt her knees go a bit weak. "I've told you the truth. What else do you want me to say? That the prime minister took vile advantage of me on the kitchen table . . . between cocoa and sweets . . . and while his butler and his wife looked on in shock? My saying it—even if you could persuade or coerce me—would never make it true." Her voice lowered, pulsing with anxiety. "I cannot accuse a man of wrongs that never happened . . . no matter what crimes he may have committed against others."

Something in those tense and quiet words arrested Pierce. Her protestations of respectability were either remarkably well rehearsed or genuinely believed. A moment later he shook himself mentally. Of course they were rehearsed; she was a professional "maiden," an expert at pretending respectability. But her gambit might indicate an ambition to better things, which could prove the key to her cooperation. He changed his strategy accordingly.

"You asked who I am." He smiled smoothly. Experience had taught him that nothing exerted quite as lubricious an effect on an ambitious young thing as the sound of a title. "I suppose it is only fair that I introduce myself. Pierce St. James, sixth earl of Sandbourne"—he nodded with exaggerated gallantry—"at your service." When he captured one of her hands and bent to plant a kiss on her palm, he caught a whiff of something familiar. He stilled and inhaled again, closing his eyes, concentrating on it.

Biscuits. Good Lord—her hand smelled like biscuits— those fancy ones dipped in chocolate! He quickly grabbed her other hand and sniffed, finding it smelled the same. His eyes flew open. She was leaning stiffly back at arm's length, looking at him as if he'd lost his senses. This bizarre confirmation of her story knocked his assumptions about her night's activities into a cocked hat. He had to admit the possibility that the old man *had* fed her cocoa and biscuits. And if so, perhaps he *had* refrained from sexual indulgence and *had* plied her with his hypocritical "reform" nonsense instead.

The possibility infuriated him. He had just spent an entire evening in heated pursuit of a major political stroke, only to have his efforts reduced to naught by a whiff of chocolate-dipped biscuits.

"What on earth are you doing?" she demanded, trying to free her hands.

"Making your acquaintance, I believe," he said curtly. *Making a bloody fool of myself,* he said to himself, glaring down at the cause of his frustration. But his irritation gradually faded as found himself looking into her very blue eyes, noticing streaks of blond emerging in her hair as it began to dry, and watching the rapid rise and fall of her breasts. Suddenly one desire supplanted another. "If you cannot give me your betrothed's name, then give me yours," he continued in a milder, almost conciliatory tone. When she hesitated, he offered her choices: "Polly? Maude? Lizzie, perhaps?"

"Gabrielle."

"Truly?" He smiled, and she couldn't help thinking it was the same sort of smile a man gave a prime beefsteak just before he took a knife and fork to it. "That's a very romantic name. Tell me, *Gabrielle,* what was a decent and virtuous young woman like yourself doing out in the Haymarket in the middle of a raging downpour?" The sardonic way he emphasized the words "decent" and "virtuous" rankled her.

"Getting lost . . . getting wet . . . and getting into trouble," she said, bracing. With every exchange he was edging a worrisome bit closer. "I suppose I should thank you for providing me with the names of my two kidnappers, sir. At least I shall know who to bring charges against, later."

That took him aback for a moment, then he laughed heartily, purging the tension that had risen between them. As he sobered, an ironic humor lingered in his eyes.

There was a discreet knock at the door, and two liveried servants entered, one with a coal bucket and the other with a bucket of champagne and glasses. Gabrielle's heart rose as she eyed the half-open door. But she had no conveyance . . . no money . . . no shoes. . . . When the earl stepped into her line of sight, blocking the way, her heart sank again. The servants went quickly and efficiently about their business, then withdrew, leaving behind cold champagne and a hot fire. When the door closed, she gave in to her need for warmth and hurried to the hearth.

Heat flowed up her arms in waves, and gooseflesh appeared over her shoulders. It was a moment before she felt a nudge at the nape of her neck and realized that *he* was partly responsible for that unsettling reaction in her skin. Whirling to one side, she checked the buttons at the back of her dress and found the top two unfastened.

"I thought you might like to step out of those wet clothes and let them dry," he said with a voice that was low and silky with concern. "I wouldn't want you to take your death of the grippe, in my company."

He might be a good bit more handsome than the count, she thought darkly, but he wasn't much more subtle. This was the second time today a man had tried to divest her of her clothing in an attempt to drag her into some amorous entanglement or other. Two kidnappings, two seductions. What other torments would she have to suffer in pairs before the day was out?

"I shall keep my clothes on, thank you," she insisted, trying to contain her anxiety. "And if I die of pneumonia, my death will be on your conscience." She met his gaze with narrowed eyes. "Assuming you have one."

"Oh, I have one," he said, surprisingly unaffronted. "But, I haven't heard from it in years, and I do not intend to let you interfere with that perfectly splendid state of affairs. Here . . ."

He brought a chair from the table to the hearth, pushed her down on it, and sank onto one knee beside her. When he pulled her skirts up to expose her shins and wet undergarments to the heat of the fire, she gasped, seized them, and they found themselves in a bizarre tug-of-war over her petticoats. He finally relinquished his hold on her skirts and snagged her wrists instead.

"See here, Gabrielle—or whatever your real name is—

don't be tiresome. It's not as if no man has ever seen your legs before."

"Gabrielle *is* my real name," she declared with her face crimson. "And no man *has* ever seen my limbs before." Desperate circumstances called for desperate measures, the ultimate distraction, the *truth*. She summoned every bit of nerve she possessed.

"If you must know what I was doing out in the Haymarket," she blurted out, "I had a fierce argument with my mother and ran out of the house to walk off my anger. I kept walking and walking . . . before I knew it, I was lost, caught in the rain, mistaken for a 'street woman,' forced into a carriage and then a kitchen, and finally escaped . . . only to be snatched off the streets a second time and accused of all manner of depraved indulgence." She squirmed slightly on her seat, feeling the warmth he radiated almost as strongly as she felt the fire. "It may sound ridiculous, even foolish, but that is exactly what happened. And now all I want is to go home."

He caught her gaze in his, probing her startlingly blue eyes for the truth. There was something intriguing about the odd combination of tenuousness and self-possession in her. One minute she seemed a frightened young woman, the next a tart-tongued young chit with pretensions to gentility and a strong rebellious streak. Just as striking was the blend of freshness and sensuality she exuded. Every step, every sway of her hips, every twist of her shoulders and sweep of her lashes, carried the promise of carnal pleasures. And yet, if he were honest, those enticements seemed largely unintentional. Like the scent of biscuits on her hands . . . simple and real . . . impossible to counterfeit. On impulse, he raised her hand to his face again and breathed in, confirming his earlier perceptions. The scent was fainter, but still there. *Biscuits*.

"You smell wonderful." His voice was like a purr as he

began an olfactory exploration of her, skimming her wrist and following a trail of scents up her arm and across her shoulder, while murmuring descriptions of what he encountered. "There is a veritable cloud of roses about you . . . *ummm* . . . a clovelike scent to your neck . . . the hint of lemon rinse in your hair . . ."

Gabrielle watched his romantic overtures with genuine horror. Of all the dangers she had faced this night, this was the worst. Pierce St. James was determined to seduce her, and a seduction would ruin her chances of making a marriage forever. Talk—maybe if she could get him to *talk*—

"The earl of Sand—something?" she said, pushing on his chest and managing to put an inch or two between them. "Tell me again, my lord . . . earl of what?"

"Sandbourne," he said, running his hand down her cheek and bending his head to nuzzle and kiss the palm of her hand. "Lucky girl. A prime minister and an earl in the same night," he murmured, losing himself to passion, by degrees.

"A real earl? I mean, with patents and robes and a seat in the House of Lords?" she demanded, holding her breath until he murmured something in the affirmative. "Well, that certainly must keep you busy. I mean, what with fine houses and holdings and estates—you do have them, don't you?"

"I do," he said raising his head to savor the eagerness of her. Her avid interest in his rank and wealth brought a faint curl of triumph to his kiss-reddened lips. "All of the standard luxuries . . . estates, houses, carriages, bank accounts, family jewels . . ."

"How lovely," she said, as calmly as she could with her heart thudding wildly. "And I imagine you must travel a great deal—winter in the south of France, that sort of thing."

"Occasionally," he murmured, unbuttoning her cuff and working her sleeve up her arm with kisses and nuzzles. "I don't like to be away when Parliament is in session."

"Or away from your wife and children, I suppose."

"I have no wife or children," he murmured, pursuing her as she scooted to the edge of the chair and sat teetering on the brink of falling.

"That's a pity," she said, meaning every word of it. She had hoped that the mention of a virtuous wife and innocent children might divert him from his designs on her. "Still, I'm sure you have plenty of time for them. After all, you are probably no more than . . . what . . . thirty-five?"

"Thirty. Such delicate skin . . ." With each adoring murmur along her skin, he leaned progressively closer, until he was pressed intimately along her side; shoulder, waist, and hip. "Shaded like peaches and sweet cream." One of his arms slid around her waist, holding her in place on the chair, while the other hand began to stroke her cheek and feather fingertips down the bridge of her nose and across her lips. "You feel like fresh rose petals in dew . . . so cool and silky . . ."

"Please, your lordship—no—" She shoved harder against him, nearing full panic as her talking strategy went up in flames. Inexplicably, Rosalind's voice filled her head, recounting an axiom from her Rules of Romance. *A true lover appreciates a woman with all the senses . . . sight, hearing, touch, smell, and taste.* She had the half-rational thought that his lordship must have studied in the same amorous school as her mother. He was sniffing, staring, stroking, and whispering . . . any second now she expected to be nibbled as well.

By her mother's standards, the earl was a prime specimen of the accomplished and desirable lover . . . handsome, smooth, masterful. In fact, she thought with growing despair, her mother would probably be delirious with joy if she could see what was happening to her at this very moment!

She jerked her head as he aimed his mouth for hers, and his lips grazed her jaw instead, then dropped a string of light kisses around her throat. When she felt the rasp of his tongue and telltale tug of her skin, she cringed. Was this what she had to look forward to? A lifetime of being continually sniffed, ogled, handled, and nibbled by men with rampaging passions and extravagant pedigrees?

Passions and pedigrees. She froze. For one breathtaking instant, her present danger intersected her larger dilemma of how to wrest control of her life and future from her mother. And at that critical juncture stood her current abductor. Tall, dark, and undeniably handsome, he fairly oozed worldliness, sophistication, and sexual accomplishment. If anything he said was to be believed, he was a nobleman, a peer of the realm . . . wealthy and unmarried and thirty years old . . .

He was *exactly* what her mother wanted for her.

Her thoughts raced wildly as his hands began to roam her waist, rising up her sides, searching the shape of her beneath the damp layers of her clothes. Then he was sliding to a seat on the chair beside her, and the next instant, she was being lifted and dragged onto his lap.

The heat of his body beneath her bottom and the feel of his hands gliding over her waist and up her back should have generated either panic or outrage in her. But just now, with her limbs aching from cold and tension and her thoughts fastened tenaciously on turning her predicament into an opportunity, she suppressed those alarming sensations. All she could think was that the libidinous earl could be the answer to her prayers.

"Wealthy, handsome, and thirty," she whispered, pushing on his shoulders and managing to put a bit more space between them. "Tell me, your lordship . . . do you play polo? Are you simply mad about horses and racing?"

"I've a respectable string of ponies." He overcame her resistance and resumed his intimate inventory of her neck and other ear.

"And do you go to the theater often? How is your Shakespeare? I imagine you must have a whole raft of sonnets tucked away inside you." She bit her lip and quelled a massive urge to shiver as his hands slid up her sides.

She thought he mumbled something like: "One or two."

"And what about music, your lordship? You have such a lovely, deep voice . . . do you sing? Perhaps play a musical instrument?"

She held her breath as he stilled, mid-nibble, and raised his head to look at her. His skin had taken on a ruddy cast and his eyes had a dark, luminous quality that, even to her novice's eye, spoke of dangerously aroused passions. He frowned, and she felt his hands tighten possessively on her waist. The moment of truth had come.

"Polo ponies, Shakespeare, sonnets . . . now a singing voice?" he said, fighting to recall and make sense of that barrage of questions. "Inquisitive little thing, aren't you?"

"You're perfect." She took a steadying breath. "Wealthy, knowledgeable, accomplished . . . undoubtedly an expert in all sorts of amorous matters."

"Good of you to notice," he said dryly, mentally fanning the steam from his senses as he focused on her and caught the sense of purpose in her expression. "I wasn't certain you were paying attention."

"Of course, it really would be better if you were married," she hurried on, mentally measuring and evaluating each line and feature of his face, tilting her head this way and that, trying to view him from her worldly mother's perspective.

"It would?" He returned her scrutiny with a hint of incredulity.

"Absolutely. It would demonstrate how settled, stable, and dependable you are. That, and . . . my mother says that a man who has to bear with a wife probably deserves a mistress."

He gave a short, surprised laugh. "Your mother says that, does she? She sounds like a very interesting woman."

"Men generally seem to think so," she said, squirming gingerly on his hard thighs and wondering what he would do if she bolted from his lap.

"Uncomfortable?" He had noticed her movements. "So am I." Over her protests, he gathered her up in his arms and carried her to the divan.

Dropping her unceremoniously among the pillows, he sank over her and pinned her on her back against the tufted velvet with the weight of his chest. She barely had time to bring her hands up between them. "Noooo—"

"Come now, Gabrielle . . ." His voice was low and ragged.

"I don't think this is at all wise, your lordship." Panicking at the determined glint in his eyes and the urgency of his body against hers, she pushed with all her might and turned her face away. "It's only fair to warn you that if you continue in this behavior, you're letting yourself in for a grave disappointment."

"Nothing short of your turning out to be a longshoreman littered with tattoos could disappoint me, sweetheart." He gazed hotly at her ill-concealed breasts. "And from what I can see, that's not bloody likely."

"Trust me, your lordship, a man of your expertise and experience would most certainly be disappointed." She drew a jerky breath and looked up at him, forcing back the waves of terror pounding at the edge of her awareness. "You may have noticed . . . I am not very adept at this 'passion' business. My amorous skills are dismal, at best." His smile lost a degree or two of heat. "Oh, it's not that my mother hasn't tried to instruct me. The problem seems to be that I haven't shown any particular aptitude for the amorous arts. That . . . and I have an abysmal lack of interest in the subject."

"What in hell are you talking about?" he demanded.

Whether it was prudent or not, whether she had thought it through fully or not, the time had come to try out the desperate plan that was still half formed in her head.

"It's something of a story, I'm afraid . . . but, if you will just be patient . . . You may recall, I said I was out on the streets tonight because of my mother—that we argued fiercely." She saw his impatience rising and backed up to start again. "First you should know . . . my mother is a very beautiful and elegant woman, and for years she has been the mistress of a wealthy nobleman who—"

"Stop!" He raised a hand, glowering. "What the devil does your mother have to do with any of this?"

"She has everything to do with it . . . and with the proposition I'm about to make you."

"Proposition?"

He stared at the tousled hair spread around her, at the smooth shoulders and ripe breasts barely hidden by her ruined garments, at the wild jumble of feelings visible in her face. She was the most improbable and exasperating female he had encountered in quite some time. She had squirmed, evaded, and resisted him . . . protested, dissembled, and avoided him . . . since the first minute he set eyes on her. Now, with him poised on the brink of making mad, passionate love to her, she lay beneath him apologizing for her ineptness as a woman of passion and dragging out a sordid family history by way of explanation! And as if that weren't enough, she announced that now *she* intended to make *him* a proposition.

It was just too much for his jaded sensibilities to resist. Exotic, rapacious, or even rapturous sex he could have anytime. It wasn't every night he was propositioned by a self-confessed lousy lover . . . who had a noble father, a yet-to-be-chosen fiancé, a flaming courtesan for a mother . . . and the air of a cranky debutante. She had to be one of the most entertaining street tarts in London. And, for some unfathomable reason, his fingertips itched when he looked at her.

"What sort of proposition?" he demanded, shifting to one side, on his elbow.

"Well, it's a rather unusual one. And I would have you understand that I am compelled only by desperate circumstances to so desperate an act." She paused to gather her courage and announced with great gravity: "You see, I've turned nineteen and my mother thinks it's time I fell madly and passionately in love."

"She does, does she?" He bit his lip. "I wasn't aware there was such a strict timetable for such things. Rather like British Rail, is it? 'Young girls with names beginning with the letter 'G' depart for amorous bliss promptly at seven twenty-three . . .'"

She gasped and pushed violently with both hands, forcing him up onto his arms above her as she tried to wriggle away.

"Whoa—come back, here!" He caught her.

"I assure you this is no laughing matter," she said hotly. "This afternoon, she introduced me to a detestable French count, and I . . . well, I didn't react favorably to his manner of wooing, and he left in a terrible huff. My mother was furious. You see, she wants me to take a lover and have a grand and glorious romance, like she did.

Something for the ages . . . a fiery, scintillating affair of the heart and body and soul . . . a love to be immortalized in sonnets and celebrated in Italian opera."

He studied her with rising incredulity. "And you find that objectionable?"

"Don't you see, she insists that I become a courtesan, like her."

"And what is wrong with that? I would think being the grand romance of a wealthy and generous nobleman might have definite advantages for a young girl."

"For some other 'young girl,' " she retorted stubbornly. "I haven't the slightest wish to be 'the hunger in a man's eyes' or 'the fire in his soul.' "

He stared at her for a long moment, then peeled himself from her tense form and rolled from the divan to stand. Jerking his vest down, he gave her a turbulent look.

"I need a drink."

She closed her eyes and fairly melted into the ruby velvet cushions beneath her. It had worked!

Hearing a scrape of glass raking metal, she sat up and braced on her arms. The blood drained from her head, clearing her vision but leaving her flushed and a bit unsteady. She scooted to the edge of the divan, tucked her skirts securely down about her ankles, and prayed she didn't lose her nerve. She had come this far . . .

Shortly he returned to the divan with two tall, fluted goblets filled with a sparkling golden wine that contained tiny bubbles. She hesitated, then accepted the glass he offered her, giving it a suspicious sniff. "This is 'champagne,' isn't it?" She made a face and held the glass well away from her nose without tasting it. "My mother is mad about the stuff. It's terribly *romantic*."

"And, I take it, *you* are not." He took another sip and eyed her over the rim of his glass.

"I haven't a romantic bone in my entire body," she said

with a perverse bit of pride. "I can't abide staying up until sunrise and then sleeping all day with squashed cucumbers drying on my face. And I loathe wearing bosom enhancers and being stuffed into dresses that don't have any shoulders . . . and milk baths and risqué stories and oysters on the half shell and the smell of cigar smoke . . ." He choked on a swallow of wine and stared at her. She realized how strident she sounded and halted to take a steadying breath. "I simply have no desire for a life of extravagant love and soaring passions."

"You haven't?" he said, lowering his empty glass, watching her keenly for telltale signs of pretense. "I thought all young girls wanted to fall madly and thrillingly in love . . . to capture a man's eye, his heart, and his fortune."

"As you pointed out, I am hardly a 'young girl' anymore." She gave him an adamant look, as if expecting a rebuke or rebuttal. When none came, she softened a bit, confessing matter-of-factly: "That . . . and . . . I don't have the juices for it."

Pierce wasn't sure what sort of tale he had expected to hear from her, but he certainly wasn't prepared for the blend of innocence and matter-of-factness that she displayed toward carnal matters. And there was something oddly unsettling about her sitting there in her ruined dress and bedraggled hair, forswearing girlish dreams of love and all the pleasures, intrigues, and agonies of human desire. Her story of being forced by her mother to take a wealthy lover was plausible enough; he had known others who found their way into the demimonde in that very fashion. But none of them had resisted their pampered fate for long —or protested it out of a professed lack of feminine desire. *Juices.* Good God. Did she honestly believe she had no passion or desire in her?

There was a new spark in her blue eyes when she

looked up again, and her next words threw him into even greater confusion.

"What I need, your lordship, is a *lover*. Someone my mother would accept as a suitable protector. Someone with wealth and sophistication and a noble pedigree." Her face began to glow with expectation. "You wouldn't have to do much . . . just come to my mother's house, declare your undying fascination with me and behave as if utterly besotted." In the ensuing silence, a few additional duties occurred to her. "And be generous. And attentive, at least at first." She warmed to the images forming in her mind. "Then my mother will think me safely settled with a generous protector and leave me to find a suitable hus—"

"Just a moment," he interrupted, scowling. "Your proposition is that I present myself as your lover . . . to your *mother*?"

She nodded earnestly. "In return, your lordship, I could pay you. And, of course, I would also reimburse you for whatever flowers, chocolates, and love tokens might prove necessary. When I turned nineteen, I began receiving a sizable income from an inheritance left me by my great aunt Theodora. Money is no object."

"Money?" He lay back on one elbow on the divan, staring at her. Could she be serious? She certainly seemed to be. He thought for a moment. She wanted to buy him. Never before, in all his sensual exploration and indulgence, had a female offered to *buy* him. The possibilities in that idea sent a tantalizing stir through his blood.

"You propose to purchase my services as a lover, for money?"

"Not as an *actual* lover. As a lover in name only," she clarified, adding, "And only for a few weeks."

The notion captured his jaded fancy, insinuating itself into his highly developed sense of the absurd. *In name only.* The term applied to marriages, not affairs. And it was that very fact—the perfect irony of pretending to sin—that appealed to the social scapegrace in him. What a delicious game that could be. And how very interesting of her to propose such a thing.

He slid his gaze over her curvaceous form and lush, intriguing mouth . . . which just now was set with concentration. Even if she was serious, the prospect of *not-sinning,* in close consort with this toothsome bit of muslin, was a novel and utterly delicious one. And when the novelty and charm of illicit abstinence grew tedious, as it undoubtedly would, there would be an even more stimulating prospect at hand: the leisurely erotic discovery of the curious and unpredictable creature inside Gabrielle's appealing body. There certainly would be endless opportunities . . . the inevitable consequence of the closeness required by such a pretense.

Better yet . . . if he could manage to wring some political benefit from her bizarre proposition, then this night wouldn't be a total waste.

"I have more money than I will ever spend," he replied. "No, if I did agree to help you, it would have to be for something far more interesting. Or important."

"Such as?" She held her breath as a calculating look settled over him.

"I might be willing to pose as your lover if you would be willing to see the prime minister again and report to me on it."

She frowned. "See him again? You mean, let him 'rescue' me?"

He laughed wryly. "If he is so inclined. Meet with him again and, afterward, tell me everything the old vaulter says and does."

That was all? Just talk to Old William again? Eat biscuits and drink cocoa? The memory of William's fervent exhortations to purity and decency rose in her mind. She would have to suffer a few platitudes and improving lectures. And she would have to keep Rosalind's name out of—

What was she thinking? She had to agree to anything that would get her out of the earl's clutches.

"Agreed." She pushed to her feet, squaring her shoulders and stiffly offering him her hand to seal the agreement. He rose, fixed on the sight of her awkward gesture.

"Agreed. But I think a bargain as unique as this should be sealed with something more befitting than a clasp of hands."

Before she realized what he intended, he had pulled her into his arms and was lowering his mouth to hers. And for the second time that day she was being kissed against her will. Two seductions, two kidnappings, and now two *kisses*. Why wouldn't anyone believe that she hadn't the slightest interest in this amorous stuff?

She tried to push away, but his hold on her tightened to match her efforts, and she relented, deciding to endure it as long as it went no further. Gradually her attention shifted from her own inner turmoil to the fact that his lips seemed strangely both hard and soft against hers, and were mercifully *dry*. She considered the way he varied the pressure of his mouth on hers and canted his head, covering and massaging her lips with what she supposed— by comparison with the count's crude motions—must be some finesse. And at least he had the decency to keep his tongue to himself.

After what seemed an interminable length of time, he broke it off and straightened above her with a roused look. An instant later, he purged his expression, but not before she caught the male pique in it. She gave him an apologetic smile.

"Don't take it personally, your lordship. I just don't

have any desire for that sort of thing." Slipping from his arms, she stepped back and discreetly wiped the corners of her lips. "Now, if you would be so good as to take me home . . . or send for a cab."

"I shall send you home in my carriage," he growled, coming to his senses and giving the bellpull a fierce yank. By the time his driver brought the coach around, he was in control enough to insist that she wear his cloak over her damp clothes.

"Thank you, your lordship," she said, as he settled the heavy garment on her shoulders. "I will return it to you when you come to meet my mother. Tomorrow at five?" Unable to think of a reason to decline, he nodded. "Twenty-one Eaton Square." A rap at the door indicated that the carriage was ready. She paused with her hand on the door handle and gave him a glowing smile.

"You won't regret this, your lordship."

He stood staring at the door after she had gone, reliving that disturbing kiss, feeling again the maddening warmth and impassivity of her mouth beneath his. *No juices.* The corners of his eyes crinkled as his face warmed with a devilish smile.

"I might not regret it, Gabrielle. But you very likely will."

4

The carriage sped through the damp streets toward
Eaton Square, carrying a very different Gabrielle Le
Coeur back to the house she had fled a scant few hours
before. This Gabrielle sat smiling on the plush seat,
bundled in the earl's cloak, giddy with both release and
triumph. She had not only survived her misadventures, she
had actually managed to turn them to her advantage. That
fact generated in her a startling new sense of power and
purpose. She no longer had to suffer her mother's edicts in
daughterly meekness; she had a plan now—or the start of
one—and the means to carry it out. She had taken her first
step toward a life of her own.

But as her thoughts shifted from the memory of the

night's events to what awaited her, she sobered. Her only hope of escaping a scene with her mother was to announce straightaway that during her adventures she had met the man of her dreams and fallen madly and passionately in love. If Rosalind had a weakness at all, it was for the wildly and recklessly romantic. And the coup de grace would come when Rosalind learned the identity of her daughter's grand inamorato . . . none other than the handsome and wealthy earl of Sandbourne. All would be instantly forgiven; she was sure of it.

Now all she had to do was behave as if she were wildly and gloriously in love. And how, she wondered, did one do that?

The house was ablaze with lights when the carriage rumbled to a halt and she peered out the window. While the earl's driver was dismounting, one of the massive front doors opened and Gunther appeared with a lantern in his hand, jolting into motion at the sight of a crest on the side of the carriage. He dashed down the steps as the driver was letting down the carriage steps.

"Miss LeCoeur!" Gunther shouldered aside the coachman to assist Gabrielle himself. "Your mother has been wondering where you were."

She had more than "wondered," Gabrielle knew the instant she stepped through the doors. The gaslights of the large center hall were on high and the drawing room and dining room doors on opposite sides of the hall had been thrown back. It was as if Rosalind had turned her house into a beacon of light, hoping her wayward daughter would see it and find her way home.

"Madam—she is home!" Gunther called, propelling Gabrielle quickly across the polished marble floor.

Rosalind rushed from the drawing room, accompanied by her friend Clementine Bolt and a uniformed constable carrying his hat in his hand. They met Gabrielle just outside the doors. Rosalind seized her shoulders and thrust her back an arm's length to make a frantic assessment of her.

"Dearest heaven, Gabrielle—are you all right?" She stared at her daughter's bedraggled hair and the voluminous man's cloak she wore. "Are you hurt? Ill?"

"I'm fine, Mama, truly. I've never been better," Gabrielle said, smiling with what she hoped passed for romantic bliss. Rosalind's maternal relief was short-lived.

"Then you've a great deal to answer for, young lady—flying out the door without a word to anyone—unescorted and unprotected!" Rosalind felt the several pairs of eyes trained on them and abruptly halted, releasing Gabrielle and reclaiming her legendary poise. She turned to the constable, and her voice and manner gentled. "Thank you, Sergeant, for coming so quickly to my assistance. You may call your men in. It appears my daughter is home, safe and sound, and that is all that matters to me."

He murmured something about it being a pleasure to assist her and, with a dubious glance at Gabrielle, departed. When the door had closed behind him, Rosalind turned on Gabrielle once again with rising indignation.

"Do you have any idea how many people you have inconvenienced with your thoughtless, headstrong behavior? I've had my friends, the constables, even the servants, out combing the streets for you. You haven't the slightest notion of the dreadful things that can befall a young g-girl—" She stammered to a halt, for at that moment Gunther lifted the black cloak from Gabrielle's shoulders, revealing her ruined dress and stocking-clad toes.

"Good God. You look like a street urchin." True horror crept into her face. "Your dress is ripped—and where are your shoes? What's happened to you?"

"Oh, Mama . . . the most wonderful thing in the

world." Gabrielle broke into a beaming, rapturous smile. "Tonight I fell in love."

Of all the possible explanations for Gabrielle's appalling state, "fell in love" was absolutely the last thing Rosalind expected to hear. It took a moment to register, then she swayed and seized both Clementine's hand and Gunther's sleeve, to steady herself. For a moment she stared at Gabrielle, blinking, unable to believe her senses. Then she came to life, issuing distracted orders for sherry and a warm blanket and clamping an arm about Gabrielle to drag her into the drawing room.

"Love? In the streets? And looking like a drowned rat?" She pulled Gabrielle before the massive marble fireplace, motioning Gunther to bring her a chair. "This had better be good, my girl—this had better be good!"

"Oh, Mama, it is better than good . . . it is *wonderful.*" Gabrielle let her eyes unfocus, as if she were staring into some cherished memory that required only inner vision. "He is so handsome and strong and noble. He rescued me from some foul and depraved beasts who tried to abduct me—tried to steal me right off the street."

Rosalind clutched her diamond-studded throat.

"Oh, but you needn't worry," Gabrielle quickly assured her. "*He* was there, and he sent the wretches packing. You see, I got caught in the rainstorm and was lost—when a carriage swooped down on me, out of nowhere." She warmed to her dramatic tale, embellishing as she went along. "I screamed and fought as those hideous monsters tried to pull me inside—and suddenly *he* appeared, dashing from his carriage to come to my rescue." She clasped her hands over her heart, as if to constrain its wild response, and her mother pushed her down onto the chair Gunther had carried to the fire for her.

"Sherry, Clementine—quickly." Rosalind motioned her

friend along while staring at her daughter . . . caught up unexpectedly in Gabrielle's story.

"He pulled me from their clutches and gave them a terrible thrashing," Gabrielle continued moments later, sipping the sherry and glancing at her mother from the corner of her eye to see how Rosalind was taking it. There was heightened color in her mother's cheeks, and she seemed to be genuinely engrossed. "Afterward, I was so frightened and distraught that I could scarcely speak my name. So he took me to a lovely restaurant, where he helped me to dry my clothes and settle my nerves. Once there, one thing led to another. We talked. And he held my hands and looked deep into my eyes . . ."

Her voice and attention trailed off, seemingly into mists of memory, and she smiled with an unmistakable feminine glow. It was so utterly unlike Gabrielle that Rosalind looked up, dumbfounded, at Clementine and Gunther. The pair stood a discreet distance away, wagging their heads, equally confused by the drastic change in her daughter.

"And he gave me his cloak and sent me home in his carriage . . ." Sighing, Gabrielle came to her senses and pushed to her feet. "If you don't mind . . . I am chilled and exhausted, and I simply cannot wait another minute to get out of this wretched dress." She floated toward the door, smiling. "Good night, Mama . . . Mrs. Bolt."

"Gabrielle!" Rosalind recovered in time to halt her just inside the doors. She turned back to find her mother and the others hurrying after her. "Who is he? This man you've fallen in love with?"

"Oh, didn't I say? That is the best part." Gabrielle laughed with genuine delight, savoring her mother's expression as she announced: "He is an *earl*. And he's so unbearably handsome and so fabulously wealthy—"

"An earl?" Rosalind fairly choked on her surprise. "*Which* earl?"

"Sandbourne," she said, savoring the way her mother's face went blank with shock. "The earl of Sandbourne. Oh—and I pray you won't mind—I've invited him to call tomorrow at five to take tea with us. He is so anxious to meet you and pay his respects. Oh, I can't wait for you to meet him. I just know you'll adore him too!"

She gave a giddy twirl of excitement for good measure and then floated up the stairs on a cloud of romantic euphoria, leaving her mother standing at the base of the stairs, mute with shock and wearing a look of deepening horror.

When Gabrielle disappeared from sight at the head of the stairs, Rosalind grabbed Clementine's arm to steady herself. The carriage, the cloak, the astonishing changes in her daughter's attitude and demeanor . . .

"Sandbourne—did you hear? Only this afternoon she despised love and passion and romance, and tonight, she is in love with *Sandbourne!*" Her knees buckled. Clementine and Gunther rushed her back into the drawing room, where one helped her into the chair Gabrielle had just vacated and the other rushed to the liquor cabinet to pour her a stout brandy. She downed the drink in one unladylike gulp, but not even its fierce burn could distract her from the distress of learning the identity of her daughter's new love.

"I cannot believe it. It's a calamity of the first order," she muttered numbly. "Of all the wealthy and titled men in England, she has to be rescued by one whose reputation would make a bawd-house bully blush for shame. Why, the man's a complete libertine—a pure debauchee—"

"Won't keep a proper mistress, like a decent an' godly gentleman would," Clementine said, posting herself at Rosalind's side and patting her hand sympathetically. "Goes for fancy houses an' his friends' lady wives, the bounder. Rampin' wild, I hear."

"And as a result has set more tongues wagging than the wretched Prince of Wales. It's a wonder he hasn't been called out by some cuckold of a husband . . ." Red crept into her pale cheeks as she stared fixedly at one spot, conjuring images of what lay ahead and seeing nothing but trouble. She buried her face in her hands.

"I wanted her to fall in love with a generous, gallant, good-hearted gentleman . . . at least the first time. Someone who would introduce her slowly and carefully to the delights of love. Someone who would lavish her with gifts and affection and would be concerned for her pleasure as well as his." A moment later she raised a stricken face to them. "My little Gabrielle and the earl of Sandbourne."

Tears welled, and she fumbled about in her bodice for her handkerchief. Gunther offered her the one from his breast pocket, and she dabbed her eyes. When she spoke again, her voice was a constricted rasp.

"My baby is in love with a *swine*."

But the worst was yet to come. A moment later she remembered the rest of what Gabrielle had said and moaned in earnest.

"And tomorrow the swine is coming to tea."

An hour later, across the city, Gabrielle's newfound love was sitting by the fire in his private room at Le Ciel, nursing his second brandy in as many hours and staring into the hearth at the glowing coals. Time dragged by as he waited for his second rendezvous of the evening—the one for which he had initially engaged this room.

It had been his intention, earlier, to intercept Gladstone's female of the evening, to question her thoroughly, and then to report his findings to his political contact, here. But upon encountering the stubborn but potentially pleasurable Gabrielle, he had decided to make more extensive use of his reservation at Le Ciel. Why waste a perfectly splendid opportunity for a seduction, he thought, especially when that opportunity would yield the very evidence he needed?

If all had gone as planned, he would have plied her with champagne and mesmerizing pleasures and would have melted her defenses and coaxed her into implicating Gladstone . . . finishing just in time to be joined by a third party. But all hadn't gone as planned, and now he sat wondering how he had let things get so out of hand.

He had expected her to be a first-class tart; she showed not a single greedy or licentious tendency. He expected her to yield up a tawdry tale of the sexual fumbling of an aged reprobate who misused the license afforded reformers; but the only story she told was of being fed sweetmeats and hounded toward virtue by a self-righteous old cod. He had expected to seduce her; she had intrigued and inveigled him into something of a bargain instead.

He was left with the feeling that there was more to his "Gabrielle" than met the eye. And he didn't know whether to be annoyed or amused at himself for agreeing to such an improbable scheme. *Pretending to be her lover.* He closed his eyes, praying it didn't have anything to do with the fact that he had recently marked the end of his third decade. For it was often said that when a man turned thirty . . .

There was a soft knock at the door, and he called permission to enter. A man clad in a black evening cloak slipped inside and stood for a moment in the shadows by the door, surveying the room and its lone occupant. Satisfied that conditions were as he expected them to be, he removed his hat and strolled forward.

"You're early, Tottenham," Pierce said, turning in his direction.

"I had an unexpectedly early finish to the evening," the man responded.

"What a coincidence." Pierce managed what passed for a laugh. "So did I."

That stopped Colonel Tottenham, Conservative MP, in his tracks. He studied Pierce's mood, then went to the table to deposit his hat, divest himself of his gloves, and pour himself a drink.

"Then, I take it, you didn't get the information we had hoped for."

"You take it correctly. The old man did go on one of his night prowls. I followed him to the Haymarket, where he picked up a young girl. It was storming bloody blazes, so he took the little piece straight back to his official residence and kept her there awhile. I caught her as she was leaving and questioned her. *Nothing.*"

"Nothing?" The colonel twitched as if stung by the news. "Damnation. We wait and we watch—the old chocker finally makes a move—" He hung one arm on the mantelpiece and looked Pierce over, noting his arrogant slouch and the air of heightened intensity about him. "Are you certain?"

"Believe me," Pierce said calmly, leveling a look on him, "I tried every sort of persuasion. She claims the old man tried to 'reform' her . . . fed her cocoa and biscuits in his kitchen and preached at her."

"Cocoa and bis—? Damn and double damn!" Tottenham whirled away, tossing back his liquor and straining to control his impatience. "We know the old reprobate's weakness, his Achilles' heel, and we still can't catch him in the act." He fixed Pierce with a meaningful stare. "You know, of course, that *certain people* will be most unhappy with this development."

Pierce nodded. He knew that someone high in government—the anonymous someone who had sent Tottenham to recruit him for this task—wanted to see the powerful and self-righteous William Gladstone drummed out of office, once and for all.

The old man was an iconoclast and an extreme eccentric at best, a raving madman and a traitor at worst . . . called everything from an embarrassment to the Empire to a communist, a lunatic, and a traitor. His predilection for prostitutes was an open secret in political circles. What would be a more fitting demise to his long and controversial career than being caught flat-footed in something as sordid and sensational as a bit of sex with one of the very prostitutes that he claimed to be trying to salvage? In the public mind, it would seem a short step from corrupting the women he claimed to be reforming to corrupting the government he claimed to be leading. By association, his programs and positions would come under grave suspicion as well.

Rumors, which had circulated for years about his libidinous activities, were not enough. The prime minister would have to be accused, confronted openly with the evidence of his debauchery. And to be believed, his accuser would have to be a man of consequence and credibility—both in politics and in the even worldlier pursuits of men.

"Something's got to be done about the man," Tottenham declared angrily. "He's half senile—perched at death's door—and determined to take the upper-class down with him. He's thrown in with that whining Liberal rabble and the 'shrieking sisterhood' who blame all the nation's ills on the nobility and all the *sin* in the world on the lusts of upper-class men. They make us out to be ravening beasts and the tarts and doxies to all be 'downcast daughters' and 'sad soiled doves.' I tell you—suspending the Contagious Diseases Act is just the start. He's out to ruin the entire landed class!"

"No," Pierce said thoughtfully, "he's out to banish both privilege and sin. For everyone but himself, that is. And that, my friend, is something I cannot allow. If he allows full repeal of the acts and tries to ban all prostitution, then he will succeed in making England over in his own image . . . We'll be a whole nation of hypocrites."

And if there was one thing Pierce St. James could not abide, it was a hypocrite.

People were people, he believed. And, despite popular upper-crust delusions to the contrary, all people, great and small, were basically alike underneath their linen and beneath their layers of manners and education. They all had the very same needs and desires . . . a living, a bit of respect, and the comforts of the flesh to make life bearable. Thus, it followed that men like William Gladstone, who sat in judgment on the passions of the general run of mankind while plying their dirty little pleasures in secret, were the worst sort of hypocrites. And they damn well deserved to be called on it.

In keeping with his forthright philosophy, Pierce had developed a reputation for common sense and unflinching candor in his public life. But that same openness, carried defiantly into his private life, had brought him a reputation as a libertine and horrified his rigidly respectable mother. To those determined to expose and bring down Gladstone, Pierce's noble rank, his thorough acquaintance with the world of illicit pleasures, and his open disdain for the hypocritical breast-beaters of the world marked him as the perfect man for the task of gathering evidence and pressing accusations.

"The evening may not have been a total waste, however," Pierce continued, studying his contact. "I've gotten the girl to agree to see Gladstone again and to report to me on all he does with her. It's possible he was just dallying with her the first time, lowering her guard, getting her to trust him."

"That is something at least. I knew we could count on

you, Sandbourne." Tottenham plunked his glass down on the mantelpiece and straightened. "We have several 'spies' watching the old man—they'll keep you advised of his movements. I'll try to get information on his schedule in advance. But you never know when he'll get the *urge* and go on one of his 'night walks.' "

Pierce nodded. "I'll send word as soon as I have something. It shouldn't be long."

When his visitor was gone, Pierce sat a few moments longer, trying to decide whether to drop by his club or simply call an end to the disappointing evening and go home to bed. When Le Ciel's majordomo informed him that his carriage had returned and stood ready, he grabbed up his hat and gloves and headed for the stairs.

A light mist hung in the air, and he waved his coachman to keep his seat and reached for the door handle himself. But once on the step, he paused and looked up.

"Where did you take her, Jack?"

"Where she said, m'lord. Twenty-one Eaton Square," his driver declared.

"Back door or front?"

"Oh, front, m'lord. Definitely front."

Pierce's dampened mood slid abruptly into the sewer. "Damn."

The storm of the previous night had so drenched the city that the streets fairly steamed the next afternoon. But the rain had also scoured much of the perpetual gray of soot and smoke from the skies over London, leaving in its wake a gloriously bright sun. People high and low spilled out into the streets, parks, and boulevards, basking in the unexpected warmth and the freshly washed feel of the city. Some strolled, some hawked wares from carts, some hurried along in carriages, cabs, or wagons . . . all taking care to avoid the brimming gutters and swelling ponds that the overburdened sewers left standing in many streets.

Splashing through the midst of it all, drawing glares from pedestrians scrambling to avoid the spray from its smart yellow wheels, was the earl of Sandbourne's glossy black carriage, with its gilded coat of arms emblazoned on the doors. Inside, Pierce St. James checked his watch then slipped it back into his vest pocket, venting annoyance with a forceful breath. He was going to be more than fashionably late, which meant he would have to make an entrance of some sort into God knew what sort of situation. He had to be mad as a hatter . . . walking into a strange house to face an unknown female and lay claim to the passions of her daughter.

Both the urgency and the promise of last night's encounter had faded in his mind. Just now, his reasons for honoring their ridiculous agreement seemed almost as incomprehensible to him as the allure of the young Gabrielle. In the harsh light of day, with the memory of her charms blurred by an intervening encounter with a bottle of brandy, the only details he remembered were her renouncement of romance and passion and her utter lack of response to his kiss. If it weren't for the fact that she might prove the key to tumbling Gladstone, he would have been tempted to forget the whole thing.

The carriage began to slow, and he heard Jack calling orders to his charges. When the coach came to a stop and he descended onto the pavement, he found himself standing on a carriage turn before a large Italianate house made of gray stone and trimmed with elegant iron fretwork. He glanced up and down the row and judged this to be one of the grander residences on the square, then looked back to check the numbers above the door again. *Twenty-one.* He squared his shoulders and climbed the steps to the black lacquered doors.

He was admitted to the house by a Teutonic wonder of butler. The fellow took his name, his hat, gloves, and walking stick, then bowed from the waist and strode off toward a pair of drawing room doors . . . leaving him to stare at the entry hall and wonder if the houseman had actually clicked his heels or if he had just imagined it.

The grand hall was done in a classical arch motif and soft Mediterranean tones: glowing white and peach marble was handsomely accented by deep green serpentine marble floors, sills, and elegant statuary niche. A massive carved marble staircase seemed to float down from the upper levels in a broad, effortless spiral, and the walls were studded with Corinthian pilasters. The floor was polished to a soft luster, and the hall table and benches were grandly carved rococo pieces that complemented the classical nature of the architecture.

This, Pierce thought, coming back to himself, was far from a bordello. He felt a curious sense of uneasiness at the fact that the place the girl resided appeared to be a private residence, and a handsome one, at that. A moment later, the houseman returned to lead him through a set of double doors into a large drawing room.

He paused as his name was announced, bracing for whoever or whatever awaited him. The walls were embellished with more pilasters, the windows were large and draped with layers of heavy velvet and sheerer silk, and the furnishings were upholstered in rich tapestries and brocades. The glow in the chamber came from the palette of colors—apricot, burnt umber, peach, and ivory—and from the huge, gilt-framed mirrors hanging on each wall.

Four women sat in the center of the room, before a massive marble hearth and mantel. They were dressed in the pinnacle of fashion; each in a figured silk dress made with a bustle and train, a dramatic hat, and daintily embroidered gloves. All but one. She was gowned in a stunning loden green silk that displayed her voluptuous figure, fair skin, and light coloring to near perfection. When she rose and turned to him with an outstretched hand, indicating that she was his hostess, surprise rendered him momentarily speechless.

Perceptions that had eluded his recall for the last several hours now rushed over him, mingling with present sense. The woman who greeted him was an older, fully ripened version of Gabrielle. She had the same light hair, the same huge blue eyes, and a similarly intriguing mouth. The resemblance was nothing short of remarkable; she obviously was the girl's mother. And since she was obviously expecting him, then perhaps Gabrielle's story . . .

"Lord Sandbourne," the woman said in throaty tones that set the air humming around him. "Welcome to my home."

"Madam. It was generous of you to see me on such short notice." He took her hand and gave it a graceful brush with his lips, realizing that he hadn't a clue to her name and struggling to find a rational approach to this unprecedented situation.

"Yes. It was short notice," she said, turning with her hand still on his, leading him toward the other women, who had kept their chairs and watched him approach with ill-disguised appraisal. "But then, my little Gabrielle can be quite persuasive . . . as you must know." He smiled politely; "persuasive" was not quite the word he had in mind just now for the little schemer. "Come, let me introduce to you my dear friends." She halted with him before the chair of a petite, raven-haired, dark-eyed woman who not so long ago must have been a stunningly exotic beauty.

"Your lordship, may I present Mrs. Genevieve Francette, originally of Paris."

"Mrs. Francette," he murmured, taking the woman's languidly extended hand and doing a stiff obeisance over it. Her dark eyes were cool and thorough as they drifted over him, and he felt oddly like a schoolboy being given marks in deportment.

"And this is Mrs. Clementine Bolt," his hostess said, inserting her arm through his with the familiarity and grace of a woman used to both touching and maneuvering men.

He tried to recall what Gabrielle had said about her mother: she was both a devout romantic who loved champagne and wanted her daughter to fall gloriously in love, and a coolheaded pragmatist who insisted that her daughter's glorious love be titled, cultured, and suitably well heeled. The sensual flow of her movements, the arresting assurance of her manner, the beauty she wore so comfortably . . . he could believe she was a nobleman's prime weakness. The realization struck:

Gabrielle had told him the truth.

Coming back to his senses with a start, he found himself facing a buxom, red-haired woman whose pale complexion hinted at a lifelong battle with freckles.

"Mrs. Bolt," he breathed placing a delicate brush of the lips on the back of her hand. Her mischievous blue eyes and direct, admiring smile reminded him of a country lass in the throes of flirtation.

"And this is Mrs. Ariadne Baden-Powell," she said drawing him on to her third guest, a tall, willowy woman with chestnut brown hair, catlike green eyes, and a neck encased in a small fortune in pearls. She acknowledged him by raising one eyebrow and taking his hand in a firm handshake that left no opening for old-fashioned gallantry.

"Sandbourne," she said with a distinctly upper-crust clench to her jaw. "Good to meet you at last, your lordship. I believe we share a friend in common."

"We do? And who might that be?" he asked.

"Gerald Graves, Lord Tavistock," she answered with what could only be termed a proprietary air.

"Gerald? Ah, the *old* Lord Tavistock," he said, wishing to recall it the moment he said it, then making it even worse. "Forgive me, but I thought he had died."

"He did. Last year." Mrs. Baden-Powell said archly, shifting on her seat and looking as if the fact still generated turbulent emotions in her. "In my arms."

"Well," he said, caught off guard by the visibility of her grief and his belated realization that she had been the old boy's mistress. What was the accepted form for addressing grieving mistresses? He settled for: "My . . . condolences . . . upon the loss of Tavistock. He was a very fine gentleman."

"Indeed he was. Of the old school, of course. Noble, valiant-hearted, and generous to a fault," she responded, pinning him with a look that declared *him* to be suspect in each of those areas.

"Then perhaps you knew Addison Savoy, Lord Kenyon," his hostess declared, steering him toward a straight-backed parlor chair situated at the center of that circle of high femininity. "He was an especial friend of our Genevieve's. And Dickie Howard, Lord Bartlesford, was a dear companion and close confidante of our Clementine's."

He nodded to each woman, in turn, realizing that they were all mistresses of deceased noblemen. He managed to say something marginally polite about each of their losses, while glancing surreptitiously at his hostess and wondering to whom *she* belonged. Someone wealthy—he flicked an eye around their opulent setting—and spectacularly generous. He knew most of the titled and many of the wealthier men in England and had seen them out and about with their lights of love. But he couldn't recall ever setting eyes on Gabrielle's beautiful mother. . . .

"As I said, it was good of you to join us for tea," she

said, turning a smile on him that was carefully crafted to appear gracious without implying acceptance of him. "I must confess that I was terrified by Gabrielle's report of her misadventure. I owe you a great debt, your lordship."

He returned the smile a bit mechanically, wondering what the inventive little Gabrielle had told her. "It was the least a gentleman could do, madam."

"I think we might dispense with the 'madam,' Lord Sandbourne. I am generally addressed as Mrs. LeCoeur." Her smile warmed from icy to a moderate chill. "Or you may address me as Rosalind, if that would make you more comfortable. In view of the relationship you have come to seek with my daughter, I would not think either too familiar."

Rosalind LeCoeur. His jaw loosened before he could check his reaction. The same Rosalind who was the duke of Carlisle's mistress? Since Pierce had been abroad in society, the fabled beauty had not been seen in the demimonde's traditional haunts: the races, the fashionable restaurants and risqué parties, and the theater. After the death of the duke's wife, more than ten years ago, the staid peer had all but retired from society, favoring the company of his long-term mistress over that of society's tyrannical doyens.

Suddenly he knew who Gabrielle was. She was the mysterious "love child" Rosalind was widely rumored to have produced with the duke. Gabrielle was a duke's daughter . . . a famous secret . . . the tantalizing product of a grandly passionate and illicit union. His eyes widened. What *had* he gotten himself into?

"Tell me, your lordship," Rosalind said, watching his changing expressions with a discerning eye, "why is it you have never formed a significant alliance with a lady? It is my understanding that you have never been married or betrothed, and that those in the know would be hard pressed to name a single lady with whom you have been in love." Her summary left no doubt that she was acquainted with his freewheeling reputation.

"I-I have been a man who enjoyed his freedom, Mrs. LeCoeur," he said, still recovering from the revelation of Gabrielle's identity. Shifting uncomfortably on his chair, he cast about for a plausible explanation for desiring a change in his singular and hitherto hedonistic mode of living.

"Indeed," she said, lifting an eloquent eyebrow. "But, a titled man with a considerable fortune who has no wife and has had no affairs of substance . . ." Her gaze raked him like subtle claws. "It gives rise to certain . . . questions."

"Questions?" he echoed, feeling his gut contract.

"Are you quite certain it is a *mistress* you want? and not a 'bully companion'?"

He visibly stiffened. Her matter-of-factness rivaled her daughter's! Not since schoolyard foolery had anyone suggested that his tastes ran to anything but women. "Madam. I am *quite* certain." He desperately seized upon what he hoped would pass for an explanation. "Of late, the lure of stage lights and fast company seems to have lost much of its appeal. I find I now desire . . . a different sort of companionship . . . a deeper and more thoroughgoing experience of love."

"*Alors*—you claim to have been in love before?" the Frenchwoman said.

"For how long?" the aging country girl asked, leaning forward an inch.

"With what sort of woman?" the Baden-Powell creature demanded, lowering her chin, looking as if she might charge at any moment.

Muscle by muscle, his body tensed with shock. He was accustomed to a subtle bit of bargaining in acquiring his pleasures, but nothing in his varied and worldly experience had prepared him for sitting in a civilized drawing room, defending his amorous history over tea . . . before a quartet of astute and unflinching women of the world. He straightened irritably. He did not intend to spread the details of his involvements before them to be picked over like the carcass of yesterday's hen.

"What man of experience has *not* been so engaged by a member of your fair sex?" he said, surprising even himself with so rational and diplomatic an assertion. "Suffice it to say: early attachments are seldom lasting ones. One's judgment requires time to mature. But, I confess, I had not realized the full extent of my change of heart until I saw Gabrielle." He watched Rosalind cast a sidelong glance at her friends, who returned it with speaking looks that he was at a loss to interpret.

"And just what was it about our Gabrielle that captured you so, your lordship?" Rosalind asked with that cool, impenetrable smile.

"Captured me. Yes. Quite. The perfect way to express what happened the instant I set eyes on Gabrielle. . . ." He shifted again; his chair seemed harder and less hospitable with each passing moment. He glanced about. "Will she not be joining us? I had expected to see her . . ."

"But of course," Rosalind said, pinning him with a look that was unabashedly critical as it lowered to his empty hands. No flowers, no chocolates, no token of esteem and affection, it said clearly. He unfolded his hands and spread them tightly, palms down, against his thighs. "It is only that, in such delicate matters, some things are best left to *la maman*," she continued. "You must understand: Gabrielle is a tempestuous young girl, whose fiery passions and emotions sometimes run ahead of her judgment. As her mother, I must exercise *restraint* for her and see to her best interests." The glint of determination in her eye said that despite her voluptuary profession, she possessed the necessary amount of that austere virtue. "Tell me, Lord Sandbourne, are you a gaming man?"

"I sit a few rounds, from time to time," he said, stiffening back and feeling the wooden carvings on the top of the chair digging into his spine.

Rosalind nodded, glancing at the others, who again communicated something with their eyes. "You belong to a number of clubs, I assume. Do you normally dine there of an evening, or do you prefer your own cook?"

"My own cook, most evenings." From the sidelong glances they exchanged and the looks on their faces, he wasn't certain how his answers struck them.

"Clubs and restaurants can be so noisy and difficult," Rosalind announced, phrasing her agreement in terms oblique enough to discourage optimism. "How much better to have a quiet meal in the company of a kindred and comforting companion."

In short order he was asked a dozen more questions, ranging from how long he had employed his valet and cook, to the size and character of his wine cellar in town, to how much of the year he spent in the country and whether he intended to travel abroad in the coming year. Additional inquiries elicited from him the facts that he seldom entertained at home, had no intentions of marrying in the foreseeable future, and kept open accounts at Asprey and Co. and Garrard's, jewelers, at Agnew's gallery in Bond Street, with the perfumer Floris, and at Liberty's, Harrods, and a number of the finest haberdashers, wine merchants, and silk drapers in London.

Clearly, he was being interrogated with regard to his reliability as a potential protector, and with a forthrightness that quite shocked him. But their insufferable curiosity did not end with his social habits, personal tastes, and fiscal condition; it extended to his very person. Four pairs of experienced eyes surveyed him thoroughly, if discreetly, from stem to stern. He could feel them analyzing the quality of his barbering, the cut of his coat, the wear of his boot heels, and the grace of his gestures . . . even the way he moistened his lips. And if the intimate probing and faint luminosity of their gazes meant what he thought they did, his sensual potential and amorous equipage were also being judged . . . with professional precision.

It was all he could do to keep his seat, much less his poise. No one in polite society—not even the most brazen of mamas—would have dared *mention* his solvency, personal tastes, or amorous reputation, much less question them. But, here, in the demimonde—this underlayer of society, which existed to stimulate and satisfy upper-crust males like him—apparently nothing was taken for granted; rank and wealth, even desire itself, were subject to challenge. Here, things were appallingly reversed; women assessed and passed judgment openly upon men, the way men were wont to evaluate females in the so-called respectable world.

And the only clue to how he was faring in their estimate lay in the bewildering play of glances between them, a form of communication that mortal men were not privileged to understand. A sort of . . . "feminese."

After a pause, Rosalind fixed a searching look on his burning face and smiled at whatever she saw. "I am still waiting for your answer, your lordship, to the question of what it was about Gabrielle that you found so captivating." He could have sworn the lot of them edged forward in their seats—lady hawks eyeing their helpless prey.

"She is quite lovely," he said a bit testily, seizing the first thing that came to mind. What *maman* would not wish to hear that her daughter was ravishing? "Stunning, in fact. Exquisite. Beautiful beyond bearing."

"Perhaps . . . if your tastes run to shoeless, dripping wet, terrified schoolgirls," Rosalind responded, with a vinegar-and-honey smile. He tightened his grip on his knees.

"She is clever and delightfully . . . unpredictable," he declared emphatically.

"Which was evident, no doubt, from her penchant for strolling the London streets at night, alone, and in the middle of a raging downpour." Rosalind raised her chin a notch, positively daring him to try yet another vapid bit of flattery.

He took a deep breath and leveled a sizzling look on his chief inquisitor, seeing her in a new light. Despite her romantic proclivities, she was apparently accustomed to dealing with the realities of relations between the sexes in a forthright manner. In the matter of her daughter's future, she insisted on truth, not ephemeral niceties. Very well, he would give her "truth" . . . and then see if, like most women, she claimed to want it while secretly preferring the sweetness of deception.

"To be honest, I cannot for the life of me understand what I find so compelling about the little vixen." He glanced from one elegant courtesan to another, dropping all pretense of romantic delicacy and with it, much of his tension. "All I know is that my fingers itch, my blood pounds in my veins, and my loins begin to burn whenever I look at her. Last night she made me laugh, made me think, and made me *stop*. God knows, that alone puts her in a class by herself." He saw the way their eyebrows rose and knew his defiant candor had just sealed their opinion of him. He risked little by adding: "I want Gabrielle a great deal. And I am willing to be generous."

There was a long moment's pause, in which he could hear the ticking of the gilded mantel clock above him and the thudding of his heart in his ears. Then Rosalind rose abruptly and reached for the bellpull. When her Viking houseman arrived, she draped her hand on the back of her chair and struck a dramatic pose. Pierce fully expected to be thrown out of the house on his ear. Instead, she gave the houseman a dignified nod.

"Gunther, please ask my daughter to join us."

5

On the floor above, Gabrielle sat at the writing desk in her boudoir, sealing an envelope. "Please, *cherie,* take care," her maid, Rue, entreated from across the desk, anxiously eyeing her ink-smudged fingers and the red sealing wax she was pressing onto white vellum. "There is not time to change your dress . . . His lordship is already here."

"I'm finished," she declared handing the little Frenchwoman the letter. Rue immediately laid it aside and began rubbing the ink from Gabrielle's fingers with a damp cloth. "Remember, you are to deliver it as soon as I go downstairs. Promise me, Rue."

"*Oui, oui* . . . I promise."

Gabrielle had spent the better part of the night pacing and thinking, fleshing out her plan to find a husband and marry as quickly as possible. The greatest difficulty seemed to be finding men of suitable standing and temperament and approaching them on the notion of matrimony. There had to be some logical, safe, and respectable way of obtaining introductions to suitable gentlemen. Every possibility she conjured ended in a mountain of obstacles . . . until Rue delivered her morning tray, on which lay copies of *The Times* and the *Pall Mall Gazette*. Newspapers!

Suddenly she had known exactly what to do.

Rue dragged Gabrielle to her feet to put final touches on her cascade of ringlets and fluff the row of ruffles that plunged down the front of her bodice. One of the upstairs maids had already brought word that Lord Sandbourne had arrived. Now Gabrielle looked at the clock and realized a quarter of an hour had elapsed and her mother still hadn't sent for her.

"What could be taking them so long?" She paced back and forth. "What could she find to talk about with him for a quarter of an hour?"

"She is *la maman*. She speaks of you, *naturellement*," Rue answered, with a very French shrug.

"I don't want her to speak of me." Gabrielle lost some of the color in her cheeks. "She is supposed to be impressed with the earl, call me down to tea, see how enraptured we are, and . . ." She scowled, deciding just what the next logical step in their passionate affair should be. ". . . and then release us with her blessing for a carriage ride or a walk in Hyde Park."

"Since when does your *maman* do what she is supposed to do, eh?" Rue wagged her head. "She is a mistress of the game, *non?*"

Gabrielle stumbled back against the divan and sat

down, heedless of the fragile flounces that trailed down the back of her skirt. Rue had a point. There were a few things Gabrielle hadn't had time to consider in her plan . . . chiefly, her mother's shrewdness in matters of romance. With rising concern, she thought of the tidbits of erotic wisdom Rosalind had tossed off in her presence. Her mother probably couldn't have achieved the pinnacle of London's demimonde without learning how to read the lust in a man's eyes and gauge the sincerity of his promises, whether passionate or financial.

Adding to Gabrielle's anxiety was the possibility that, if pressed, the worldly and libidinous Lord Sandbourne might prove a less than convincing suitor. Just now she was having some difficulty recalling what it was about him that made her think he would appear to be the perfect lover. What if, in her desperation, she had misread him?

"He's down there with her right now," she said with a groan, as the magnitude of her attempted deception came crashing down on her. Her mother was "mistress of the game," and Gabrielle was a mere novice . . . who would prefer not to learn the game at all.

Just as she pushed to her feet, Gunther appeared at the door to summon her to the drawing room. She hurried to the pier glass for one last rehearsal of a "besotted" smile. The maid was at her heels in an instant, pinching her cheeks and clucking over the silk violets she had flattened by sitting. "Really, Rue." Gabrielle tried to shield herself from the maid's primping fingers.

"But, you must be glowing—pink with delight, *non?*" Rue said, leaving no room for dissent as she batted Gabrielle's hands away and pinched on.

"As if anyone would notice," Gabrielle grumbled, wincing through the rubbing that followed, then ducking away and hurrying for the door.

But they did notice. The moment she appeared in the

drawing room doorway, four pairs of feminine eyes fastened on her rosy cheeks and nervous smile, evaluating their sincerity and potential allure. Quickly, those perceptive gazes slid downward over her person, assessing the display of her ripe young curves and predicting the earl's reaction to them. He should find her seductively girlish dress and torrent of blond curls nothing short of riveting, they decided, nodding covertly to one another and settling back on their seats, awaiting the coming encounter.

Gabrielle paused in the doorway, feeling their scrutiny and donning her best distracted-by-ecstasy smile. But as she surveyed the room, her heart sank at the sight of an all too familiar circle of fancy figured silk and feathered hats . . . juxtaposed against one lone chair.

"Here she is now," her mother said, rising with a smile that had more maternal admonition than indulgence in it. The earl was on his feet in an instant, turning to her. For a moment Gabrielle was struck dumb.

He was tall, broad shouldered, and surpassingly elegant, clad in a finely tailored black double-breasted morning coat, charcoal gray trousers, and a dove gray silk tie. His dark hair was parted on one side and brushed casually back, framing his sculptured features and fathomless brown eyes that fairly brimmed with passionate potential. She caught her breath, trying to reconcile this paragon of masculinity with her memory of the man she had struck a bargain with less than twenty-four hours ago. He had the same features, the same hair, the same dark, worldly gaze. But somehow, in the light of day, in her mother's drawing room, he seemed so much taller and more imposing, so much more powerful and self-assured, so much more *male*.

"Gabrielle," he said, drinking her in with his eyes and producing a convincing smile in response to what he saw. The warmth of his greeting might have reassured her, if she hadn't glanced up and read in his eyes an unsettling swirl of determination. She extended her hands, more in an unconscious gesture of self-defense than in welcome. He seized both as if they had been offered to him, smiled, and bent to brush them with his lips.

"Gabrielle, my dear, we were just having a chat with your Lord Sandbourne," her mother's voice intruded, making her realize that she was still standing just inside the doorway with her hands captive in his, staring at him. "Come and sit, dear. Gunther is here with the tea."

Your Lord Sandbourne. The words rang in Gabrielle's mind, proclaiming that her plan had successfully cleared its first hurdle. But, as he led her to the empty chair beside her mother, she could feel Rosalind scrutinizing every nuance of her behavior toward him and sensed that her delirious new love was still on trial. She thought it best to stare longingly at him as he returned to his chair, and used the opportunity to scrutinize his erect carriage, the fluid power of his movements, and the sensual acumen evident in his face, trying to see him as her mother must. A trickle of relief ran through her. He was perfectly irresistible . . . in a worldly, carnal, and intimidating sort of way.

Catching herself engrossed in the symmetry of his features and the power latent in his long frame, she blinked to free her vision and found him examining her with an openness that in the drawing rooms of proper society would have been considered an affront to decency.

Pierce watched her cheeks grow pink and her lashes flutter down with embarrassment and felt his manly indignation sliding. The mystery of what had brought him here was solved. She was nothing short of captivating. He let his eyes drift down over her straight shoulders, full bosom, and narrow waist, visually stripping away the coy ruffles that disguised them to memorize the tantalizing curves beneath. Hell—she was a full-blown beauty.

Whoever had chosen her garments had understood well the perennial male fascination with innocence tainted by awakening desire. Their attempt to make her appear sweet and virginal, while simultaneously displaying the ripening of her body and sexual potential, was a brilliant success.

Every aspect of her appearance radiated a summons to sensory delight, and even knowing that things were not what they seemed, he felt himself responding to that carefully crafted invitation with roused attentiveness. The visual softness of her honey blond tresses, the creaminess of her skin, and the translucent cling of her dress generated that oddly tactile response—that tantalizing itch—in his fingertips once again. And even the fact that his carnal interest in her was being closely observed and measured against some inscrutable feminine standard didn't seem to deter his stubborn impulses.

When Gunther had finished laying out the tea cart, Rosalind presided over the serving with small talk about the oncoming summer. "We usually go to the seaside for much of the summer heat," she said with deceptive casualness. "But the duke is still away on one of his grand hunting safaris, and I thought that it might be prudent to stay in town, to help our Gabrielle become better acquainted with the city. And you, your lordship, will you abandon the city for the summer?"

"I had considered it." He accepted a cup of tea and stirred it with slow, deliberate strokes that drew Gabrielle's attention. Around and around, she followed the movement of his hand, watching the way it cradled the spoon and feeling an odd swirling sensation in her middle. "My estates in Sussex are near the shore, and the sea breezes are pleasant." He intercepted Gabrielle's gaze with an intimate smile. "But now I believe I shall stay in London. Summer in the city also has its . . . pleasures."

Gabrielle broke that contact, taken aback by the

directness of his regard and the insinuation in his words. But as she accepted a cup of tea an instant later and caught the scrutiny of her mother's friends, she remembered and reminded herself that he was supposed to appear aflame with desire for her and returned him an anemic smile.

"*Alors,* your lordship, you seem to have suffered no ill effects from your harrowing encounter of last night," Genevieve Francette said, using her comment as an excuse to look him over. "I understand you gave quite an accounting of yourself."

"My harrowing encounter?" He paused mid-sip and flicked a glance at Gabrielle.

"Them vile ruffians . . ." Clementine Bolt declared, popping the rest of a biscuit into her mouth and munching. "Ought to be horsewhipped, that's what." She dabbed crumbs from her mouth. "Out in York that's what we'd do."

"Ruffians?" He blinked, then frowned at Gabrielle, who realized instantly what was afoot and forced her smile broader to conceal her panic.

"I told Mama about the way you *rescued* me. How you gallantly charged in to save me from those horrid men . . . who tried to drag me into their carriage," she said, signaling him with widened eyes to follow her lead and go along with the tale.

"Ah, yes. The men in the carriage," he said, after a perilously long pause. "It was dark and raining and I was so concerned for Gabrielle that I took no notice of their faces."

"Who would have thought you had such a passion for 'rescue work,' Lord Sandbourne," Ariadne said tartly, drawing sly chortles from the others.

"And how *genereuse* of you to carry our little Gabby to a restaurant to recover," Genevieve added.

"Indeed," Rosalind put in, then after a perfectly timed pause, pinned the earl with another scalpel-sharp look. "I don't believe Gabrielle mentioned the name of this restaurant." She offered him the tray of biscuits. "I only ask because she seems to have left her slippers there."

"Oh, didn't I say?" Gabrielle hurried to answer for him. "It was—"

"The Monmortaine," Lord Sandbourne inserted before she could finish.

Gabrielle gave him a startled look, which she covered a moment later with a halfhearted smile. He apparently didn't want her mother to know he had taken her to a restaurant that catered to appetites having nothing to do with food. "And as for my slippers, I believe I—"

"Lost them in the street, during the scuffle," the earl provided, catching her eye in a bit of teasing that fairly flaunted the fraudulence of his answer. Alarmed by his boldness, when the credibility of their story was already stretched quite thin, she shook her head, hoping that it would seem she was chastising him for his teasing.

"The Montmortaine." Rosalind lifted the teapot and used it as an excuse to fix the earl with a skeptical stare. "I know it well. More tea?"

The cups were filled once more and talk veered mercifully to other things: the fashions at Ascot, the best place to hire riding horses in town, the state of the streets after the heavy rain . . .

Pierce gradually relaxed, sensing the worst was past. Whatever the reason, Rosalind LeCoeur was keeping her doubts about him and her questions about their admittedly unconvincing story to herself, allowing the bizarre interview to proceed.

Gabrielle, however, was on tenterhooks, maintaining her pretense of girlish adoration while watching Lord Sandbourne fend off her mother's curiosity. He proved to be as adroit with skeptical mothers as he was with stubborn daughters—answering some questions, sidestepping others —holding his own against her mother and that trio of expert courtesans. But repeatedly, as she scrutinized his performance, she found her attention narrowing and fixing on his expressive mouth, the subtle movements of his shoulders, and the language of his worldly eyes. More than once she was jarred by the sound of her mother's voice and realized she had been lost to what was being said around her. She could only dissemble and pray her embarrassment would be seen as a sign of being overwhelmed by her "beloved."

It was a great relief to all when the Napoleon clock on the mantel struck the hour of six. Rosalind immediately deposited her cup on the butler's tray and leveled an imperative look on her guest. Taking his cue, Pierce rose to place his cup on the tray and take his leave. The time of decision had finally come.

Gabrielle slid to the edge of her chair, her back rail straight, looking to her mother with a hopefulness that was entirely genuine. As Pierce positioned himself beside Gabrielle's chair, Rosalind hesitated one final moment, studying the way they looked together and luxuriating in the high drama of the moment.

"So good to have met you, your lordship." Rosalind rose and met Pierce's inquiring look with a ruthlessly neutral expression. "We would have you call upon our Gabrielle again. Tomorrow. Shall we say . . . three o'clock?"

Gabrielle felt like her bones were melting.

"Three o'clock would be most agreeable," Pierce responded, taking Gabrielle's hand. "But I fear, the hours until then will seem the longest in the history of the world."

He kissed her fingertips while gazing into her eyes . . . a gesture she knew was meant for their audience, but which still produced a disconcerting shiver in her. As quickly as appearances permitted, she extracted her hand from his to slide it demurely into the crook of his arm.

"Come, your lordship . . . I'll see you to the door."

Steering him out the drawing room door and across the entry hall, she lengthened her stride in order to give her skirts a bit more sway and make certain that her flounces brushed his trousers as they walked. Then as they waited near the door for Gunther to bring his hat and walking stick, she felt her mother's gaze and edged closer to him.

"You did it—she will accept you as my lover!" she whispered with compressed excitement, hoping that her mother would interpret her animation as romantic delight.

"Lucky me," he said with a sardonic half smile, glancing down at her hand, which was squeezing his arm. "You might have told me who you were last night, Gabrielle LeCoeur . . . daughter of the duke of Carlisle."

She pulled her hand away and felt her cheeks reddening. "Illegitimate daughter of the duke's mistress," she corrected quietly. "You wouldn't have believed me." He stiffened but couldn't honestly deny it. "And it doesn't make any difference in our agreement. You still need help with the prime minister, and I still need a lover."

She halted, wondering if now he would cry off, now that he knew who and what she was.

He stared at her, searching her upturned face, with its intense summer-sky eyes and long amber lashes, and wondered the same thing. Should the fact that she was the daughter of a duke of the realm make a difference? It didn't seem to make a difference to her mother, who was obviously intent on securing her a wealthy lover. A faint smile crept over his face. If he were honest, the fact of her illicit nobility added a certain piquancy to the scheme. She was a love child, the product of a grand and sweeping passion, who claimed to have no passions of her own. The challenge to his curiosity, his cunning, and his sensual pride was too much to resist. She certainly *did* need a lover. In fact, he had never met a woman who needed a lover more.

His warming expression betrayed his decision before he spoke.

"Exactly what am I to plan for . . . when I come to pick you up tomorrow at three?"

"A ride in the park would be good." She smiled, visibly relieved. "Or a visit to a cathedral, a library, or a museum. Someplace serious or sober or sensible."

"Serious, sober, or sensible? Romantic little thing, aren't you?" Her purposeful manner gave him pause. "Just what sort of infamous doings do you have planned, once you have escaped your mother's thrall?"

She started to say something, but after a glance toward the drawing room, she thought better of it and produced a beaming smile instead. "We can discuss that tomorrow, when we have a bit more time and privacy."

Time and privacy. He studied her smooth skin and sapphire blue eyes, feeling a rustle of anticipation. Capturing her hands, he pressed a soft, lingering kiss on each.

"Until tomorrow at three." With a last sweeping glance at her, he turned to Gunther and motioned for his hat and cane.

She stood for a moment after the door closed behind him, touching the backs of her hands and feeling a bit dazed by the early successes of her scheme. It had worked! She whirled and raced for the stairs, glowing with newfound confidence. If all went as planned, within a month or two she would be a safely married woman.

Rosalind and her lady friends watched from the drawing room as Gabrielle lifted her skirts and flew to the stairs the minute the door closed behind the earl. To their experienced and observant eyes, she appeared to be the very picture of a young woman in the first intoxicating throes of love—transported, glowing. But, being mistresses of artful illusion themselves, they knew full well how deceiving appearances could be.

"What do you think?" Rosalind demanded, crossing her arms and planting herself before her panel of amorous experts.

" 'Andsome devil," Clementine said with a naughty twinkle in her eyes. "Did you see them I-can-see-right-through-yer-muslin eyes? them come-let-me-nibble-ye lips? Temptation on the hoof, I say. Sin just waitin' to happen." And the wistful lust in her eyes said just whom she wished it would happen to.

"Lord, Clementine," Ariadne said with a sniff of disgust, "you are so easy."

"O' course." Clementine lifted her chin with defiant good humor. "It's part o' my charm."

"He's a first-rate bounder," Ariadne declared, spearing Clementine with a glare and smoothing the folds of her fashionably draped skirt as she delivered her judgment. "He's smug and arrogant, and he's never been denied a thing in his life. I know his sort. He's a taker not a giver . . . naught but trouble for a green young girl."

Rosalind began to wring her hands.

"*Non, non,*" Genevieve said, reaching out to give Rosalind's arm a comforting squeeze. "It matters not how many women he has known; he has not *loved* before. Of that I am sure. And until a man loves . . ." She shrugged. "Well, who can say what love will make of him, eh?"

"All I know is . . . 'e's built like a stallion and moves like a tomcat," Clementine said impishly. " 'E'll make one mighty fine bed warmer on a cold winter night."

"Bed warmer, *humph.* You're getting old, Clementine," Ariadne chided. "He's wild as a March hare, rich as

Croesus, and handsome as Lucifer. That's a recipe for ruin. And I don't care if his kisses are like volcanic fire and he can take a girl to heaven thirty-nine different ways . . . he's just not worth it."

"Ahhh, but did you see the light in *la petite's* eyes?" Genevieve raised a finger of exception. "Perhaps *she* will think he is worth it."

"It doesn't matter what she thinks," Rosalind declared sharply, stepping into the fray. "She is much too inexperienced and hardheaded to decide what is good for her. Which is why I must do it for her." She began to circle the room, giving her train of delicate silk flounces an absentminded kick at each turn. Her scowl caused much-dreaded worry lines between her brows. "He is much too handsome to suit me. I'd prefer someone a good bit less experienced and a great deal less sure of himself. And that pathetic yarn they spun of him rescuing her . . ."

"What do you think really happened?" Ariadne asked.

"I haven't a clue." Rosalind paused to stare at a mental picture of her daughter and the earl, side by side, and her crow's-feet deepened. "All I know is . . . yesterday she was physically ill over a mere kiss, and today she is feverish to take 'Lord *Scandal*bourne' as her lover."

"Well, you can't just toss 'im out," Clementine countered. "He's too rich an' handsome an' titled. Why, he's a prime catch!"

"And the first gentleman *la petite* has shown willingness for." Genevieve waved a hand, drawing their attention. "Think, *mes amies*, of the way they look together."

Each woman conjured a vision of Gabrielle and the earl as they had stood by the front doors . . . her delicate form yielding to his touch, his dark frame taut with reined desire. They were nothing short of breathtaking together, a study in contrasts—darkness and light, power and vulnerability —one a gentle seduction and the other a dangerous allure.

And they had scarcely been able to take their eyes from each other during the encounter.

"Like Adonis and Aphrodite." Ariadne's rigid shoulders softened.

"He looked at her like she was made of sugar." Clementine wagged her head. "An' him with a powerful sweet tooth."

"In his eyes, in his soul, there is the hunger, *oui*? And the way she watched him . . . he has struck 'the spark' in her, I am certain," Genevieve added wistfully.

"A fine lot of help you are." Rosalind interrupted their separate romantic reveries. Then, as if their digressions had only focused and defined her intentions, she strode to the serving cart and picked up the cup he had used, regarding it with a fierce new resolve.

"I don't trust either of them. His sudden desire for an established love . . . her abrupt change of heart . . . I will not throw away my daughter's blossoming passions on a ravening beast, even if he does own half of the Bank of England." With her new maternal instincts at high quiver, she set her jaw and raised the cup that stood proxy for Pierce St. James.

"So you are mad about my daughter, eh, Sandbourne?" she demanded, her countenance filling with determination. "Well, we shall see about that."

Pierce arrived at Maison LeCoeur promptly at three o'clock the next afternoon, intending to collect his new inamorata and spirit her off in his carriage. He was shown immediately into the drawing room, where he discovered Rosalind posed artfully amidst satin pillows and spring flowers, alone and awaiting him.

"I see you are prompt, Lord Sandbourne," she said, lifting an eyebrow in the direction of the clock. That tartly delivered observation spoke volumes about his status in her household; he was still very much on approval.

"What man would not hurry to Gabrielle's side?"

"Indeed." Her smile did not quite extend to her eyes as she rose and took him by the arm, turning him back to the entry hall. "But, surely you will agree that there are some things that must *not* be hurried, especially in these delicate matters." He slowed and stiffened, certain he was being tossed out on his ear. She merely smiled and gave his arm a tug, directing him toward the stairs.

"As a man of the world, you must appreciate that a young girl's heart and passions—to yield a bounty of delight—must be cultivated with care." She watched his reaction carefully. "Gabrielle has had so little experience with men. I think it best to proceed slowly . . . to give her a chance to know you before she is introduced to . . ."

"Pleasure." He made himself say it, though it somehow dried his mouth.

"Exactly. I knew you would understand." She urged him up the sweeping marble steps. "To that end, I have arranged for you to see her in the shelter of familiar surroundings—her own boudoir—for the next several days." He stopped abruptly in the middle of the stairs, scowling.

"Her boudoir?" He clamped his jaw for a minute to forbid the escape of any stray expletives. "That is"—*ridiculous,* he thought—"unnecessary," he said. "I am well aware of Gabrielle's status. I have planned a carriage ride, this afternoon. Nothing more."

"Quite out of the question," Rosalind said, meeting his aristocratic air with equal hauteur. "There are proprieties to be observed. I could never allow Gabrielle out in public in the company of a man with whom she has no *established* relationship."

Proprieties? This was the demimonde, for God's sake,

he thought furiously. What the hell kind of proprieties could they possibly have to observe here?

"You mean to say that I am not allowed in public with her?" he demanded, his voice tight with the strain of remaining civil.

"That is exactly what I mean to say," Rosalind said, with a hint of condescension, as if his lack of sagacity in these matters disappointed her. Taking his elbow again, she urged him along. "But if things progress as hoped . . . it shouldn't be long."

"*How* long?"

"I would never presume to say, your lordship." She raked him with a practiced feminine glance that contained equal parts assessment and flattery. "I rather think that is up to you. But then, a *true* lover appreciates the prelude as much as the pleasure itself . . . don't you think?"

As she led him down a broad, lavishly appointed hallway, Pierce's mind raced to make sense of his bizarre situation. A *true* lover. This was some sort of a test of his intentions. In a matter of moments he would be closeted away with Gabrielle, given permission—more like orders— to romance and seduce her. It was either decamp now, this very minute, or find himself trapped in a beautiful young girl's boudoir for days on end . . . tutoring her endlessly in the arts of love.

Pretending to tutor her.

Good God. What had he gotten himself into?

As he strode along he thought frantically of her striking face, her shapely curves, and sparkling eyes. He thought of the way she surprised and amused him. Then, almost as an afterthought, he remembered Gladstone. . . .

By the time they reached the ornate double doors, his face was frozen in a polite mask that barely covered the turmoil he was feeling inside. Rosalind paused with her hand on the polished brass handle, commanding his attention to make one last point.

"I entrust Gabrielle to your expertise, your lordship," she said, with an unmistakable shimmer of warning in her gaze. "And to your restraint."

Then, she opened the door and waved him inside with a fierce little smile.

6

Pierce strode purposefully into the room, his eyes crackling with irritation and spun on his heel as the door closed behind him, keenly aware that a portal of decision had just closed as well. There was no going back now. He was obligated, by pride as much as agreement. And despite Gabrielle's assurances and his confidence in his ability to hold his own in a ticklish situation, he was beginning to think he might regret this bit of sensual intrigue. Decisions made by the lower half of a man's anatomy were seldom seconded by his common sense. And this decision had "loins" stamped all over it.

Gradually the sight of the gilt-trimmed door insinuated itself into his consciousness, and he turned slowly, surveying the place where he would pass the required time in close confines with Gabrielle. It was a large sitting room that glowed warm and golden, like a softly polished tiger's eye. Gauzy sunlight coming through a large bay window added luster to the exotic gold and burnt umber brocades that covered walls and furnishings. Underfoot was a thick Persian carpet in amber and burgundy tones, and nearby, a huge, pillow-strewn divan was grouped with matching Queen Anne parlor chairs in front of a carved marble fireplace. On the far end of the room stood a writing desk flanked by floor-to-ceiling shelves filled with books and natural wonders, and in the middle sat a grand piano surrounded by lush ferns and potted palms.

But the set piece of the chamber, the focus of that display of evocative splendor, was Gabrielle herself, perched on the edge of a chair with the streaming light from the window behind her setting her honey blond hair aglow and brushing golden highlights over the delicate, weblike silk of her dress. For a moment he stood, just breathing in the soft, roselike fragrance that permeated the chamber. *Her* scent. And as recall joined recognition, he exhaled slowly and felt his irritation draining, recounting his reasons for involving himself with her in the first place . . . boredom, passion, and the prime minister of Britain.

"Your lordship!" Gabrielle sprang up, reading in his turbulent expression his displeasure at getting so much more than he had bargained for. "I apologize. I had no idea she would lock us up together because I'm a—a—"

"*Beginner,*" he supplied, with a rare bit of tact, emerging from his intense sensory immersion into a strangely improved mood. "And just possibly because she believes me to be a bounder and a high-living cad who can't be trusted with a young girl." He came to lean an arm on the edge of the piano.

"Hardly," she declared, so intent on her own indignation that she missed the hint of the sardonic in his tone. "I am certain she finds you a sterling prospect." She scowled. "I am the one who is suspect . . . being an ungrateful 'modern' girl who has resisted her mother's attempts to instruct her in the necessary allurements and who only two days ago declared she wanted nothing to do with love or romance." She heaved a disgusted sigh. "I am afraid it's my fault you're being locked up with me for days on end. She is worried that I won't behave as a proper mistress should."

He studied her for a moment, realizing she was serious, and broke into a wry smile. "A proper mistress . . . Now, there is an image to ponder. And here I thought the whole purpose of a mistress was impropriety. It just goes to show how things have changed with you 'modern' girls." He looked her over with a twinkle in his eyes that spoke of private amusement and of complicated, worldly intentions. "By the way, I've been meaning to ask: exactly what does it mean to be a *modern* girl?"

"Well, I'm not entirely clear on that, myself," she said, fighting the urge to cross her arms over her breasts and shield them from his gaze. It was a very good thing he wasn't pursuing her passions in earnest, she thought; she would be totally out of her depth with a man like him. "But I believe it has to do with thinking too much, and having opinions of your own, and not meekly obeying your mother when she tries to run and ruin your life."

"Good Lord—by that standard, *I* would probably qualify." He laughed, a soft, seductive rumble that vibrated her fingertips, then he pushed off from the piano and strolled around her boudoir, trailing his fingers over the silk-clad walls, gilded picture frames, and polished mahogany.

She heaved a quiet sigh of relief. He was taking their confinement better than she had expected.

"Well, Gabrielle," he said, "what do we do now?"

As she watched him appreciating the chamber's assemblage of erotic textures and exotic hues, her anxiety began to rise again. The room was cannily crafted to evoke a lush, romantic aura—furnished, textured, and perfumed to pique sensory hungers and turn a man's mind from the burdens of rank and duty to amorous dalliance. Just setting foot across the threshold was halfway to a seduction. And the last thing she needed was Lord Sandborne in an amorous mood.

"Well, I believe I am supposed to charm and impress you with my accomplishments and graces. And you are supposed to respond with . . ."

"Generosity?" he supplied, clamping his hands behind his back as he paused to look up at a painting of a sun-drenched seascape.

"Gifts would be excellent."

"Eagerness?" He strolled to the huge mirror above the mantel, then to the window to take in the view of a small tea garden that surrounded the terrace below.

"I suppose," she responded cautiously, considering his formidable elegance and wondering what, if anything, could make a man of his experience *eager*. "Whatever we do, we must make it appear that we are wholeheartedly engaged in romance."

"Speaking of appearances . . ." He halted on his circuit about the room. "How will your mother know when we're 'romantic' enough to be let out on our own?"

Surprised, she pursed one corner of her mouth and considered it. "I haven't the faintest idea."

At that very moment, just outside the door, Rosalind was fretting under the watchful and sympathetic eyes of her majordomo, the upstairs maid, and Ariadne Baden-Powell, who had come to support and advise. Rosalind halted and put her ear to the door for a minute, then paced back to them in frustration.

"I can't hear a thing," she declared in a furious whisper, then rolled her eyes heavenward. "Please, God, just don't let her be going on and on about how to tell Liszt from Wagner and Pre-Raphaelite from neoclassicist, the way she did with the poor count." She clasped her hand over her heart as she recalled the rest of Gabrielle's behavior with her last suitor. "She could be getting sick, even as we speak."

She turned to glare at the door, and her gaze fell on the keyhole. A lady of breeding and refinement would never stoop to such a thing. However, a desperate mother—especially one unaccustomed to "mothering"—had to get her information however she could. She hiked her skirts with a determined expression and sank onto her knees to put her eye to the keyhole. But as she positioned herself, her dress caught under her and she fell against the door with a soft thud.

In a flash, Gunther was helping her up and spiriting her down the hall, away from the door. But after a few moments, when the door didn't open and their heart rates returned to normal, they crept back. And soon Rosalind was at the keyhole once more, staring in mounting frustration at a bright window and an empty divan.

Pierce's exploration of the chamber had carried him past two portraits of elegant women posed in sylvan settings and brought him up before the shelves lined with books at the far end of the chamber. He paused to study the books and ticked off the names.

"Shakespeare, Donne, Blake, Pope, Keats, Byron—the great poets!" He perused more of the bindings, taking note of the authors' names, and his eyes widened at the selection on the second shelf: "What have we here? Wesley, Pascal, John Locke, Voltaire, Descartes, St. Thomas Acquinas . . ." The contents of the third shelf astonished him. "And Homer, Virgil, *The Orations of Cicero,* the plays of Euripides, the *Dialogues of Plato.* And Ovid, no less." He slid the volume from the shelf and turned to her. "Your father certainly has elevated tastes in reading matter."

"My father?" His assumption that such reading matter must belong to a man irritated her. "Those are *my* books. Really, Lord Sandbourne, wouldn't you prefer to have a seat—"

"Yours?" He turned the elegant little volume over in his hands, drew his chin back, and stared at her skeptically.

"Yes, mine," she insisted, feeling oddly exposed under his critical glare. A reckless impulse made her add: "They were required."

"By whom?"

To refuse him an answer might only make him more determined to find out. The plain truth, she knew, was the only cure for a case of aggravated curiosity.

"By my mother. At least by proxy. They were required at Marchand." When he looked puzzled, she explained, "L'Academie Marchand, a private school for English girls in the village of d'Arcy, just outside Paris. My mother sent me there when I was seven years old. And, except for an occasional holiday, that was where I lived until my nineteenth birthday." Her face and posture softened a bit.

"Madame Marchand, our headmistress, was something of a bluestocking, I'm afraid. She had a passion for reading and discussion and insisted her pupils become literate in a number of areas. I loved to read and so became one of her prime protégés. It was she who accompanied me on my tour last year."

"Your tour?" He studied her with narrowing eyes. "What tour?"

"My grand tour . . . at least I believe you could call it that. My mother insisted I visit the great capitals: Paris, Rome, Vienna, Athens, and Geneva. Madame Marchand, who acted as my guide and chaperon, managed to fit in a few lesser-known but far more interesting places, as well."

"Your *mother* insisted you travel?" He didn't bother to hide his surprise.

"She was quite adamant about it."

"But a 'grand tour' is a *male* rite," he said with a bit of manly indignation.

"Precisely." When he scowled at her, she smiled. "You see, my mother believes that a gentleman of substance desires an interesting woman, someone who can stimulate all of him, his mind as well as his passions. A man of importance requires a partner for his learning and accomplishment: a mistress who can converse intelligently on a wide range of subjects and is cultured and well traveled."

"So she made sure you studied and traveled and learned." He paused, seeing the broader scope of her mother's plan and recalling something she had said. "She was preparing you to be a mistress."

"The perfect mistress."

"But you don't want to be the perfect mistress," he concluded for her, eyeing her with open speculation. "What do you want to be, Gabrielle?"

"I believe I have already said." Her heart pounded as she raised her chin to a determined angle and took the volume of poems from his hands. "I intend to become a *wife*."

Given her previous statements and opinions, he wasn't exactly surprised by her announcement. But somehow "wife" didn't fit the picture of her that even now was being revised and enlarged in his mind. She was beautiful, bright, startlingly well educated, and had more than her share of self-possession . . . a far cry from the delectable little tart he had expected on their first encounter. And he could see from the set of her jaw and the glint in her eye that she was quite serious about her ambition. As she stood there, her delectable curves awash in ruffles, clutching a volume of Ovid's poems, he thought of the obstacles she faced and found himself voicing his question aloud.

"And just how do you intend to accomplish that, Gabrielle?"

"By distracting my mother and finding a husband." She assessed him for a moment, thinking, and then slid the book back into the empty slot on the shelf and turned back to him. "That is where you come in, your lordship."

He looked as if he'd been doused with a pail of icy water. "Me?"

"Absolutely." She saw the indignation rising in his eyes and quickly reassured him. "You asked what we would do when we are out and about. Well, I intend to use the opportunity to search for a husband."

He straightened, his shoulders inflating with male outrage. "See here, Gabrielle, there are some depths of degradation to which even the most depraved of men will not sink. And hoodwinking fellow bachelors into marriage is one of them."

"No one is asking you to 'hoodwink' anyone. All you have to do is call for me each day and take me out and about until I find a husband. I have it all planned." She watched him grappling with the notion and sensed that, being a man, he needed a bit of 'logic' to help him accept what was plain as the nose on his face. "The way I see it, we're really both out to do the same thing: catch a man. In my case it's a husband, and in yours it's the prime minister. And I can't see any reason why we shouldn't help each another."

It did make sense, in a labyrinthine, feminine sort of

way, he thought. But the notion of being an accomplice to that age-old female ritual, the husband hunt, still made him feel uneasy . . . as if he were somehow betraying his sex. He took a deep breath and paced across the room, thinking, his brow furrowing.

As he neared the doors, suddenly there was a thump against the wooden panels, loud enough to cause both him and Gabrielle to start. It was followed by a faint, unidentifiable whisper of noise, then all was silent again. She started for the door, but he held up a hand to halt her and motioned for quiet with a finger against his lips. He stole toward the door, staring at the brass handle and the large hole in the lock below it. Pressing an ear to the panels, he pointed sharply, indicating someone was just outside the door. A moment later, he crept stealthily back to the desk and sorted through the writing materials in the drawer.

Finding the bit of sealing wax she had used the day before, he held it up and whispered, "I believe I have just discovered how your mother intends to learn whether or not we are 'romantic' enough."

He squeezed and kneaded the wax in his hand to soften it, then went to the door and stuffed it unceremoniously into the keyhole. Gabrielle was appalled by his implication that her mother would stoop to something so vulgar as peeping through keyholes . . . and equally chagrined by her suspicion that he was right.

When the keyhole was plugged, he pulled her to the center of the room, keeping his voice low. "She may not be able to see us, but she can still hear us. Perhaps you'd better play something."

"The piano?"

"I assume you play," he said with a hint of sarcasm, "since there is a piano here."

"But I—" This was not the time for anything heroic. Her mother was not one to give up easily, she knew, and could very well be outside, listening. If so, the longer she delayed, the longer it might take for her mother to release them.

Furious at Rosalind's endless manipulations, she seated herself on the bench he held for her at the piano, and she studied the keys. He stood near her shoulder, watching, waiting to pronounce a verdict on her efforts.

"What *shall* I play? Something suitable for the occasion, obviously. Ah!" She gave him a defiant little smile and put her fingers to the keys.

When the notes began to string together into a recognizable melody, the smugness in Pierce's expression disappeared. And as she warmed to her playing, his spine straightened and his jaw loosened in gentlemanly shock. His gaze fastened on her nimble fingers, flying over the keyboard, punching the ivories with what could only have been called an excess of enthusiasm. And the words to the music began to run maddeningly inside his head . . .

All around the mulberry bush, the monkey chased the weasel . . .

Outside, her mother was wilting with horror, being supported by Gunther and fanned with Ariadne's handkerchief.

"Do you hear?" she whispered, frantically. " 'Pop Goes the Weasel'—she's playing 'Pop Goes the Weasel'! What's gotten into her?"

But Rosalind's distress was due to worsen. In a few moments, when the weasel was duly "popped," the music died—only to start up again with the slightly more melodious, though equally inappropriate music hall ditty, called "Twiggez-vous." "*Ohhh!*" Rosalind clamped an elegant hand to her forehead and sent the housemaid running for her salts. "The humiliation! Years of classical training at the piano . . . a fortune in music lessons . . . and she plays him French beer hall songs!"

Gabrielle paused at the end of the next verse to gauge Pierce's reaction. He was leaning on the side of the piano, watching her with a stunned expression, and she challenged him to sing the next verse.

"What—me? sing?" He laughed shortly at the absurdity of it.

"Well . . . I suppose we are not all born musical," she said, oozing a uniquely feminine sort of condescension. She ran expertly through another chorus while gazing steadily at him, and he straightened, realizing she was serious. "Or perhaps you don't know the lyrics . . ."

Nettled by her forthright challenge to both his pride and his male dignity and reserve, he sniffed. "Of course I know the words . . . along with everyone in the entire East End of London." Soon his reluctant baritone blended with her music, growing gradually louder and more confident.

When he had run out of verses, she went straight into another song he recognized: a rollicking rendition of "Whoops, Alice!" He knew the words to that one too and rendered them with as much dignity as it was possible to maintain while singing about a four-hundred-pound girl who gets stuck in a window while eloping.

After an extra chorus, she finished with a musical flourish and looked up at him, her cheeks rosy and her eyes sparkling with mischievous pleasure. He was breathing as if he'd run a foot race; his face bronzed and glowing. He sat down on the bench beside her, holding himself taut. She drew her hands from the keyboard. For a long, moment they stared at each other, breathing with the same rhythm, their pulses racing, their lips parted and eyes glowing.

Neither spoke; each was reluctant to disrupt the strange sense of connection that had risen between them.

But after a moment, she lowered her eyes and dusted her fingers over the keys, and he shifted uncomfortably on the bench.

"Where in heaven's name did you learn a thing like 'Whoops, Alice!'? Your mother will be scandalized . . . probably bar you from ever playing again."

"No, she won't," she said with a prim little smile. "I'll just tell her that you specifically requested it. I'll tell her it's *your* favorite song."

He choked out a laugh. Then, sobering, he took a deep breath and tugged down his waistcoat. "You are a saucy bit, Miss LeCoeur. I can see your mother has her hands full with you."

"She has indeed." And the look she gave him made him wonder if he might have his hands full as well.

Time slipped away as Gabrielle played several more common ditties and then a few country songs she remembered. When she was reduced at last to a musical rendition of "Old King Cole," she knew it was time to stop. A discreet knock at the door confirmed it.

Gunther stood outside with a pained expression. "Your mother requests that you and his lordship join her in the drawing room for tea . . . before he departs."

As they trailed the majordomo downstairs, Gabrielle stole glances at Pierce's now unreadable face and braced for the worst. And yet, she couldn't bring herself to repent or even regret her behavior. Not only had it kept both her mother and his amorous impulses successfully at bay, it had also given her a shameless amount of pleasure.

In the drawing room they found Rosalind and Ariadne Baden-Powell waiting, a bit pale and tight-lipped but otherwise models of matronly courtesy. They poured tea and made small talk as if determined to take a stopped keyhole and a bizarre program of beer hall tunes and nursery songs in stride. Their worldly aplomb had been sorely tested—the tilt of their chins proclaimed—but they had seen and heard stranger things in their years in the demimonde.

When the clock struck half past five, Pierce expelled a discreet sigh of relief and stood to take his leave. Gabrielle rose to see him to the door, feeling her mother's gaze boring into them all the way to the front door. She took special pains to stand close and look up at him with a beaming smile.

"Well, that wasn't so bad," she said, hoping he would agree.

"If you don't mind having your eyebrows singed. Your mother must be made of pure phosphorous. Rub her the wrong way and . . ."

"Yes . . . well . . . Perhaps you'd better bring me something when you come tomorrow. My mother sets great store by a man's generosity." She halted and looked up at him with a trace of anxiety. "You will come tomorrow?"

He nodded.

She relaxed. "I know—*flowers*. Bring me a huge bouquet of flowers. Smelly flowers—they're her favorite kind."

He considered her a moment. "I'm not supposed to be courting your mother," he said calmly. "What is *your* favorite kind?" The notion struck her with unexpected impact. *Courting her.* She glanced up and found his eyes dark and serious.

"I don't think I have one," she said, feeling a shiver run down her spine. "Any flowers will do. I'll write you out a bank draft, tomorrow, to reimburse you for the expense." She stepped back, offering him her hand. His gaze intensified as he held it a moment before pressing a soft kiss on her palm.

"Tomorrow at three." He nodded curtly, donned his hat, and strode out the door.

She stood for a moment, staring at the door after Gunther closed it. Phantom warmth remained in the center of her hand, the lingering heat of his kiss . . . the touch of those handsome, supple, expressive lips. She shook herself mentally. Worldly lips, expert lips, filled with irresistible half-truths that smoothed the way for both his will and his passions. He was the sort of man that mothers usually warned their daughters about. She scowled. Not *her* mother, of course . . .

She turned to the stairs, but was halted abruptly by the sound of her name.

"Gabrielle!" Her mother's strident tones floated out from the drawing room, and she realized she was caught. "I should like to have a word with you, young lady!"

That evening, Pierce dined at Brooks's, indulged in a few hands of cards in the venerable club's game room, then wound his way to his imposing mansion in Hyde Park. He wasn't in the mood for male companionship just now. Since five-thirty that afternoon, he had been feeling restless, physical, and aroused . . . and he knew exactly where to lay the blame.

There were a number of pleasure palaces in St. James that would welcome his money and presence, he knew. And should he be inclined to more private indulgence, there were several loosely married ladies who would be more than eager to put his needs to rest. But the relief he needed had nothing to do with those all too transient pleasures. He couldn't get Gabrielle out of his mind. And he knew in his very sinews that he would not be satisfied with a substitute, however lovely or accommodating or inventive.

Anticipation was a unique sort of pleasure, he had

learned; one that required a certain maturity and a surfeit of other pleasures to desire and then to learn to enjoy. It manifested itself in a divine and languid tension that heightened awareness and in a poignant, almost painful appreciation of sensation. It made a man notice things like the many different colors in a woman's hair, the subtle language of her movements, and the variations of texture in her skin. And it tutored him on the inner workings of his own body, on the capacity of each vessel and sinew, as his blood coursed and his breathing quickened and his muscles tensed with wanting.

Tonight, Pierce St. James was being tutored in spades.

He arrived at his house earlier than expected, to find his butler, Parnell, waiting for him, pacing alongside the great curved stairs of the entry hall. Whether it was a glimpse of the fellow's ashen face or something more subtle and primal in the air itself, he felt a chill that announced a dread presence in his house. As Parnell hurried to take his hat and gloves, Pierce sensed what the fellow would say even as he began to speak.

"I tried to reach you at your club, my lord . . ."

"When did she arrive?" Pierce demanded, glancing up the stairs.

"Just before five." Parnell leaned closer and lowered his voice. "I said you might not be home until quite late. Perhaps you could return to your club . . ."

Pierce felt a new kind of tension coiling around his stomach, beginning its merciless squeeze. He had looked forward to spending the balance of the evening in his study, with a good book, a fine brandy, and a fat cigar. His plans were ruined. It was either flee his own house or find himself trapped and run through an emotional mangle intended to make a perfect bedsheet of him—render him flat and colorless and endlessly conforming.

"Send word to Jack not to unhitch the horses," he

ordered, snatching his hat and gloves back from Parnell and heading for the door. Just as he reached it, the sound of his name rang out in the entry, and he froze.

"Pierce!" An imperious female voice with all the charm and lilt of a hot locomotive brake, burst out over the hall. "So there you are. And about time, too."

The flurry of swishing silk and the emphatic clack of heels on marble steps galvanized him. He turned like a block of granite. Descending the stairs was a robust woman in her fifties, with hair streaked with gray and a face rounded—though not softened—by time and appetite. Her movements were brisk and energetic, and her dark eyes were bright with internal fires. She strode across the entry hall with her emotional weapons stoked and primed. Instinctively, Pierce took a step back.

"I sent word this morning that I was coming, but your wretched houseman"—she flung a contemptuous hand at the red-eared Parnell as she drew up before Pierce—"wasn't at all prepared for me. I've spent the last two hours airing and freshening my own rooms. Scarbury never would have permitted such sloth. My quarters would have been ready at a moment's notice, or there would have been hell to pay!" She leveled a glare on the butler that said she was more than ready to step into the old butler's shoes and serve up a bit of perdition herself.

"What are you doing here, Mother?" Pierce demanded.

"I was under the impression that this was still *my* home as well," she declared, turning back to her stony son, "—at least until you come to your senses and take a wife." She settled back on her heels, with her hands clasped, assessing him with a look of disgust. "As if any *decent* woman would have you."

"Mother—" he warned with a growl.

"Not that it is any real concern of yours what I do—since, God knows, you have no natural feelings toward your family—but I've come to London for a bit of shopping."

"Shopping?" He narrowed his eyes, scrutinizing the aristocratic features, once-dark hair, and unholy arrogance that had served as templates for his own. He crossed his arms, resolved to wait as long as necessary. There was more to her visit, he was sure of it, and if he waited in unblinking silence, she would eventually tell him what it was. One moment passed, then another, and the quiet became burdened with the bitterness of old clashes and the specters of expectations unmet and dreams denied.

Stubbornly, he stared at her and she at him. The air around them heated.

"Very well," she said, discharging the tension unexpectedly and lowering her pitch and tone to what, for her, was a conciliatory level. "I have been talking with Lady Marjorie, Countess Havershom. She has a niece . . . a lovely and quite respectable girl . . . and I think you should—"

"Damnation!" he thundered.

"Pierce St. James—I will not be sworn at in my own house!" she barked back. "I have come to see to it that you do your duty to your family and your title, that you take a respectable wife and make an heir. Decency and duty may not be to your tastes, but they come inextricably bound to the wealth and privilege you so enjoy with such abandon. You have obligations to the family, and I intend to see that you honor them. I want you married by the new year, and I want a grandchild by the Christmas after. And I swear to you, you will not see a farthing of my inheritance until you have married and produced an heir."

"Damnation!" Shoving his hat on his head and his hands into his gloves, he spoke curtly to Parnell. "Tell Jack I'll be waiting on the turn." The butler took off through the house at a run, and Pierce jerked open the front door.

When he stalked defiantly out the door, she started and went after him.

"How dare you walk off when I am still speaking?" she demanded, following him out onto the landing as he strode angrily down the front steps. "Come back here—I haven't finished with you, young man!"

But he had finished with her . . . a number of years ago. She stood on the landing and watched him climb into his carriage and rumble off into the night, escaping her . . . just as his father always had. And in the midst of her outrage and turmoil, she felt the same deep and painful sense of loss growing within her. She turned back to the house, wilting slowly, and mounted the stairs to her old chambers, feeling her bones speaking to her of the many years they had climbed those stairs. By the time she reached her rooms the fires that had crackled in her eyes were dying, snuffed by the same faults and hurts that over the years had turned every new start into a false hope.

She assured her maid that everything was all right, then sent the girl to the kitchen to fetch her nightly posset of warm milk and brandy. When she was alone again, she went to the window and parted the lace curtains, staring into the darkened street below.

Why was it always the same thing? Why was it they couldn't be in the same room, the same house for two minutes without a bloodletting? She saw his life so clearly . . . saw the possibilities in it, saw the disappointments and regrets in store for him. She recognized them because they were some of the very ones she had experienced. And because of their turbulent history, she was helpless to make him see it.

All she wanted for him was a good and decent family life with someone who was clever and reasonable and good-hearted, someone who was strong enough to withstand his gales and blasts and soft enough to love him in spite of them. But, she knew too well the way he had lived his life in recent years, and she feared that no decent, honorable, and loving woman would have him.

If only he weren't so much like his father—so handsome, so licentious, so arrogant. And so utterly contemptuous of *her*.

"All you can do is try, Beatrice," she said quietly. "All you can do is try."

Like a twelve-year-old, Pierce thought, staring out the carriage window as he sped through the night. That was how his mother treated him whenever they were in the same room for more than two minutes. She refused to relinquish one jot of the power she wielded as the Countess Sandbourne and spared no opportunity to try to run his life and make his choices for him.

In the last several years she had made it her crusade in life to see him married and converted to her brand of respectability. She was determined to shackle him to some pampered and extravagantly pedigreed female whose notions of life came from Eugenics Society journals and who swooned at the sight of her own ankles. She wanted him hobbled and broken, made into one of the dismal wretches who lined the walls of ballrooms dressed in the grim uniform of the upper-crust male—counting their drinks, complaining of their feet, and praying that neither their skill nor their corsets would fail during the next waltz —society's matrimonial geldings.

And despite her oft-repeated exhortations to produce her some grandchildren and secure himself an heir, he had long known that her true reason for wanting to see him sacrificed upon the altar of matrimony was that she simply couldn't bear the thought of him enjoying himself. Well, she could keep her cursed money; he didn't need it. He wasn't about to submit to her tyrannical demands, no matter how urgent the requirements of duty and dynasty. If he had to *beget,* then he would just bloody well do it at sixty, when he had no juices left for anything else.

He sat back in the cushioned seat, calmer now for having purged the vitriol from his system, and his gaze fell on the seat across from him. Juices. How had *that* gotten into his mind? A moment later memories filtered into his awareness; a snatch of white silk, a burst of robin's egg blue, the scent of biscuits. His mood improved steadily as he turned his thought to the possibilities of "three o'clock tomorrow."

Anticipation.

As the carriage halted before the exclusive Brooks's Club, he alighted, whistling a tune. When he put words to the melody in his head, he stopped stock-still. He was humming: "*Whoops, Alice! . . . the lad-der is bend-ing . . .*"

7

The next afternoon Pierce arrived at Maison LeCoeur as required, with an armful of flowers. He had spent the morning raiding every florist in London for a bouquet befitting the occasion. And in describing his needs to deferential shop attendants, he quickly discovered that he wasn't at all certain of the occasion. He was either courting or seducing a young girl, willingly or under protest, in pretense or in earnest . . . all depending on where he was and who he was with at the moment. And he needed a gesture to impress, not the girl—who was well-nigh unimpressible—but her eagle-eyed mother with his reckless generosity and the fevered depths of his desire. Just what sort of flowers were appropriate for a pretense of gripping passion and impending sin? For a seduction within a seduction?

Now, as he stood in the entry hall, waiting to be shown upstairs, the blended fragrance of jonquils, tulips, and hothouse roses wafted up from the two bouquets lying in his arms. Unable to decide, he had finally bought an assortment that combined the best of "spring" and "smelly." And he was glad of it when Rosalind floated out of the drawing room and greeted him. She eyed with approval the abundance of flowers in his arms and breathed in deeply as she resumed her original course toward the dining room.

By the time he trotted up the great staircase behind Gunther, he was feeling rather confident. He had passed muster with the amorous expert in the family and now anticipated the glow of delight in Gabrielle's blue eyes when he told her so.

Thus, he was unprepared for the way she accepted his gift with girlish enthusiasm—"*Ohhh,* how lovely, your lordship! They're glorious!"—and then tossed the flowers onto the tea table the instant the door was closed. He stood feeling a bit unmanned as she hurried to the door and listened, focused entirely on the impact his gesture was making *outside* that chamber.

"I think that went well." With a wilt of relief, she turned her back to the door and inquired, "Did she see you? With the flowers?"

"Of course."

"Excellent." She strolled closer, looking him over in a rather businesslike fashion, noting with approval his handsome charcoal coat and pinstriped trousers. "After yesterday, something a bit more traditional was probably in order. My mother had a few well-chosen words for me after you left."

"I can imagine," he said, wishing he couldn't.

"I must say, I was a bit surprised to find her so rigid in

her notions of romance," she said with a puzzled look and a shake of her head. "She thinks you have a rather eccentric taste in 'musical foreplay' . . . whatever that is."

He groaned quietly.

A moment later, a knock on the door startled them both. When she answered it, there stood Gunther, holding a large crystal vase filled with water and a pair of heavy shears. "Madam thought you might wish these," he said, glancing smoothly past her into the room for a glimpse of Pierce.

She accepted the vase and shears, closed the door, then carried them to the tea table, where the still-wrapped bouquets lay, and turned to him with fresh determination.

"Well, your lordship, what shall we do to pass the time today?"

He studied the stubborn glint in her eye and glanced at the flowers. "Aren't you going to at least put them in water?" He tucked his chin, annoyed by her attitude toward his gift. "—after all the trouble I went to find suitably romantic flowers?"

She expelled a long-suffering breath, picked up both bouquets, and plunged them, tissue and all, into the vase. Then she turned back from the table with a folding chessboard in her hands. "How about a game of—"

"That's it?" He planted his hands on his waist. "You're just going to leave them there . . . like that?"

"She expects me to arrange them for you," she declared calmly. "That is why she sent up the vase and shears. Flower arranging is one of the romantic arts, you see. It's supposed to demonstrate my flair and sensitivity for aesthetic pursuits. That, and it's supposed to inflame your" —she thought better of her choice of words—"good opinion of me." She held up the chessboard. "Now, how about a game of—"

"What will happen when she learns you didn't arrange them?" he demanded.

She hesitated, trying to think of an excuse, and produced a vengefully cheery smile. "I'll just say that you kept me far too busy."

"And have her think I've been appallingly 'eccentric' again? *Ohhh*, no." He tugged down his vest and strode to the table, looking over the flowers and shears, evaluating the size of the task. "If you're not of a mind to do it, then I shall."

He lifted the flowers from the vase and tore the soggy tissue from them. But there he paused, uncertain how to proceed. Under her watchful eyes, he seized a tall purple spike and plunged it down into the vase, where it promptly keeled over and lay sticking out at an angle. He tried adding a few more stems, but had to hold each in place, so that soon his hands were too full to pick up more flowers. She watched him and bit her lip to keep from smiling.

"It helps if you cut the stems. The flowers don't droop as much and they will get more water," she offered. As a second tangle of blossoms grew, she came to lean against the table and watched the determined set of his mouth. His long, graceful hands moved with such gentleness over the flowers that she felt an odd sort of emptiness growing in her stomach. It wasn't quite a hunger; it was more like . . . a longing. She rubbed her waist, thinking it was strange. She had never experienced such a consuming desire to arrange flowers before.

"There are rules to flower arranging, you know," she said, leaning over to choose a few taller spikes to plant in the center of the vase and brace with others.

"Rules?" He snipped the end of a stem and thrust it with defiant randomness into the vase. "Rules are made to be broken."

"Don't be silly." She frowned at him. "Rules are there to

provide order and safety and security . . . even beauty. You see, formal arrangements are done to a geometric form that will both please and uplift the beholder . . . the most popular being a triangle." With a finger, she traced the shape that was formed by the stems she had just placed. He folded his arms and stroked his chin with his thumb and forefinger, considering it and her.

"But flowers don't grow in perfect triangles in nature. No more than people in their natural state grow in precise, orderly patterns and turn predictably into modest, honest, virtuous, and dutiful souls. Rules aren't natural." He leaned closer to her. "And nowhere is that more obvious than in the ridiculous rules society lays down regarding men and women and how they must behave toward one another."

"Which rules?" she demanded, looking up, suddenly intensely aware of how close he was standing.

"The hypocritical rules about who can ride in a carriage together, dance together, sit together, eat together, even *speak* together. And touching—God forbid!—you practically have to hang out the family pedigree to be permitted to touch a woman in any meaningful way. Pleasure is outlawed in any and every form." He snipped off the end of another stem with a vengeful flourish. "The entire purpose of such rules is to give some people an excuse to disdain and gossip about others. Think . . . if there weren't any rules, there couldn't be any scandal. No scandal; no gossip. Then what would the dragons of society do?"

She paused, her attention piqued, searching his face. He had just revealed more of himself than he knew. In the depths of his handsome eyes she glimpsed a past littered with broken rules and very likely broken hearts as well.

"Is that why you agreed to pose as my lover?" she asked quietly, holding that insight carefully and wondering what it meant to her. "To break a few rules?"

He searched the clear, perceptive blue of her eyes and felt a dry, whispery sensation in his middle, as if her gaze had brushed something unexpectedly sensitive inside him. He looked quickly away and seized another blossom, giving the stem a snip.

"I am here as a result of a bargain, remember? I want proof of the prime minister's perfidies, and I think you're the one to provide them"—he flicked a glance around them —"if I can ever get you out of this blessed chamber."

She took the blossom he handed her and placed it with care in the vase, then paused to study him again. "Why do you want to discredit the prime minister?"

"It's simple. He's the prime rule maker, the standard setter, the leading arbiter of what is good and proper and allowable in government and society. And he conveniently exempts himself from his own rules. He demands decency and morality of others, while placing no such constraints upon his own behavior. That makes him a hypocrite, in my view. And if there is one thing I cannot abide, it's a hypocrite."

She paused in the midst of stripping a few extra leaves from a stem and thought of the old man who had dragged her into his kitchen and tried to get her to change her ways. He had seemed perfectly, even frighteningly sincere to her.

"What if he isn't a hypocrite?" she said. "What if he really is trying to help those women change their lives. Heaven knows, someone needs to help them."

"And what would you know about 'those women'?" he said, piqued by her audacity in challenging his opinion.

"I happen to know a great deal about 'those women,' " she declared, tossing the flower she held onto the table and setting her hands on her waist. "Prostitutes, tarts, roundheels, trollops, soiled doves . . . I've made the acquaintance of a number of them. And I can tell you that they often live very bleak and difficult lives." She interpreted his glower as both disbelief and disapproval.

"It's true." The spark struck in her eyes confirmed her words. "D'Arcy, the village where I lived in France, is home to a large foundling hospital, run by Catholic sisters. Many women came from Paris to leave their babies with the nuns." Her face grew sober as her gaze fastened on some inner scene. "Most had to walk the twelve miles from the city limits, carrying the child they would give up. Some wept much of the way. Others were too weary or too hardened to do more than just make the journey. They spoke of the horrors of their lives with deadened voices that came from deadened spirits. Some claimed seduction as the cause, but many were far beyond such attempts to salve pride and simply admitted there had been so many men that they had no idea who the father of their child was.

"Mme. Marchand led us to the hospital and orphanage each week to do charity work. I saw the women who came, and as I grew older and spent more time there, I heard their stories. I held the children on my lap and watched the mothers walk away . . . some with hearts that were breaking and would never mend."

She came back to the present and found herself staring into the flowers, but seeing the faces of children. For some reason she added, as much to herself as to him: "Those women need someone to speak with them, to speak for them. And for their children. Especially the children. They had no part in their mothers' wretched choices, but they had to pay for them, all the same." She glanced at him and was halted by the intensity of his stare. Blushing, she picked up the flowers again and began to pluck excess leaves from the stems. But there was no censure in his face or his silence, and gradually she was drawn to continue.

"Working with the children was the best part of what we did. We taught the littlest ones how to dress themselves and how to talk. We read stories to them and taught them songs. As they got older, we taught them to write their letters and their names, eventually how to do sums. And when they were old enough, we began to teach the boys to garden and the girls to sew." Her eyes grew luminous. "One of the hardest things about leaving France was leaving them. I don't think I could ever leave a child of mine. I don't know how anybody could."

Pierce watched her remembering her time in France and saw the power of those memories in the sadness that settled in her expression. The strength of her views was a bit unsettling, for it was clear that she spoke from experience. And that experience had marked her in profound and unusual ways—with a mesmerizing clarity in her words, a softness in her eyes, and an unmistakable depth in her conviction. He felt an odd tightness in his chest. A minute later, she looked up, shaking off that somber mood to put the final two blossoms into the arrangement.

"I'm going to have a dozen children," she declared, forcing a lighter tone as she gathered up the stem cuttings and debris and rolled them up in the soggy tissue.

He smiled, scarcely able to take his eyes from her. "And you say you're not romantic."

"I most certainly am not," she said, glaring as if he'd accused her of something vile. Then she uncovered the chessboard she had placed on the table earlier and lifted it. "Ah, there it is. I assume you play. Most gentlemen do."

"Chess?" He winced and put his hand to his stomach as if the prospect disagreed with him.

"It's one of my favorite pastimes."

"It's deadly," he said with a surly tone.

She studied him for a moment, realizing a compromise was called for.

"I'll make you a bargain. Play chess with me today and

tomorrow you can choose what we do." She saw the spark her proposal struck in his eyes and immediately amended it. "Within reason, of course."

A smile spread slowly over his features. "Of course."

There was some disagreement over the venue for their joust of intellects, and they settled on a compromise: the divan with the chessboard propped on pillows between them. He suggested she take the white, since it was her favorite color.

"White is *not* my favorite," she said, puzzled. When he stared pointedly at her dress, she held up a flounce disdainfully between two fingers. "Surely you don't think I dress this way because I like it?" She rolled her eyes and began setting up the black chessmen on her side of the board. "I'm nineteen . . . well past the 'maiden trade,' as you so succinctly put it," she said, quoting him. "The white and ruffles are my mother's idea. She and her friends think I should look as young as possible until I dispose advantageously of—"

She reddened and concentrated on arranging her playing pieces. His chuckle said he knew exactly what her mother wanted her to dispose of advantageously. And when she couldn't resist stealing a glance at him, the light in his eyes said he wouldn't mind being the one to help her dispose of it.

Wicked man. The heat that rushed into her cheeks was humiliating.

"It's your move, your lordship," she declared.

"Not until you call me Pierce," he insisted. After a brief silence she relented.

"You have the first move . . . *Pierce*." It didn't feel right to call him that. It was so . . . personal. Still, he hesitated, and when she looked up, he looked rather smug.

"I have already made the first move, Gabrielle."

And what move was that? she wondered. The move

into her boudoir, into her thoughts, into her stray imaginings? She gave him her best no-nonsense glare. The man was a master at double meanings.

"Truly, Gabrielle. I have made the first move." He gestured to the board and she looked down to find that he had indeed moved a piece, pawn to queen three.

They played at a leisurely pace, trading pieces and being courteous and civil, as the tradition of the game required . . . until she took his queen in an unexpected move and he protested. It was a legitimate capture, she argued. It was a sneak attack, he insisted, launched while he was distracted by the play of light in her hair. She laughed and said that he shouldn't have been staring at her in the first place. To avenge her strategy of distracting him with her treacherous charms, he vowed a full assault upon her king. And he would take no prisoners.

But in point of fact, he took several in quick succession: four of her pawns, a knight, and a rook. She gasped, scandalized by his lack of gallantry and promptly seized his bishop, three pawns, and *both* rooks. He nabbed her bishop and wiped out her pawns. She retaliated by taking his knight and several pawns and then chasing his king into a corner.

"Bloodthirsty wench!" he sputtered, moving his king into a pocket of his own pieces, then realizing too late that he had also moved into a trap. He started to pick his king up again, and she cried foul.

"You took your hand away!" she declared, her voice rising, her eyes narrowing.

"I did no such thing—my hand is still right here—" He sat up straighter, lifting the piece and waggling it. "When I remove my hand, my turn is finished, not an instant sooner."

"You did take your hand away—now it's my turn . . ."

•   •   •

At that moment, outside the door, Gunther was passing by on one of the errands Rosalind had concocted for him, duties that took him past Gabrielle's boudoir at regular ten-minute intervals. Alarmed by the sound of their raised voices—arguing about whose hands went where—he headed for Rosalind's boudoir to report.

"The wretch!" Rosalind, who was sitting with Clementine and Ariadne, gasped and shoved to her feet. "I *told* him she was new at this—"

Before anyone could respond, she was out the door, heading for Gabrielle's chambers. Her friends caught up with her at about the same time her better sense did.

"I have to know what is going on in there!" she whispered, motioning for quiet as the muffled sound of Gabrielle's impassioned voice reached them through the doors. Her anxiety soared. "I have to do something."

"Whatever ye do, ye mus' be discreet," Clementine counseled sagely.

"Discreet, hell—call the constables and have the bastard carted off!" Ariadne declared in a fierce rasp.

Rosalind waved them to silence as Sandbourne's deep, wicked laugh seeped through the cracks around the doors. It was enough to rouse her maternal instincts to fever pitch. She turned on Gunther with a flame in her eyes. "Champagne—hot or cold—it doesn't matter. Just hurry!"

As he ran for the wine cellars, she wrung her hands, paced, and listened. It seemed like forever before he came rushing back with a rattling tea cart draped with linen and laden with a silver ice bucket and goblets. Frantically, she waved him toward the door and gathered her friends back against the wall, out of sight. He knocked and waited, tugging his vest down and recovering his breath and dignity.

The door opened and he rolled the cart inside.

Moments later he exited and the door closed behind him. His ears were red as he faced his mistress and reported: "It is chess. They are playing chess."

"Chess?" Rosalind felt her friends' shock and tried to hide her own distress. "Well, she is new at this, after all." She met their incredulous looks with an upraised chin. "And his lordship seems to have peculiar tastes. Perhaps he finds 'taking the queen' stimulating."

"Champagne. Again." Gabrielle stood with her hands on her waist, glowering at the distinctive green bottle canted inside the silver ice bucket.

"Well, I believe I am ready for a little refreshment," Pierce said, rising carefully so as to not upset the chessboard. "Losing is dashed thirsty business."

He opened the champagne and poured. He laughed at the sour face she made each time she took a sip and warned that she probably should acquire a taste for it . . . since the current fashion in better circles was to serve champagne at *weddings*.

With a withering glare, she looked about for some way to get rid of the wretched stuff and poured it into one of the palms by the piano. He watched her, thinking about her objections to romance, wondering what had caused her great antipathy toward things that most young women her age cherished fond hopes and dreams of.

"Just what do you have against romance and passion, anyway?" he asked. "I've experienced a generous sampling of both and have always found them rather pleasant."

"Oh, it's not that I have anything against them . . . as long they're not foisted upon me," she declared lightly, as she came back to the divan and began to set up her side of the board again. "But, personally, I think they're overrated. All that heart-racing passion and knee-trembling excitement." He noted a rise in her shoulders and faint tightening of her mouth, though her tone remained light. "Rapture and splendor require a great deal of preparation and maintenance, you know.

"Take food, for example. Grand romance requires an elaborate diet: oysters, Turkish apricots, champagne, caviar, lobsters, pomegranates, chocolate—which are all very dear. Then there are the rafts of servants required to clean and freshen everything—the linen and laundry bills alone are staggering—and there are florists and jewelers and perfumers. The decor in a boudoir must be updated frequently to keep the surroundings interesting, which means new curtains, furnishings, and carpets. And of course, there must be regular changes in a mistress's wardrobe, lest *she* become a bit *passé*. That means hours at the dressmaker's and more hours in toilette. Every garment, no matter how great or small, is scrutinized for its allure. And that doesn't begin to account for the hours spent reading papers, books, and journals, keeping current as a conversationalist." His eyes were glazing over. She chuckled and changed course.

"I've tried to tell my mother it's not for me, but she refuses to listen. She insists that I am destined to take my place in her world and is adamant about turning me into a seductress of the first water . . . like her."

"The perfect mistress," he supplied, turning it over in his mind, seeing it from a new perspective. He hadn't imagined so much work went into something as seemingly spontaneous as passion. "But, you've decided to become a *wife* instead. Forgive me, sweetness, but what makes you think you would like wifery any better than mistresshood?"

"Wives don't have to bother with all that romantic nonsense. They don't have to worry about constantly pleasing a man and keeping him enthralled and satisfied. They have a *contract* for life."

He started with surprise, then hooted a laugh. She grabbed for the toppling chess pieces and reddened.

"It's true. In marriage, *he* provides the income and the residence and the place in society; *she* creates and maintains a home, and takes care of his needs and the children. It's a much neater, tidier arrangement all around. Nobody has to worry about the ecstasies of love or stoking the fires of romance or being continually swept up in great tempests of passion."

He watched her lift her chin and realized she was serious. She believed that marriage was a dry, bloodless, sexless bargain . . . an assignment of roles and resources made with society's blessing. Where would she get such an idea? And why on earth would she want such a thing?

"Well, Gabrielle, I don't want to disillusion you, but I've seen a number of marriages in my time, and I don't think any of them have been quite as neat and tidy as you make it sound. In fact, marriage can get downright messy at times."

"Well, it can't be any more messy or difficult than maintaining a scintillating love affair for twenty years." She looked down to escape his gaze and began busily setting up the chess pieces. "If a husband gets tired of a wife, he can't just walk away and refuse to ever see her again . . . so a wife is much freer to do and to be what she wants."

A husband cannot just walk away. It was a telling comment, and it didn't take much thought to deduce the source of that idea. It was a glimpse of her mother's life, through her eyes. By her own words, her mother was the perfect mistress . . . a seductress of the first water. She was also a woman who had spent her life, or at least the last twenty years of it, constantly making herself alluring to a man who could throw her over at any moment.

Suddenly Gabrielle's idea of marriage as a cold, passionless contract made perfect sense. It was her mother's outlook, a courtesan's view of the world—a woman could have either passion or security, not both—and Gabrielle had adopted it.

For the first time he thought of the women of the demimonde as persons, not just sexually eager sports, attainable beauties, or agents of male pleasure. Over the years he had known mistresses to pass from man to man, and it had never occurred to him that they might worry or suffer from such a change, or that they might have to work hard at the elegance and sensuality that seemed so effortless for them. Pleasure had always been easy for him, and he didn't want to think about whether it had been easy for the women who had pleasured him.

"So you intend to trade the treacherous glories of passion for the dull security of marriage, do you?" he said, not realizing that he had voiced his observation aloud until she answered him.

"I do," she said, forcing her chin and her spirits up. "I intend to make a nice, ordinary life with a decent, ordinary sort of fellow who will go about his business and leave me to mine."

"Sounds just like a few marriages I have known," he said dryly. Then he fixed her with a suggestive look. "Have you considered that if he *truly* leaves you alone, you may never have your 'dozen' children?"

Her face heated. "Play, your lordship. It's your move."

They played another game of chess, which she also won, and then Gunther arrived to summon them downstairs to tea. She told the majordomo that they would be along presently and closed the door.

Pierce surveyed her as he strolled toward both her and the door. Every hair was in place, her face was still properly pale, and every ruffle was still as pert as it had been when he was admitted to the chamber. One look at her and her mother would realize—as he did too clearly—just how far his intended seduction had missed the mark.

She noticed the scowl on his face as he stared at her. "What is it? Am I a mess?" Her hands flew over her hair and swept anxiously down her bodice and skirt.

"Not at all." He crossed his arms and stroked his lip, studying her with a rueful eye. Amorous impulses that had been waylaid somewhere between flower arranging and chess were beginning to reassert themselves. "Indeed, you look positively untouched . . . a fact your mother is sure to hold against me." He smiled rakishly. "After all, I am supposed to be introducing you to the delights of love."

"Oh. I see. That could be a problem." She tried to think of an out, but found her mind strangely sluggish. Moments ticked by and still she had no ready answer. She frowned uneasily. "Then, I suppose you'd better 'touch' me."

He savored the response that registered in her as he settled close to her and ran his knuckle down the side of her cheek. It was soft and cool. He could feel the tension in her, sensed her awareness of him, and felt the sweet essence of her curling through him on every breath he took. He reached for a lock of her hair and rubbed the silky strand between his thumb and forefinger. When he gave a tug, the curl popped free and dangled just above her shoulder.

Guided by instinct, he removed one hairpin and then another, loosening curls. The feel of that silk gliding through his fingers sent a curl of heat through his blood. He was seized by a powerful urge to pull it all down around her shoulders and plunge his hands into it. Resisting that impulse, he turned his attentions to her ruffles; crumpling her puffed sleeves, trapping her bodice frills and wilting them with the warmth of his touch.

Gabrielle was skittish, tensing at every motion, holding her breath each time he brushed her skin. Her heart was beating steadily faster, hammering against her ribs.

Suddenly, there was a strange, empty feeling in the middle of her, and she was having a devil of a time swallowing. All she could see was his hands, stroking her face gently, caressing strands of her hair, devastating her girlish ruffles with a touch so whisper light that it was maddening.

She found herself drawn to lean into him, wanting to fulfill the promise of those delicious little nudges and tantalizing brushes with a more direct and purposeful contact. And when he dragged his hands over the ruffles that flowed over her breasts, she knew she should protest, but couldn't summon a single word. When his hands withdrew, she blinked and looked up to find him gazing down at her with warm, inviting eyes . . . dark, flattering eyes . . . eyes she had been avoiding for the past two hours.

"Are you through?" she managed in a dry whisper.

"Not quite." He surveyed her with those worldly eyes. "I think you need something more." A soft smile appeared. "Oh, yes. One thing more."

His head lowered toward hers, which took a moment to register. She managed to bring her hands up between them.

"Are you certain this is necessary?" She braced against his chest, staring helplessly at his mouth, knowing what he intended.

"Ah, yes, Gabrielle," he murmured, continuing his descent. "This is very, very necessary."

Slowly, sweetly, with more restraint than he thought possible, he kissed her. It was like sinking into a field of sweet clover on a warm summer's day, soft, fragrant, and awash in unexpected warmth. He fitted his lips to hers, feeling a tantalizing hum of sensation in his lips, something just less than a tingle but tantalizingly more than just the pressure of skin on skin. He'd never felt anything like it.

And it seemed that the longer the kiss went on, the stronger the sensation became. . . .

She was drowning in sensation . . . firm, supple lips . . . no longer dry . . . no longer still. Her lips parted as her head sank to one side, accommodating his mouth . . . yielding, exploring the stunning new sensations he created by moving his mouth over hers. It was nothing like the last time or like the time before that with the count. This was delicious, so unexpectedly pleasant. And as her perceptions widened, she realized that her entire body, from her racing heart to her watery knees, was responding in some way to that oral caress. Then his tongue raked slowly across her lips, and she held her breath . . . waiting and wanting . . . wanting what, she did not know.

Without warning, it was over. His head lifted, his mouth abandoned hers, and she came to her senses feeling boneless and disoriented. She was standing in the circle of his arms, pressed hard against him, scarcely able to focus her eyes.

"There." He thrust her back an arm's length and looked at her. She looked exactly the way he had imagined she would after being thoroughly kissed: her skin glowing, her hair faintly tousled, her eyes dark as midnight. Her expression was filled with softness, vulnerability, and, unless he was mistaken, a sense of discovery. She had just learned the pleasure and the power of a kiss.

"Perfect," he pronounced her.

She felt perfect. And not even coming back to her senses could dispel the warmth suffusing her skin and collecting into a pool in the middle of her. She floated down the stairs on his arm, wrapped in a pleasant haze, aware of the stares of her mother and her mother's friends, but too absorbed in the revolution going on inside her to care what they might think. When he left, she drifted up the stairs, still under the powerful influence of his presence.

From the drawing room, Rosalind watched her floating up the steps with a dreamy look that signified something momentous had occurred. She resettled herself on her chair with a maternal "tsk."

"Her hair, it was mussed," Genevieve declared wistfully.

" 'E give her a good kiss an' a tousle, that's what." Clementine chuckled.

"A pawing is more like it," Ariadne said with a sniff.

They looked to Rosalind, and there was a moment's pause before she announced her opinion of the day's wooing. It was cautiously optimistic.

"Well, at least this time she wasn't sick."

Upstairs, as she sat on the foot bench at the end of her bed, Gabrielle fingered her startlingly sensitive lips and wondered at the strange lethargy that lingered in her. She had never imagined that such an intimacy—mouth to mouth, lips to lips—could be so pleasurable. It certainly explained the attention given to the glories of "the kiss" in poetry, plays, and romantic stories.

She shook herself to dispel that sensory fog and made herself think critically about it. After examining the evidence, she decided that her reaction was probably the result of a sense of intimacy created by their shared pretense. He was her partner in deception, and a heightened air of excitement always surrounded the clandestine. No doubt that was what made it seem so enthralling. And prolonged exposure to his worldly charm, at such close range, must certainly have an effect after a while.

Further, it wasn't as if she was totally incapable of

feeling pleasure. She positively adored a long steamy bath of an evening, followed by the caress of a soft silk nightdress and the slide of cool satin sheets against her bare limbs. And at times she got the most intense cravings for almonds and chocolate, or the taste of raspberries with clotted cream. Thinking of food inspired the insight that kissing might be something one had to acquire a taste for . . . like horseradish or escargot.

Yes. Well. That certainly put it all in better perspective, she decided. There were several perfectly logical and understandable reasons for her reaction to his kiss. It was nothing to worry about, really . . . as long as she made sure it didn't happen again.

8

Taking a virgin mistress was proving to be every bit as arduous and involved a process as taking a virgin bride. That annoying conclusion occurred to Pierce on the third day of his bizarre courtship as he stalked up and down Regent Street, going from shop to shop, searching for a gift suitable for his mistress-to-be.

The gift had to be something feminine, expensive, and highly personal . . . indicative of the deepening level of intimacy between them. But it also had to be in keeping with his appreciation of Gabrielle's freshness and innocence. And harder still, it would have to meet the approval of her worldly, refined, and highly critical mother. After two interminable hours stalking around Liberty's,

Dickins and Jones's, Hamely's, and half a dozen smaller shops, he was still empty-handed and growing testier by the minute. Everything seemed either too explicit or too subtle, too ordinary or too much the grand demonstration.

Gabrielle was right, he realized. The wooing, the gifts, the thought and energy involved in exalted gestures, and the constant, all-encompassing scrutiny—this romance business was nothing short of exhausting. He wouldn't have to expend this much effort in applying to marry the prime peach of this season's crop of debutantes!

In respectable society, there would be a few dances at cotillions, a stolen kiss, a whispered query and a blush of response, and then it would be off to the study with the old man for brandy and cigars and the ritualized blessing. He would see his name linked to the peach's in newsprint, then on invitations, and from then on, everyone would leave them alone in the parlor, in darkened corners, and on the bridle paths in the park. No questions asked. Nobody would demand to know his amorous history or call into question his motives. And certainly no one would dare inquire about or pass judgment on his erotic tastes and passionate sensibilities. There would be no expectations of soaring romance or desperate, feverish, soul-rending . . .

Hold on. He stopped dead in the middle of the sidewalk, realizing Gabrielle was right again; marriage *would* be easier, especially for a man of his rank and station. And respectable marriage would be a hell of a lot less intrusive into his private character, personal habits, and manly dignity.

What in hell was he doing, putting up with this charade? Who knew how long it would be before he could take Gabrielle out and dangle her before Gladstone's eyes? Sooner or later the old man would seek out another tart, probably one a good bit more eager to earn a fast "fiver." If Pierce had the sense God gave a turnip, he would just turn around and walk away from the entire scheme. He turned on his heel and at that moment found himself facing a shop window containing outrageously expensive French shoes.

And there in the window—in exquisite white silk brocade, adorned with a blue satin bow and rosettes—was a pair of party slippers with dainty spool heels. The fires of discontent in him died as he stared at those shoes.

White like her dresses. Blue like the ribbons she wore in her hair.

He strode into the shop and bought them on the spot.

Promptly at three, he arrived at Gabrielle's house, with the tissue-wrapped package under his arm. After standing inspection for her mother in the hall—and feeling a certain vengeful satisfaction at the way she eyed the box he was carrying—he was shown up the stairs to Gabrielle's boudoir. He found her seated on the window seat, staring down into the tea garden below. She rose and greeted him with a beaming smile . . . which lasted only until the door shut.

"I've brought you something." He held out the box to her.

"Does my mother know?"

"She saw the box as I came up." He put it into her hands and folded his arms, waiting for her to open it.

"It would have been better if she could have actually seen it." She gazed ruefully at the white tissue and the blue satin ribbon. Placing it on the tea table, beside the vase filled with yesterday's flowers, she went to the desk to get out her bankbook. "But it's still proof of your generosity. Just tell me how much—"

"I didn't bring it for your blessed mother, Gabrielle, I brought it for you." He glowered at the sight of her pen poised above a blank bank draft. "I spent half a day picking it out—the least you can do is open the damned thing."

She glanced at the box, then up at him in genuine

dismay. "Oh, but I could never accept a gift from you, your lordship. Why, it wouldn't be proper."

"Let me get this straight. You *can* accept it if I give it to you as part of a pretense, but you *cannot* accept it if I give it to you as myself, person to person." He gave her a furiously sardonic smile. "Forgive me—I do tend to get a bit lost in the ethical intricacies of these things. You pretend to be my lover and spend hours locked away with me, purportedly engaged in wild, illicit passion. But you refuse accept a trifle from me because it might offend your precious notions of propriety?" Picking up the package, he stalked over and thrust it into her hands.

"Open it!" he demanded.

She hesitated, surprised by the intensity of his reaction and confused by the intensity of hers. Her heart was beating faster and her mouth was beginning to dry. A gift. For her. From him. She told herself it was probably a bad sign—first a kiss, then a gift. She flicked a glance around the suggestive opulence of her boudoir and worried that he was being influenced by their unfortunate surroundings.

Still, she would have to open it sooner or later; her mother would expect a report. She carried it to the window seat and began to remove the ribbon and tissue. Inside was a black pasteboard box embossed with a gold emblem touting a shop in Regent Street. She lifted the lid and uncovered a pair of shoes—dainty party shoes with elegant French heels—made of white satin brocade and trimmed with a delicate blue bow and ribbon rosettes.

"If they don't suit you as a gift," he said, with a hint of gruffness, "think of them as reimbursement for the pair I pitched out the carriage window."

A gift of shoes from a man to a woman was considered shockingly suggestive and highly improper. But considering the "proper impropriety" of their strange relationship, a gift of shoes from him to her was somehow rather fitting. And if she had chosen for herself, she couldn't have found a pair that delighted her more. Even the color was perfect. She stroked them gingerly, then, without quite realizing what she was doing, pressed one to her heart as she looked up.

"They're beautiful. But, the ones I lost weren't nearly so grand."

The shimmer of pleasure in her eyes caused a queer fullness in his chest. It was something like an ache of need, only it registered too high in his body to be recognizable as any of his usual desires. He took a deep breath, trying to force it down into his loins, where it undoubtedly belonged. And as she set the shoes back in the box, he felt a slightly irrational urge to prolong the curiously intimate feeling between them.

"Aren't you going to put them on?"

"Oh, well . . . I don't think . . ." She looked at them, then at the plain black slippers on her feet.

The next instant, he was on one knee beside her, and before she could protest, he had seized one of her feet and removed her slipper. When he slipped one of the gift shoes on her foot, there was a space between her foot and the shoe. He sat back on his heel, looking at it in dismay.

She watched the red creeping up his neck and collecting in his ears. He had expected them to fit. He apparently hadn't considered that they might not be the right size, and that made her suspect that he probably had never bought shoes for a woman before. The sight of his embarrassment and disappointment caused something in the middle of her to soften dangerously. Just at that moment, he seemed so human, so ordinary. So accessible.

"Well, clearly these won't do," he declared, starting to remove the slipper.

"No." She brushing his hands away. "They're fine." With a determined smile, she took off the shoe, ripped off a piece of the tissue wrapping, and stuffed it into the toe. She gave the other one the same treatment, then stood and lifted her hem a few inches to gaze at her feet. With the stuffing hidden in the toes, the shoes appeared to fit perfectly. "They're beautiful."

He stood beside her, looking at her feet, then staring into her eyes when she lifted them to him. He felt a conflicting swirl of embarrassment and relief and bruised male pride. The overture he had intended to turn into a seductive gift had been reduced by his thoughtlessness to an empty romantic gesture, fit only for impressing her mother. Until she rescued them. Oddly, he didn't feel embarrassed at all now; he felt nothing but pleasure. And he didn't want to think about why.

Tearing her gaze from his, she busied herself setting the box aside and rediscovered the book she had been reading when he arrived. It reminded her of what she had intended to tell him the minute he came through the door.

"I have some bad news, I'm afraid." She waved him to a seat on the sofa and joined him, walking carefully in her tissue-stuffed shoes. "After yesterday, I'm forbidden to play chess with you again."

He clapped a hand to his heart. "I'm devastated."

She scowled. "I'm serious. And so was my mother when she lectured me last night on the dangers of appearing too much the bluestocking. 'A woman who flaunts her learning has a great deal yet to learn,' she insisted. And she drew up for me a list of appropriate activities, things guaranteed to charm a gentleman."

"Guaranteed?" He raised his eyebrows. "I should like to see that list."

"At the very top of it was"—she made a face—"poetry reading."

"Poetry?" He winced.

"I confess, that was my first reaction too." She leaned forward, energy flooding into her countenance. "But in this case, I think she may be absolutely right. I also think she may be *listening*." With a glance toward the door, she stood up, opened the slender book she held.

"So much for doing what I wanted today," he grumbled.

" 'There was an old lady of Harrow,' " she read in a mock stentorian voice.

> " '*Whose views were exceedingly narrow.*
> *At the end of her paths*
> *She built two birdbaths*
> *For the different sexes of sparrow.*' "

She watched his jaw drop, savoring his surprise, then with a mischievous grin launched straight into another.

> " '*There was a young lady of Riga*
> *Who smiled as she rode on a tiger;*
> *They returned from the ride*
> *With the lady inside*
> *And the smile on the face of the tiger.*' "

"Limericks!" he declared, laughing and leaning back against the pile of cushions.

"Well, it *is* poetry. In the loosest sense, of course."

"Loose poetry." He wiped his eyes. "My favorite kind. Read on."

He watched her defiance of her mother's edicts on romance with fresh insight. Her reading, like her piano selections that first day, was nothing short of rebellion, a full-scale insurrection against her mother's overwhelming requirements.

He understood rebellion, the need to throw off another's suffocating demands and expectations and strike out on a path that was purely your own. He had been embroiled in it himself for years. But her sort of rebellion—intelligent, civilized, a diabolical imitation of obedience—was so fresh and unexpected. So engagingly inventive. So deliciously playful. So very much like *her*.

As she laughed and her eyes sparkled, he slid the book from her hands, rose to read a few limericks himself, and took a stand with her.

"Limericks?" Rosalind gasped. Gunther had just brought word of what Gabrielle was reading to the earl behind closed doors. "But, I spoke with her. I specifically told her to read him classical poetry or the sonnets of Shakespeare."

With Genevieve at her heels, she hurried through the halls to Gabrielle's chambers and halted several paces from the door, inclining her head to listen intently. Lord Sandbourne's deep voice rumbled forth, but she couldn't make out his words at first. Gradually, his baritone voice raised and became all too understandable.

> " '*There was a young lady of Kent*
> *Who said that she knew what it meant*
> *When men asked her to dine,*
> *gave her liquor and wine . . .*' "

Rosalind grayed and staggered, steadying herself on Genevieve's arm. "Ye gods, it's *him*—he's reading her limericks," she whispered hoarsely, her disbelief turning to horror. "Beer hall tunes and now *limericks*—the man is a cultural wasteland!"

After several more recitations, Pierce paused to let Gabrielle catch her breath. He studied her glowing face and jewel-bright eyes.

"I've a weakness for limericks," he confessed. "I've

committed to memory every one of that lot *Punch* published some years ago."

His gaze traveled up and along the sinuous line of her body as she leaned back against the pillows of the divan on her elbow, her legs drawn up to the side so that just her ankles dangled over the edge. Her unconsciously erotic posture and relaxed mood radiated a warmth he found irresistible.

He started toward her, his gaze fixed on those ankles, those shoes . . . *his* shoes . . .

A knock at the door startled them both. He motioned her to keep her seat and answered it himself. Gunther trundled a cart past him, depositing it in front of the divan with word that her mother had thought they might like some refreshment.

As the houseman opened the bottle of champagne, Pierce strolled about the room with his hands clasped behind him, using the opportunity to take slow, deep breaths. By the time Gunther withdrew, Pierce had managed to reclaim his control, if not his good humor, and found himself standing before her bookshelves, staring at the titles of the books.

"I must say, Gabrielle, you do have a rather wide-ranging taste in literature. From 'loose poetry' to classical treatises to the plays of the great masters." He came to pour two glasses of champagne and offered her one. She declined, but then recalled her mother's vigilance and rose to pour it into the potted palm.

"If I had known they had such things in a girls' school, I'd have petitioned for entrance to one myself."

She smiled, settling once again on the divan. "Well, I wouldn't lay the blame entirely on Marchand." She looked toward the window, focusing on something far away with a look that was the essence of longing and regret.

"You miss it, don't you . . . your French life."

"Yes." She came back to the moment from wherever she had been. "Ironic, really. I hated it at first." She took a deep breath. "Lessons, tutors, a bright and unconventional headmistress—my mother had seen to everything. *Almost.* I don't believe she had counted on all that learning producing a person with ideas of her own. She must have thought of me as some sort of dutiful sponge, soaking up whatever culture was put in my way and rendering it up upon command." She broke into a small, defiant smile. "And she hadn't counted on my complete lack of desire."

He studied the rebellious glint in her eye. She had convinced herself she had no passions . . . when all a person had to do was watch her play the piano, listen to her talk about the French women and their children in the foundling home, or experience her laughter to know that she was a very passionate woman. He smiled to himself. It was a mark of her sexual inexperience. And inexperience was an easy thing to remedy.

"About these lackluster 'juices' of yours . . . Whatever gave you the notion that you have no passion in you?"

"I should think that would be perfectly obvious," she said, sitting up primly and feeling heat blooming in her cheeks. "My aptitude and responses are dismal at best."

"They are not."

"Really, your lordship." She slid to the edge of the divan.

"*Really,* Gabrielle." He leaned back on the cushions and looked her over appreciatively. "I've had some experience in these matters, and in my judgment you show a good bit of promise. Though, I admit, you could do with a bit more in the way of enthusiasm."

"The question of my sensual capacities is moot," she declared hotly. "I'll have no need of them, now or later. I remind you, your lordship, I intend to become a *wife.*"

"Indeed? Well I have known a few wives with considerable 'juices.' "

His laughter washed over her, drenching her with confusion. He found her notion of wifehood highly amusing. Insufferable male! He seemed to think his experience with illicit *amour* made him an authority on all relations between the sexes. She turned to her desk, trying to recoup and to think of something to keep him busy.

Her eyes fell on the books on the top shelf of her collection, then drifted down to light on a book stuck on the very bottom shelf. Smiling, she stooped to pluck it from the shelf, and when she would have stood up, she found him bending over her, watching her intently. Instead of pulling back to give her room to straighten, he remained where he was . . . so that she had to either press back against the bookcase or find herself nose to nose with him.

Something within her refused to quail at this bit of male intimidation. Or perhaps something in her simply wanted to experience being death-defyingly close to his satiny lips and dark velvet eyes again. She came up slowly, face to face, eye to eye, and nose to nose with him.

His lips were parted slightly, and she could feel the soft eddies his breath made as it moved across her skin. His eyes were warm and filled with shimmering lights that seemed to be internal reflections of things known and things experienced, just waiting to be explored. Through those windows on his soul she glimpsed unplumbed secrets —pleasure, sadness, pain, pride, and a thousand more vagaries of the human heart and mind—beckoning to something nameless and half formed within her.

Waves of sensation poured over her, rich and liquid, clinging to her senses, running down the inner walls of her body . . . thick like cream, sweet like honey. She could see the heat-bronzed texture of his skin, could smell the sandalwood and starched-cotton scents of his garments blending with the wine on his breath. She could almost hear the beating of his heart . . . slow and inviting . . . patient and waiting. It was such a basic and seductive rhythm.

Her gaze drifted to his mouth and she waited, entranced, scarcely breathing. Like a glacier, he moved without seeming to move, melting toward her and, by the inexorable force of his movement, scouring and changing the landscape of her senses. And suddenly, as if a suffocating layer of frost were being scraped away from her senses and her spirit, need began to grow, warm and nascent inside her. She felt the pull of longing, fresh and painfully strong, the tension between the almost and the certainty, the wanting and the having. She suddenly ached for the feel of him, craved the pressure and taste of his mouth. She wanted. For the first time, she truly wanted the intimate physical contact of a kiss.

And he was so close. The slightest movement . . . across a space of less than an inch . . . would bring her that heady satisfaction. But she waited, absorbed in the wonder of newborn desire, certain that there would be forever to have and to savor that inevitable sweet conclusion.

Then abruptly he pulled back, staring hotly at her, and turned away.

She staggered—unkissed, untouched—and quickly turned back to the bookcase to hide her shock and reassemble her defenses. What on earth had gotten into her? It took several minutes to banish the embarrassed heat in her countenance, before she could turn back to the divan. He was seated, sipping his warming champagne, watching her with an unreadable expression.

"Here it is," she said, relieved to find her voice normal. She held up a book titled *Aesop's Fables*.

"Ye gods." He dragged a hand down his face with a

martyred air. "We're now reduced to parables and morality tales. What's next? Bedtime stories?"

"Oh, I don't think we'll be here quite that long." She opened the book. "I'm especially fond of the one about the fox and the grapes."

She read that fable, then another and another. But, instead of falling asleep, Pierce found himself falling deeper and deeper under some strange and beguiling spell that had begun with his risky gambit at the bookcase and still exerted an effect on his senses. He had meant to pull her into his arms and kiss her, and to keep kissing her until he managed somehow to raise the passionate responses she so desperately denied possessing.

But somehow, staring into those azure blue eyes, glimpsing in them the irresistible glow of inner discovery, he hesitated in seizing that moment. Something was happening inside her, and he found just watching the shimmering, shifting lights of becoming in her eyes unexpectedly fascinating. In that moment he sensed her rising desire and understood that she was beginning to feel the nearness and the need between them in the same powerful way. Apparently *not-kissing*, like *not-sinning*, had an erotic appeal all its own. Near, but not quite near enough. With her it was tantalizing.

Now he sat watching her take the parts of the fox, the crow, the weasel, the rabbit, and the turtle, knowing she was doing it to distract them both and somehow not caring. He laughed at her charming make-believe menagerie, thinking of all the human creatures that lived inside her: the prim little schoolgirl, the naive miss, the adamant bluestocking, the stubborn daughter, the petulant debutante, the conniving urchin, and most interesting of all, the tempting, voluptuous woman who had yet to make her presence fully known.

Gabrielle seemed to be a composite of every female to

whom he had ever been attracted. No, he decided, she was different. He shifted his heated frame to a more comfortable position, as she lowered her voice to imitate a wizened old owl. Entirely too different. Too interesting. Too complicated. And too damned desirable.

Something that had been nagging at the edge of his awareness ever since he had stood on the street outside the shoe shop that morning, finally emerged into his consciousness. Somewhere in the midst of flower arranging and music hall songs and chess games and limericks, somewhere in the slow, tantalizing revelation of the person inside Gabrielle, his plans to use her as a foil to gather evidence against Gladstone had fallen apart. Knowing her as he now did, he could never subject her to the old man's perversity, or to the questioning and examinations that would be required to validate her "evidence" afterward.

It was a blow to his schemes, but it wasn't fatal. Sooner or later, Gladstone would take to the streets again, to take advantage of some other desperate woman under the guise of helping her. And Pierce would be there to intercept her and start the wheels in motion to put an end to the old man's hypocritical policies and his government.

With that decided, he turned his attentions to Gabrielle, watching and listening, now free to concentrate on exploring and enjoying and claiming her lush presence and person for himself.

Later, just as Gabrielle was launching into another story, Gunther appeared at the door to request their presence in the drawing room for tea.

"But, it's not yet five o'clock," Gabrielle protested, then caught herself and glanced at Pierce. All she could think was that there wouldn't be any time for "touching," and she prayed that her shameless thoughts didn't show in her face.

"Your mother was most emphatic, Miss Gabrielle. I was to fetch you immediately." Gunther stood in the doorway waiting, his unbending efficiency speaking her mother's annoyance plainly.

Gabrielle smoothed her skirt and sent a hand to her hair. Pierce tugged at his vest and made sure his tie was straight. They trailed Gunther downstairs, stealing glances at each other behind his back, like guilty children. Beer hall tunes and nursery songs, limericks and then Aesop's fables —they had brazenly trespassed the rules of high romance and now were being called to account.

In the drawing room, they found Rosalind with her friends Genevieve Francette, Clementine Bolt, and Ariadne Baden-Powell waiting for them. All through tea, Rosalind made it a point to converse on cultural topics and to give a nod to Gabrielle's numerous cultural accomplishments whenever possible. More than once she alluded to her daughter's skill at the piano and was less than subtle in praising Gabrielle's "exquisite soprano" and her "musical reading voice." By the time she managed to work in a few words about the way the duke of Burgundy had declared that Gabrielle danced like a floating feather, Gabrielle was certain she knew what purgatory must be like.

Rosalind's message was dismally clear. Their style of courtship was straining the bounds of credulity for a grand passion. If continued, their behavior would lead to questions about the seriousness of his lordship's intentions.

But, when Gabrielle walked Pierce to the door, there was a stubborn glint in her eye. "I think another gift is probably in order. Something precious and expensive. My mother believes that *generosity* in a man covers a multitude of sins."

As soon as the door closed behind him, she lifted her skirts and hurried for the stairs. But she wasn't quick enough.

"Gabrielle!" Her name came roaring out of the drawing

room in an icy blast, freezing her in her tracks. "I would have a word with you, young lady."

Gabrielle stiffened and clamped a ruthless hand on her rebellious impulses. She managed to get through the lecture that followed by repeating over and over in her mind: *Only a few more days . . . a few more days and I will be free to get on with finding a husband.*

9

Pierce spent a good part of that evening in a dark, chilled carriage parked outside the Reform Club on the Pall Mall, waiting for Gladstone to leave. The later it got, the less the likelihood that the old man would decide to do a bit of "walking" on the way home and the more irritated Pierce became. By the time he trailed Gladstone to his home, watched as most of the lights were extinguished, and headed home himself, he had had plenty of time to think about his situation with Gabrielle and was in a ripe mood indeed.

The control that Rosalind exerted over Gabrielle—and by association, over *him*—was intolerable. He was a peer of the realm, for God's sake. He wouldn't stand for *his* mother's scheming and manipulation, why should he stand for *hers*?

If Rosalind were a man, he knew exactly what he would—he stopped dead. What was the matter with him? She was an adversary, just the same as any political opponent, and she had to be treated as such. In politics, sound strategy was to discover an opponent's weaknesses and exploit them. And he already knew Rosalind's prime weakness: she was a devout romantic. Only when she believed that he and Gabrielle were grandly and passionately in love, would she release them from the boudoir. And she could only judge whether or not they were convincing lovers by the level of her own romantic feelings about them.

Then it wasn't Gabrielle he needed to ply with gifts and romantic gestures—it was Rosalind!

With that revelation keenly in mind, he spent the next morning acquiring and sending several cases of Perrier-Jouet and a number of excellent clarets and burgundies to Maison LeCoeur, to express his gratitude and largesse toward his soon-to-be mistress and her mother. Then he arrived on the doorstep himself, promptly at three, with his arms once again full of flowers.

The atmosphere was noticeably warmer toward him in the drawing room, where Rosalind sat with her covey of friends. And it got warmer still when he presented her with a massive bouquet, declaring that her arrangements were always so superb.

She was flattered speechless at first, but she recovered as he turned to go and suggested that surely he meant them to go to Gabrielle instead.

"Oh," he said with a wickedly charming smile, "I've brought her some as well." He turned so that she could see and lifted a dark-colored earthen pot in the crook of his other arm. It hadn't been visible at first, tucked away at his side, against his dark coat. Her eyes widened on what appeared to be three grizzled sticks with a few stemmy green shoots sticking out of them. He nodded and excused himself to make for the stairs, carrying with him the deliciously stunned look on her face.

After a moment of silence, Rosalind turned to her friends with an unsettled expression. "At least he is making an effort . . . in his own peculiar way."

"He brings blossoms to *la maman* . . ." Genevieve said.

"An' he brings 'er dried up sticks in a pot," Clementine declared with a scowl.

Ariadne, who had been staring at the door, broke free of her reverie and turned with a look of annoyance. "It is a rosebush, Clementine, not 'sticks in a pot'! The shoes were too easy, and the wine too ordinary." She glanced back at the doors with a wistful expression. "But a rosebush. Who would have thought the bounder had such a streak of romance in him?"

Pierce took the steps two at a time, outpacing Gunther, who halted in some pique at the top of the stairs and left him to his own devices. He found Gabrielle waiting for him, wearing another frothy white confection and a long-suffering look. She brightened and bounded up from the divan when he entered. Then her gaze fell to the pot.

"What's that?"

He smiled and held it out to her. "A rosebush. For you."

She scowled, accepting it. "Did my mother see it?"

"Of course. She was enthralled."

"She was?" She lifted the pot and regarded the shrub with a dubious expression.

His smile tightened. "Of course. It's a hauntingly romantic gesture."

"It is?"

"It most certainly is," he said, propping his fists on his waist. "It is symbolic of our growing affection. It is a raft of extravagant metaphors rolled up in a pot of soil. In fact, it's a whole bloody treatise on our present and future love."

"Oh. Well." She forced a polite smile. "That's lovely of you." Then her politeness melted into worry. "Do you think she understood all that?"

"I expect she'll figure it out," he said testily. "She is a professional romantic."

She took a deep breath, realizing that she had offended him. "I, on the other hand, am a ghastly amateur. Forgive me. It's just that I had something of an extended lecture last night, and I thought we agreed you would bring something suitably expensive and—wait!" She had been struck by inspiration. Holding the pot, she looked it over with rising appreciation. "A rosebush belongs in a *garden*! Oh, Pierce, you're a wizard."

"I am?"

She flashed him a radiant smile, grabbed him by the hand, and pulled him out the door. "You've found the key to the prison. Where better to tend our blossoming love than in a *garden*?"

Down the stairs and back through the morning room they went, to the doors leading to the terrace and the garden at the rear of the house. She paused to pull the bell, then they stepped out into a bright afternoon and a walled garden filled with nooks and vine-covered bowers and the sound of sparrows chirping above the faint clatter of the distant street. A paved stone terrace set with rattan furniture lay at the center of three stone paths that radiated outward, like the spokes of a wheel, between beds of grass and new plantings. There was a tang in the air, the smell of freshly tilled soil that spoke of spring and new growth.

When Gunther arrived, she sent him for tools,

fertilizer, and water. As the houseman collected the materials from the gardener's shed, she had an idea and glanced up at the house to locate her window. She pulled Pierce out along the path to a spot clearly visible from her room, where a cleared flower bed lay waiting for the gardener to prepare it for planting.

"If we plant it here, I can see it from my window . . . and think of you every time I look at it." She looked up at him. "Is that romantic enough?"

It was more than romantic, he thought, it was arousing. Intensely so. When he looked down into her sparkling eyes, his gaze got tangled in them. For a long moment he stood feeling the warmth of the sun, the cool air, and a sudden, absorbing awareness of her freshness and sensuality. Gunther's arrival with the tools and watering can was all that kept him from kissing her on the spot.

Gabrielle dismissed the houseman and, straightaway, sank onto her knees beside the bed, grinding her pristine voile into the dirt that had spilled onto the grass.

"Gabrielle, your dress—"

"Oh, I can't be bothered with a dress," she said determinedly, patting the ground beside her, insisting that he join her. "Not when I'm so overcome with the *romance* of the moment." Challenged to match her sacrifice in the name of gloriously impractical love, he planted the knees of his expensive trousers in the dirt beside her. Beaming with mischief, she thrust a spade into his hands and ordered, "Dig."

Pierce, as it happened, knew nothing about gardening or roses. Gabrielle, on the other hand, had done a good bit of gardening at Marchand and knew something about the cultivation of French roses and their English counterparts. She insisted that the soil be turned all around the area before digging a hole for the bush. In the combined warmth of the sun and with the exertion of digging, Pierce soon overheated and had to peel off his coat and lay it across the branch of a nearby flowering cherry.

"You gardened . . . in a French girls' school?" He balanced on one hand stuck in the soft dirt, wielding the trowel forcefully with the other. Then he raised up onto his knees and held up one dirt-caked hand. "In dirt?"

"What other kind of gardening is there?" She smiled. "It is a highly commendable pastime for ladies—considered quite 'improving.' It is also considered quite romantic."

"It is?" He scowled, wriggling his dirt-caked fingers. "Oh, yes. Silly me. I can feel myself being swept away."

"Dig," she ordered, pointing to the modest dent he had made in the ground. "It is universally agreed that a woman in a garden is something of an enticement." He gave a snort of disbelief. "It's true. The beauty and natural harmony that abound in a garden illuminate a woman's own graces and display her at her best." She lowered her voice and leaned closer. "Personally, I suspect that the effect has more to do with the strong scents and earthy textures." She paused, amused by the sight of him in so undignified a posture. "Or, as Mme. Marchand said, it just may have to do with the fact that men adore the sight of a woman on her knees."

"Who is on whose knees here?" he grumbled.

A short while later they were both on their knees, one adding the bonemeal and milled peat while the other mixed it in the soil. Together they removed the bush from the pot and set it in the hole, and together they scraped and packed and tamped and watered. Their shoulders bumped and their hands brushed, and when they reached for the trowel at the same time, he held her hand for a moment before relinquishing it and the tool.

Whether from the work or from his nearness, she found her breath coming faster and became aware of where every point of her body was in relation to every point of his. Her gaze flitted surreptitiously over his shirt and vest, lingering on how they molded to his body as he moved, and somehow she felt her corset and the strain of fabric across her shoulders and breasts in a new way. Then when they straightened to begin "watering in," she saw how his waist tightened and his thighs flexed as he lifted the heavy metal can, and felt her own waist and thighs tighten in response.

She could scarcely take her eyes from him as he stretched to extend his reach and make sure the far side of the bush was properly watered. How was it that by just removing a coat he seemed so much more human . . . so much more male?

When he finished and turned, she found herself nearly nose to nose with him again and abruptly sat back on the edge of the grass.

"Why did you bring me a rosebush?" she asked, raking the soil with her fingers.

"To be perfectly honest, I thought a grand romantic gesture was called for. And what was more fitting for a 'rosebud' than a rosebush?"

"A rosebud? Just what is that?"

"I'm afraid that's what we bounders call pale, perfect little debutantes, with their delicate constitutions and impossibly dewy eyes." When she looked up, he had a devilish twinkle in his eye. "Behind their backs, of course."

"Have I just been insulted?"

"Not really." He reached out to brush a streak of dirt from her cheek and only made it worse with his dirty hand. He tried again with his handkerchief. "As a rule, 'rosebuds' are highly desirable. They're bred, pampered, and groomed like prime thoroughbreds and then rigorously schooled in all the female graces and accomplishments. They play and sing sweetly. They sketch and do watercolors and read poetry with great flair. They converse brilliantly, and arrange flowers artistically, and sip champagne modestly, and dance divinely . . ."

"That's not me!" Her rebellion flared.

"You think not?" He laughed and seized her hand, letting his gaze skim the curve of her body as she sat curled on the grass at the edge of the flower bed. "Granted—you play beer hall songs instead of sonatas, read limericks and fables instead of sonnets, pour your champagne down some poor potted palm, and force men to do your flower arranging for you. . . ." He sat down beside her and laid his arms across his upraised knees. Then he gave her a slow, sweeping look that caused her heart to skip. "But, you work so hard at not being appealing that it has something of the reverse effect."

"It does?" She felt a shiver that could only be called pleasure.

"It does." He glanced at the rosebush they had just planted together. "In that respect, you're probably more a rosebush than a rosebud."

"Now I'm a rosebush?" she said, looking dismayed. "What does that mean?"

"Without pushing the entire metaphor ridiculously far, let me just say . . . you're infinitely more fascinating than the typical rosebud. More complex, more textured, more complete. And the thorns you affect don't detract from your beauty or desirability any more than a rose's do from its. Thorns—keep life interesting."

"They do?" There was a curious flutter in her stomach.

"Yours do," he said, his voice lowering. "One look at you is all a man needs to know that someday you'll blossom. And one taste of you is all a man needs to make him want to be there when you do."

She found herself staring, entranced, into his dark eyes: knowing, provocative, inviting. A thousand mysteries inside him. She couldn't swallow. A moment later she came to her senses and pulled her chin back, trying to think of something to dispel the jittery warmth rising inside her.

"One of your rosebush metaphors, no doubt," she whispered, averting her gaze. "Very effective. I'm sure my mother would be impressed."

"There are more," he said—too quietly. She couldn't help looking back at him and was immediately caught up in the glint of sun in his hair and the bronzed texture of his skin. Her fingers fairly itched to touch his tousled hair, his strong jaw, his soft lips. "You are a rose, sweetheart. A flower of great beauty and delicacy . . . so fragrant and soft." He reached out to run his knuckles down the side of her cheek and she couldn't seem to pull away from that touch. "Your skin feels like silken petals." He leaned closer, then still closer, lowering his dark head and following the line of her shoulder, breathing in her scent. "*Ummm,* you always smell like sun-warmed roses to me. Like summer love in a country meadow. Like desire among the wild roses."

He slid his hand back along her ear, into her hair, and used it to nudge her head closer to his. She watched his gaze settle on her mouth and was helpless to suppress the sweet tangle of emotions rising in her. He wanted her. She could feel it like a tangible thing, reaching for her, taking hold of her. In that moment she wanted nothing more than to feel his lips against hers, to be with him in that country meadow . . .

"And like a rose, sweetheart, you need tending . . . otherwise, you won't open properly." He was so close that his breath bathed her lips. "Let me tend you, Gabrielle," he whispered, filling her vision, her senses, her erratic heart with the sultry persuasion of his revealed desire. "I want to see you blossom." Just before his lips touched hers, she heard him say, "I want to feel you unfolding in my hands."

Wave after wave of sensation washed through her

senses, reaching the pleasure-starved roots of her being. His patient wooing and tender persuasions had finally penetrated her deepest recesses. She wanted to claim the need in her, to open those forbidden chambers where need and vulnerability and response had been locked away. She wanted to unfold . . . to feel herself opening, growing . . . to know what it was to feel deeply and fully . . . to embrace both him and her own long-denied yearnings.

His lips finally touched hers, and a dizzying flush of warmth rushed through her, spreading through her lips and face and trickling down her throat in rivulets of pleasure. She inclined her head, yielding to his tutoring, instinctively imitating his gentle pressure, complementing the angle of his mouth with hers. His hands slid around her waist and drew her slowly toward him, enfolding her with exquisite care.

Then he tilted her back, bracing over her, holding her to him as they sank together onto the moist, tilled ground. The unexpected weight of his chest drove the breath from her for an instant. She gasped in surprise, and his tongue sought that opening, tracing the sensitive inner surface of her lips, tasting her, dipping provocatively into her mouth. Each stroke of his tongue was like liquid fire that set her tingling, burning.

She had never experienced anything so potent, so pleasurably intimate, so wholly involving. Every part of her was stimulated and responded with a furl of pleasure, a tingle of warmth, or an ache of longing. Her body hummed, resonant with pleasure. He must have felt it, for he murmured approval and whispered her name as he poured long, fluid kisses down the column of her throat. His hands slid from beneath her to begin tracing her shape, seeking her through her clothing.

His long fingers closed over her breasts, finding the

line of her corset and the soft flesh above it. Pleasure streamed from all over her body to collect in a delicious burning fullness at the tips of her breasts. She arched against him seeking the warmth, the solidity of his frame and released the sides of his shirt to slide her hands up his sides and around his back. She pressed her tingling breasts harder against his chest, melting against him, wanting to match every curve and hollow of his body with the mounds and valleys of hers. Closer, she wanted to be closer . . .

"They're in the garden?" Rosalind stopped in the midst of putting the final touches on an arrangement of the flowers Pierce had brought her and stared at Gunther. She had just instructed him to deliver the usual champagne to Gabrielle's boudoir and he had informed her that the pair was not there. "Whatever are they doing?" she demanded, emptying her hands of scissors and blossoms and looking to her friends, who were seated around her in the drawing room.

"They began by planting, madam," the houseman said with a sniff.

"That rosebush," she said with annoyance, before catching the intimation that more had occurred. She scrutinized her majordomo's impassive face. "They *began* by planting? Dear God—there's no telling what sort of outrage they're perpetrating on my poor garden." She snatched up her skirts and started for the door, drawing the others up and along with her.

The best view of the garden was from Gabrielle's boudoir. Deciding quickly, she led the others up the stairs and invaded her daughter's sitting room. But on the way to the window, she caught sight of the yellowed palms by the piano and turned aside to investigate.

"I don't know what they're doing in here," she said

with alarm, examining the drying fronds, "but whatever it is, it's killing my potted palms."

"There they are," Genevieve said, standing at the window, pointing.

Rosalind rushed to join her, and the others crowded in around them, staring down into the walled and thickly planted garden. There, where a patch of tilled earth and a border of clipped green grass met, lay two figures—one light and one dark—entwined. Even from a distance, it was clear that they were deeply and mutually engaged in amorous indulgence.

"Would ye look at that," Clementine said, shaking her head.

"It would seem they are lovers indeed." Genevieve smiled softly.

"That rosebush has worked its spell, I'd say," Ariadne murmured wistfully. "You know, 'the lady and the gardener' was always one of my Gerald's favorites."

"My little Gabby has a lover," Rosalind said in a whisper, watching her daughter discovering her passion. A jumble of feelings rose in her as that evidence of Gabrielle's powerful physical attraction to the earl melted her doubts. Her eyes began to glisten.

The four of them stood watching for a long time, their faces softening, each recalling memories of youthful pleasures and the thrill of passionate discovery. When Genevieve glanced at Rosalind, she saw emotion welling up in her friend and reached for her hand, reassuring her. Ariadne reached for the other one, and Clementine patted her shoulder. After several minutes, Rosalind roused and sighed with a bittersweet smile.

"I believe I've seen all I need to see," she said thickly, giving her friends' hands a squeeze as she turned away from the window. "Come, let's give them a bit of privacy."

•   •   •

The constraints of clothing, time, and place finally seeped through the sensual haze that had enveloped them. Pierce raised his head and dragged a hard breath, working to focus his eyes. Feeling strangely thick and heavy from the weight of blood in his loins, he pushed up onto his elbows and looked down at Gabrielle. Her skin was flushed, her lips were swollen with the effects of his kisses, and the centers of her eyes were dilated with desire. She was the very image of a woman aroused.

The sight of her unfolding passions aroused something new and unexpectedly sweet inside him. She was his, he sensed, in a way she would never be any other man's. He had just awakened pleasure in her . . . proved to her that she was no different than the rest of humanity, that she had the same desires and passions, the same need to be touched and loved. And now that he had finally roused her passions, he knew that he wouldn't be satisfied until he claimed them in full.

Gabrielle lay beneath Pierce, feeling dazed and molten. Wild, glorious currents of liquid heat were swirling through her limbs and pouring into the core of her. She ached and throbbed in places she hadn't even realized could provide sensation, much less such divine and enthralling pleasures. As he moved away, she suffered a mad impulse to drag him back, to join their mouths again, and to feel his body pressed tightly against hers once more. But as he pulled her upright with him, some internal balance swung back into place and her molten wits began to solidify and function again.

Molten. Liquid. That realization blew through her consciousness in an icy blast, condensing the steam in her senses into a sobering shower of self-awareness. Dearest heaven, it was a short step from liquid to . . . This stirring sensation meant she had . . .

The realization rattled her to the very core of her being.

This tumult of feeling meant she was susceptible to pleasure and capable of passion, deep, knee-trembling, heart-racing passion. He had kissed her, and she had responded by embracing and touching and wriggling, like a pure wanton. Her eyes widened and she fingered her newly sensitive lips. How had this happened to her?

She glanced up to find Pierce beside her, brushing his trousers and ruined sleeves, and she stared hungrily at his bronzed face and dark eyes, absorbed in the riveting sensuality of his movements. It wasn't just her, it was *him*. She hadn't stood a chance against his good looks, sophistication, and vast carnal repertoire. With his knowing eyes and tender hands and irresistibly wicked smile, the man could probably pull an amorous response from a post. And she wasn't exactly made of wood.

Determined not to let him see how deeply she was affected, she shrugged off his assistance, scrambled to her feet, and began tidying the skirts that only a short while ago she had declared were of no consequence. From the knees down, her dress was full of dirt and there were smudges on her bodice.

When she straightened and turned to him, Pierce froze. "Gabrielle," he choked out, trying not to laugh, "your dress!" He seized her by the shoulders and turned her around. "And the back is even worse."

"It is?" She strained to see over her shoulder and found the entire back of her bodice covered with dirt. "Oh, dear! I have to get inside and change before my mother sees this and—" She halted and glanced away in embarrassment.

"—thinks I've been playing 'the gardener and the lady' with you?" He snatched his coat from the tree branch and settled it around her shoulders. "Here, this will cover the worst damage."

" 'The gardener and the lady'?" she said, scowling as they hurried down the path toward the terrace.

"A very old game . . . started in the Garden of Eden."

They hurried through the morning room and down the hallway, heading for the stairs. But as they rushed across the entry hall, Rosalind's voice floated down from the stairs above them and they halted in their tracks . . . *caught*.

"Here they are now," Rosalind said with a pleasant lilt, speaking to her ever-present trio of women friends. But as she neared the bottom of the stairs and the disreputable state of their appearance came into focus, her smile faded. "Dearest heaven—what's happened to you?"

There they stood, looking like a pair of overgrown urchins: he in a begrimed shirt and trousers with dirt-caked knees, and she in a soiled and grass-stained gown and his smudged coat. They had ruddy, dirt-streaked faces, and their eyes glinted guiltily as they pressed closer to each other.

"His lordship brought me the loveliest rosebush," Gabrielle said, forcing a smile. She was determined to behave as if standing in the entry wearing a ruined dress and gentleman's coat was the most normal thing on earth. "We just planted it."

"And I'm afraid we had forgotten just how messy an undertaking gardening could be," he added gamely, putting a dirty hand to his chest and nodding over it with admirable aplomb. "Sincere apologies."

Rosalind blanched at the state of his sleeves and ignored the "*tsks*" from her friends as she continued down the stairs. "I suppose these things happen when your minds are filled with . . . other things," she declared with strained graciousness. "But heavens, we must see you set right. Gunther!" She called to the houseman, who was striding through the entry with a freshly polished candelabrum. When he emptied his hands and hurried over, she ordered, "Take his lordship's coat and see what you can do with it. See to it he has what he needs to freshen up . . . perhaps one of the duke's spare shirts. They look to be about the same size."

Before Gabrielle could prevent it, Gunther was pulling Pierce's coat from her shoulders. At the sight of her ruined dress, her mother gasped, and her mother's friends made startled noises that were perilously close to laughter. Pierce cleared his throat uncomfortably. Desperate to get away, she lifted her chin and nodded to her mother, "Mama," then slipped her arm through his and urged him up the stairs.

"If you'll follow me, your lordship," Gunther said, appearing at their side the moment they reached the top of the stairs.

Gabrielle saw Pierce's mouth twitching, suppressing a smile, as he disentangled his arm from her hand and followed the houseman.

It wasn't until she arrived in her boudoir and glimpsed herself in the mirror over the mantel that she fully understood her mother's reaction and Pierce's response. Against the still white front of her bodice directly over her breasts were two large, dark handprints.

10

R ue helped Gabrielle change her dress and wash, then pulled her to the dressing table and gave her hair a good brushing. There wasn't time to put it back up the same way, so Gabrielle had her leave it down, bound with a simple ribbon, instead.

She found Pierce sitting on the window seat in her boudoir, sipping a glass of champagne as he stared down at the garden below. He set his glass aside and regarded her with a suspicious look. Her face was rosy with embarrassment, but deep in her eyes he glimpsed a sparkle of unrepentant glee.

"You're going to blame me for this little incident, aren't you?"

"I am," she said with defiant cheeriness.

"Brazen chit." He scowled. "Now I'm to be responsible for rolling you around in the dirt like some crazed heathen. Have you given any thought to the possibility that she may decide I am too 'eccentric' to be your lover?"

She shook her head. "That won't happen."

"What makes you so certain?"

"You're a man, a *wealthy* man. You're permitted any number of 'eccentricities.'" Her smile tightened. "Men can be and do whatever they want, as long as they pay the bills. It's my mother's prime axiom."

"A rather cynical statement for someone who has devoted her life to passion and romance."

"Oh, she never actually says it . . . she just believes it." Feeling vaguely uncomfortable, she glanced away from his perceptive gaze and spotted a book of plays lying on the tea table. "There they are." When she returned with it, he was still watching her intently.

"If she's never said it, how do you know she believes it?"

"For the last twenty years, her every decision, every impulse, and every thought have been shaped by one man's desires. Yet he could stay or go as he pleased, do or demand whatever he wanted . . . because he was willing to keep her in luxury." Her chin rose. "It's her golden rule, all right."

He studied the emotion rising in her, then gestured to the opulence around them. "It seems a fairly straightforward proposition, to me. A bit of pleasure for a bit of luxury."

"That's the way it seems to you, is it?"

"Frankly, yes. I mean, she must have had some choice in the matter. And she chose to make a man happy and satisfied in return for a very comfortable life."

"Yes," she said tersely, "she had a choice. In fact she

had a world of choices. And she chose him . . . every time."

The spark in her eyes caught him aback for a moment. There was obviously something here he didn't understand, something important . . . a key piece of the puzzle of why she was so determined not to believe in love and romance.

She turned away to replace the book in the case, but he caught her by the arm and pulled her to the window seat with him. "Really, your lordship, your champagne—" She tried to rise.

"—will wait." He held her firmly. "You don't think she should have chosen the duke."

She fixed her gaze on her whitened fingers as they gripped the book and she tried to sort through the jumble of thoughts clamoring for expression inside her. When she raised her face to him, her mouth was a sober line and her eyes were luminous.

"In every choice, something is kept and something is discarded. In always choosing him and her grand passion for him, my mother discarded some things that should have been at least as precious to her as he was."

He studied her eyes and discovered the traces of old hurt in their depths. Her face filled with personal feeling, an expression remarkably like the one she had worn when speaking of the children who were given up by their mothers to the foundling home. After a moment he made the connection in his mind and understood her passion for those abandoned children. She had been abandoned herself, after a fashion.

"Things . . . like you," he said, to himself as much as to her.

"Yes, me. Among other things," she said, with a remnant of bitterness. "She sent me away so that I wouldn't interfere with her grand affair. But I soon discovered I had a great deal of company in my fate. Nearly every girl at

Marchand was considered 'underfoot' somewhere or other. After a while, with Mme. Marchand's help, we came to terms with it and turned our energies toward learning and growing. We read and talked and studied, and learned to serve, and learned to rely upon ourselves."

She looked out the window, and her voice lowered. "Then, just as we had developed a worth of our own, our families and guardians remembered we existed and began to reel us home, to dispose of us as family assets. The other girls were brought home to become wives. I, however, was sent on a grand tour and then brought home to become a 'trinket'—something for a man to play with."

"I hardly think a liaison with a man of means would make you a 'trinket,' Gabrielle." He felt a stab of guilt. Mistresses and professional beauties were often referred to in such terms in the clubs. But until now he had never considered it particularly arrogant or belittling—until now, when he thought of Gabrielle being spoken of in that way.

"What would I be, then? Selling my body for a life of comfort, pretending always to want whatever my current lover wants, pretending to need only what he is willing to give?" She had scarcely allowed herself to think such things, much less speak them aloud. But suddenly she felt a desperate need to speak them, and for some reason she wanted him to hear them, to understand why she could never accept her mother's plans for her.

"I don't want to live the way my mother has . . . constantly paring myself into a man's idea of desirable or worthwhile. My mother had a choice." Her voice dropped to a whisper. "I only want the same chance to choose for myself. What is so wrong with that?"

Nothing, he thought ruefully, watching the passion flickering in her glowing face and feeling a curious tension building in his body. Nothing, except that it was too simple. And life had taught him, long ago, that nothing was ever quite as simple as having a free and clear choice.

"And what would you do with that choice, Gabrielle?" he said thickly, wishing he could give her that freedom, wanting to—he halted that thought, wrestling with the seduction of her heartfelt revelations. "—except choose another man, another set of expectations?"

"I would not choose a *man*," she declared. "I would choose a *marriage*. I would choose a life in which my body and my feelings and my accomplishments would be my own, not the conjugal property of a man."

He studied her determination. "To the best of my knowledge, marriage also involves a man, sweetheart. And I cannot help but wonder where you think you'll find one who won't exert a few 'property rights' from time to time."

She felt her eyes stinging and looked down to hide the tears collecting in them. "I'll find one. One who can appreciate that a woman must be more than a head of hair and an eighteen-inch waist." He lifted her chin and held it, searching the prisms of moisture in her eyes. "Is being a whole, real person too much to ask?"

"No." That single, powerful syllable reverberated all through him. Perhaps it was his experience of those same longings for choice and freedom that made him vulnerable to them in her. Or perhaps it was the sweet and satisfying rebellion of her spirit that drew him to her. Or perhaps it was the uniqueness of her mind . . . or the genuineness of her heart . . . or the pull of her oddly jaded innocence . . . "It is not too much to ask."

In that quiet moment, sitting in the shaft of sunlight streaming through the window, he felt an irresistible sense of connection to her. They had come from such different worlds, such opposite circumstances to arrive at this common place.

She felt it too: a powerful and tantalizing sense of

oneness, an understanding that somehow went deeper than words. It was a closeness that went beyond their pretense and even their mutual attraction. He truly had listened to her. And in that moment, staring into his worldly brown eyes, the protective barriers inside her lowered yet another notch.

He leaned closer. She migrated toward him.

A knock came on the door, startling them. He stood up abruptly, and she turned aside and began brushing her skirts and smoothing her hair.

"Ten minutes of five." He reached for his watch and made note of the time. "I fear we've displeased the goddess of romance, yet again. She's sent for us early."

Gunther was outside with the now customary summons to tea. Gabrielle closed the door and turned to find Pierce standing just behind her, staring at her with a warmth that betrayed roused feelings. She cleared her throat.

"Do I look all right?" She ran a hand down her hair. "No smudges . . . nothing disarranged?"

"You're perfect," he declared softly, meaning every syllable of it. She glowed, golden, full of warmth and vitality. He simply had to touch her.

For one shimmering moment, she felt the stroke of his hand on her cheek sweeping across her very heart. The peculiar ache in her chest sank into her stomach and she recognized it for the hunger it was . . . a physical need for contact, for pleasure. For *him*.

The realization nearly undid her. She had fallen completely under his spell. Even knowing he was a worldly and complicated man, an arrogant and devious and possibly even dangerous man, she had opened herself to him the way she had opened to no one else in her life. Just being with him, she felt more vital and alive and powerful, more womanly and passionate and vulnerable. It was wonderful. And it was terrifying. Her plan to find a husband and marry—to put herself beyond the destructive reach of passion—was jeopardized more with each moment she spent alone with him.

"Please, your lordship," she said, jolting back a step. "I think we've had more than enough touching for one day."

"You do keep forgetting my name. *Pierce*," he insisted, in a voice that was oddly husky.

"Pierce," she said, nodding. Then she stepped around him and headed for the door with her cheeks ablaze.

Rosalind received them alone in the drawing room. Throughout tea she could scarcely take her eyes from Gabrielle, as if searching her daughter for the answer to the question that weighted her brow and sometimes made her halt with distraction before reaching the end of a sentence. Pierce and Gabrielle exchanged glances, wondering if she was contemplating some maternal retribution for their earlier indiscretion. But when the clock struck half past five, Rosalind rose with a serene expression and an announcement that put an end to both their anxiety and their confinement.

"I must say, your lordship, your manner of courtship is certainly unconventional." She drew herself up and looked him over with her discerning eye. "But it is also clear, after today, that it is quite effective. You have shown yourself to be a generous and considerate lover. I believe you and Gabrielle are ready for the next step in your relationship."

Gabrielle swayed on her seat, and Pierce looked a bit startled by the announcement. They looked to each other, then to Rosalind, uncertain what she meant.

She sighed. "You are free to continue your relationship wherever, whenever you will. You may go out . . . to the opera or the park, riding or on picnics."

The joy that filled Gabrielle's face was heartfelt as she

put her arm through Pierce's and ushered him to the door. "Free—at last!" She gave his arm a squeeze before releasing it. "Your rosebush worked. You truly *are* a genius."

The sight of her glowing pleasure struck him in a very vulnerable place. He didn't feel very much like a genius just now. He felt annoyed.

"Well, of course." He forced a smile. "And now that we're allowed in public together, what do you want to do tomorrow?" The gleam in her eyes made him realize she was going to say something about a husband, and he quickly preempted it. "Besides *that*."

She gave it a moment's thought. "A carriage ride. Shall we say at three?"

Pierce ate dinner at his club, took a brandy in the bar, and declined to round out a table in the card room. He felt surly and deprived and out of sorts, and he had no one to blame but himself.

He had participated in Gabrielle's rebellion, expecting to give her a taste of the tantalizing pleasures locked inside her and then claim her delectable person and passions for himself. But today he had not only roused her passions, he had also glimpsed the depths of her heart as well. And the resulting clash between his worldly intentions toward her and his growing feelings toward her had awakened his long-dormant conscience.

Knowing how she loathed her mother's way of life, how could he seduce her into it? But if he didn't seduce her, what was he to do with his growing desire for her? And to complicate matters, just as he was melting her reserves and reaching for her passions, her blasted mother decided to release them from their confinement, and now she was free to pursue her marriage plans—with the help he had promised her!

To top it all, he was about to become one of those

beings that men loathed worse than the Devil himself: a matchmaker.

Pierce arrived on time the next day, wearing his best charcoal gray coat and matching pinstriped trousers and a charcoal felt top hat. His arms were full of flowers, for Gabrielle and her mother. And when he saw Gabrielle in her powder blue shot silk dress with its long bodice, elegant bustle, and snugly fitted sleeves, looking ripe and womanly while still suitably demure, the pleasure in his smile was genuine. Under Rosalind's doting gaze, he greeted Gabrielle and ushered her out the door with a haste that satisfied Rosalind that he was eager to have her daughter all to himself.

For her part, Gabrielle was understandably both nervous and excited. The world seemed a new place as she descended the steps of Maison LeCoeur on Pierce's arm and, with his help, stepped up into the fine black landau that awaited them. The sun seemed brighter, the breeze warmer, and the greenery in the square across the street seemed more lush and vibrant. Both vehicles and foot traffic moved briskly in the streets, and the moist air had a buzz of expectation in it. She was making a new start, taking her first steps toward securing a husband and a respectable life.

As the carriage lurched into motion, she settled back against the seat, adjusting her short-brimmed hat with its pert blue and gray feathers to be sure its veil was securely in place, checking her handbag, and making certain her bustle wasn't being disarranged.

Pierce watched her primping with a scowl, realizing that he had never, not once in all the time he had known her, seen her behave in such a manner. *Primping.*

Today marked the start of a new phase of their relationship, an intensely personal association for which there was no precedent in either polite or impolite society. They weren't quite respectable, going about without a chaperon, but neither were they quite a scandal, riding in a sedate landau with the top down, seated respectably across from each other. They weren't family or business associates or lovers. They weren't even officially acquaintances. When she looked up at him through that demure veiling that somehow both cloaked and enhanced her eyes, his attempt at defining their relationship got snarled in a tangle of feelings that included both pleasure and irritation.

"All right. You've said you have a plan," he said, giving his tie an unnecessary straightening. "I think it's time you tell me what it is."

Infused with new energy, she turned to him. "First, we must go to the offices of the *Pall Mall Gazette*." When he just stared at her, she fished about in her handbag for a slip of paper bearing the address. "It's on Fleet Street . . . number—"

"I know where it is," he said. "What I want to know is why we're going there."

"I've rented a box there, and I need to collect my mail," she declared, drawing a folded piece of newspaper from her purse and handing it to him. Circled in black ink was an advertisement from the *Pall Mall Gazette*'s "Personal" section, reading:

> Refined young woman of means and excellent
> education seeks a younger gentleman of standing
> and high moral character. Object: matrimony.
> Must love children. Reply by letter to Box 47.

"Yours?" he choked out, giving her an incredulous look. "You *advertised* for a husband?"

"I most certainly did." She straightened defensively. "I don't have family or the usual social contacts to provide candidates. Correspondence is a perfectly logical and acceptable way of making an acquaintance, in the absence of a proper introduction. And this way I can evaluate the applicants without risk to my privacy or safety." Struck by the indignation in his face, she braced for a protest or sarcastic comment.

But he couldn't fault her common sense without sounding petty and mean-spirited. A woman, alone, in search of a husband, had to make reasonable provisions for safety and privacy. The fact that she had taken such sensible steps irritated him, and he didn't want to think about why. After an uncomfortable moment, he sat forward and called the *Gazette*'s address to his driver. When the driver nodded and the carriage lurched faster, he sat back with a cool expression and a terse: "Well, *this* should prove interesting."

The *Pall Mall Gazette* made provisions for responses to advertisements for a fee. When Gabrielle applied at the appropriate desk of the bustling newspaper office for the responses to her advertisement, the clerk checked his files and made out a bill. After paying the box rent and waiting for what seemed an eternity, she was handed a wire basket with the stamped metal tag bearing the number 47. It was filled with letters. Something cold and cramped in her relaxed at the sight of so many responses. Under his gaze, she stacked and arranged the envelopes in one arm, then slipped her other through his and announced she was ready to go.

"How many are there?" he asked when they were again seated in the carriage. Immediately he regretted it. She counted the letters in her lap with unabashed pleasure and looked up.

"Twenty-three. Surely I will find a number of reasonable prospects out of such a response." She selected a letter, intending to open it, but his hand on hers stopped her.

"Wait—you can't just read them and decide based on whichever one takes your fancy." He gave her a smile that made her feel as if she was being patted on the head. "You should think for a moment about what it is you are looking for . . . develop some *criteria* for judging which of your prospective husbands would be best suited to you."

She leveled a gaze on him, annoyed by the veiled sarcasm in his tone. No doubt all this was quite amusing to him. "I already have, your lordship. I know precisely what I am looking for in a husband."

"Do you indeed?" He sat back and crossed his arms with a patrician air.

Reaching into her handbag yet again, she drew out another piece of paper and handed it to him. "Here is the list of qualities." The way his nostrils flared and his mouth tightened was quite satisfying. "Ranked in order of importance."

Pierce jerked open the paper and stared at her list, scarcely able to read it at first, for his irritation. How dare she be so logical and detached and . . . *prepared*?

"Honesty," he read aloud, "charity . . . generosity . . . education . . . tolerance . . . moral rectitude . . ."

"Go on," she said, when he lowered the paper to stare at her. "I believe 'love of children' comes next, then 'kindliness' and 'good manners' and 'cleanliness' . . ."

"Obviously," he said, reddening at being caught flat-footed in groundless male condescension, "you have given it a great deal of thought."

"I have." She looked at him with a steady gaze. "And now I think I'd like to see what my first prospective husband has to say." Pulling a letter opener from her purse, she slid it under the flap of the first envelope. He glared at her handbag in annoyance.

It would have been a perfect validation of her plan if the first letter had been from a gentleman who was honest, charitable, generous, and well educated. But in fact, the first letter was not from a man at all. It was written by a woman on behalf of her nephew who was a sergeant in the army, posted in India, and due to return to England in several months. He would need a good situation and a wife as he "settled in."

The next three letters were no better. One claimed to be heir to a sizable estate, wrongfully deprived of an inheritance and eager to have the support of a wife in seeking legal redress. Another was from the typesetter who had assembled the type for her advertisement. Struck by the "most excellent composition" of her words, he had immediately deduced that she would understand his "most meticulous nature." Since "meticulous" was not on her list of qualities, she went quickly on. The next fellow was a packet-coach driver who had seen her ad while in London to either "deliver testimony at a trial" or "deliver terrible lot of mail," depending on which way his writing was interpreted. He was most keenly interested in whether or not she could cook something besides "banes an burley"— whatever that was.

But the fifth letter was from a prosperous London merchant, owner of a flourishing ready-made clothing concern. His letter was written in beautiful hand and worded with unmistakable refinement. He loved children and looked forward to raising his own with "proper paternal devotion." Heartened to have a sound prospect at last, she set it aside and continued.

There were a few more agreeable surprises—three more, to be exact. One was a mill owner in the town of Reading, west of London, another was vicar of a church in

Brompton, and the last, and most distinguished, prospect proved to be a member of the peerage . . . a "Baron Colchester."

Gabrielle eyed the stack of "suitable" letters; only four sound prospects out of twenty-three. Privately disappointed, she made herself focus on the fact that all four held true promise and reminded herself that she only needed to have *one* to marry. When she roused from her single-minded concentration, arched her back, and looked around, she found herself surrounded by letters and empty envelopes on the seat and realized the carriage was stopped at the side of a treelined street. She dimly recalled the driver putting the top up, at Pierce's direction, to give them more privacy and some protection from the breeze that flirted with the corners of the letters.

Pierce was seated across from her, watching her with a frown. "Was it worth it?"

"Of course." She sat straighter. "I have four very fine prospects."

"*Hmmm*. And where shall we go next, Miss LeCoeur?"

"To a stationer's, if you don't mind," she said with as much dignity as she could support just now. "To reply to these"—she lifted the stack—"I shall need to lay in a supply of papers."

"If you are determined to do this, why waste time writing to the ones you've chosen?" He gathered up the rejected letters, raised the seat beside him, and stuffed them in the stowage underneath it, leaving her with only her four "very fine prospects" in hand. "Why not go and see them? Have a look and see what they are like before you respond." He smiled and waved a magnanimous hand. "My driver and I are completely at your service."

11

Gabrielle would have preferred to deal with her suitors on paper, for the present, but she sensed a challenge beneath Pierce's offer and could not refuse. She did manage, in the name of decency and logic, to insist that she remain unannounced to her potential husbands to allow for a proper introduction via letter, later. And as the carriage rumbled along the streets, she clutched the clothier's reply in her hands and felt her stomach drawing into a knot of aprehension.

The "prosperous clothing concern" of Calvin Londsdale was not located on Oxford Street, as indicated in his letter, but a block away, fronting on something of an alley that had no street sign. They found it only because Pierce's driver stopped several people to ask and finally located "Londsdale's place." The shop entrance was set into the side of a large brick building, and for a prosperous concern, it appeared strangely run-down—lacking in paint, with display windows stuffed with a jumble of cheap garments and knitted goods faded by the sun. Traffic was brisk in and out of the door, and when Gabrielle and Pierce stepped inside, they found the shop crammed with tables and counters piled with "ready-mades," which were being examined by customers in clothing that clearly announced their modest means.

Gabrielle backed a step, where she bumped into Pierce. Her plan that they remain inconspicuous was instantly forfeit; they were considerably better dressed than anyone else in the place.

"Lookit wot we got 'ere! Well, guv'na," a buxom shop attendant declared pushing her way through the customers, eyeing Pierce's dignified looks and Gabrielle's elegance. "Wot can we do fer ye?"

"Just having a look, my good woman," Pierce said with a genial tone. Then he lowered his head and his voice. "And just where would the proprietor of this establishment—Mr. Londsdale—be?"

"In th' workroom . . . out back," she said, jerking her thumb toward the curtain hanging over a doorway at the back of the shop. While she went back to her customers, Pierce and Gabrielle made their way toward that doorway and into a short, dingy corridor beyond. Gabrielle's every instinct was to head for the nearest exit, but with both Pierce and her pride at her back, she couldn't abandon her quest for a glimpse of her first suitor. She found herself stepping into a huge workroom filled with stale air, dust, and lint . . . and benches and tables crammed with young boys, stitching rough garments.

"What are you doin' in here?" came a roaring challenge,

startling them both. They turned and discovered a thin, knotty man with lank brown hair and watery eyes glaring at them. "If yer from that 'society'—ye can jus' take yerself straight back out that door. I told you—I give th' little cabbagers three squares an' a dry place to sleep."

Waving his hands, he bustled them back into the corridor and into the shop, but not before Gabrielle caught sight of a dozen little faces with huge, dark eyes that had looked up at her in dull surprise. "Prosperous" Londsdale protested that he had improved their ragamuffin lives by taking them off the streets and "keepin' 'em too busy for trouble. And I don' deserve to be hounded by the likes o' you for it!"

Gabrielle soon found herself out on the street, with her elbow in Pierce's tight grip, being propelled along toward the carriage. Holding her hat, she resisted long enough to look back at the dingy establishment and sputter: "Horrid man—he runs a 'sweatshop' . . . using children. Why, the oldest among them couldn't have been more than twelve." Then she looked up and caught Pierce's amusement and glared at him. "He's a liar, a fraud, and an opportunist. He probably *paid* someone to write his letter for him. Something ought to be done about men like that!"

It took a while for her to calm and regain her poise when they reached the carriage. She kept seeing the children's faces and thinking about how the wretch claimed to be helping them. It was hard to put behind her, but after they were underway again, she lifted her chin and tried to focus on the possibilities that lay ahead. Drawing the letter from her second prospect out of her handbag, she perused it. "Well, I'm certain that Vicar Trowbridge will prove much more suitable. How far is Brompton from here?"

Several minutes' drive, south and west, were all that was required to reach Brompton, but it took a bit longer for them to locate Holy Trinity Church. It had been surrounded and all but overwhelmed by a large and impressive bit of construction going on around it. When they were able to reach the church, through the lorries and maze of wooden walks, they were greeted inside by an irate clergyman whose face was set like red granite.

"Have you ever encountered such lunacy in your life?" the fellow demanded, gesturing to the doors and the confusion in the street beyond. "They're out to ruin this church, they are—wretched papist conspirators. Building their cursed oratory right virtually on top of Holy Trinity. It's an insult, I tell you. And they're doing it on purpose— to ruin my parish!" He halted and took a deep breath, smoothing his split collar and his nerves. "Well, I don't intend to let them get away with—" He halted and regarded them suspiciously. "What do *you* want?"

"The vicar of the church," Pierce said after a moment, and Gabrielle nearly gasped. "I wonder if he is here."

The clergyman drew himself up to give them a thorough looking over. Their fashionable appearance worked a miraculous change in his demeanor. He gave them a stiff, joyless smile and folded his hands together in ecclesiastical forbearance. "I am Vicar Trowbridge. What do you want of me?"

What indeed? Gabrielle's eyes widened and she backed a step, looking at the gaunt, graying man. His letter had portrayed him as being a dedicated churchman devoted to music, holy charity, and doing good works . . . but in person he appeared to be a dyspeptic sort who vacillated disagreeably between "irascible" and "unctuous."

"We're here to see the church," Pierce said, when she didn't speak. He looked around the sanctuary, marking the fine windows and handsome architecture. "A lovely setting for a wedding." He glanced at Gabrielle. "Don't you agree?" She barely restrained herself from giving him an elbow in the ribs.

"Ah." Trowbridge looked them over with a judgmental frown, making the obvious assumption. "Well, I do marry persons from outside the parish . . . if they meet with my approval and my conditions. You see, I believe marriage is taken much too lightly these days. Men ignore their responsibilities and allow women to come and go as they please . . . abroad in the streets without proper protection or supervision." He gave Gabrielle a suspicious look, then turned to Pierce. "Young women today require a firm hand." He closed his hand into a fist, seizing the reins of some mercifully hypothetical female. "Take my advice, sir, 'spare not the rod of reproof, lest you allow your wife to stray from the path of righteousness.' "

Gabrielle gave the clergyman a scathing glare, turned on her heel, and headed straight for the doors. Pierce gave the indignant clergyman a sardonic shrug. "These *modern* girls."

They were in the carriage and well underway before she could swallow the anger lodged in her throat and speak. "The pompous wretch. Writing to me of charity and love, claiming to seek holy nuptial bliss with a woman of good character, when what he really wants is a plodding beast of matrimonial burden. A marriageable *ox!*"

But her anger at the opinionated vicar was also fueled by the smile broadening on Pierce's face, as her second matrimonial prospect turned out to be nearly as disagreeable as the first. She stared out the side of the carriage, her face hot and eyes stinging, refusing to look at him. It was bad enough to have her matrimonial hopes dashed in such a drastic fashion, but to have it happen before *him.* . . .

Pierce gave orders to his driver to take them about in Hyde Park, then sat back in the seat across from her, watching her deal with her anger and embarrassment and getting lost in the sight of her. God, she was gorgeous when her blood was up—those rosy cheeks, those flashing eyes, the irresistible pout of her lips . . .

He had started this husband-hunting expedition in a testy mood, but with each marriage prospect that turned to ashes, his spirits had improved. He couldn't believe someone as unique as she could find a suitable mate from a common newspaper advertisement. And, to his relief, her initial experiences had just borne him out.

Still, there was always the possibility that she might find someone close—someone dull and agreeable and earnest and virtuous and bearable enough—and might tell herself that she could make do with him. He sat back in the rear-facing seat and took a deep breath as they rolled into the park and along one of the carriage lanes. He just had to hope that her other prospects would prove every bit as disagreeable.

Shortly, they were overtaken by a burst of hoofbeats, and as he sat forward with a scowl two men in riding clothes drew even with the carriage and hailed him.

"Sandbourne! I thought this was your rig!" A tall, strikingly handsome young man in a fine black coat and top hat reined in beside the carriage. His head snapped sharply to the side when he spotted Gabrielle in the seat across from Pierce, and his handsome face lighted with pleasure. "I say, Sandbourne, you have stunning company today. Hold up and give us a chance to meet your guest."

Before he could prevent them, his two acquaintances were calling orders to his driver, reining in, and leaning against the sides of the carriage, staring at Gabrielle.

"Ruffians—can't a man have a decent ride in the park without being accosted by the likes of you?" Pierce growled.

The pair of horsemen ignored his irritation, looking Gabrielle over with admiration that narrowly trod the bounds of decency. Feeling their gazes roaming her, she looked to Pierce with an expression that communicated her concern about how he might explain her. When they refused to be put off, demanding he act the gentleman, he expelled a hard breath and said flatly: "Very well. Gabrielle, my dear, these inconsiderate bounders are Peter Atcheson, Lord Arundale, and Harry Shively, recently become Viscount Shively. Remember their names and faces and avoid them at all costs. They are not to be trusted."

"Come on, Sandbourne, don't dare fill that pretty head with lies. You mustn't believe a word he says," tall, blond Arundale said to her, with a smile that she suspected had probably charmed the socks off many an unsuspecting girl. "We're decent sorts."

She looked at Pierce with a clear question in her eyes.

"I shall probably regret this," he grumbled, turning to them with a disapproving expression. "May I present my cousin, late from France . . . Gabrielle . . . *LaSande*."

"Mademoiselle," Arundale said, bowing from the waist.

"Miss LaSande." Muscular, broad-faced Shively nodded, scarcely taking his eyes from her. "Ye gods, Sandbourne, I didn't know you had relations in France . . . especially pretty ones."

She nodded to them and explained: "My father was French. The connection is on my mother's side." They seemed to accept Pierce's fiction without much question. A cousin could be close or far: close enough to explain their being in a carriage together, far enough to explain why she was unknown in England.

"I say, if you've just come from France"—Arundale regarded her with a glint of speculation—"then perhaps you've been to the follies in Paris."

"That will be enough of that, Arundale," Pierce said quietly, fixing him with a steely look. "Gabrielle has certainly *never* been to the follies."

Arundale studied Pierce, taking in the deadly earnestness in his tone and the warning in his eyes, then laughed ruefully. "Well, I shouldn't have thought so. But after all, they are quite famous. Where in France is your home, Miss LaSande?"

"I lived for most of my life in a village just outside Paris, called d'Arcy." She answered but volunteered nothing more, and her reticence only seemed to inflame their curiosity.

"Lovely city, Paris. I have been thinking of making the trip this autumn," Shively put in, then brightened, gazing at Gabrielle. "We were just on the way to Blaisdell's for a bit of refreshment. Do join us, Sandbourne, and allow us of the joy of gazing upon your pretty cousin for a bit longer. Perhaps she will consent to give me advice on points of interest in Paris." He was so boyish and so charming, Gabrielle couldn't help smiling.

"Come on, Sandbourne, don't be a stick about this," Arundale said genially, giving her a lingering glance. "We'll be on best behavior."

That was how they came to be sitting in Blaisdell's fashionable coffeehouse at five o'clock that afternoon, flanked by two handsome gentlemen intent on learning more about Pierce's stunning young "cousin." After her initial anxiety passed, Gabrielle relaxed into her role as a demure but well-traveled young woman, deferring to Pierce at times with a naturalness that supported the notion of kinship.

As she warmed under their attention, she also seemed to blossom; her cheeks colored and her eyes began to sparkle with pleasure. In answering queries about Paris and the Champagne district of France, she was nothing short of captivating. Shively and Arundale vied to get her coffee and biscuits, to see that she had a comfortable chair, and to sit as near her as Pierce's glowering presence would allow. They flirted shamelessly with her, and, to her credit, she acknowledged it but declined to play the coquette.

In short, she gave every indication that she was indeed the little-known cousin from France . . . a genteel young woman, whose beauty was undeniable and whose good sense was a credit to her. But no matter how circumspect she was, Pierce's face and mood steadily darkened, and she was at a loss to explain his increasing surliness.

He was somewhat bewildered himself at the intensity of his mood. The sight of two of his frequent companions in debauch trying to charm and impress Gabrielle sent him into a slow burn. He could see their minds working behind their handsome smiles and smooth manners . . . as he had seen them do so many times before, as his own had done on just such occasions. Given the chance, they would test both her breeding and her virtue to the very limits. Bastards, he thought. And he backed them off with sharply placed responses that established subtle boundaries around Gabrielle.

They eyed his glowering form and smiled all the more eagerly at her. The undercurrent of tension between Pierce and his friends grew until Gabrielle withdrew from the conversation and reminded "Cousin Pierce" that he had promised to have her home in time to dress for dinner.

"Home? Don't tell me you are staying with St. Pierce and the Dragon?" Arundale said, looking Pierce over as if seeing him in a new light.

"The dragon?" She looked to Pierce, who cleared his throat and gave Arundale a cutting look before responding.

"My mother," he explained. "I'm afraid your 'dear Cousin Bea' has a rather different reputation with my friends. She isn't as accommodating with everyone else as she is with you."

"Oh," she said, lowering her eyes to hide her surprise at his fabrication. Then she recalled the original question. "No, I'm not staying with Cousin Beatrice and Cousin Pierce. My mother and I have taken lodgings of our own in

Eaton Square." She looked to Pierce again. "And now I really should be going home."

It was the perfect excuse, and Pierce pounced on it. But Gabrielle's new admirers wouldn't let her go until she promised to speak to them again the next time they saw her. She smiled, adjusted her hat, and agreed.

Pierce spirited her out the door and into his carriage, his face like a thundercloud.

"Nice young men, your friends," she said when they were underway.

"They're womanizing louts."

"They are handsome and well mannered. I found them rather charming."

"They're randy, irresponsible adolescents."

"That must be why you like them so much," she said tartly. It was hardly like a man of his worldliness to warn a woman about a fellow rake's intentions. *Unless* . . . he feared she was entertaining matrimonial thoughts of them and intended to set her off them by labeling them as jaded and undesirable. She thought of his horror at the notion of helping trap a fellow bachelor into marriage. He was protecting them from her designs, from the ignominy of an inappropriate match. Why the nerve of him! She was good enough for him to lust after and try to seduce, but not good enough to marry one of his pedigreed companions.

Pierce was so preoccupied with his own thoughts that he scarcely noticed the indignation rising in her. His mind's eye was full of images of the way his friends had admired and flattered and cozened her—as far as the limits of decency would allow. The speculation in their faces said they were wondering if Gabrielle was really his cousin or just some new bit of fluff, a potential "trinket" to add to their collection of sexual playthings. The wretches. If they had the slightest inkling that she was the illegitimate daughter of a mistress—even the fabled love child of a duke

—their handsome smiles and courtly manners could turn quickly ugly and base. He had seen it happen before. And the thought of them treating Gabrielle in such a manner made his very blood boil.

"So"—she broke the silence with a terse comment—"your mother's name is Beatrice. And, I take it, she has a *lovely* disposition." She gave him a vengeful smile. "That certainly explains a great deal about *you*."

Stung, he sat upright and impaled her with a look. "You know, you bear a striking similarity to my mother. I hadn't seen it until just now. Both of you are ruthless in your pursuit of respectability. And both of you are perfectly fanatical about marriage as a means to secure it."

When she seemed startled by his response, he smiled grimly.

"Let me tell you about your soul-mate, 'Cousin Beatrice.' My mother is about as pleasant as a rogue sow . . . and just about as maternal. She drove my father from his own house and, since his death, has spent the last decade trying to run and ruin my life just as she tried to run and ruin his. The only two aspects of my life she cannot bend to her control are my politics and my sex life, though she would dearly love to get her hands on both of them. The fact that I am not married and settled dutifully under her thumb regularly throws her into apoplexy. And I would rather cut off my right arm than give her the satisfaction of trapping me into a proper marriage."

The blast of his anger so shocked her that she had to drop her own in order to handle it. She had unwittingly touched a raw nerve in him. And as he broke off his angry discourse and sat staring out of the carriage, she put the pieces together. He was the product of a bitter and volatile marriage, which had poisoned his notions of marriage and family life. And he loathed his mother's attempt to control him by marrying him off . . .

Suddenly she understood. His reason for helping her. The defiant intensity of his sensuality and the dark current that sometimes ran beneath it. His revulsion at the prospect of inveigling another man into marriage. His attraction to her, based on her illicit birth and her rebellion against her mother's expectations. She understood his cynicism about marriage and his comments about her tidy view of it. She understood his anger. She understood *him*.

The only thing she didn't understand was why—now that there was little chance of him seducing her—he continued to bother with her.

Across the carriage from her, he was roiling inside, asking himself the same thing. What was it about her that wouldn't allow him to let her go? Why was he ferrying her around the city so she could look for a husband when he personally despised marriage and thought her ideas of it bordered on the ludicrous? He glanced at her and saw her look away quickly. She had been staring at him, and now he returned that interest.

She was warm and lovely, intelligent and spirited. And determined to have a life that was different from her mother's. She was so determined that she was willing to trade a life of luxury and pleasure for the right to make that choice.

Part of him wanted to see that she got what she wanted —a respectable life, a marriage. And part of him wanted to take her back to his house and his bed and make mad, passionate love to her until . . . Until what? Until she admitted she wanted him more than she wanted respectability? Until he somehow satisfied this bone-deep hunger that seemed to be growing inside him? Until he got her out of his system?

When he deposited her at her door, he stood for a moment on the steps, shifting from foot to foot and wondering if he was losing every bit of his sanity. "If we're going to Reading tomorrow, we shall have to leave earlier than three. I shall have to call for you at one."

She looked up at him with an expression of surprise and relief that made something in his chest constrict. "I wasn't sure you would still be willing to help . . ."

"Whatever else I am, 'Cousin Gabrielle,' I am not a quitter."

He gave her hand a sardonic kiss, and as he rode off in his carriage, he added, to himself: "Even when quitting is the only sane thing to do."

The next morning Gabrielle arranged for the cook to fill a hamper with food and wines and sought out her mother to explain that Pierce would call for her early to take her on a picnic in the country. But Rosalind had just that morning received word that the duke had landed in Portsmouth, a month earlier than expected, and would be making his way north to London to join her in a two or three days.

Rosalind had gone into an immediate flurry—ordering her boudoir freshened and made ready, selecting foods and flowers, and dragging out her most provocative garments for evaluation. She was so preoccupied that she waved Gabrielle off with a distracted, "Of course—of course— have a nice time, dear."

When Pierce arrived to collect her, Gabrielle had Gunther carry the hamper out to the carriage and settle it in the boot. Pierce stood looking at her a moment, savoring the sight of her in her teal silk dress with its soft, ruched bodice and her picture hat rimmed with yellow flowers and draped with yellow and teal ribbons. Then, with a deep breath, he reached for her hand and helped her up into the forward-facing seat.

"Your mill owner from Reading doesn't stand a chance," he said smoothly as he settled on the seat beside her.

"You think not?" She was genuinely surprised by what seemed a compliment.

"I'm sure not." He glanced away and adjusted his tie. "You'll undoubtedly turn both of his heads."

She just managed to keep from smiling.

The tension between them was still present beneath the surface, but they both were determined to be civil. They spoke of the weather, the shocking news in the papers of the discovery of a cache of explosives and plans by the Irish-American dynamitards to destroy a number of public buildings in London, and of the controversial principle of Home Rule for Ireland. Time and miles flew by in the bright sun. By midafternoon, they were in Reading, inquiring as to the whereabouts of Wright's Mill.

They were surprised to learn it wasn't a knitting mill at all, as she had been led to believe by the fellow's letter. It was a grist mill, set on the banks of a modest stream. And next to it was a rather rough-looking house with a warped roof that had been propped up with hastily nailed planks. They stepped down out of the carriage, into the middle of the afternoon's trade—farmers, householders, and bakers' apprentices with handcarts, awaiting the results of the day's milling.

As they drew near, they could hear laughter coming from just inside the main doors. Shortly, several men spilled out into the yard, their faces ruddy and glowing, their fists wrapped around tankards of ale. When one of the bakers' boys called to a short, thickset man wearing a canvas apron and asked if his employer's flour was ready, the man turned on him with a booming voice.

"O' course it's ready, boy! A man is as good as 'is word. An' I give mine. Bring yer cart round to the side door. Will be easier loadin' from there." What followed was a flurry of orders and activity that set the yard and the mill humming. With a judicious blend of cajoling, bullying, and good-natured curses, the stocky miller accomplished the delivery of feed grain, bakery flour, and the filling of various householders' orders in what must have been record time.

Somewhere, in the midst of that bustle, Gabrielle realized she was looking at her potential husband, Mr. William Wright. And it wasn't long before he looked up, caught sight of her, and stopped dead.

"What can I do for ye, sir—you an' yer pretty laidy?" he asked striding across the yard and brushing flour from his shock of wheat blond hair and his broad shoulders as he came.

"Perhaps you would let us see the inside of your mill," Pierce said, pleasantly. "It's been quite a while since I've seen the inside of such a works . . . and I doubt my cousin has ever seen a grist operation, close at hand."

"Sure enough. Only, I can't be responsible for yer fancy clothes, ma'am." He scowled at Gabrielle's dress, but then raised his gaze to her rosy face and grinned broadly. He was missing a couple of teeth. "Ye'll have to be careful."

He showed them around his mill, pointing out with pride the longevity of its use—more than two hundred years of milling on that very site. He eyed Gabrielle, embarrassed her with his gruff flattery, and made her flinch when he cleared his throat and spat. To his credit, each time, he begged her pardon and explained it was the constant dust.

By the time they climbed back aboard their carriage, she was greatly relieved to get away and feeling a huge burden of guilt for her unworthy thoughts.

"He's a good man. A fair and honest man," she said aloud, but mostly to herself. "He works hard, and he probably deserves a good wife and a house full of children . . ."

Pierce watched her grappling with the conflict between her liberal principles and her own bred-in-the-bone sense of class distinctions. He was a good man . . . But the unspoken remainder of that sentence, they both knew, was: *of the working class.*

"And he's about as suited to be your husband as a prize boar," he said, taking responsibility for saying what for her was unspeakable. "He spits and scratches. He likes his ale and his bluff stories and giving his workers an occasional boot in the backside. Just imagine him across a chessboard or ordering wine in a restaurant or even wearing a shirt with a collar." He smiled wryly. "Though, now that I think on it, you might just find common ground if you read him a few of your limericks or played him a few choruses of 'Whoops, Alice!' . . ."

She folded her arms irritably and turned her shoulder to him, staring out at the fields they were passing. "You really are intolerable, sometimes."

"Sometimes." He watched her struggle and felt a powerful impulse to make it easier on her. "And sometimes I am right. You couldn't abide marriage to him any more than *I* could. You haven't wronged him. And it's not a great failing in you. It's just a fact. But of course, being an eminently logical sort—you already know that."

She cast him a look from the corner of her eye, then turned back to the countryside. She hated that he was right. And she hated even more that he was being so decent about it. It would make things so much easier if he would crow and swagger and be insufferable.

"So, who is next on your list, Cousin Gabrielle?" he said brightly.

"A baron." She refused to look at him. "Baron Colchester, in Kingston-upon-Thames."

After a stop in a shady grove, and a picnic that grew increasingly more tense, they resumed their course back to London, by way of Kingston-upon-Thames.

They asked after the baron in a number of reputable

hostelries and mercantile establishments in the town. The fact that he was universally unknown did not bode well for Gabrielle's hopes. When they finally located someone who knew of him, they were nearly through Kingston-upon-Thames and back on the road to London. Following an inscrutable set of directions, they turned down one country lane after another, searching for what was reputedly "old Colchester's" house.

The road grew too rough and rutted for the big landau. When Pierce and Gabrielle got out to walk what promised to be the last bit of the way, she could scarcely bear to have him touch her or look at her.

When the tumbledown farmhouse with derelict plow and hay wagon in the overgrown yard came into view over a rise, her heart sank all the way to her stomach. Pierce called out to whoever might be at home. As they approached the house, a tall, gaunt man who looked to be in his late fifties stumbled from the farmhouse door, shielding his eyes from the bright sun.

"That you, boy? This is the second time this week you've been late with my bot—" He stopped at the sight of them, weaved, and squinted. "Who are you?" His eyes were bloodshot, his complexion sallow, and he looked like he hadn't had a either a haircut or a decent meal in months. The slight breeze carried scents of stale drink, sweat, and unwashed linen to them.

Gabrielle looked to Pierce with alarm. "We were out for a ride and our carriage got stuck," he said. "I was wondering if we might borrow your horses to free it."

"Got no horses," the fellow said with something of a slur. "Sold the bolters off ages ago." He turned to stagger back to the house, and Pierce tried again.

"Then perhaps you could offer us a bit of shade and something to drink. We've had a dusty walk up the road."

He waved his arm irritably and lumbered toward the house. "There's the well."

When the front door slammed behind the man, Pierce went to knock on it. "I do hate to trouble you further," he said tautly. "But could you tell me where we are?"

"You're on my land . . . and I'll thank you to f-fix your rig and get off."

"Whose land? Who are you?" Pierce demanded.

"Baron Colchester—now get off!"

When the door slammed a second time, Pierce strode back to Gabrielle, turned her by the arm, and escorted her forcefully down the lane.

She was too stunned to protest, too humiliated by the rude treatment they had just received from her most "noble" suitor. He was a vile, drunken old wreck, apparently looking for a woman to keep him in the style from which he had fallen. And with his rough rebuke, her last and best hope for a quick marriage had crashed.

By the time she reached the carriage, her face was stiff, her shoulders tight, her whole body was rigid with self-control. If he said one smart word to her, one casual I-told-you-so, to add to the burden she was carrying, she would smack him—she truly would.

Jack had managed to turn the landau, and when Pierce handed her up and climbed aboard himself, she sat stiffly at the far side of the carriage, avoiding his gaze. They were turning onto the main path when the fatal comment came.

"Well, you might never ride another horse or drink another drop of lemonade . . . but at least you'd be a baroness."

The stinging in her eyes became a surge of hot tears, and once they started flowing, she couldn't make them stop. She fumbled blindly about in her handbag for a handkerchief and discovered that it was the one thing she hadn't thought to bring. A folded square of linen appeared around the shoulder she had turned to him. Accepting it, she dabbed at her eyes and held herself rigidly. What was the matter with her, breaking down like this? She tried to tell herself one more disappointment didn't matter. She could go back and search again the letters she had received. She could place another ad. She would find a decent husband . . . somewhere . . . sometime . . . eventually . . .

Pierce watched her struggling with her tears and her pride, and his hands curled into fists. Just then he would have given almost anything for five minutes alone with rummy old Colchester. As she strained to control her emotions, he slowly lost the battle with his . . . growing more furious, aching to plant his fist in someone, ready to take on the whole damned world for her with just bare knuckles.

But he couldn't. What was making her cry was not something a man could use his fists against. It was an idea, a possibility, a desire in her. And she was trying against overwhelming odds to make that possibility a reality.

She deserved better than this—better than unscrupulous sweatshop owners, priggish vicars, swaggering millers, and broken-down peers. She deserved a home, a loyal and sensible husband, a secure future. She deserved her choice.

"Gabrielle," he said quietly, reaching out to touch her arm. She flinched as if his hand burned her.

Tumult erupted in him. Seizing her by the arm, he dragged her back against him and wrapped her in his arms. She struggled briefly, pushing and saying "no." But he refused to release her and after a moment she stilled. And after another moment she buried her face in the lapel of his coat and began to cry in earnest.

He listened to her sobs and felt every breath and shudder of her frame. She was so warm and soft, and so very miserable. The scent of her hair filled his head, and the sense of her despair filled his heart. For a long time he just held her. Gradually her tears ceased and her body began to relax against him, drawing warmth and comfort from his presence. After a while, he shifted back and raised her face to his on one finger.

Her eyes were red, her cheeks were flushed, and her lips were . . . the most irresistible thing he had seen in a very long time. His gaze fastened on them, and he became aware of the heightened sensitivity of his own, of the rush of his blood and the thickening in his loins, of the desire he had managed to set aside for these last three days. She was so lovely . . . He knew just how she would taste . . .

He lowered his head, and she made no attempt to avoid his mouth.

Her eyes closed, her lips parted. Her hand came up to weave her fingers into his hair. There was nothing else in the world that could fill the aching hollow inside her.

Suddenly they were spiraling deeper into a passionate kiss, hungrily tasting each other, touching, stroking. She arched against him, and he pressed her back into the soft carriage seat, his hands covering her back, her shoulders, her waist and hip. She wasn't wearing as much boning . . . felt softer, more accessible as he searched the shape of her through her clothes.

She wrapped her arms around his neck, feeling a storm rising inside her, willfully ignoring the warnings of her battered reason and sensibility. Passions long denied now demanded release and expression. And the warmth and vitality of his presence, of his desire poured through her in a rich, life-giving flood, assuaging the hurt and loss.

Pierce suddenly lifted his head, alert to some change in their surroundings, and she struggled back to reality through the steam in her senses. He said something, but not to her, then relaxed his hold on her. She looked up to find him moving away with regret in his eyes.

Sitting up, she realized they were stopped at the side of the narrow lane, within sight of the London Road. Knowing traffic was generally brisk on that road, Jack had stopped to warn Pierce and to offer to put the top up. The sense of why he had thought it prudent to stop brought a belated flush to Gabrielle's face.

Moments later, she sat across the carriage from Pierce, smoothing her skirts and repinning her hat, which had been knocked off during their kiss. She knew she should feel guilty, but somehow she didn't. His kiss had restored some balance, filled some void within her. It was the only good thing that had happened to her all day. It felt honorable and decent and right somehow, and it took a while for her to understand why. In reaching for her just now, in embracing her through her pain and frustration and tears, he had intended his kiss for comfort as much as passion. It meant he saw her as a person . . . not just a desirable "trinket."

But as the spell of his kiss gradually wore off, she was left with the painful awareness that nothing had really changed. She had eliminated all of her marital prospects, still needed a husband, and still had no future. She glanced at Pierce. Her feelings for him were growing ever more powerful and compelling. And she hadn't the slightest notion of how to combat them, except to find another man —a *husband*—and let marriage put her dangerous passion for him safely beyond her reach.

As they pulled onto the London Road, Pierce watched her fixing her hat and reclaiming her control, now as calm and proper as she had been improper and out of control minutes before. In spite of himself, he began mentally searching through his acquaintances, trying to think of a man who might make a reasonable match for her. He thought of the lords, MPs, bank managers, secretaries and under secretaries in government bureaus, industrialists, and out-and-out merchants that he knew. And he couldn't think of one man, married or single, whom he believed could equal, appreciate, or even understand her.

Then he realized there was *one*.

But there was no man less suited for marriage or less likely to marry her.

He wrestled with both his higher and lower impulses, and the contest was decided by his newly resurrected conscience. As much as he wanted her, he would have to give her up to what *she* wanted: a respectable and passionless future. He would have to help her find a pleasant, safe, tolerably dull husband . . . a man who would understand how wonderfully unique she was and wouldn't try to control her too much.

Praying that such conscience-ridden thinking was not a harbinger of more soul-searching and moralizing and ways-mending to come, he vowed to keep his desires to himself and, for once, *be* the gentleman he usually just pretended to be.

When they arrived at her home, she slid to the edge of the seat, obviously expecting him to dismount first. Instead, he took her by the hand and made her look at him. The traces of sadness in her eyes caused a peculiar fullness in his chest.

"I'll help you," he said quietly.

"What?" she said, feeling her heart beginning to skip beats at the sincerity she glimpsed in his handsome face.

"I'll help you find a husband—a proper husband. Someone with lots of money and little enough sense to leave you to your own devices. I'll introduce you."

"You will?" She felt as if a dark husk had just slid from her heart, and she forced a smile, hoping he wouldn't notice the moisture rising in her eyes. "What a rotten thing to do to me, Pierce St. James, to help me and make me beholden to you for the rest of my natural life."

"Oh, I expect to be paid," he said, trying not to see her tears. "When you're settled, you'll have to write me a limerick, once in a while," he said, his voice strangely thick. "And, of course, you can name your firstborn after me."

She somehow managed to get out of the carriage and make it up the steps and inside the house. When the doors closed behind her, she leaned back against them and let the tears come.

12

A message from Colonel Tottenham was waiting for Pierce when he arrived home that evening: Gladstone was likely to "walk" that night. Pierce crumpled the paper and ran his hands over his face. It meant another miserable night in a damp carriage—following, watching, waiting—when there were a thousand things he'd rather be doing.

He trailed Gladstone from a dinner at his friend Lord Rosebery's, to his official residence in Downing Street, and then waited for the old man to emerge once again and head for the Haymarket or the East End. But Gladstone didn't leave his house again that night. Sometime after midnight, well after the lights in the household had been extinguished, Pierce ended his vigil and went home, seething about the faulty intelligence he had received.

Thus, the next morning, when word arrived at his house that Gladstone intended to go out again that night, he was vaguely annoyed. The fact that Tottenham wasn't able to tell him where Gladstone was going only added to his deepening mood. He had other things on his mind.

He had promised Gabrielle introductions. The fact that he had agreed to help her snare one of his fellow bachelors into marriage was proof of her detrimental effects on him. Clearly, the sooner he got her safely married off, the better. He gave some thought to what might be a proper and dignified venue for such introductions and sent word to her that they would attend the Gilbert and Sullivan operetta *Iolanthe* at the Savoy that night.

Thus, he stood, that evening, in the entry of Maison LeCoeur, watching with a surge of pleasure as Gabrielle floated down the steps in a haze of midnight blue silk chiffon. For the first time since he had known her, she was wearing a fashionable, lower neckline and her hair was swept up in a sophisticated style. Her movements were sure and womanly, and her eyes were bright with the womanly pleasure of knowing she looked her best. She was nothing short of breathtaking.

"I shall have to call a dozen men out before this evening is over," he grumbled good-naturedly as he pressed a kiss on her hair, for her mother's benefit, and tried not to inhale her perfume. Her quiet laugh set his fingertips tingling.

But the minute they stepped into the lobby of the Savoy Theater, Pierce revised his estimate of a dozen duels —upward. It seemed that every man they passed halted in the middle of his conversation and turned to watch her walk by. Pierce saw them staring at her figure and her neckline and, knowing his reaction to them, now wished that she were wearing something much more concealing. A wave of whispers and murmurs spread through the assemblage like ripples through a pond, and before long they were surrounded by a number of handsome young drakes in full evening dress, all greeting Pierce like an old friend and seeking an introduction to his stunning companion.

With each request for an introduction, he felt more pressed and irritable, and he finally excused them both and ushered her into their box to escape. As the overture began and the curtains rose, he was glad for the darkened theater; it hid the grimness of his mood.

At intermission, when they emerged and descended onto the mezzanine, where champagne was being served to the more affluent patrons, they were again beset by an even larger group of gentlemen, headed by two familiar faces. Lord Arundale and Lord Shively had seen them in their box and headed for them as soon as the last note of the first half sounded.

Gabrielle stayed close by Pierce's side and returned their greeting, while declining to respond to their extravagant praise. She did her best to deflect their interest, but her modesty only seemed to inflame their desire to impress her through flattery. Shively tried to engage her eyes directly, and Arundale contrived to stand beside her and managed to run his hand up the curve of her back before she could pull away. His only response to her cool, censuring look was the glitter of unrepentant pleasure in his eyes.

As a predominantly male crowd enlarged around them, Gabrielle was perilously close to becoming the sensation of the evening. Gowned ambiguously between "rosebud" and full flower, she was too beautiful to be entirely pure, too modest to be anything else. She was a tantalizing mystery: an unknown "cousin" that the rakish Lord Sandbourne seemed to actually treat as a cousin. His protective stance and respectful attendance on her, a major departure from his usual behavior, gave credence to the possibility of kinship.

News of the earl's lovely cousin sifted down through the less fashionable and more sedate layers of theatergoers, as well. Among that group was one whose interest in Lord Sandbourne's new companion had a rather different motive.

As he descended from his borrowed box to the mezzanine, William Gladstone caught sight of the libertine lord who had become one of the thorns in his political side in the last three years. His dark eyes slid to the earl's lovely companion, a supposed "cousin." The "introducing houses" and brothels of London were filled with women who began their descent into degradation as a "pretty cousin."

Poor thing, he thought to himself, caught in the jaded earl's clutches. If only she knew the pain and disgrace that lay in store for her with that opportunistic beast.

Drawn by the irresistible combination of beauty and the hint of illicit passion, the prime minister edged through the crowd to get a closer look. As the young woman smiled warily, enduring the press of people demanding introductions, something in her voice and the shape of her face seemed hauntingly familiar to him. Light hair . . . square face . . . memorable blue eyes. He watched for a while, trying to remember where he had seen them. Then she said something about "my mother," and his eyes lighted with surprise and recognition. He knew that voice, that face, those eyes. He knew where their owner had come from, and he knew the trouble she was in. He turned and made his way from the crowd, his brow knitted with concern.

The attention Gabrielle attracted gradually overwhelmed her. The avid smiles and hungry stares, the press and heat of that throng of male admirers grew steadily bolder and more oppressive. When she drew back against Pierce and looked up at him, there were traces of panic in her eyes. She whispered that she needed to find the ladies' retiring room, and Pierce obliged by making a path through the crowd with his sizable frame, then ushering her down the hallway toward the ladies' room. He seemed relieved when she proposed that she remain there until the opera resumed.

With her nerves on edge, Gabrielle endured the stares and chilled silences of the other women and thought of the crush of men outside. The attention thrust upon her was more frightening that flattering. Those men with their heated stares and suggestive smiles . . . she shivered, just recalling them.

Somewhere, she told herself, there had to be a man willing to marry her despite her illegitimate birth and extravagant education. But tonight, as she searched each face and form that loomed up before her, hoping one would strike some spark of recognition in her that would say he might be the right one, her hopes had begun to sink.

One was too boy-faced, another too visibly arrogant, another spit when he spoke, another's fashionable lisp set her teeth on edge. The next was too sly, and the one after that too jaded . . . or too lusty, or too pretentious, or too eager. A lord, a knight, an MP, and a banker . . . After a while their names and faces began to run together. Then she had looked up at Pierce's powerful, reassuring form and realized why they all seemed so lacking. In her mind, she was comparing their qualities to Pierce's wit and consummate self-assurance, to his honesty and compassion. And she realized, with a sinking feeling, that Pierce's formidable shadow would probably cast a pall over her future husband as well—no matter how good or decent or honorable he proved to be.

When the ladies' room was empty and sufficient time had passed for the performance to start, she opened the door and peered outside. The hallway seemed deserted. Taking a deep breath, she stepped out into the corridor and started for the main mezzanine and the steps to the boxes.

As she passed the cloakroom, someone grabbed her arm and pulled her into the dimly lit room, then thrust her back amongst the cloaks and wraps. She would have screamed, but a hand clamped over her mouth. As she focused on her captor, with her heart pounding, she found herself staring into a familiar pair of dark eyes set in a craggy face and beneath a familiar cap of wiry white hair.

"Mr. Gladstone," she whispered as he removed his hand.

"You *are* the one," the old man said, frowning. "I knew it—I've a memory for faces."

She was too stunned to speak again. Her mind crowded with conflicting memories and feelings; Pierce's charges against him, Gladstone's righteous zeal, her unfulfilled bargain with Pierce to gain information about him, fear of discovery. . . .

"You were telling the truth, then. And Sandbourne was the nobleman your mother insisted you take to your bed. If I had known his identity—"

"No, no—he wasn't the one my mother pressed me to take." Her voice sounded tight and desperate in her own ears.

"Then she lost no time in finding you a worse one. The man is nothing short of contemptible—makes no secret of his sordid affairs and makes no apologies to the poor women he seduces and ruins. Just to be in his company is to suffer a blow to a woman's reputation." He stepped back to look her over, then shook his head. "I cannot bear to think of what he has done to you—"

"He has done *nothing* to me," she protested. "However

it may appear, I am *not* Lord Sandbourne's mistress. I told you the truth before, and I'm telling you the truth now. He is a friend, who has agreed to pose as my protector so that my mother will not press me to take someone else." She halted, realizing that the entire tale of her deception would only muddy the waters, when she needed desperately to clear them. "I have never taken a lover. Not then, not now."

"Not *yet*, you mean," he said, straightening and taking her by the arm. "Then there may still be hope. Come, my child, I shall see you are secreted—"

"You don't understand." She wrested her arm from his grip, realizing that his opinions of Pierce were every bit as dire and flawed as Pierce's opinions of him. "You don't know him as I do. He has become a dear and trusted friend." With every word, his incredulity deepened. "Truly, Mr. Gladstone, he is a wonderful man. We've spent a good bit of time together in the last week, and he has gone to great lengths to help me. He has taken my part against my mother's designs and has given me his protection and the use of his carriage. He is patient and thoughtful and decent. He's been nothing but honest and forthright with me. He is helping me to find a husband."

"You poor child—"

"You must believe me." She grew desperate as she realized just how improbable her story must sound to him, how absurd it would have sounded to her only a week ago. "The earl is no threat to me or to anyone." But as soon as she said it she thought of Pierce's designs on Gladstone himself and looked down, hoping that awful knowledge wasn't somehow evident in her eyes.

"Something must be done," he said with quiet indignation.

"No!" She looked up, reading his determination in his piercing eyes. Her only hope, she realized, was to be perilously candid with him. "My only hope is to make a marriage, and I will never make an honorable marriage if my name and the circumstances of my birth are made part of a public scandal." As the thought of "scandal" crossed her mind, she realized there was still more at stake. "There are my parents to think of."

"Yes . . . your parents." He studied her rising alarm and reached for one of her hands, to hold it comfortingly between his. "Who is your father, my girl? You have spoken of him as a titled man. Does he know what is happening to you?"

She looked down at her hand, captive in his, and smiled bitterly. "He is off on a great hunting safari, somewhere. He takes no interest in me. You must understand, my mother has been his consort for more than twenty years and—"

"Twenty years?" The number clearly astonished him.

"I suppose now you will doubt that, as well. But it is true." She curled her fingers around the old man's hand and squeezed, pouring every bit of her desperation into her plea. "After tonight I will have a number of marriage prospects, but they will all disappear at the first breath of scandal. If you have any care for me, any thought for my best interest, then you will do nothing, nothing at all. God willing, I will soon be a respectably married woman and all of this will be forgotten."

Before he could stop her, she jerked her hand from his and dashed out into the corridor and along the mezzanine to the steps leading to the boxes. He lurched to the door and watched her hurrying back to the earl, and his hands balled into fists of frustration at his sides. The treacherous Sandbourne had done his work well on the girl . . . had her believing he was gallant and noble and that he would help her find an honorable situation with a husband. He had promised her a marriage, of all things, when his antipathy for marriage was almost legendary in the clubs.

She was headed for heartbreak and infamy; he was certain of it. He had never seen a woman in greater need of a rescue.

He tugged his vest down and gave his rumpled evening coat a brush as he made his way back to his own box. Something would have to be done. And the sooner the better.

"Did you catch the name of that young girl with Sandbourne?" Gladstone asked a trusted acquaintance, Edward Hamilton, as the glittering lobby of the Savoy slowly emptied of people after the performance. Together, they watched the earl escorting her quickly through a cordon of male admirers and into his carriage.

"I believe he introduced her as Gabrielle La—something." Hamilton shrugged.

"Gabrielle La*Something* . . . whose father is a nobleman and whose mother is a high courtesan . . ." Gladstone considered it for a moment. "Have any of the higher-ranking lords been absent from the country for a while . . . say, on a hunting safari?"

Hamilton thought for a moment. "Come to think of it, Carlisle applied to the queen some time ago for some sort of African jaunt. I saw his letter."

"Carlisle? The duke of Carlisle?" Gladstone's dark eyes flickered as he searched some internal vision. "He had a mistress, didn't he? I remember now—a liaison of long standing. What was her name? Rosamund . . . Rosalind . . . something . . ."

"LeCoeur." Hamilton came up with it after a moment. "Now, there's a name I haven't heard in a long time. They used to be the talk of the 'upper ten.' There was even a child, I believe."

"A *daughter.*" Gladstone's eyes widened with recognition, and his shoulders straightened. New determination filled his aging frame. "So, that is who she is.

The duke of Carlisle's love child. Small wonder she's terrified of dragging her father into it." His eyes narrowed. "Well, perhaps it's time someone made the duke—and others like him—tend a bit of what they have sown."

He clapped his friend on the shoulder as the next coach drew up. "Here is your carriage now, Hamilton. Do me a good turn, my friend. Follow Sandbourne's carriage for a bit and see where he takes the girl. It is imperative that I learn where he takes her. Send word to my residence. . . . I'm going straight home."

It took the entire second half of the performance for Gabrielle's racing heart to calm. She expected Gladstone to lead a pack of constables into the box at any moment to seize Pierce and charge him with some hideous offense against moral decency. When the performance continued, uninterrupted, her panic slowly subsided, and she began to think. Her second encounter with Gladstone put her in a very difficult position with Pierce. She didn't know whether or not to tell him about seeing the prime minister, knowing now that there was great animosity between them, and knowing how wrong they were about each other. Pierce hadn't said anything about her part of their bargain in several days. And nothing she could report of her conversation with Gladstone would help Pierce prove anything against him. In the end, it was that fact that made her decide not to tell Pierce about her meeting with him. It was probably best just to let the entire issue remain at rest.

When the singers took their final bows and Pierce ushered her to the cloakroom, then out to his carriage, she searched the crowd without catching so much as a glimpse of William Gladstone. But they were halfway home before she finally heaved a sigh and relaxed. When Pierce's hand reached for hers in the darkened carriage, she looked at him and her heart skipped a beat.

"We won't do that again," he said, watching her tension draining.

"It was overwhelming. All those . . . *people*." She meant *men*.

It *had* been overwhelming. And infuriating. Pierce had come within an inch of losing his temper and his vaunted self-possession. They had jostled and ogled and leered at her as if she were meat on a spit and they were starving. Then they flattered and cozened and appraised her with insultingly transparent intentions. It was humiliating to belong to the same sex.

Earlier, he had believed that Gabrielle was searching for a husband in too low a class. But, in truth, tonight had shown him that higher class was no guarantee of manners or decency or morality. The plain-spoken mill owner from Reading had shown more basic decency toward her than any of the randy "gentlemen" they had just encountered.

In the quiet darkness, he saw her eyes shimmering, felt her hand trembling in his. A streetlamp suddenly shone through the coach window, casting a golden halo about her. Then it faded as abruptly as it came, leaving her lingering image in his mind, bathed in light. She was so lovely, so bright, so desirable . . . and so damned illegitimate.

Tonight, watching the behavior of London's upper-class males and her reaction to them, he realized that there probably wasn't a man amongst them who would give her what she wanted. No man with any pride or passion would marry a woman as beautiful and sensual as her, deposit her in some prosy little house in the country, and pretend she didn't exist for months at a time. And any man who *would* do such a thing to her probably didn't deserve her.

His thoughts went around and around, on that dismal track . . . which gradually narrowed and focused his reason to one final, drastic conclusion:

There was no such thing as a good marriage for Gabrielle LeCoeur.

He stared into her tense face as he helped her down from the carriage and saw her to the door. All of his instincts told him that she had just taken stock of the possibilities for her future, as well. And she was intensely miserable.

He gave her a smile and stroked her pale cheek.

By the time he climbed back into his carriage, he knew there was only one course left open to him. The most decent and noble thing he could do . . . was to make her his mistress in earnest.

Pierce arranged to call for Gabrielle promptly at three the next day, with the expressed intent of taking her riding in Hyde Park. He arrived on horseback to collect her, with another mount in tow, looking inexpressibly elegant in a black coat, buff riding breeches, and tall black boots. Her mother had not provided for new riding clothes, so she was able to dress comfortably in the riding habit she had always used in France: a hunter green tailored cashmere jacket, a black skirt, and a black hat made in the style of a gentleman's top hat.

The air was damp and cool, and high clouds kept the sun from being too bright. If it hadn't been perfect weather for a ride, the prospect of being outdoors and on a horse again would still have made it seem the balmiest of days to Gabrielle. It was a true liberation—from her mother's frantic household and from the tyranny of her own thoughts. They rode through Rotten Row, which at this time of day was all but deserted, then along the curving lake known as the Serpentine. They were stopped twice by acquaintances of Pierce: one the heir to a mercantile concern and the other a career diplomat. Each time Pierce made proper and congenial introductions.

Both gentlemen showed interest in pursuing an acquaintance with her. They were both pleasant fellows, reasonably attractive, gracious, and well-mannered. Gabrielle tried to smile and be polite, but she felt alarmingly empty at the prospect of spending her future with either of them. Those meetings, and her disturbing reaction to them, subdued her spirits and dampened her enjoyment of the rest of the afternoon.

Pierce watched her sobering mood and her attempt to be gracious and pleasant to her potential suitors, and he felt a guilty relief that she hadn't reacted more favorably to them. It only confirmed and supported his plans for the rest of the afternoon.

After a while, he consulted his watch, then led her down through the city to St. Margaret's Church, on the grounds of Westminster Abbey. The organist was practicing in the empty church, and with a finger to his lips, Pierce bundled Gabrielle up the rear stairs to the choir loft in the balcony. There, he took off his coat, spread it on one of the pews, and bade her lie down on it. With some bewilderment, she complied. But soon she found herself engulfed in the most heavenly music she had heard in years. He sprawled on the floor beside her, leaning against the pew, with his head back and his eyes closed.

When the music stopped, they stayed for a while, savoring the silence.

"Why did you bring me here?" she said quietly, sitting up.

He leaned forward and looked around at the peaceful expanse before them, bathed in the dappled light from the stained glass windows. "I thought you might enjoy the music. I come here, sometimes, when I need to think or to be alone."

"Do you need to think about something?" She settled a

thoughtful gaze on him. "Is something wrong?" He rose and slid onto the pew beside her.

"Not wrong, really." He scowled, giving lie to that assurance. "It's just that . . . I'm afraid I have to ask you to make good on your part of our bargain. Gladstone is back at his scurrilous activities, and I need evidence of it. I don't like asking you, Gabrielle, but I do need your help."

She looked down at her gloved hands and prayed that none of what she had withheld from him the night before was visible in her face. "What do you want me to do?"

"Just meet him on the street and see if he wants you to talk with him. If he does, you bring him back to a certain restaurant, where I'll be waiting." He put his hand over hers. "I won't let him hurt you, Gabrielle."

She felt the warmth of his gaze and heard the regret in his tone. He honestly believed the prime minister was guilty of corrupting and misusing the women he tried to help reform, and the only way to convince him otherwise was to meet with Gladstone and report the truth of what the prime minister said and did.

"All right, I'll do it."

When they reached the stables where his carriage was waiting, he suggested that they go by the restaurant, The Montmortaine, so he could show her where she should bring Gladstone when he approached her again.

At the restaurant, he escorted her through a side door and they were shown up the stairs to a private room.

She stood near the door, surveying the dining room. It was a refined version of the room at Le Ciel, where he had taken her that first night. Instead of heavy red velvet and mirrors, this chamber was swathed in sedate moiré and dignified tapestries. The mantel and hearth were made of fine mahogany, inset with tasteful white marble, and the large divan was upholstered in tapestry and strewn with pillows of sundry shapes and colors. And, of course, the table was set for two, with china and silver, candles burning, and fresh roses.

The sight of those particular flowers sent a shiver through her, and she went to the window to look out. Below and across the street was a park surrounded by an ornamental iron grating. Lamps were just being lighted along the street.

"It's Green Park," he said, settling behind her, looking over her shoulder. "If you could see the sun, it would have set over there." After he pointed, his hand lowered and rested on her shoulder. She felt a weakness in her knees at that contact and braced, suddenly aware of how near he was . . . how warm . . . how delicious.

There was always a price to pay for "delicious," she reminded herself. Even biscuits cost three pence.

She held her breath, and he moved away, turning to the table. "Say—I've rented the room for the entire evening. Gladstone is having dinner . . . Why don't we?" He gestured around them. "Unlike Le Ciel, this place has a very creditable kitchen." He smiled and waggled his brows. "The people who patronize The Montmortaine actually do *eat*."

Before she could think of a reasonable objection, he was at the door and laying down a host of instructions with the headwaiter. When she heard him ordering salad and rarebit and a good, simple burgundy, she relaxed a bit. Removing her gloves and unpinning her hat, she laid them aside and tidied the wisps of hair that had worked free on their ride. And when he returned and held out a chair for her at the linen-draped table, she accepted graciously.

The waiter arrived with wine and a tray of bread and herbed butter. When he ordered the waiter to bring them more of the bread and butter, he caught the look on her face and grinned, explaining: "I'm afraid I'm something of a glutton when it comes to good bread." Then he amended it: "Or good food of any kind. I especially love a good beefsteak . . . cooked over hot coals, 'American' style, smothered in mushrooms and onions . . ."

The look of rapture on his face surprised her. As much time as they had spent together, she realized, she scarcely knew anything about him. She didn't know where he lived, how he spent his time, what his political affiliation was, or even whether he had brothers and sisters. Yet, she had put her matrimonial fate, the key to the rest of her life, in his hands.

"Tell me about you, Pierce St. James," she said, sipping her wine. "Tell me about your life, your schooling, your travels, your politics . . . your family."

"Not my *amours*?"

"I believe we can skip those for now," she said, refusing to be deterred.

He turned to the side, unbuttoned his coat and stretched his long legs out before him, getting comfortable. "No siblings. My father died when I was seventeen, just as I was set to go off to the continent. I postponed my grand tour . . . indefinitely."

She frowned. "Indefinitely? You mean you never had a grand tour?"

"Never. My mother refused to allow me to go off to school—always managed a well-timed bout of nerves or a sudden violent illness whenever my father mentioned sending me away. So I had tutors, an endless stream of them . . . fusty old cods with dried up . . ." He glimpsed her widening eyes and cleared his throat. "When my father died, my mother took to her bed and declared it would kill her if I left. I had to wait until I was nineteen and enlist the help of my uncles, even to escape to Cambridge."

She understood. He was a man who couldn't abide being under another's control. And his rebellion against society's rules and norms had begun long ago. "Strange, isn't it," she mused, feeling the warmth of the wine spreading through her, "how I was sent away and wished to be home, while you were kept at home and wished to be away."

He sat quietly, looking into her warm, clear eyes and feeling once again that uncanny connection with her. Then the first course arrived, and over the salad, he resumed his story. His family seat and most of his landholdings were in Sussex. He owned a large house on Hyde Park's Park Lane, and—when he wasn't being snared into wild schemes by females he mistook for tarts and snatched off the streets—he oversaw his family holdings and fortune, indulged in politics, enjoyed racing his horses and hunting pheasant, and made speeches in the House of Lords.

"In short," he said, "I led the placidly pleasurable and predictable life of an upper-class male . . . until I met you."

"Me?" She sniffed indignantly and broke off another piece of bread. "I see your game. Blame all the turmoil in your life on me, will you?"

"Not all the turmoil in my life," he said, catching her gaze in his and stopping her heart with the seriousness she glimpsed in his expression. "Just the turmoil in my heart."

Gabrielle froze. For a moment she didn't blink, didn't breathe. When she looked up, his dark eyes were compelling in a way she had never seen them—warm, alive with need. Something deep within her responded, and she felt a flutter of panic.

"I believe you were telling me about your brothers and sisters."

"I don't *have* brothers or sisters." He held her gaze fast in his. "I was talking about how you make me feel."

"Annoyed, mostly, I suppose," she said, tearing her gaze from his and reaching for her wineglass with a trembling hand. "Do take heart—if all goes well, I won't be a burden to you much longer."

He reached her hand before it reached the wineglass, and he held it until she looked up at him. "I've never met anyone quite like you. You're clever and educated and accomplished. You're unpredictable and exasperating and sometimes downright silly. And I somehow have the feeling that you intend every bit of it. Just carrying on a conversation with you is something of an adventure." He released her hand, but kept her gaze captive.

"You make me laugh, Gabrielle. You make me worry. You make me think. The sound of your voice sets my fingertips vibrating. The scent of your hair makes me a little dizzy." His voice lowered. "And when I see you walk, I can somehow feel you swaying against me."

"R-really, your lordship . . ." She pushed her chair back and stood, feeling light-headed and a little frightened. She hurried to the window, pressing her cold hands against her hot cheeks as she stared down at the streetlamps and tried to collect her wits.

"Don't say any more, please," she said in a constricted voice. "It will only complicate things, and my life is complicated enough as it is."

"I'm crazy about you." He stood several feet behind her, but his low, softly spoken words caressed her as surely as hands. "I've never felt this way about a woman. Never had a woman on my mind all the time—wondering what she was having for breakfast, what she wore to bed, or which newspaper she likes to read each morning. I've never bought shoes for a woman . . . never recited limericks or arranged flowers for a woman . . . never held a woman as she cried . . . Until now."

She could feel the heat of his desire melting her precious reserve and somehow couldn't sound the call to arms of her defenses. She just didn't have any resistance left in her. Her eyes closed and her shoulders rounded.

She wanted him.

She tried desperately to think of her future, of the man she would marry, the children she would bear. If only there were someone else, some other name or face on which to fasten her thoughts and longings. But there was no one. No one but Pierce.

He wanted her.

With breath, pulse, and thought suspended, she waited, her back still turned. Then came a rush of warmth, a powerful, bone-melting presence—the feeling of being surrounded and engulfed by him—as his hands gripped her shoulders and slid down her arms. She shivered. There was a soft rasp of fabric as his arms glided around her waist and she felt the pressure of his body against her back. She wrapped her hands over his, at the front of her waist, welcoming their warmth . . .

They stood at the window for some time in that half embrace. And as the night grew darker outside, the light of the candles made a mirror of the windowpanes. She focused on their image and felt a surge of pleasure at the sight of herself cradled in his arms. One part of her knew that he was the most dangerous thing in her world. But another part knew she had never felt so safe and protected, so alive, so wanted.

When he turned her in his arms, she allowed it.

When he lowered his head, she raised hers to meet it.

When his lips touched hers, tomorrow no longer mattered.

13

Her whole being came to life in his arms. She drank him in—the winelike sweetness of his mouth, the lean heat of his body against hers, the soft rasp of his breathing, and the salty tang of his skin. Every tilt of his head, every sweep of his tongue became her tutor. She returned him kiss for kiss, touch for touch, instinctively mirroring his movements and caresses.

"Gabrielle . . . sweetheart . . . do you know how I've waited for this?" he murmured against her mouth, then sank into another long, plundering kiss.

"Days?" she whispered weakly, as his kisses continued along her jaw.

"Months." He traced the rim of her ear with his tongue. "Years. A lifetime. I think I've wanted you forever."

The revelation of his closely guarded feelings unleashed a surge of joy within her. She felt suddenly flushed and dizzy and eager for everything he would say and do with her. He raised his head briefly to rip his coat from his shoulders and cast it aside. Then he drew her into a deep, knee-melting kiss that left her breathless. She felt his hand sliding between them, across her chest, reaching for the buttons of her jacket.

"Help me, sweetheart."

His urgent whisper set fire to her blood. In moments, her jacket was on the floor beside his, and her silk ascot soon joined it. She ran her hands up the rows of starched tucks on the front of his shirt and tugged at his tie. The bow dissolved into silken ribbons that parted to reveal a small mother-of-pearl button at his collar. She hesitated, biting her lip. On impulse, she twisted the button and released it.

With a triumphant smile, he bent and scooped her up into his arms, carrying her to the divan, pausing briefly to turn the key in the lock.

The sight, the scents, the feel of him . . . everything steamed and shimmered in her senses as she settled back on the pillows. Moments later, his chest slid over hers and her sigh of response was absorbed by his kiss. He lovingly traced her shape, adoring each line and curve of her clothed form, then began to work her buttons, nudging aside both her blouse and her inhibitions. Notch by notch the fabric parted, baring her corset and revealing her passion-flushed skin. He dragged his lips along the edge of her corset in one long, heated kiss, then sank a finger beneath the lacy rim of her corset to pry her nipple free. Swirling it with his tongue, he brought that rosy peak to a burning point . . . and began to untie her laces.

In a flurry of trembling hands, his and hers, her corset yielded and her breasts were bared to him. He rubbed each tightly budded tip with his hot cheek, then captured it in his mouth . . . teasing, tantalizing . . . teaching her the breathtaking sensations of physical pleasure. She arched against his hands, as wave after wave of pleasure washed through her, buoying her, carrying her along on powerful currents.

As each layer of garments was removed, she felt his touch changing—one minute trickling like water over her skin, the next burning like hot brands, the next reaching deep into her blood and sinews . . . caressing her to the core of her being. Following his lead, she began to explore the shape of him beneath her hands—caressing, raking, kneading . . . learning the contours of his back and shoulders, the corded column of his neck, the hard planes of his chest.

Then he shifted his body over hers, settling against the intimate heat of her body, seeking her, molding himself against her. She welcomed his weight, shifting her legs as he nudged her knees with his, to allow him to fit the hard wedge of his body tight against her sensitive woman's flesh. That intimate contact seemed to assuage the strange heaviness in her loins and the taut, drawing sensation in her woman's core. As his body flexed slightly and moved against hers, she felt a gorgeous flume of pleasure rising through her and breaking into a shower of sensation that cascaded down the walls of her body. And with each motion of his body against her, that overpowering sensation was elaborated and enlarged.

Wave upon wave of sensation broke over her, leaving her pleasure-drenched and quivering. He raised onto his arms above her, staring down at her, sliding his body against hers, watching the way her body arched and her eyes closed as desire rippled through her. It drummed in his head, in his heart, in his blood: *she was his . . . this way . . . always . . . his . . .*

Downstairs, in the private entry of The Montmortaine—the door used by the stylish restaurant's most discreet clientele —the maître d'hôtel was being beset by three men demanding to know the whereabouts of the earl of Sandbourne and his guest.

"We shall have the room number *and* the key," William Gladstone demanded, leaning into the little Frenchman's face, scorching him with righteous fire. "And don't come again with that nonsense about him not being here—I know he is here. I followed him here myself, three quarters of an hour ago!"

Indeed, since the previous evening at the opera, either Gladstone or his friend Edward Hamilton had dogged the earl's footsteps and observed virtually every movement he made. They had seen him call for the girl and take her for a ride in the park, had puzzled over the couple's visit to the church, and had deduced with alarm what was about to happen the moment the pair disembarked from the earl's carriage at the private entrance to The Montmortaine.

Gladstone had learned the previous evening that the duke of Carlisle was back in England, making his way toward London. He had sent the nobleman a message telling him that his daughter was in peril, urging him to hurry on to the city with all speed. When Gladstone saw the earl ushering the girl into the side door of The Montmortaine, he knew there was no time to waste. He dispatched Hamilton to the duke's house, praying that the nobleman had heeded his message and returned straightaway. Then he sent an urgent summons to his friend the bishop of London, declaring that a moral crisis was afoot and he was needed as witness.

The restaurateur looked at the trio of powerful men

bearing down on him—a duke of the realm and a bishop of the Church of England and the prime minister—and knew he was in trouble. "Please, Your Graces," he croaked out, "I c-cannot!"

"See here, you little vermin—" The barrel-chested duke of Carlisle seized him by the lapels and jerked him up onto his toes. "I shall take this place apart with my bare hands, if I must. My daughter is being ravished in this hellhole, even as we speak, and if you don't wish to be brought up on charges, you shall hand over the damned key!"

Gladstone and the bishop intervened to keep him from throttling the fellow, but the fury in the duke's countenance had already done its work. The maître d' led them up the stairs to the room, imploring them to recall his other patrons and be discreet. But the duke, in high dudgeon, tried the door and in a booming voice demanded, "You in there! Open this door—immediately!" When there was no response, he set his fist to the door and repeated his demand. "Open the door, Sandbourne . . . or I swear I shall break it down!"

When Gladstone and the bishop added their voices to the commotion, the maître d' glanced frantically at the heads appearing in doorways, up and down the hall, and produced the key.

Through the pleasure haze in their senses Pierce and Gabrielle heard the voices outside the door. When the pounding began, Pierce peeled himself from her body and sat bolt upright, shaking his head, trying to make his mind function. He pulled himself away from the sight of Gabrielle's darkened eyes and deliciously revealed body, to swing his gaze to the door, where someone was shouting his name and demanding entrance. In earlier days, in other beds, he would have been on his feet in a wink and heading for the nearest window. But this wasn't a bed and Gabrielle wasn't anybody's wife, and the banging and shouting didn't make any kind of sense to him.

Suddenly there were a number of voices and the pounding rocked the door in its frame. He just managed to pull Gabrielle up with him when the door flew open with a bang and the room was invaded in a rush.

He was on his feet in an instant, spreading himself between Gabrielle and the intruders, his legs braced and his fists clenched, ready to defend both himself and her. "Get the bloody hell out of—" he shouted, starting for them and stopping dead after only two strides. Into his mind and into his life burst a chillingly familiar presence.

For a long moment, he stared in deepening shock at the penetrating brown eyes, craggy features, and unruly white hair belonging to his quarry of recent days: William Gladstone. The sight of the prime minister, here, his eyes ablaze with hypocritical righteousness, sent a broadside of confusion slamming through Pierce.

"You!" he choked out. It was all he could do for the moment to grapple with the shock of being invaded at such a critical moment . . . He couldn't make any sense at all of the fact that Gladstone was the one doing it. Then his gaze broadened to take in the two men who accompanied Gladstone—both older men, one moderately short and wearing a clerical collar, the other considerably taller and wearing riding clothes, a recent tan, and a furious expression. "How dare you break in on us like this? You have no right—"

"No—*you* are the one who has no right!" The tall, robust-looking man thrust forward sharply and was quickly restrained by his two companions. "Defiling my daughter—dishonoring my family—"

"I'm not defiling anyone, I am simply spending time with—" Pierce halted, glancing over his shoulder at Gabrielle, then back at the man in Gladstone's grip. "Your *daughter*?" He stared at the strong, angular features, the graying hair, and the deep-chested physique, realizing they were vaguely familiar. Memory meshed with perception, and it struck him like a thunderbolt: this was the duke of Carlisle—Gabrielle's father!

"There is obviously some mistake here," Pierce said furiously, backing toward Gabrielle with his arms out to the sides, trying to shield her from their scrutiny.

"The only mistake here, sir, is your failure to reckon with the vigilance and honor of the House of Carlisle!" the duke declared, puffing with indignation, looking every inch the outraged father. "How dare you, sir, think to trifle with my daughter?"

"*Trifle* with . . . ?" A tide of hot chagrin washed over Pierce as he thought of how readily, even eagerly, he had dismissed the idea that Gabrielle's noble paternity should make a difference in his dealings with her. After all, it hadn't mattered to Rosalind. It had never occurred to him that the duke might have other ideas.

"I have taken Gabrielle as my mistress, with her mother's full knowledge and consent," he asserted.

"M-mistress?" The duke stiffened against Gladstone's constraint, blustering, "That is a damned lie and an outrage. My daughter is no—no *harlot*. Why, I ought to call you out and shoot you down like the lying dog you are."

The sense of what was happening finally penetrated Gabrielle's double shock of being caught with Pierce in flagrant dishabille and by her *father*. It had been years since she had seen him. Had it not been for the recent portrait of him in her mother's boudoir, she might not have recognized him. She could make no sense at all of his wrathful presence here.

"No!" She scooted to the edge of the divan, clutching her clothes together with her hands. "Please—it's not his fault!" As she made to rise, her drooping petticoat slid part way down her hips, and she sank back onto the divan with her face crimson. The bishop rushed forward, peeling off his coat and wrapping it around her.

"I agreed to meet him," she said in a shame-constricted voice, staring up at the bishop's scowl, then Gladstone's grim look, and then at her father's glare of paternal indignation. "I am to blame for all of this."

"It was most assuredly *not* your fault, my girl," Gladstone declared, coming to stand over her, searching her distraught face with a grave expression. "You were betrayed by your mother and seduced by this worldly and despicable beast. What chance did you have against such treachery? I haven't had a minute's peace since I spoke with you at the Savoy. I resolved last night to do all in my power to rescue you. The Almighty knows, someone needed to do so."

"But it's true. I wanted to be his mistress. It was my choice—I agreed to it."

"You *agreed*?" the duke said. "How dare you agree to such a thing?"

"I am nineteen." She held her ground and met his gaze. "Old enough to choose for myself."

"I don't care how old you are." The duke advanced on her, taken aback by her brazen attitude. "You're my daughter . . . and no daughter of *mine* will be permitted to make a harlot of herself!"

"Can't you see what she is doing, Carlisle?" Gladstone intervened, holding the duke back by the arm. Then he turned to Gabrielle. "It's no good protecting Sandbourne, my girl. Only last night you declared to me your desire for a decent and respectable life, a marriage. You said he was helping you to find a husband. Think, child." He waved a gnarled hand, calling her state of undress into evidence and wagging his head. "Is this how he helps a young woman to find a husband and an honorable marriage?"

Gabrielle looked up at the prime minister, her eyes stinging with shame. How could she explain that until an hour ago, that was exactly what he had been doing. How could she convey in any sense the unusual relationship that had grown up between them? The uncommon respect and restraint Pierce had shown toward her? How could she explain the delicate balance of determination and desire that had existed between them . . . or the despair she felt in realizing that she would never look at another man, never feel about another man the way she felt about him? How could she explain that for one short hour, out of all the many hours they had spent together, she had relaxed her guard and embraced the passion in herself, and in him . . . and it had brought her to this?

She couldn't say it, any of it, in a way that would make them understand. So she sat, mute, her head and heart clamoring with regret and fear.

"You have affronted my personal honor, sir. Sullied my daughter beyond all recourse . . . except one." The duke confronted Pierce with his neck veins at full swell. "You shall marry her, Sandbourne, and set this right."

"M-marry her? But that's absurd." Pierce took a step back, looking as if he'd just been gored.

He turned to glare at Gabrielle, sitting in a jumble of disheveled garments, with her fair hair tumbled about her shoulders, and her lips swollen from the ardor of his kisses. Her arms were wrapped tightly about her, as if she were holding herself together. Suddenly all he could see was the shame in the haunting luminosity of her eyes. The rest of his words stuck in his throat.

"It may indeed be absurd to expect that you act the gentleman and own your responsibility for this foul disgrace," the duke declared furiously. "Nevertheless, that *is* what I demand of you." He had watched the way Pierce stared at Gabrielle, and put his own construction on

Pierce's reluctance. "I see—you thought there would be no consequences to face because she is a bastard. Well, she is not just any bastard . . . she is a *Carlisle* bastard. And as such, she surely has blood blue enough to mate with the likes of *you*."

Pierce stiffened. He was within a heartbeat of planting his fist in the duke's pompous face.

"No, please," Gabrielle said in a choked voice. "He doesn't have to marry me. Nothing happened between us. I haven't been truly ruined."

"Haven't you?" the duke said thickly, glowering at her appearance. "What decent man would want a wife who has been demeaned in such a fashion? Whose morals and judgment cannot be trusted? What man of honor would be content with"—he looked pained—"another man's *leavings*?"

The bishop stepped quickly in front of Pierce to restrain him, holding him by the shoulders and staring up into his burning eyes. "However objectionably he puts it, the duke is right, Sandbourne. You must marry the girl. In the law and in the church, it is the only remedy for such a trespass. You chose to pursue and seduce her. Now you must live with the consequences of that choice."

The calm authority of those words somehow reached through the anger and turmoil in Pierce. *Choice.* Was that what he had made? He had desired her, sought her, and pursued her until she surrendered. He had meant to make her his mistress and give her his support and protection. But, with a few brief kisses and caresses, his entire world had been turned upside down. Now he had to make her his *wife*.

He looked at Gladstone and read in the old man's eyes an unmistakable glow of satisfaction at seeing him caught in a personal disgrace. The injustice of it—being held to account, for pleasures he had not even enjoyed, by the randy old hypocrite he had intended to catch in just such a fashion. The irony of it came crashing down on him, dousing him with humiliation. He had begun by using Gabrielle to pursue Gladstone. And Gladstone had ended by using her to ruin him.

He turned back to Gabrielle, trying to make his mind work, searching for excuses, alternatives, a way out. And he realized there was none. Together, the three had the power to wreck his reputation and his political standing if he refused to marry her. The sight of her sitting there, weighted with shame, roused his conscience to fever pitch. He had intended to help her, to protect her, and he had brought her to this. If he refused to marry her, what would become of her? But if he agreed to marry her, what would become of *him*?

Anger and confusion and humiliation boiled over inside him.

"Well, it appears you'll get what you wanted after all, Gabrielle," he said to her, with a bitterly sardonic edge. "You'll soon be a married woman." He broke free of the bishop's grasp and looked down at him. "If you would do me the mercy of applying to Canterbury for a special license. The sooner it is over, the better."

He snatched his coat up off the floor and strode out, slamming the door behind him.

After the vibrations of his angry departure subsided, the duke, the bishop, and the prime minister stepped out of the room to allow Gabrielle to dress. They stood clustered in the hallway, their faces grim and eyes downcast, not speaking. After a while, the duke cleared his throat.

"This is a most painful and demeaning incident," he said grimly. "I must rely on your discretion, gentlemen, to keep the circumstances of this marriage from becoming fodder for the despicable public curiosity."

Both Gladstone and the bishop nodded in agreement. The secret would be kept, secure among the three of them.

Or so they thought.

Just down the hall, a pair of worldly eyes peered from a crack in a doorway, glowing with devilish pleasure at recognizing two of the three faces in the hall. The shouting and banging that had so alarmed the maître d' had intrigued Peter Atcheson, Lord Arundale. He had temporarily abandoned pursuit of his own pleasures to spy on the comings and goings. After a time, he saw his erstwhile companion in debauch, Sandbourne, charging from the room with his coat in his hand and his shirt half undone. And just now he caught enough of the tall gent's words to interpret what was happening. William Gladstone . . . the bishop of London . . . *the circumstances of the marriage* . . .

He fairly crowed with glee as he watched Sandbourne's delectable little "cousin" emerge from the private chamber, minutes later. Putting it all together, he closed the door and gave a wicked laugh. Sandbourne had just been caught with his breeches down and was going to have to marry the chit!

"Arundale, you beast, you're ignoring me," came the petulant voice of his companion. He turned back to the voluptuous and accommodating creature with the indecent neckline and the kohl-rimmed eyes.

"I'll make it up to you, lovey. Wait until you hear what I just saw . . ."

At the duke's insistence, Gabrielle went with him to his house in Mayfair. Still numb with shock, she descended from the coach and was bundled through a high entry hall and up a sweeping staircase, followed by the empty echoes of her footsteps on the cold marble steps. On the second floor, she was installed in a guest chamber, where—in accordance with the duke's terse decree—she would stay until he came to get her for the wedding ceremony.

She sat down miserably on the bench at the foot of the bed, watching the door close and hearing a key scraping the lock. After a few moments, she lifted her head and looked around the elegant little room—at the delicate white French furnishings, blue flocked wallpaper, and the pretty, lace-draped bed. She was in her father's house for the first time in her life . . . not as a daughter or even a guest, but as a damaged bit of goods that had to be "set right." After nineteen years of pretending she didn't exist, the duke had just swooped down on her life, claiming jurisdiction over her.

As her numbness wore off, those last awful moments in the restaurant came flooding back over her in dark, suffocating waves. Mr. Gladstone, the duke, the bishop, and Pierce . . . all arguing, posturing, discussing her as if she were an object. But the worst of it had been the accusation in Pierce's gaze when he looked at her.

The freedom and control that he so prized had been taken from him. But the choice she sought and her dream of a decent, civil, liberating marriage had been taken from her. In a moment of weakness, in a rush of desire, the die had been cast.

And what was left? A ruined bride and a bitterly resentful groom. What sort of marriage would that be?

The duke of Carlisle went barreling through the doors of Maison LeCoeur, sending Gunther racing for Gabrielle's rooms with orders to pack her things and have her maid and her bags ready to go in a quarter of an hour.

"He's early!" Rosalind cried at the sound of his voice. She jumped up from the divan in her boudoir, ripped the black silk sleeping mask from her face, and sent her maid scurrying to bring her most exotic dressing robe. But before she could change her loose-fitting tea gown, the door to her private sanctum banged open and the duke stood in the opening, looking as if he had just ridden hell-bent all the way from Africa.

"Augustus, *darling!* You're here!" She rushed to him with outstretched arms, her eyes glowing with surprise and pleasure.

"How dared you?" he thundered, stopping her in her tracks.

"How dared I what?" She stood teetering, blinking with confusion. "What is wrong, my darling?"

"How could you, Rosalind?" He paced away from her, his chest heaving and his eyes hot. "My own daughter—my very flesh and blood!"

"Your daughter? Gabrielle?" She gasped, thinking that something must have happened to her. "Is she all right? Tell me!—she isn't hurt, is she?" She hurried to his side and seized his sleeve.

"She's worse than hurt—she's ruined," he declared, shaking her hands from his arm and stalking away. "And I am told *you* are to blame."

Rosalind blanched. "Ruined? What are you talking about?"

"As I was making my way north from Portsmouth, I received an urgent message from William Gladstone saying that my daughter was in grave peril. I rushed to London and discovered that my daughter had been the victim of a foul and depraved seduction . . . by the earl of Sandbourne—one of the worst scapegraces in London. And when I confronted him—caught him in the very act—the scoundrel claimed *you* had initiated and endorsed it!"

"A seduction? That's absurd, Augustus. How could he possibly seduce her? They were already lovers . . . or were to be soon." His nostrils flared, and she realized she needed to explain. "Gabrielle is mad about him. And I believe he sincerely loves her. Why, he's courted and wooed her . . . shown her nothing but the greatest generosity and consideration. I admit that, having heard his reputation, I had reservations about his character. So I put him to the test. And he proved himself more than worthy. I gave them my blessing only a few days ago."

"Good God—you admit it openly!"

"Of course I do." The raw indignation in his eyes alarmed her. In all their years together, she had never seen him like this. "I brought her home in January, after her schooling ended and she had toured a bit. It was time to get on with seeing to her future, and I decided to find her the best situation possible: a good and gallant gentleman to take care of her and love her."

"Without a word to me," he charged. "You didn't bother to consult *me* or ask my permission or to discover what *my* plans were for her."

"*Your* plans?" Rosalind gasped. "You've never had plans for her—you've never even acknowledged her." As the shock of his anger wore off, she began to think. "You never asked about her, and whenever we were in Paris and I mentioned visiting her at her school, you seemed bored or impatient and refused to accompany me."

"I knew perfectly well where she was!" the duke blustered, red-faced. "I—I was not without responsibility toward her. If you'll remember, I *paid* for that fancy school."

"No! You paid for *me*!" Rosalind swayed closer, her eyes blazing, her chest heaving. "*I* paid for the school! She was always a LeCoeur . . . my daughter, my responsibility. You made that quite clear when she was born, and I bowed to your feelings and kept her out of your way. I have always taken that responsibility quite seriously, including finding her a suitable protector—"

"A *protector*?" He sputtered. "You sought to turn my daughter—my own precious seed—into a common *harlot*.

And worse, you gave her to a man whose only redeeming feature is the depths of his pockets." He stalked closer to her with his eyes burning. "I was hauled to The Montmortaine by none other than the prime minister himself. And in front of him and a bishop of the church, I was forced to witness the sight of my own daughter, half naked, in the arms of a high-living swine. I've never been so humiliated in my life."

He was humiliated? What about Gabrielle? By his account, he and those others had burst in on Gabrielle and the earl while they were making love, possibly even for the very first time.

"My poor Gabby—she must have been mortified!" She grabbed the duke's arm. "Where is she? What's happened to her? I have to go to her."

"She is at my house," he declared with a dreadful calm, "where she will stay . . . until the vows are duly and legally spoken."

"Vows? What vows?"

"Marriage vows. He's a high-living rake who has seduced the girl. Without vows she is little more than a tart to him. She is being married by special license, as quickly as it can be arranged. Possibly a day or two . . . as soon as an agreement can be reached. I've come to collect her things and her maid."

Rosalind stood looking at him, feeling the cold that had gripped her heart beginning to spreading through the rest of her. She had never seen him like this . . . so righteous and proper and possessive. So judgmental.

Without vows she is little more than a tart. Those words turned over and over in her head, and she felt them somehow turning and shifting the earth under her feet. "But, Augustus, *we* have never spoken marriage vows . . ."

"Don't be absurd, Rosalind." He scowled furiously. "You are my mistress."

"I see." She could scarcely breathe.

He squared his shoulders and started for the door. "The vows will be read by the bishop of London, in one of the chapels . . . as early as tomorrow. I shall send word when it is done."

"When it is done?" She hurried to intercept him. "What do you mean?" But from the way he refused to meet her eyes, she knew. "You mean that I shouldn't attend the wedding." She went weak in the knees and caught herself on the back of a nearby chair. Her world was suddenly reeling. "But I'm her *mother*."

"For God's sake, Rosalind, show a bit of sense," he said with a final, imperious blast. "She is marrying an *earl*."

He strode out the door with his patrician pride at full billow. The sound of him bellowing orders to Gunther and the maids drifted back to her through the open door. The scurrying and thudding of feet and the clank and swoosh of trunks continued for some time. And then all was quiet— hideously quiet.

Rosalind stood just as he left her, motionless, frozen in disbelief.

She might be Gabrielle's mother, he had just informed her, but she was—first and foremost—his mistress. And mistresses were forbidden to appear at society weddings, even if they were the mother of the bride.

"My God. After all these years . . ." She swayed and had to catch herself to keep from falling. "He's treating me like a common tart!"

Pierce went straight from The Montmortaine to his club, ensconced himself in the bar, and proceeded to work his way to the bottom of several stout brandies. The barman, watching Pierce's intake and knowing his usual self-imposed limits, took it upon himself to find Pierce a bed in the sleeping rooms above and to steer him into it. Thus it was nearly noon next day before he arrived once more at his own house in Hyde Park.

There was a healthy growth of beard on his face, his hair was rumpled, his eyes were bloodshot, and he was walking as if he were afraid his head would topple from his shoulders at any minute. But his racked exterior was only a pale reflection of the damage the previous day had wrought inside him. Guilt, anger, humiliation, indignation, chagrin, regret, mawkish melancholy . . . there wasn't a single dread emotion in the entire human repertoire that he hadn't wallowed through in the night just past. And each had left behind some trace of itself in passing.

That Gladstone had humiliated him—trumped him at his own game—was bad enough. But that he had used Gabrielle to do so made it damn near intolerable.

Somewhere in the middle of his second brandy the previous night, while going over and over the disaster in his mind, he realized that the old man had spoken to Gabrielle of the Savoy and of the fact that Pierce had offered to help her find a husband. Both were things Gladstone would have known only if he had seen and spoken to her at the theater. With further thought, Pierce realized that Gladstone couldn't have known where they were going to be today. He hadn't even told Gabrielle his plans for the afternoon. The old man must have set someone to watch them . . . looking for an opportunity to "rescue" Gabrielle.

The fact that he had been watched and followed in an attempt to discredit him, sent a bolt of outrage through him. It was worse than ungentlemanly. It was low and cowardly. It was mean-spirited and calculating. It was patently *un-British*. For the moment, it escaped him that he had done the very same thing to Gladstone.

But, if truth be told, the worst part of the entire thing was that the old man had used Gabrielle to get to him. He had seen her with Pierce and plied his hypocritical "rescue" nonsense with her to . . . When a further possibility occurred to him, he felt as if all the blood in his body had drained to his feet.

Had she been a part of a scheme by Gladstone, from the beginning? A plot to humiliate him socially and discredit him politically? What could be more damaging than the scandal of a seduction and a forced marriage? He thought of Gabrielle and her mother and the entire crazy situation—limericks and chess and flowers and that bizarre courtship. Was the "command romance" all just an elaborate ruse? Or had Gabrielle been used as well, in a cold-blooded attempt to wreck his career?

As he entered his house, his stomach was roiling, his head was throbbing . . . and there wasn't an answer in sight. He was in no mood for talk or tension or temper, but the instant he set foot in the dining room, he was confronted by all three in the person of his mother. She was arranging flowers on the main table. At the sight of him, she stopped to give him a thorough looking over.

"You could at least shave and change your clothes . . . maintain a pretense of respectability after spending an entire night in God knows what depravity."

He halted halfway across the dining room, straining for control of his volatile mood. "Is that any way to speak to your only son when he is about to make you the happiest woman alive?" he snarled.

"What are you talking about?"

"You're getting your heart's desire. I'm going to be married," he announced, trying not to choke on the word. He reached for the bell, thinking that her startled look was at least some compensation for the trauma and upheaval he was going through.

"Married? To whom?" She dropped the flowers in her hands.

"Yes, your lordship?" The butler stepped through the door from the kitchens.

"I want a 'morning after' breakfast," Pierce ordered. "In my chambers. I'm going upstairs to have a bath and a bit of rest." He cast a meaningful glare at his mother. "I don't want to be disturbed for the rest of the day . . . unless it's a message from my solicitors or the bishop." The butler nodded and withdrew.

"I don't believe you," Beatrice said. "What eligible woman of good birth and breeding would possibly agree to marry you?"

A muscle in his jaw jumped as he constrained himself. "It will be very quick—a day or two at most. By special license. You'll just have time to buy a new hat, if you hurry." He started for the door.

"I demand to know who she is—this woman you're marrying!" But for all her bravado, she gripped the edge of the table, bracing for the worst.

He paused at the threshold. "I am marrying my mistress."

As he left the room, Beatrice took the vapors for the first time in weeks.

More than an hour later, lying on the reclining bench in her chambers with a vial of salts in her hand and a cold cloth on her forehead, Beatrice had managed to battle through her shock and her anger enough to think about it. He was marrying his mistress? Good Lord, she hadn't even known he *had* a mistress!

The wretch—he was doing it on purpose, just to spite her.

But on second thought, she realized that there must be more involved. It was one thing to have a mistress; many men did so without the slightest blemish upon their reputations. But it was another thing entirely to marry one. It smacked of poor judgment at best, weak or depraved character at worst. Men who married their mistresses were made laughingstocks in proper society . . . considered gullible or hopelessly entangled in a woman's petticoats.

Pierce knew that just as well as she did. And while he would go a long way to annoy her, she knew he was not one to cut off his nose to spite his face.

That meant there was more to it. The more she thought about it, the more certain she became. And she determined to learn just what had happened between Pierce and his bit of fluff that gave this woman a power over him that his mother had never managed to wield.

14

Gabrielle's wedding day dawned gray, wet, and depressing, and went steadily downhill from there. Rue spent two hours fixing her hair and helping her dress, attending to every detail of her appearance . . . only to have the duke declare that a white dress, even a deep cream white with a burgundy underskirt and burgundy velvet trim, was wholly inappropriate.

"I liked it better when I didn't have a father," she muttered to Rue, as he hauled out her pale blue satin and ordered her to wear it, instead.

The carriage ride was suffered in abject silence, and when they arrived at the church—St. Mary's of the Something-or-other—it was raining so hard that they had to wait in the carriage until the torrent subsided. She fleetingly recalled another rainstorm, one that had started Pierce and herself on the way to ruin . . . and the altar.

By the time the coachman handed her down to the church steps and helped her to the doors, she was feeling light-headed and a bit sick at her stomach. Her father grabbed her by the elbow and propelled her into the vestibule. As he steered her down the aisle, she realized Pierce was not yet present. At the front of the church the bishop waited, along with William Gladstone, an older woman whom Gabrielle recognized as Gladstone's "Catherine," and another, thickset woman in a dark gray dress and a stylish feathered hat.

It was eerily quiet in the chapel. The sound of Gabrielle's heels on the slate floor echoed about the stone walls. She felt conspicuous and guilty and utterly friendless. Her heart sank a bit lower as the duke edged away from her, as if separating himself from the taint of her infamy, but kept a firm hand on her elbow.

The bishop did his best to greet her warmly, which was generous of him, considering that when he last glimpsed her she had been half clothed and bearing passion's evidence plainly on her face. He spoke quietly to her, asking if she was prepared and if she wished anything special read. When she looked up, she found the woman in gray glaring at her with a ferocity akin to a slap in the face.

There was a creak of hinges at the side door. Pierce was entering the church. He stood a moment, lowering an umbrella and brushing rain from his sleeve. His dark eyes and chiseled features, once so familiar to her, seemed perfectly unreadable as his eyes met hers.

After terse greetings, they approached the altar railing, where the bishop directed them to their appropriate positions.

Just as he opened his service book, Gabrielle's name

rang out from the back. Gabrielle turned in surprise and found her mother sailing down the aisle toward her, dressed in a buttercup yellow floral silk and a yellow picture hat, at least a yard across, dripping with yellow silk roses and green satin ribbons.

To Gabrielle, Rosalind looked like the veriest breath of spring as she approached with open arms and a beaming smile. It was the first bit of human warmth Gabrielle had been offered in three days. Without a thought for possible consequences, she wrenched free of the duke's grasp and was soon caught up in her mother's embrace.

"Are you all right, Gabby?" Rosalind whispered in a strained voice, then after a moment thrust her back to look at her. When Gabrielle nodded, Rosalind gave a sigh of relief and scowled at Gabrielle's simple dress. "Ye gods— you're being married in *that*?"

"The duke chose it." Gabrielle was blinking away excess moisture in her eyes.

"Well, that explains it," Rosalind said, with a tight smile.

"I didn't think you would come," Gabrielle whispered. "Knowing how you feel about marriage . . ."

"Not come?" Rosalind cupped Gabrielle's cheek in her hand. "However I feel about marriage, my feelings about *you* are far stronger." She paused to swallow the emotion that clogged her throat. "Go now, my dear, and say your vows and become a wife. That is what you said you wanted, after all."

"But it's not what *he* wanted," Gabrielle whispered, looking so miserable that Rosalind sighed and leaned close to her ear.

"Of course not. He'll get what *he* wanted tonight. Now, you must promise me that tonight you will wear nothing but a bedsheet and a smile." She squeezed Gabrielle's shoulders. *"Promise me."*

"I promise," Gabrielle murmured, blushing.

When the startled bishop asked who the latecomer might be, Rosalind spoke for herself in a clear and ringing voice: "I am Rosalind LeCoeur, the mother of the bride." The bishop glanced at the red-faced duke, then asked Rosalind to have a seat in the first pew on the left side. Rosalind noticed the woman wearing the dreadfully drab gray satin dress and a fierce scowl occupying the first pew on the right. She gave the woman a defiantly cheerful smile.

There were no more interruptions as the bishop called the company to order and began the service of marriage. The duke placed Gabrielle's hand in Pierce's and stepped back, transferring his recently assumed ownership and authority over her to Pierce.

Gabrielle found herself standing beside him, feeling small and powerless and overwhelmed by the promises she was required to make. Love, honor, and obey. What did that mean? To have and to hold, in sickness and in health, in wealth and in poverty . . . she was promising to abide with him, to care for him, to hold his honor and his comfort and his trust as she would her own?

There was a pause, and Pierce took her by the shoulders and turned her to him, startling her from her swirling thoughts. In something of a daze, she watched him remove her glove and place on her finger a gold ring set with a sizable ruby surrounded by small diamonds. In full, clear voice, he promised to be faithful and diligent as a husband and to cherish her always in holy Christian love.

She looked up into his eyes. Dark eyes. Turbulent eyes. Yet, in their depths, she glimpsed another, deeper current of feeling . . . one she was relieved to recognize, one she had touched and known. Tenderness. Warmth. Passion.

This was not just a "husband," she realized, this was *Pierce*. Pierce who brought her fancy French shoes. Pierce who sang with her and made her promise to write him limericks and to name her firstborn after him. Pierce who listened to her, and laughed at her and with her, and taught her that she did have passions. Pierce who held her when she cried.

Could she honor him . . . cherish him . . . abide with him? The knot of tension in her stomach began to relax. In the midst of those daunting promises, she managed a tenuous smile. There was no one on earth she would rather "abide" with.

Pierce stood staring down into her blue eyes, into her warming, trusting face . . . and felt a loosening in the control he had imposed on himself for today's events. He had spent most of the morning preparing himself to face Gladstone, the bishop, his mother, the duke . . . and realized the moment he set foot in the church that the one he hadn't prepared for—the one he hadn't even allowed himself to think about—was the one against whom he most needed a defense. Gabrielle.

There she stood in her blue dress with her pert hat and demure veil, promising to love and honor and obey him . . . to cherish him in all the conditions of their lives. Those summer-sky eyes could almost make him forget all about Gladstone and humiliation and treachery and the fact that he was being forced into a trap he had long regarded as only a half step above oblivion. Almost.

He looked up and caught sight of Gladstone's stare. The disgrace and humiliation of his situation were resurrected, fresh and intensely painful, in his mind. And it all had begun with *her*.

When the bishop pronounced them man and wife, he hesitated in suggesting the groom kiss his bride. But Pierce needed no prompting. He seized Gabrielle by the shoulders and gave her a long and lusty kiss that had a number of purposes . . . defiance, expression of anger and frustration, declaration of possession, assumption of authority . . . everything, in fact, except pleasure.

Then he stepped back and, with his next breath, demanded the papers and the register to sign. When that was done, he turned to the witnesses.

"My bride and I will be departing shortly for Sussex," he announced sardonically. "I am sure you all will understand that the schedule leaves no time for the customary wedding breakfast." With a savage glare at Gladstone and a bitter look at his mother, he scooped Gabrielle up in his arms and carried her out of the church.

As he kicked open the outer doors and headed for the carriage, her foot bumped against the railing then brushed one of the columns on the front portico of the church. "Pierce, please—" she gasped, but at that moment he stepped out into the cold rain and she had to shield her face from the cold drops. When he stood her on the carriage step, she balked at entering and pointed back to the church doors.

"My shoe—I lost my shoe!"

"I'm getting soaked—" He pushed her inside, then climbed in after her.

"But my shoe—" she said, scrambling to the cross seat and peering anxiously out the rain-streaked carriage window, trying to locate the shoe on the portico. When he rapped on the carriage roof and the coach lurched into motion, she stared at him with genuine distress.

"It's a shoe, Gabrielle," he said with icy impatience. "You have others."

"Not like that one," she said, staring at him as if seeing a stranger. Then she reached down and plucked the other one from her foot and tucked it protectively into her crossed arms. It was a dainty party slipper with spool heels . . . made of white satin brocade . . . trimmed with bows and blue ribbon rosettes. He looked up at her with a furious expression, then jerked his head and fixed his gaze on the window.

"Damnation."

She hugged the shoe to her, battling back tears of frustration, and knew beyond all doubt that in gaining a husband, she had just lost her dearest friend.

After a short stop at Pierce's Hyde Park house, where Pierce took care of several details, including the posting of a terse but dignified marriage announcement to *The Times*, they did indeed leave for Pierce's estate in Sussex. Gabrielle protested that she had to wait for her maid and her baggage to arrive from her father's house, but he informed her that he had already sent a carriage to collect them and carry them straight on to Thorndike, his family home. Then when she insisted she could not go anywhere without shoes on her feet, he sent his houseman into his mother's wardrobe to borrow a pair for her to wear. They were underway in less than an hour.

In the carriage, Pierce produced a blanket and a pillow and suggested that, since the trip would take at least seven hours, she get some rest.

"Pierce, please . . . I think we should talk."

"I despise long carriage trips—they put me in a foul mood. And the only thing I hate worse than the ride is idle chatter during it. Go to sleep, Gabrielle."

Distraught at his deep anger and his high-handed manner, she realized that pressing him now would only make things worse. She removed her hat, wrapped up in the blanket, all the way to her chin, and tried to do exactly what he suggested, rest. Sleep didn't come easily; her thoughts and feelings were chaotic, and the feel of his constant gaze on her was difficult to bear. But at length the rocking and jostling of the coach lulled her into a troubled sleep.

She didn't awaken until Pierce gave her shoulder a shake and announced that they would soon arrive. The carriage was slowing and swaying as it executed the final turns, and she sat up, blinking, and looked out the darkened windows. In the distance, through a stand of old trees, she could see house lights. As they drew nearer, she made out the shape of a stately Queen Anne house nestled in a rolling countryside and surrounded by clumps of trees. When they reached the front court, a number of servants came hurrying out the front doors to greet them. They had received word of his marriage and impending arrival when the coach that carried Rue and Gabrielle's baggage arrived earlier. And for most of the afternoon they had been busy cleaning, polishing, and preparing for their master and new mistress.

Pierce lifted her down onto the gravel drive and introduced her to Onslow the butler, Frieda the housekeeper, Millie the cook, and Old Stanch, the head of the stables. He declared that she would meet the others later, and ushered her inside. With a hand clamped tightly on her elbow, he directed her through the soaring center hall with its crystal chandelier, split staircase, and marble floors, and up the stairs to the portrait-lined gallery that ringed the hall. It was a beautiful house, she thought, solidly built and tastefully decorated, at least what she was so far permitted to see of it.

He showed her to a stately bedchamber filled with somewhat oversized furnishings and a massive bed bearing a gilded crest at the head. After laying down orders for her to bathe and rest before dinner, he turned and walked out.

She stood in the middle of the room, holding the hat she hadn't had time to put on, feeling confused and abandoned and guilty. He was furious with her . . . undoubtedly blamed her for the whole affair. And he was probably right. It was her fault.

In her moment of truth, confronted with that most primal of decisions, she had chosen *passion,* and from that moment on, she had lost all control of her life. Since then, she had been pushed and pulled about; ordered to "sit," "stand," and "stay" like the veriest hound; dragged, carried about, and dumped in a bedchamber like a piece of baggage. She had been told what to wear, what to say, what to sign . . . and now was being told when to sleep, when to bathe, when to rest . . .

Once she had believed that marriage would bring her a bit of freedom, the chance to be her own person. But that was before she dabbled in passion and as a result had been forced to marry Pierce. The man she had once considered her closest friend had been made her lord and master, and now was turning out to be a tyrant. She understood too well that *marriage* was what had worked that devastating change in him.

The door latch clicked, and she looked up to find Rue coming toward her with a sympathetic expression. When she put out her hands, Rue took them and smiled at her.

"It is not so bad, *chérie,*" the Frenchwoman said tartly. "At least this great pile of rocks has piped in water."

At that moment, the fledgling tyrant was pacing the walnut-paneled library on the floor below, trying to expunge the distress in Gabrielle's eyes from his mind and conscience.

He had just had several long hours in the coach to think about his situation and put it into perspective. What he had to do, he saw quite clearly, was to seize control and exert proper husbandly authority from the start. She had managed to get him to marry her, but that didn't mean she had the upper hand.

That was what women wanted, he knew—the upper hand with a man. It was their way of exerting control over the world around them. They might not have the vote or the right to own property or to succession to titles, but as long as they had men to control and manipulate, they were far from powerless. That was the entire point of marriage, he had realized some time ago—snaring men through their own weakness and then gaining control of their money, their passions, and their emotions.

That was exactly what his mother had done to his father—demanded and berated and usurped, until the lusty and independent earl left her to establish a separate life altogether. It hadn't escaped Pierce that Gabrielle bore more than a passing similarity to his ruthlessly proper and respectability-obsessed mother. And he didn't intend to let what happened to his father happen to him.

Just thinking about it in such logical and forthright terms made Pierce feel a great deal better. He had come across clever, contriving, even formidable women before, and he'd managed to escape their snares. In fact, he'd *lost* control with Gabrielle precisely because she didn't seem to *have* any control—over him or anything else. He hadn't seen that her subtle appeals to his rebellious spirit and her neatly timed surrenders to his sensual enticements were slowly lowering his own defenses . . . until it was too late, and he was trapped.

But he saw it now. The clever chit. And he was going to use that knowledge to his advantage. If he had to be married, it would be on his own blessed terms.

The warm bath that should have been soothing wasn't. The rest that should have restored her didn't. And Rue's usually reassuring chatter wasn't at all reassuring. All Gabrielle could think about was the night ahead, the seven-foot bed looming in the midst of the chamber and the look in Pierce's eye as he exited earlier. By the time he arrived, she was as tense and fragile as a new bowstring.

He acknowledged her with a nod, then strolled to the

fireplace and leaned an arm on the mantel as he watched the old butler and the other servants trundle in the food and lay the table with linen, china, and silver. He had changed into a loose-fitting jacket and removed his collar and tie. By the glow of candlelight, he looked bronzed and powerful—consummately sensual and in control. She had difficulty getting her breath.

When the door closed behind the servant, he held the chair for her and let her know that he, too, was recalling what happened the last time they sat at a table together. "I doubt we'll be interrupted this time."

She took a seat and felt him pause behind her chair for a moment before taking his seat across from her. He served the food and poured the wine from the cart by the table, and they spoke in single syllables until the main course. This was her wedding supper, she thought dismally, and there was only tension between her and the man with whom she would share her life. The pain of that realization made her determined to try to do something about it.

"Your house is beautiful," she said, in a conciliatory tone. "And the servants have been both diligent and pleasant."

"Yes, they are. Something of a miracle, actually, since they have to put up with my mother for months at a time." He looked up with a cool smile. "Did I mention that she lives both here and in my city house? Unavoidable, really. She owns a considerable interest in both houses." He cut his beef roast, stuffed it into his mouth, and chewed for a moment. "By the way . . . you mustn't be put off by the way she calls you 'that tart.' I'm sure she'll get over that in a few years, and the two of you will get on famously."

She couldn't swallow what was in her mouth. It took three sips of wine before she managed to get it down. "Was she the lady in gray, at the church?"

"She was." He spooned the creamed potatoes into his

mouth and gave a sigh of satisfaction. "That was a new hat she was wearing too. Quite an honor, actually. She seldom spends money on 'fripperies.' Very frugal sort, my mother. Makes Onslow reboil the tea for belowstairs. Knits tea cozies and potholders out of all her end skeins." He took a long drink of his wine and gave her an irritating smile.

"And she has rather fixed ideas about proper behavior for ladies. No riding horseback for a female in her household. And no spirits for females under forty. She's not overly keen on piano music. And she believes that a woman without a cap is a . . . well . . . not respectable. But her greatest loathing is reserved for people who laugh too much and for *loose women*." He smiled and took a huge bite of buttered bread. "Just a few items to keep in mind . . . as you 'settle in' here at Thorndike."

But it was not the bread or the wine that made him smile. The glare his mother had given Gabrielle at the vows that morning had indeed branded her "that tart." Now, reboiling tea and knitting potholders, women in caps and no piano music—he was purposefully trying to intimidate her. And—*curse his black heart*—it was working.

"Don't you care for rarebit?" he asked, gesturing to her untouched plate. "Pity. It's one of Millie's specialties. And what with my mother's notorious cheese paring, she seldom gets the chance to cook it."

Her heart was pounding, her hands were icy; she simply had to say something.

"Pierce . . . I'm sorry about all this." She concentrated on keeping her voice low and level. "I didn't want this any more than you did."

"Didn't you?" He put down his fork and knife and sat back, his genial taunting instantly gone. "I find that hard to believe. But then I have only myself to blame. You stated quite plainly, from the start, that marriage was your goal. I was just distracted enough by your novelty, and arrogant enough about my own experience with women, to actually believe that your designs were on somebody else."

"They *were* on somebody else . . . *anybody* else!" she declared, irritably, clenching her cold hands in her lap, seeing the full range and depths of his suspicions and appalled by them. "You're not exactly the husband I had in mind, you know. You're much too worldly and unpredictable and carnal and arrogant . . . Merciful heaven, you're arrogant. You know what my mother's friends called you? Rue told me. 'Temptation on the hoof.' *Aggravation* on the hoof is more like it. *Tyrant* on the hoof also comes to mind. I can see now why the prime minister wanted to protect me from you. My only regret is that he didn't succeed."

"Oh, he succeeded, all right. He did exactly what he intended to do all along . . . humiliate me. What I want to know is: Was the marriage part his idea or yours?"

She stared at him, stunned by the implication that she and Gladstone had conspired together against him. After all the time she and Pierce had spent together and the things they had shared with one another . . . how could he think such things about her? The ease with which his view of her had been poisoned by his contempt for Gladstone made her want to shake him.

"Over and over, I've told you the truth and you haven't believed me. I told you that Mr. Gladstone tried to rescue me, that he preached at me and fed me cocoa and biscuits . . . You didn't believe me. I told you my mother insisted that I take a lover . . . You didn't believe that. I told you I had a plan to look for a husband . . . You scoffed until you saw it all with your own two eyes. You've disbelieved nearly everything I've ever said to you. Why should I bother to tell you the truth again?"

"Because I want to hear your explanation," he said,

leaning forward, his eyes glinting darkly. "Because I find your fictions . . . entertaining."

She jerked her chin back, feeling as if she'd just been slapped. "Then, you'll have to find another diversion," she said, tucking her arms around her waist. "I'm not in the mood, just now, to be reviled and pilloried as a schemer and a liar."

"You did see Gladstone at the Savoy that night," he charged.

After a long, volatile moment she answered.

"Yes."

"You told him I was helping you find a husband."

"Yes. And he told me you were a bounder and a beast, and that I was in danger." She gave him a furious look from the corner of her eye. "I should have listened."

"Why didn't you? Because I was too wealthy and noble a 'prospect' to let get away?" he said with a taunting edge.

"No." She looked down at her plate, refusing to say more. After a few moments he pushed his chair back forcefully and strode to the fireplace. When she looked up, he was standing there with his legs braced and his arms crossed, staring at her.

"Why didn't you listen to him?"

How could she admit that she had thought he was generous and noble and compassionate and genuinely decent? That she was grateful for the restraint and the respect he had shown her? That she trusted him? That she was crazy about him? Instead, she gave him another truth . . . one a good bit less threatening.

"For the same reason I didn't tell you I had seen him. Because it was clear to me that he was just as determined to be wrong about you as you were to be wrong about him. Nothing I said about you made a difference to him, even though it was entirely the truth." When it struck her, she couldn't keep from saying it. "Come to think of it, you and

Mr. Gladstone are really very much alike." The flare of anger in his eyes was immensely satisfying. "You're determined to believe he is a hypocrite and a debauchee, despite the fact that he has tried three times—in his own way—to rescue me. And he refuses to believe that you could possibly behave in a decent and compassionate and helpful way . . . or that you could possibly be my friend."

Fearing she might have already revealed too much, she reached for her wine and took a drink, welcoming the warmth that seeped through her. When she looked up, he was standing closer, and she quickly rose and put her chair between them.

The dark, unreadable expression on his face worried her. But whatever he had in mind, she was determined that he would at least hear the truth from her.

"Both you and Mr. Gladstone are more than eager to judge something by its outward appearance. But things are not always what they seem. I should think you, of all people, would know that. Who in their right mind would believe that you and I spent hours locked away together and were not lovers? Yet, it was true. Who would believe that while you and I were out alone together in your carriage all we did was talk and look for a husband for me? But that was just what we did." The fierceness in his face made her stomach quiver with dread, but she went on.

"And who would believe, looking at us now, that for a brief while we were really, truly friends?" She slid her gaze to his and her knees weakened. "But we were." Her voice dropped to a dry whisper. "At least, I thought we were. And while it might look to you as if I conspired and schemed against you, I swear to you, I did not. I would never have done that to you, Pierce. Or to me." The smile she gave him was self-mocking and tempered with pain. "You see . . . I knew you well enough to know that you would make a much better friend than a husband."

He knew it was a mistake to stand there listening to her. Her quiet, melodious voice. And her logic. And—dear God—she had a way with words. It just wasn't possible to pull away. She was so damned appealing. And so earnest. And with every word she pulled up memories inside him: the time they spent together, the secrets and the laughter they shared. She called him a friend, and there was genuine regret in her voice. It was that trace of sadness, that longing for what had once been between them, that finally got to him.

Damn her. She *had* been his friend.

Now she was his wife.

Confusion roiled powerfully in him. Suddenly all he could see was the luscious pout of her mouth, the soft curves of her breasts. Suddenly all he could remember was the constant tension of wanting that he had kept in perilous balance with the pleasures of anticipation. All he could think was that tonight, the anticipation was finally over. He had the right—the obligation—to take her. Tonight she would be his. And tomorrow, with body sated and sanity restored, he could get on with his life.

An explosion of heat roared through his blood.

"You judge things by appearances too, sweetheart," he said, edging closer. "What makes you so sure you won't like me as a husband? I may have hidden abilities . . . secret assets. What may seem like arrogance may be well-deserved confidence. What seems like worldliness may be experience that will serve you well. And what seems 'unpredictable' may keep you happily entertained tonight."

He came closer . . . until he was only a foot away . . . close, but not close enough.

"Try me as a husband, sweetness," his voice dropped to a husky, irresistible throb. "I might surprise you."

15

The glint in his eyes, the subtle tightening of his shoulders, the way his lips parted and his hands clenched at his sides . . . She read those signs of arousal and realized that her lips felt thicker and more sensitive and her skin was warming in response. The sharpness of his tone and his accusations were being softened and blurred by the desire rising between them. How they had come to this point, face to face, in his bedchamber, in his house, didn't seem to matter as much as the fact that they were alone, at last, and aware of each other in the most elemental and compelling way . . . as a man, as a woman.

The tips of her breasts began to tingle, and deep in her body, that delicious tightening sensation was occurring again. With him only a foot away, looking at her as if she were a chocolate truffle, she was suddenly feeling echoes of all the wild and erotic sensations she had experienced three days before. It was as if her arousal had been just frozen in time, awaiting the proper moment and the right provocation to resume.

Her shoulders softened, and the dark centers of her eyes widened. Her lips reddened; she licked them, staring at his. He watched with an unholy surge of pleasure as she responded to the suggestion in his voice and his intensifying gaze. She wanted him. And he wanted her.

Perhaps she leaned toward him first; or perhaps he reached for her. They were suddenly in each other's arms, pressed hard together, kissing hungrily at first, then more responsively. He shifted his feet further apart to brace himself, and she arched slightly to rub the aching tips of her breasts against his ribs. He ran his hands roughly over her, claiming every part of her, feeling her shape through her garments, possessing the softness of her body and the willingness of her heart. She slipped her hands inside his jacket, ran them along his waist and up his back, absorbing some of his determined heat.

She felt the hard swelling of his desire against her body and realized from its proximity to her own sensitive woman's flesh that it would ultimately satisfy her intensifying desires. She pressed harder against it, against him, wanting to be closer, wanting to learn all there was to know . . . wanting to try him as a husband and a mate.

He felt the seeking movements of her body against his and drew back long enough to pull her to the bed. There he sat down and pulled her onto the feather mattress beside him. In a blink she was on her back with him braced over her, smiling.

"I think it's only fair to warn you, your lordship . . . you may be in for a disappointment. I'm not very skilled at this sort of thing," she said, her eyes glowing, asking him to remember. His grin broadened. Apparently he did remember. "It's not as if my mother hasn't tried to instruct me . . ." She stiffened with her hands against his chest. "Wait—I'm supposed to take off my clothes."

"We'll get around to that," he murmured.

"No, I think I'm supposed to do it . . . I promised."

"Promised whom?" He scowled, puzzled.

"My mother," she declared, pushing him aside, sitting up, and sliding to the floor beside the high bed. "She made me promise I would wear nothing but a bedsheet and a smile for you."

"God. I might have known."

"She said you should get what you want tonight."

"Remind me to thank her. Someday." He lay back with his head propped on his elbow, watching her fumble with her buttons and lacing.

"She said it's only fair, and I suppose she's right." She shed her bodice, then worked the button of her skirt and the ties of her petticoats, stepping out of her shoes and skirts all at once. Then she paused, in her corset, drawers, and stockings, and chewed the corner of her lip. "I do need a sheet . . ." She looked a little uncomfortable. "I'm not sure I can do this . . . without one."

Shortly he was ripping back the covers and dragging one huge linen sheet from the bed. After a few contortions, she managed to shed her corset cover and corset.

"Do you think you could . . . hold up the sheet for me?" She blushed, when he laughed. "Well, I am just learning."

"And rather quickly, I might add." He held the sheet up and watched the shadow she cast, with the candles behind her. She drew off her camisole, then slid her drawers down her hips and stepped out of them. He watched the tantalizing outline of her bare body, mesmerized, as she rolled her stockings down her legs, one at a time. Her shadow shrank as she came to take the sheet from him and wrap it around her.

She stepped back and smiled. "There." Then she thought of her hair and reached up to check it for pins. "Shall I take down my hair, or are you supposed to do it?"

"I don't think there are hard and fast rules for such things. At least there had better not be. Come here." When she padded over to him in her bare feet, kicking her sheet out of the way, he grinned and told her to stand still. Sinking his fingers into her hair, he took a deep breath and pulled pins, one after another, handing them to her. When her hair was a mass of curls around her shoulders, he took a hot breath, snatched her up, and bore her back onto the bed.

The hairpins in her hand went flying as he covered her sheet-clad body with his and captured her mouth in a kiss that made her toes curl and her fingers dig into his shoulders. Soon his clothes were on the floor beside the bed, and he was working his way inside her sheet with her.

The sight and feel of his big, hot body against hers should have been at least a little shocking. She had never imagined seeing a man without his clothes, or being naked herself in a man's presence. But somehow, she knew this wasn't "a man," this was "Pierce." And his body was long and hard . . . so different from hers, so reassuringly like *him*. The broad mounds of his chest, the powerful columns up the middle of his back, and the sleek caps of muscles at the top of each shoulder fascinated her. Everything about him was as she might have expected: solid and beautifully tapered. The textures of him beckoned to her fingers . . . from his silky lips, to the faint scratchiness of his jaw, to the crisp hair that trickled down his chest. She loved the way the sinews of his hands worked as his fingers closed possessively over her breast.

He seemed to know exactly where to touch her, how to caress her, until her body felt like a deep and spreading pool of liquid heat, simmering with need and response.

"You're so beautifully curved," he murmured, running a finger along the outer curve of her breast. "And marvelously responsive." He brushed his palm over her nipple in circles, around and around, watching her shiver in response. Then he raked those same inquisitive fingers down her side and watched her squirm. "*Ummm* . . . ticklish too, and prone to laugh when embarrassed." When she pulled his head down to hers and ran her lips over his, he hesitated for a moment, murmuring, "And so delectably eager," before giving her the kiss she wanted.

He kissed and nipped and caressed his way down her body. His hand slid intimately across the curls at the base of her belly, and she stilled, concentrating on that sensation, remembering. Gradually, his fingers slid along that hot, sensitive cleft . . . parting, stroking, teasing. She shivered and tilted her pelvis, pressing against his hand. Her eyes were closed, her breathing shallow as he found the aching center of her response. With each stroke of his fingers around that burning pleasure point, chords of response vibrated all through her. Pleasure seeped along every nerve and fiber, thick and clinging, building continually within her. The slow, hypnotizing circles made by his hand gradually heightened and tightened her arousal . . . lifting her . . . higher . . .

Suddenly, she was propelled upward on a swell of sensation and flung through an unknown barrier. Her overstuffed senses seemed to burst and shatter as shock waves of sensation shuddered through her. She arched and contracted, writhing against his hand, scarcely able to breathe, numbed to all but those powerful torrents of pleasure.

As wave after wave of pleasure broke through her, he

cradled her against him, murmuring reassurances and stroking her hair. Slowly the storm in her gave way to a soft, permeating ache in her deepest core, a wanting not satisfied by the gale of pleasure she had just experienced. Somehow he understood what was happening in her . . . for he gave her a sultry, dark-eyed smile and slid his body over hers.

The feel of his weight, pressed all along the length of her body, satisfied part of her craving for the feel of him. But it wasn't until he fitted his swollen flesh against her burning center that she understood the tightness, the tension lingering in her loins. With slow, gentle thrusts, he entered her lush receptive heat, pausing here and there to kiss away the anxiety caused by those foreign sensations. This was what she had wanted and needed—this joining, this sheathing of his flesh in hers.

It was stunning, the pleasure, the warmth, the sense of oneness she felt with him. She looked up into his eyes, reading in him the same desire, the same pleasure she was feeling. Instinctively, she met his deepening thrusts, giving herself to him without reserve, wanting his pleasure as much as she wanted her own. They moved together in a slow, mesmerizing crescendo of loving, savoring the glide of flesh on flesh, exploring each sweet rush of sensation. That same breathtaking tension built in her loins, only sharper, keener. And when she shattered those bright and brittle boundaries of sensation, he followed her into those steamy realms of release.

They lay together for a while, still joined, their limbs entwined . . . letting their hearts and bodies return to normal. After a time he withdrew and propped himself up on an elbow beside her, to look at her, to luxuriate in the sight of her rosy breasts and sated blue eyes.

She smiled. And he smiled.

"Just for your information," he murmured, brushing

her hair back from her damp and glowing face, "I think your mother meant for you to wear that sheet and that smile . . . *now.*"

She realized what he meant and covered her burning face with her hands.

"Although 'before' was quite delightful as well," he said with a laugh, pulling her hands away from her face and kissing them gently. "Tell me, sweetness, what other interesting instructions did your mother give you?"

The sun had been up for some time when Pierce awakened and propped himself up on his elbow beside Gabrielle. He watched the slow, even rhythm of her breathing, took in the rosy blush of her skin, and lost himself for a time in the curve of her lips, which, even in sleep, seemed an expression of her pleasure with the night just past. But perhaps it was the deep, lingering pleasure in him that made him see that in her.

He couldn't recall ever experiencing a night like the one just past. And he had certainly never felt like this before on a morning after. Usually after a night of heated indulgence, he felt wrung out; his senses were discharged and empty, and his body was mercifully dead to sensation. He couldn't wait to haul himself from the bed and go home to a hot tub of water and several uninterrupted hours of sleep. And there was always the personal aftermath . . . having to confront his partner in pleasure in broad daylight, to pay her risqué compliments and make pacifying promises about a "next" time.

But just now he felt warm and full and his body hummed with a low vibration that seemed paradoxically both peaceful and energizing. He felt he could take on all comers in a footrace, or ride a wild stallion, or swim the whole blessed English Channel before breakfast.

He felt like waking her up, just to see the look—*that look*—in her eyes again.

Never before while making love had he stared into a woman's eyes and watched the effects of his lovemaking registering in the depths of her. His eyes were usually closed or fastened on some erotic combination of shape and motion. But last night he had looked into Gabrielle's eyes and hadn't been able to look away. Something had held him, absorbed him, made him want to see what was happening to her and within her. He had seen the anxiety, the awe, the delight, and the discovery born in her and watched as every motion of his body etched an impression into her mind and heart. He saw the longings in her before her body expressed them, saw the pleasure exploding in her depths well before its tremors rocked him.

He had given her pleasure, and she had given it back to him, with all the eagerness and generosity her sweet little body could manage. Making love with her was astonishingly like doing anything else with her . . . warm and enthralling and a bit unpredictable. As her longing turned to pleasure and her desire was transformed into a glow of satisfaction, he found himself discovering it all anew with her, through her. And as alluring as the discovery of her passions was, it was equaled in full by the stunning pleasure of discovering it all again himself.

Now, watching her sleep, he wanted more of that unique and enchanting pleasure. He wanted to wake her up and love her again and again. He was still hungry for her, and he understood that it wasn't just physical. He wanted to tickle her and listen to her laugh . . . wanted to stroke her and feel her shiver . . . wanted to be the center of her curiosity and her attention and her discovery, as he had been last night. He wanted to be the center of her world, the way she was becoming the center of—

His heart stopped for a moment, convulsed, then

lurched and beat wildly to make up for missed beats. His gut tightened, his blood surged, and his skin contracted in the first case of gooseflesh he had had since he was a boy. The intensity of his longing suddenly broke through the barriers passion had erected between his emotions and his instinct for self-protection.

It was happening again—that unholy seduction of his senses, his pride, and his better judgment. She had gotten to him. After making mad, passionate love to her all night long, he was lying here, watching her, wanting her, wanting more. The crushing tightness in his chest made him break out in a cold sweat. How many times would he have to take her? Or would this ravenous appetite for her never be satisfied? Somewhere in the night, in the taking of her passion, he had lost a bit of himself.

Sitting up slowly, he realized that every time he tried to quench that soul-deep thirst in him, he would fall just a bit deeper into her thrall, under her spell. She would have just that much more power over him. Soon he wouldn't be *him* at all, but some haunted, pathetic wreck of a man, devoid of will and determination of his own. Look at him—panting after her as she slept, hanging on her every breath and every sigh.

With gentle ferocity, he peeled his skin from hers and slid from under the sheet. His heart was pounding and his mouth was dry as he bolted from the bed and stood watching her with rising panic. Something in her reached right to the core of him and touched long-buried needs and responses. She had already aroused his conscience and hitherto unknown impulses for protection and possession in him. What was next?

This was a test of his manhood, his very personhood, he realized. One misstep, one moment of weakness, and he would find himself forever relegated to the matrimonial drone's corner of society's ballrooms—counting his drinks, complaining of his arches, wincing his way through interminable waltzes . . .

Gabrielle awakened to Rue shaking her shoulder and calling her name. She shifted languidly and felt a burst of discomfort in her loins and a dozen small steamy aches in her limbs.

"Hurry, *chérie,* your husband awaits," Rue said, hurrying to her unpacked trunk and throwing it open. "Downstairs . . . at breakfast."

Gabrielle sat up and quickly snatched the sheet up around her. *Your husband.* That had a very nice sound to it, indeed. She looked beside her at the bed, where he had slept, and smiled, giving the pillow that still bore the impression of his head a caress. In a moment she was out of bed, wrapped in a sheet, and hurrying to the basin in the dressing room.

Despite Rue's urgent fluttering, she dressed carefully in her best eggshell silk, printed with purple and blue violets. It was past ten before she rounded the gallery and descended the stairs. Pierce was standing in the entry hall, speaking with Onslow and Frieda, and she could tell the instant she set eyes on him that something was wrong.

His back was rigid, his jaw was set, and his hands were clamped behind him, as if he was containing something within himself. When he spotted her, he dismissed them and strode to the bottom of the stairs to meet her. Ignoring her smile, he seized her by the wrist and pulled her into a cavernous walnut-paneled drawing room.

"I'm sorry I am so late; I had no idea I had slept so long," she said breathlessly, at a loss as to how she might have offended him. "I'm usually an early—"

"I have to leave in a few minutes, and I thought it would be best to set a few things straight before I go."

"You're leaving?" She leaned against the back of a large,

overstuffed chair, alarmed by the drastic change in his demeanor. "Where are you going?"

"Back to London. I have business to attend to." He strolled a few paces away, refusing to look directly at her. "Since this will be your home for the foreseeable future, you should know what you may expect. I have given orders to Onslow and the staff that your wishes be accommodated in every regard. You may continue to use my chambers, until you decide which rooms you wish to claim for your own. If you wish to ride, you may use the stables. Besides the household funds, I have arranged a certain stipend for your personal needs. Should you decide to make changes in the house, you will need to write me in London with the details. And as to my mother . . . when she is here, she usually spends her time in the west wing and dines in her rooms."

He glanced at her, then quickly away. "I think that covers the essentials. If you have questions, ask Onslow and Frieda. They've been in this household longer than I have." He turned to go.

"Pierce—" The sense of what he was proposing finally seeped through her disbelief. He was leaving her. Now— this minute! "Wait!" He halted in the doorway, turning just his head to her. "When will you be back?"

"I cannot say. I have a good bit of work to do. Parliament *is* in session."

"But you cannot just leave . . ."

"I *cannot*?" When he turned partway, she saw the anger her words sparked in him. "Giving orders already?"

"Orders? No . . . I only meant . . . can't it wait a week?" There was no softening in his face, and she knew she would have to be more direct. "We were just married yesterday. Why did you bring me here if you were only going to go—" She halted, and her eyes widened.

"I brought you here to see to it that you have exactly

what you wanted," he declared tightly. "You wanted a sensible, reasonable marriage . . . with a dull, ordinary sort of fellow who wouldn't make demands on you and would allow you to run your own life . . . well apart from his. I had no wish to be married at all. But since I am, I realize that a sensible, reasonable marriage is precisely what I want as well . . . with a dull and obedient sort of woman who will keep to her place and who understands that I wish to run my own life . . . well apart from hers. How fortunate that what we both desire, a tidy legal arrangement, is quite within our grasp.

"This is your new home, your new life." He gestured sardonically to the handsomely decorated room. "I sincerely hope you find it everything you expected."

He turned once again and strode out into the hall, where his hat and walking stick lay on the center table. Stunned, she hurried after him.

"Pierce?"

When he had donned his hat, he couldn't resist one last look at her. He found her stopped a short distance away in the center of the hall, staring at him with her face pale and her eyes like bruised violets. She seemed so innocent and so bewildered—and so damned irresistible. Against his own better judgment, he let his gaze roam her, memorizing every detail—the delicate, springlike flowers of her dress, the lustrous gold of her hair, the lush curves of her body, the ripeness of her reddened lips, the longing and confusion in her face. The air between them heated. He took a sharp breath and felt a blast of dry heat searing his lungs.

Turning on his heel, he strode out the open door.

She stood in shock, listening to him give instructions to Jack and hearing the carriage door slam. Then she rushed to the door and caught a glimpse of him through the window of the carriage as it rolled past. He was looking the other way.

Gripping the doorframe for support, she watched the carriage move, praying that at the last minute it would turn and carry him back to her. But it rumbled on until it disappeared into the trees that overhung the drive near the main road.

Stumbling back into the house, she found old Onslow in the entry, watching her with a scowl on his face.

"Will you be having some breakfast, your ladyship?" the august old houseman asked with a frown of concern. "Or shall I clear away in the dining room?"

"I am not hungry, thank you," she said woodenly, turning toward the steps. Her knees weakened, and she just managed to make it to the bench that nestled against the wall between the two branches of the split staircase. *Gone.* It would have been more merciful if he had just refused to marry her at all . . . instead of speaking binding vows with her, whisking her off to his country house, making mad, passionate love to her . . .

Passion.

Once again, she had succumbed to it, and once again she paid the price.

Tears made it difficult to see as she dragged herself up the stairs to the rooms they had shared. She couldn't have been more wrong . . . about the fact that she had no passions, about the possibility of having some control over her own life, about the meaning of Pierce's loving . . . and even about the nature of marriage itself.

Apparently a husband *could* just walk away.

That evening, Pierce blew through the doors of his London house, with his body and his mind grimly braced to withstand the turmoil that threatened to overwhelm him. And, as invariably occurred when he was troubled and in need of comfort, the first person he encountered was his irascible and domineering mother. She was coming down the stairs as he started up, and they met in the middle of the steps.

"What are you doing here?" she demanded, blocking the way and glaring past him and all around the entry hall for evidence of his newly acquired "baggage." "Where is she —your bit of fluff with the shocking pedigree?"

"My *wife* is at Thorndike," he declared hotly.

"You left her there? Alone?" Beatrice seemed genuinely shocked.

"Afraid she'll try to make off with the silver?" he said irritably.

Beatrice's eyes narrowed as she searched his tense and angry face. "Well . . . things must have been dismal indeed if you've abandoned her after only one night." She drew herself up to deliver a coolly calculated thrust. "You'd think a professional tart would take a bit more pride in her work."

Neither of them was prepared for the explosion of anger her verbal gouge set off in him. He sprang forward, sending her back against the wall, and shoved his burning face close to hers. He could barely contain his anger.

"She's *not* a damned tart! She has had one man in her entire life." He jerked a thumb at his chest. "*Me.* And that was just last night. Is that bloody well clear?"

Beatrice stared at him, eyes wide with astonishment. After a pause that fairly crackled with heat, she gave a nod. He drew back sharply. She watched him withdraw once again behind stony walls of self-control as he whirled and took the rest of the stairs by twos and threes.

The echoes of a door slamming wafted down to her as she stood, still frozen, on the step. Never in all their confrontations had she seen him on such a ragged edge. And, to her knowledge, never in his life had he behaved so protectively over a female. This Gabrielle wasn't a tart, he insisted. But if she wasn't, then just what was she?

Beatrice wobbled on down the stairs, thinking about the fire in her son's eyes and the fury with which he had just proclaimed the girl's virtue and laid exclusive claim to her passions. Clearly, something about the chit had gotten to him—gotten right under his skin. She knew the signs all too well.

And what sort of woman could do that to her worldly and decadent son?

Settling herself in her knitting chair in the drawing room, she took out her latest needlework project and made her needles fly as she resurrected the sights and sounds of the marriage in her mind.

The girl was a bastard—the love child of the duke of Carlisle and that flamboyant creature in the monstrous yellow hat. When the bishop had introduced Pierce's future father-in-law, Beatrice had been caught flat-footed, gaping at the duke like a perfect fool. The girl was the acknowledged offshoot of a duke of the realm—her blood almost as blue as Beatrice's own . . . or Pierce's. And while bastardy was a terrible blight in respectable circles, Beatrice had lived too long and seen too much to condemn a person solely on the circumstances of his or her birth.

She turned a mental eye to the girl herself: blond and lovely and surprisingly demure, considering the influence of that gaudy flowered female who claimed to be her mother. And virtuous, according to Pierce. Beatrice doubted her jaded offspring could have been easily fooled on such a point.

As Beatrice considered her new daughter-in-law, she recalled that Gabrielle had seemed strained, even a bit frightened when facing Pierce before the bishop. A good sign, there. A bride with any sense should be frightened at the prospect of vowing away all control of her life to some man who would use it for his own convenience. And Pierce had done exactly that—bedded her and left her to fend for herself in a strange house after only one night . . .

Beatrice's hands suddenly dropped into her lap, still clutching her knitting needles. She sat up straight, her heart beginning to pound and her eyes widening as the importance of it rumbled through her. Dear God, he had left the girl at Thorndike after only one night. Bedded and abandoned her. *After just one night.*

Damn. It was happening again.

Snatching up her tapestry bag of yarn and needles, she sailed out the doors and up the stairs. "Sophie!" she called. When her maid appeared, Beatrice had thrown open her wardrobe and was pulling out an armful of dresses.

"*Oui*, madam?"

"Get my cases and start packing my things. We're leaving for Thorndike, first thing in the morning!"

16

The next morning dawned gray and damp over the Sussex countryside . . . and in Gabrielle's heart. At Rue's badgering, she submitted to cool compresses to reduce the swelling around her eyes, then finally hauled herself from the bed and took a bite of breakfast from the tray Rue had brought. She insisted upon wearing some of her oldest clothes—relics of her schooldays in France—and putting her hair back in a plain chignon. There was no one to impress here, she insisted when Rue tried to persuade her that a bright dress and a proper coif would lift her spirits. Only the hope that moving out of Pierce's chambers would separate her from the disturbing memories they contained convinced her to set out with Onslow to choose other accommodations.

There were two suitable sets of chambers nearby; one across the hall from his, and one adjacent to his, but neither seemed appropriate. She asked that he show her additional rooms, but nothing appealed to her, and she insisted on looking at the rooms on the floor above.

The uppermost floor of a country house, even a grand estate, was usually a functional, unpretentious space, with lower ceilings and few of the architectural blandishments common on the floors below. It was for children, nurses and tutors, servants of visiting dignitaries, and poor relations; there was no need to extend luxury to such as them. But whoever had planned Thorndike clearly had thought otherwise; the ceilings were just as high as in the lower floors, the windows were as plentiful, and the doors and finish work, while more modest, were still substantial.

In fascination, she went from room to room, opening doors and peering under dustcovers. Here was the nursery, and there was the schoolroom, and still further along was the playroom. School desks, a rocking horse, pails of wooden blocks, shelves of books, and a piano draped with a sheet, all stood silent, keeping vigil until the next generation of St. Jameses arrived.

Further down the hall, they came to a modest but comfortable set of rooms with plenty of sunlight, a recently plumbed bath, and an adjoining room large enough to serve as a sleeping room for Rue. Gabrielle brightened. "This is wonderful." She went to look out the huge windows that overlooked the entry court, a grand sweep of front lawn, and a duckpond beyond.

"It's perfect. I'll make these my rooms." She turned to old Onslow, who blinked and stared at her as if she'd lost her wits.

"Not these, your ladyship." He shook his head. "These are governess rooms."

"Well, we don't have a governess just now," she said, suppressing the thought that she might never have or need one. "And until we do, these rooms will do nicely for me. If you'll please send up the housemaids and get them started scrubbing down the walls and airing the rugs. We'll need a new mattress, new curtains for the windows, some pillows, and a chair or two from downstairs. I'm sure it will be quite comfortable."

If Onslow was distressed by her choice of accommodations, Rue was horrified. "*Non, non, chérie*, you cannot do this!" She looked around her proposed quarters in dismay. "It is so small—so drab—and so far away from . . ." Gabrielle's scowl stopped her before she said what was on both their minds: so far away from Pierce's rooms.

At Gabrielle's insistence, and under her direction, the staff labored through much of the afternoon cleaning and freshening the rooms, locating acceptable furniture, and preparing to move her things upstairs. By dinnertime, she felt a bit better. Perhaps this was just what she needed, a chance to take her life into her own hands. Perhaps some independence and solitude would help her see things in a more comprehensible light.

As she stared out the window at the setting sun, she caught sight of a carriage rolling along the road in the distance. Her heart slowed for a time, then picked up speed as the large black coach entered the cover of the trees, then emerged on a course for the front doors of Thorndike.

"It's him! He's back!" She started for the door, then turned back shaking her hands with anxiety. "How do I look?"

Rue held her back long enough to remove her apron and give her skirts a good brushing. There was no time to change clothes or bother with her hair. Soon, she was running down the upper hall, hurrying down the steps, then racing down another long hallway to the gallery, where she finally slowed to a more dignified pace. Her cheeks were rosy, her eyes were bright, and her heart was pounding as the front doors opened and Onslow stepped inside with two large valises in his hands.

At the half landing, Gabrielle halted, staring into a face that was hauntingly familiar, but of both the wrong age and the wrong sex to be the one she had hoped to see. Descending the steps slowly, she watched the woman conferring with Onslow and frowning. By the time Gabrielle reached the main floor, she felt an icy chill and knew beyond all doubt this was the much-dreaded Beatrice. The first words out of the woman's mouth confirmed it.

"So, you're the one who trapped my son into marriage, are you? I am Pierce's mother, Lady Sandbourne." She came forward, giving Gabrielle a thorough looking over, letting her gaze linger on the simple blouse and skirt and the uninspired style of Gabrielle's hair. "And *you* are . . . ?"

Gabrielle came within a hair's breadth of saying: *that tart.* "Gabrielle LeCoeur . . . St. James, I suppose." Flustered under the woman's critical regard, she curtsied as she had been wont to do when Mme. Marchand introduced her pupils to the local nobility. It didn't have quite the same effect as it had had in France.

"Well, I never." Beatrice stiffened visibly. "Such cheek!"

It took a moment for Gabrielle to realize what she had done wrong. Curtsying to a woman of the same rank . . . Pierce's mother had taken it as a bit of mockery. "I'm sorry, Lady Sandbourne." She tried to fix it. "Forgive me. I am not accustomed to addressing countesses as equals."

"Do you make a habit of impertinence, Miss LeCoeur? Along with poor judgment?" Lady Beatrice demanded imperiously.

"Poor judgment?" Gabrielle blanched. Which poor judgment was Beatrice referring to? The idiocy that made her proposition Pierce in the first place? The momentary lapse into passion that got her caught in flagrante delicto with him? The hopeless muddle she was making of her introduction to her mother-in-law?

"Onslow tells me you have chosen to sequester yourself on the top floor in the governess's rooms." She came forward, jerking the fingers of her gloves forcefully. "Obviously you are new to the workings of a substantial household, otherwise you would know how ridiculous it is to have the wife of the master housed any place but near the master's chambers. Even worse, you failed to consider the hardship and inconvenience to the staff. A number of our servants are getting on in years, and it is grossly unfair to think of making aging servants traipse up and down an extra flight of stairs just to see to your whims."

Gabrielle's face was on fire as she glanced at Onslow, who looked down. "I'm sorry. I hadn't thought of such things."

"Quite obvious enough, without your stating it." Lady Beatrice dropped her gloves on the hall table and reached up to unpin her hat. "Now that you have thought of it, choose either of the apartments across from or adjacent to my son's, and be done with it."

With that, Lady Beatrice laid down a string of orders that made it dismally clear who was in charge here and exited up the stairs to the west wing. Gabrielle tucked her chin and headed for the drawing room. Once inside, she sank down onto a window seat and stared out into the deepening gloom, just managing to keep her composure and hold back her tears.

Though the air was fairly crackling with angry tension at Maison LeCoeur when the duke arrived the next afternoon, he scarcely noticed. Rosalind had sent several messages asking him to come—the previous evening and this morning—but he had delayed coming because he was furious with her for appearing at the church in defiance of his wishes. Her behavior of late had appalled him, and he knew that when he saw her again, he would have to set her straight on a number of things.

Now it could be put off no longer. Pausing outside the drawing room, he took a deep breath, squared his shoulders, and girded himself for one of the most onerous duties a man could face: the disciplining of his mistress.

He found Rosalind standing by the fireplace, wearing a high-necked dress and an angry expression.

"There you are. At last." She gave him a glare that stopped him in his tracks. "Are all your trunks unpacked and your hunting trophies hung? Are your guns cleaned and oiled for storage and your shirts all laundered? Have you caught up on all the parliamentary gossip and visited your barber and your bookmaker? Are the cats all fed?" Her gaze sharpened to a razor's edge. "How good of you to finally think of me, after attending to such urgent and weighty matters."

"Rosalind . . ." he said, completely taken aback. Everything he had intended to say to her somehow deserted him. "What's gotten into you?"

"What has gotten into *me*? I sent for you last evening and this morning, and again this afternoon, because I desperately needed you," she declared. "Where have you been?"

"Don't be absurd," he said, tucking his hands into his waistcoat pockets and puffing with manly outrage. "I cannot just drop everything and come running whenever you get a bit hysterical."

"*Hysterical?*" She propped her hands on her waist and moved closer to him, her eyes hot. "Clementine brought me word that Sandbourne is back in London—alone. She saw him outside Brooks's last night. That means he has abandoned Gabrielle in Sussex—just dragged her out to some moldy old pile of bricks in the country and dumped her there!"

The duke crossed his arms and glared at her. "It's none of my business if he did. He's married the girl and what he does with her from now on is his concern, not mine . . . *or yours.*"

She straightened and lowered her arms to her sides, seeing him as she had never seen him before.

"No, she was never a concern of yours . . . until you decided she was a threat to your precious family honor. The name of Carlisle wasn't even involved until you came charging home and barged into the situation.

"Heaven help me, I told myself you loved me and that our love was all that mattered." She stalked slowly closer. "Marriage vows and a place in high society didn't matter to me. And after all your gifts and protestations of love, I believed it didn't matter to you either. But it did, didn't it? I never saw that, never understood it until the other night. You said I wasn't a harlot and, in the next breath, forbade me to attend my daughter's marriage!"

"Rosalind, cease this at once!" he thundered, grabbing her by the shoulders. "I have loved you and taken care of you . . . placed you above all others in my life!"

"Have you indeed?" She shoved back in his arms, the turmoil in her heart visible in her eyes. "Would you have married me? When your wife died . . . when you were free again . . . I never asked. Perhaps I didn't want to know. But I am asking now. Would you have married me ten years ago?"

He stared into the face he knew so well, into eyes he had seen so often glowing with desire and pleasure and love. Marry her? Marry his mistress? How could he have?

He had an heir to protect, obligations, a place to maintain for his son in society. If he said yes, now, would it pacify her?

She searched his gaze and read in his eyes the thoughts he dared not speak aloud. He was deciding whether or not to lie to her, she realized. Whether or not to buy another little bit of her soul with the counterfeit currency of easy assurances.

"Don't you dare say it," she said, her voice scraped raw on jagged emotion. Wresting free, she stumbled back. "I devoted my entire life to your comfort and pleasure. I have loved you openly and honorably. And this is the respect you show me—ordering me about like a servant, demanding I keep to my 'place' . . . expecting that I can be bought with a simple lie.

"I am just a mistress, a *harlot,* to you after all." Scalding tears flooded her eyes and spilled down her cheeks. "Well, I'd much rather be an honest harlot than a lying hypocrite like *you.*"

"R-Rosalind—you—y-you—" He stammered and clenched impotent fists, caught somewhere between astonishment and outrage.

Rosalind rushed to the door and jerked it open. Her whole body was trembling.

"Since you have such a terrible loathing for harlotry, Your Grace, I shall do you the service of removing my offensive presence from your life. As of this moment, our relationship—the *arrangement* we had—is over. Finished. And I'm certain we shall both be greatly relieved if you never darken my door again."

She strode out into the hall, calling for Gunther. When the houseman came running, she seized his sleeve. "Show the duke out, and send for the locksmith straightaway. I want every lock on every door in this house changed by tomorrow night."

As the duke burst out into the entry hall, bellowing her name and demanding she come back downstairs that instant, she continued defiantly up the steps and down the hall to her private chambers. There, she stood in the middle of her boudoir, waiting, breath and movement suspended, until she heard the duke's angry oath and the slamming of the front door. Then she slammed the door to her chambers, threw herself on her bed, and broke into sobs.

Later that night, a tense, somewhat haggard Pierce entered the bar at Brooks's. He ordered his usual scotch whisky and considered sitting a few hands of faro in the Subscription Room. But just as he was about to make his way from the small room that housed the bar, Arundale and Shively entered with Edward Dimsdell, Lord Catton, and two others, and they spotted him.

"Ye gods—there's the bridegroom now!" Arundale crowed.

Every muscle in Pierce's body contracted as if he'd just taken a blow to the gut. The announcement of his marriage had come out that morning in *The Times*. He should have known someone would bring it up if he had little enough sense to show his face in clubland that night. He wasn't thinking clearly or he'd have stayed home. Before he could escape, they were bearing down on him in those tight quarters and offering him their hands and their sly smiles of congratulations.

"Lucky bastard, you," Arundale said with a quick knowing glance at Shively.

"So your pretty 'cousin' wasn't merely a pretty cousin, after all, eh, Sandbourne?" Shively laughed.

"Not such a *distant* relation now, I'll bet." Lord Catton rolled his eyes.

They had a good laugh at Pierce's expense, ignoring the bronzing of his features and the hardening of his eyes. "But what's this? Married one day and already he's haunting the clubs." Arundale's voice was thick with insinuation. "That is something of a disappointment. I would have guessed your voluptuous little Gabrielle would provide more than a single night's . . . *entertainment.*"

Pierce reacted instinctively. Seizing Arundale by the coat, he drove him back across the bar and smashed him against the wall, setting it trembling and the other club members in the bar into an outcry.

"That's my countess you've just referred to as common 'entertainment,' " he snarled. "Don't ever make that mistake again, Arundale. You'll not live to regret it." He released the young lord and stormed out of the bar.

Arundale straightened his coat and tie and brushed off the impact of the attack when other members crowded around to see if he was all right. "I am fine. Apparently Sandbourne has lost all sense of humor about the subject of marriage. A pity." He smiled with innocent-looking malice. "The rest of us find the circumstances of his marriage quite amusing . . ."

On the afternoon of the fifth day of Gabrielle's marriage, she pleaded a headache and asked for a tray in her rooms to avoid yet another interminable meal under the critical glare of Pierce's mother. In the last two days Lady Beatrice had monitored her activities, declaring the stables, the gardens, the kitchens, and the work buildings off limits to her. But even in her rooms she was not safe from the woman's control. That morning, a huge pile of linen had been sent to her rooms. When Gabrielle stared at it, bewildered, old Onslow explained that Thursday was always Lady Beatrice's mending day. The message was clear; she was expected to comply with her mother-in-law's habits and notions of economy, household management, and decorum.

Gabrielle retreated in turmoil to the nursery on the

floor above. There, she wandered around, touching the hand-carved swinging cradle in the corner and the low, narrow bed that looked as if it had seen a bit of use. Examining the books on the shelves, she wondered about the children who had spent time here. Inevitably her thoughts came to Pierce. She imagined him here, as a little boy with dark hair and irresistible brown eyes. She wanted that little boy . . . and a whole house full of others just like him, with ruddy cheeks and warm brown eyes full of mischievous laughter. She wanted hugs and bedtime stories and frogs in the schoolroom, and tea-and-bread-sandwich picnics in the garden . . .

Downstairs, Beatrice was standing on the gallery, frowning at the untouched tray of food Onslow was holding. "Didn't touch a morsel this time either, your ladyship," the old butler said, then looked up at her and wagged his head. "She's miserable, she is."

"Or simply too precious and finicky for her own good," Beatrice declared, glowering at the old houseman, who glowered back. After a moment she relented. "All right, I'll go and have a word with the chit." She started off, but Onslow's voice halted her briefly.

"She ain't in her chambers, your ladyship. She's upstairs in the nursery."

"What the devil is she doing up there?"

"Looking, touching things, I imagine . . . like she done before. Fancies it up there. She likes children."

"Does she indeed?" Beatrice mulled over that bit of information, adding it to her growing knowledge of the girl. When she reached the first landing of the stairs, the first strains of music reached her. She stopped, immobilized by the faint but recognizable strains of a melancholy sonata. Gabrielle was playing the piano in the schoolroom. Beatrice stood for a moment listening. Piano . . . the girl played beautifully . . . clearly, from the heart.

Gabrielle turned to find her mother-in-law standing behind her with her face flushed and her eyes bright with emotion.

"That instrument is hideously out of tune." Beatrice put a hand to her temple. "In future, please confine yourself to the lower floors and to more productive pursuits." She closed the cover over the piano keys with a clack and gave Gabrielle a look that made her slide from the stool.

When she was gone, Beatrice stood there a moment, staring at the piano and then at the door. The girl was lovely and well mannered and accomplished, probably a better catch as a daughter-in-law than she could have hoped for, considering her son's reputation in respectable circles. And Onslow had said she loved children. That boded well. But, it would take nothing short of a miracle to make a success of a marriage with Pierce. And it remained to be seen whether the girl was indeed that miracle.

Gabrielle was on the verge of tears as she headed down the stairs. Just as she reached the main staircase, she caught sight of Onslow hurrying through the entry hall and then peering out the side window. Straightening his coat and looking a bit flustered, he headed for the door. She slowed on the half landing, realizing someone was arriving.

When the door opened, in rushed a storm of swishing silk and swirling perfume . . . a veritable typhoon of extravagant femininity.

"Dear God—they said the place was out in the country —but no one said *which* country! Why, we must be halfway across France by—" Rosalind halted in the midst of tilting her blazing red "cavalier" hat to the proper angle, jerking the matching crimson military-style jacket down into place, and brushing at her tailored black serge skirt. Pinning the stunned butler with an imperious look, she demanded: "Where is she, my daughter? What has that beastly wretch done with her?"

"R-really, madam—"

"Very well, I shall find her myself!" Rosalind brushed past the butler to rake the entry hall with a critical glare, then headed for the open doors of the drawing room. "Gabrielle! Where are you?"

"Mother!" A tide of relief washed over Gabrielle.

She ran down the steps and in a heartbeat was engulfed in a smothering hug.

"My dearest—are you all right?" After a thorough squeezing, Rosalind thrust her back an arm's length to look her over. "I've been worried sick ever since Clementine brought me word two nights ago that Sandbourne was back in London *alone.* I kept imagining you in some dreadful old country pile, abused and heartbroken—" Taking Gabrielle's face between her hands, she searched the traces of puffiness around her daughter's eyes. "The wretch—bedding you and then abandoning you the very next—" She halted as an even worse possibility occurred to her. "The bounder did at least *bed* you, didn't he?"

"Mother—please!" Gabrielle pulled back, her reddened face answering for her.

"Then, he has some nerve, stuffing you away in the country. But you needn't worry, my dear. I have come to see you through your wretched time of trial. I shall not abandon you this time."

"What on earth is all the commotion—" A voice came from the stairs above, drawing their attention upward. Lady Beatrice was standing on the stairs, gripping the railing, staring at Rosalind in extreme agitation. "What is *she* doing here?" she demanded, apparently of Gabrielle.

"This is my mother, Lady Beatrice. Mrs. Rosalind LeCoeur." Gabrielle stepped instinctively in front of her extravagantly attired mother.

"I know both who and what she is," Lady Beatrice declared, descending the stairs with her back rod-straight and her eyes crackling. "What I want to know is what she is doing *here* . . . in this house."

Gabrielle steadied herself, caught between two overwhelming and diametrically opposed forces. "My mother is here because . . . she . . ."

"I am here because I learned that your bounder of a son abandoned my daughter after only one night," Rosalind charged, stepping from behind Gabrielle. "I came to be certain she is all right and to comfort her."

"To sponge off the rich relations, you mean," Beatrice declared shortly, folding her arms.

"It can scarcely be called 'sponging' when I have brought provisions and staff, not to mention some of Gabrielle's dower goods with me." She glanced around the center hall with a scathingly critical eye. "From the looks of things, she will need all of what I have brought her and more to make this place habitable."

Beatrice reacted as if slapped. "It is clear that one must be blunt with a creature of your ilk," she declared, advancing on Rosalind, who held her ground with a haughty look. "It is unthinkable that a woman of your 'profession' would inflict herself upon a decent and respectable house. By coming here you embarrass your daughter and call attention to her distasteful origins."

"There is nothing *distasteful* about Gabrielle's origins," Rosalind declared, her nostrils flaring and her chin lowering. "She was born of a great love and a soul-searing passion."

"I will not stand for such talk in my house!" Beatrice was suddenly on her toes, her fists clenched, her ample bosom puffed with outrage.

"What? *Passion?* It's probably the first time the word has been uttered in this house in a generation!"

"Please!" Gabrielle lurched between them, sending the dueling mothers each back a step. "Mother, this is not your house!" Then she turned to her mother-in-law and straightened to her full height. "It is unfortunate, Lady Beatrice, that my mother's presence offends you. But she has come a very long way, and it would be positively un-Christian to turn her out."

Beatrice settled back on her heels, struggling with her outrage at being spoken to in such a fashion, in her own house, not to mention being reminded of her Christian duty by someone with such a flagrantly "distasteful" background. Giving Gabrielle a narrow glare, she retreated in a huff to the unsullied reaches of the west wing.

Gabrielle's knees wobbled at the realization that she had just defied her mother-in-law. Somehow she knew she was going to pay for it.

The next moment, Rosalind was at the door, beckoning to a number of familiar faces—Gunther, Aberdeen the cook, Colette, Rosalind's lady's maid, and Lucia, the head parlor maid who functioned as Rosalind's housekeeper. Dear heaven, Gabrielle thought miserably, she couldn't escape her past even in exile in the netherlands of Sussex.

Rosalind had brought two carriages, containing herself and part of her household staff, and a wagon, bearing a generous stockpile of provisions; she had intended to be prepared for whatever disgraceful circumstance she found Gabrielle in. Among the provisions were two trunks of fine linen, barrels of hand-painted china, silver flatware, and several very fine paintings, intended as a part of Gabrielle's "dowry." Rosalind had also arranged for the transport of Gabrielle's grand piano, which wouldn't arrive for another day, due to the care with which the instrument had to be transported.

It took only an hour or two to settle everyone into sleeping quarters, but it was clear that it would take—as Onslow so succinctly put it—"until hell freezes over" for Rosalind and her staff to settle into anything more than that at Thorndike. Gabrielle introduced Gunther to old Onslow, Aberdeen to Millie the cook, and Lucia to old Frieda. Each of Rosalind's staff was rebuffed by his or her Thorndike counterpart . . . but refused to be deterred. By evening, each had invoked Gabrielle's name to set himself or herself up with duties paralleling those of the Thorndike staff.

By dinner, tensions were cresting in the house. Nowhere was that more evident than in the kitchens, where two cooks and two sets of dishes were separated by the narrowest of margins, and in the dining room, where the two mothers were separated by the length of a twenty-foot table.

When the food was served—plain cottage pie on the St. James end, braised beef tips in Madeira on the LeCoeur end—Gabrielle found herself again caught squarely between two mothers and two menus, representing two entirely separate and irreconcilable worlds. Seated halfway between, Gabrielle was served by both Gunther and Onslow, but she couldn't seem to swallow a bite of either cuisine.

"Thank God, I thought to bring you some decent wine and brandy. This place is as dry as a bone," Rosalind remarked, lifting her glass to Gabrielle.

"Better bone dry than half embalmed," Beatrice declared with a disdainful sniff. "Spirits slow the mind and loosen the virtue. They should be outlawed for women under forty."

"Under forty?" Rosalind sat forward with a recklessly defiant smile. "By that standard it would be another *ten years* before I could touch a drop of brandy."

Beatrice's eyes narrowed. "Is that so? That does surprise me . . . since I've heard that you were started in your dubious 'trade' by none other than Admiral Lord Nelson, who we all know died in 1805."

"Mother, please!" Gabrielle's entreaty stopped

Rosalind's hot response before it was uttered. Rosalind gave a *"tsk"* of annoyance and shifted irritably in her chair. But she couldn't stay silent long.

"You're not eating, Gabrielle," she said. "And poor Aberdeen has come so far and worked so hard to make you something tasty."

"She shows considerable sense," Beatrice put in. "Wine, red meats, and rich foods are not good for a young girl."

"She is not a young *girl* anymore," Rosalind said archly. "Your son saw to that."

"Well—I never!" Beatrice's hands came down on the table with a smack.

"Come now, I'm certain you must have . . . at least *once!*"

"I will not be spoken to in such a manner"—Beatrice was on her feet in a flash—"in my own house . . . by a common *tart!*"

"*Former* tart!" Rosalind pushed up from her chair with her head held high. "I am no longer in that profession."

For a moment there was an utter and awful silence in the great dining room. Gabrielle's horror at the outbreak of open hostility was overcome by her shock at her mother's bold announcement. "Mother—what are you saying?"

"I meant to tell you in a different way, my dear." Rosalind steadied herself against the table and lifted her head to a defensive angle. "I've left the duke. Forever."

For a moment, Gabrielle just stared at her, unblinking, scarcely able to fathom what she was hearing. Her mother and the duke . . . separated?

"Why?"

Rosalind came down the side of the table opposite her, swaying, her eyes alight with internal fires. "Because he's a despicable swine. The lowest and meanest kind of a hypocrite. He was incensed that I arranged a future for you without his permission . . . accused me of trying to sell you into harlotry. I tried to tell him you were in love with Pierce and he was in love with you, and that I had secured your future as best I could. He was outraged—sputtered and blustered about *his daughter,* as if you were some bit of property upon which another man had dared poach. Him and his johnny-come-lately fatherhood . . . His real concern was his own precious name and family reputation. The vaunted 'House of Carlisle.' Then to placate his precious male notions of 'honor' and 'decency,' he proceeded to sell you into something even worse than harlotry—a forced and loveless marriage."

She leaned over the table, and her voice lowered to a passionate rasp. "Do you know . . . he forbade me to attend your wedding? Apparently I am an embarrassment to him. The wretch! To think of all the years I gave him . . . all the love and care and passion . . . all the times he said it didn't matter what society said."

Hurt and anger boiled over into scalding hot tears. "What kind of love can it be if a man is ashamed to acknowledge the woman he beds as the mother of his child?" As the tears burned streaks down her face, she whirled and made straight for Gunther, who stood nearby with a newly opened bottle of claret. Snatching the bottle from his hands, she sailed out the doors.

Gabrielle was stunned. The one constant in her life had been the soaring love and searing passion of her mother and her father. She had felt rejected by it, and had, in turn, rejected it as an example and a guide. But she had never once doubted it.

Poor Rosalind . . . learning after so many years that the great love that had dictated and circumscribed her life was not what she had always believed.

Oddly enough, Gabrielle felt no vindication, no satisfaction that Rosalind was at last learning the price she had paid for her grand passion. Gabrielle felt only sadness and a pang of sympathy. She, too, had paid the price of passion.

Rousing to the feel of Beatrice's gaze on her, she excused herself to her rooms.

Beatrice watched Gabrielle leave and, in some shock, sank back into her chair at the table. After a time, she looked up at Gunther and beckoned to him.

"Is there any more of that claret?" she mumbled. "I believe I could use a taste of it, myself."

17

In the world of the London clubs, word traveled quickly of the earl of Sandbourne's matrimonial demise. Whenever he appeared at Brooks's, the Carlton, or the Saville, where he held memberships, he was greeted by stiff congratulations, awkward silences, and curious stares on the part of his fellow members. More than once he turned unexpectedly and saw a whispered conversation stop and heads jerk guiltily. Finally, in the bar of the Saville, liquor loosened the tongue and the discretion of Edward Dimsdell, Lord Catton, enough for him to offer condolences —giving Pierce a glimpse of the rumors that swirled, unseen, around him.

He had been brought to the altar by force. The gossips

had somehow gotten wind of that devastating fact and had either ferreted out or astutely guessed that it was a seduction gone awry. The details, however, varied from version to version. According to some gossips, he was guilty of seducing his beautiful lady cousin; according to others, he had gotten snared by his own contriving mistress; and still others spread a tantalizing tale of his being caught with the bastard daughter of the duke of Carlisle . . . the love child born of his longtime mistress.

By its very nature, gossip selected out the more dramatic, and before long the most widespread and credited account was the most sensational one. The tale of a seduction, an angry duke, and of the prime minister's involvement in forcing Sandbourne to the altar made juicy telling in clubland and beyond. Just how far beyond, Pierce was appalled to learn when he responded that same evening to a summons from Colonel Tottenham.

It was after twelve when he arrived at Le Ciel and was shown up the stairs to a room just across the hall from the one where he had attempted to seduce Gabrielle that first night. The red velvet decor was disturbingly familiar, so much so that he had difficulty, at first, concentrating on the introductions Tottenham was making. Two of the three men were well-known Conservative members of parliament, Cornelius Harrison and William Tyburn, and the third turned out to be none other than Everett Sewell, the private secretary of Benjamin Disraeli, the former prime minister and lifelong enemy of William Gladstone. And suddenly Pierce knew the identity of the highly placed "someone" who had recruited him for the task of gathering evidence on Gladstone.

"We were most aggrieved to hear of your situation, Sandbourne," Tottenham said gravely, pouring him a whisky and waving him into a chair at the table.

"My *situation*?" Pierce's gut tightened as he settled onto that seat, feeling their eyes focused on him.

"A damnable shame." Harrison glanced at the others. "We never would have guessed the old man might get wind of our plans and go on the attack."

"You have my personal guarantee, Sandbourne," Tottenham said, rocking forward, "that it wasn't leaked by any of my people. I have no notion how the old cod heard of your activities and managed to target you."

"Never meant to make you a sacrificial lamb, old man." Tyburn, a bluff old knight from Cobham-on-Tyne shook his head. "Sorry about the rub you are in."

"And dragging Carlisle into it . . . unforgivable. The old reprobate will stop at nothing." Sewell, Disraeli's secretary, templed his fingers and looked down his nose.

Pierce looked from face to face, reading in their comments and their eyes that they knew the truth of the "rub" he was in and of Gladstone's involvement in bringing it about. Of course they would know, he told himself, containing his defensive anger; they were men whose stock-in-trade was information. Still, it shocked him to hear his own conjectures about Gladstone's motives stated by others. Had the old man truly known that he was trying to collect evidence? Or had Pierce simply been the victim of the old man's hypocritical crusade against other men's vices?

"Sadly, what is done is done." Tottenham looked to the others, gathering consensus for his next pronouncement. "And, of course, this means we shall have to find another way to expose Gladstone's indiscretions." He saw Pierce's surprise and winced. "Sorry, old man. You're useless to us now. Any evidence you might bring against Gladstone now will be tainted. Your motives will be suspect."

Pierce scarcely heard the next several comments as they moved on to consider the possibilities. They were consigning him to a place on the political shelf. His integrity had been compromised, and now both his personal and political judgment were called into question. His marriage had gone beyond mere social embarrassment; the scandal was wrecking his political career. And he had hypocritical old William Gladstone to thank.

"Well, then, our course is clear," Tottenham was saying as Pierce came back to the present. "Everyone knows about Gladstone's depraved involvement with these prostitutes, that he thumbs his nose at decency and morality, while claiming to represent them. But, if his intelligence is as good as Sandbourne's fate would suggest, then we are undoubtedly wasting our time trailing him through the streets."

"Here, here." Harrison sat forward with a gleam in his eye. "I say we need a more direct way to catch him 'in the act.'" After a silence he lowered his voice, so that they all had to lean forward to hear. "What say we help things along a bit?"

"What do you mean?" Disraeli's man was clearly interested.

"What say we arrange a few soiled doves for him 'rescue' . . . see to it that he has a thoroughly wicked bit of debauch . . . just before several right-thinking and civic-minded gentlemen discover what is afoot and break in on him?"

Harrison looked to Tottenham, who smiled and looked to Tyburn, who smiled and looked to Sewell. Their glittering eyes and grim smiles registered an ominous note with Pierce. They were talking about *arranging* the old man's demise, not just documenting it. He squirmed, thinking of his outrage at the notion that Gladstone had plotted against him. But, as they began to suggest ways and places and times, he suppressed his twinges of conscience. Gladstone had tried ruin him politically and personally, he told himself. Why should he interfere if others now decided to return the old man the favor?

Rosalind's new status as a "reformed tart" did little to make her presence at Thorndike palatable to Beatrice. The two seemed determined to antagonize each other. Why else would Beatrice have roused the staff just after sunrise one morning to begin their annual round of spring cleaning a week early . . . and have sent them first thing into Rosalind's rooms to roll up the rugs and collect the draperies for beating and airing? Why else would Rosalind have gone storming down to breakfast in a flame red nightdress and dressing gown . . . and have insisted on having a shot of brandy in her morning coffee? Why else would Beatrice have invited the local rector to tea the next afternoon and then coaxed him to expound at length on the intricacies of passages of scripture? Why else would Rosalind have winked at the rector, then pulled out a cigar and lighted it?

As wisps of pungent blue smoke wafted across the tea cart, Gabrielle watched her mother-in-law blanching and the rector swallowing his outrage along with his tea, and her face caught fire. As the tension became unbearable, she excused herself and fled the drawing room. Rosalind hurried after her, intercepted her in the entry, and pulled her down the nearby hall, into the walnut-paneled library.

"Mother, how could you?" Hurt and resentment were visible in Gabrielle's pale skin, in the dark smudges beneath her eyes, as she faced her mother.

"It's only a cigar," Rosalind said defensively. When Gabrielle glared at her, then at the cigar she held, she had the grace to redden. "Well, I always wanted to try one, but Augustus was always so dead-set against—" Lowering her chin, she looked about for a place to get rid of it. Spotting a crystal ashtray on Pierce's desk, she stubbed it out.

"I think it's time you went home," Gabrielle said tightly.

"What? Leave you here . . . in the clutches of that great gray gargoyle?" Rosalind lifted her head. "I shall do no such thing. There is nothing more important to me or more pressing than being here to comfort you in your time of crisis."

"Nothing?" Gabrielle's eyes darkened. "You're only making things worse for me."

Rosalind's defiance faltered as she studied Gabrielle and recognized that those disturbing signs of wear and woe were in part the result of her own behavior.

"I am doing it again, aren't I? Giving in to my impulses and letting you take the—" *Consequences.* The moment she had both sought in coming here and dreaded to face had finally arrived. Reaching for Gabrielle's hands, she pulled her to the leather-clad sofa. "I'm sorry. It seems like I'm always . . . Gabby, there are some things I need to say to you, things I came here to . . ." She searched her daughter's strained face. "I know I have not been much of a mother to you. I want to tell you that if I had it to do over again, I would do things very differently."

Gabrielle watched her mother grappling with memories and regrets, and felt her own difficult emotions rising to the surface again.

"You mean, with the duke."

"I mean with *you.*" Rosalind looked down at Gabrielle's hands in hers and drew a hard breath. "I don't know if I can explain, or if you will understand, if I do. I was so young and so much in love with Augustus. I don't know if you can ever understand what I felt for him . . . how I ached just to be with him, how I craved his presence." She looked away, allowing the memories to come and closing her eyes tightly at the pain they caused. "When he was near, it was like being a little intoxicated all the time."

Gabrielle didn't want to hear it, didn't want to think of the great passion that had produced and then selfishly excluded her. But as she listened to her mother's quiet, pain-filled confession, she felt the stir of understanding in her heart. On her wedding night she had felt just such a passion. It was brilliant and breathtaking and terrifying. It overwhelmed and possessed her, expanding her senses, altering her body's internal feelings and rhythms. It wrenched control from conscious will and yielded it to some deeper and more primal urge imbedded in her very muscle and marrow. It was the kind of experience that could seize a heart . . . change a soul . . . and bend a future.

With reluctant insight, she glimpsed her mother's choice from a new perspective. For an impressionable young girl, the promise of love and the awakening of such passions had probably been too overwhelming to resist. For even with a very different past, an unromantic outlook, and grave personal experience of the price passion demanded of a woman, Gabrielle had found herself making just such a surrender.

In that quiet moment, Gabrielle felt another missing part of her heart somehow fall into place, edging out a bit more of the resentment she felt toward her mother. She was seeing Rosalind's life from a woman's perspective now.

"I think I understand."

"Do you, Gabby? Dear heaven, I hope so." Rosalind stroked Gabrielle's cheek with a pained tenderness. "When you were born, I loved you so very much . . . but I was so terrified of losing him. He was my lover, my support, my life. I knew I would have to send you away when you were old enough, and I searched out the finest school money could buy . . . a place that would prepare you for a brilliant future. I believed it was the best thing I could do for you. And I followed your progress. Louise Marchand wrote me regularly." She rose and began to pace, rubbing her hands together, growing more agitated with each step.

"If only I hadn't been so immersed in *him*. I lived my entire life for that man. I ate only what he liked and wore what he liked, read what he liked, and learned about whatever subject caught his fancy, just so I could talk with him. I played whist and faro because he liked them . . . and I nearly always *lost* because I knew he liked to win. I purged my wardrobe of pink because he wasn't fond of it. I loved horses but never rode because he said 'city riding' bored him. I was the perfect mistress. But I was only a mistress. I never had any claim on Augustus, except his desire for me."

The pain in her heart finally exploded in her face and form. "The bastard—it was all about him, you see. His needs. His desires. Yes, he gave me love. *His* sort of love. And passion and comfort. Everything I needed, in fact, except respect. I thought he was jealous to be with me and me alone"—she stared into her past, seeing it all from a very different perspective—"when in fact he had built me a luxurious little box so that I wouldn't taint the rest of his 'noble' life."

Beatrice stood outside, transfixed by what she was hearing, halted on her way to clear them out of the library and send Rosalind packing from the house. She had seen them on the sofa, glimpsed tears in Gabrielle's eyes, and caught part of Rosalind's confession. Since last night she had been plagued by Rosalind's revelation in the dining room. The woman's story was so different from her own— yet they had the same regrets, the same pain, the same need to reach out to a child they had lost . . .

"Don't let it happen to you, Gabby." Rosalind knelt by Gabrielle's feet, seizing her hands. "Don't let him put you into a box. You're a wife . . . you needn't be a slave to a man's desires. You can have a respectable life. I wish I could help you—but I honestly wouldn't know where to begin. God knows, I never thought to hear myself say this, but perhaps you can learn from Pierce's mother, use her as your example. She knows what it takes to be a wife—"

"*No.*"

That single powerful syllable stopped both their hearts. They turned to find Lady Beatrice standing in the doorway with her hands clasped so tightly that they were whitened, her dark eyes mirroring the turbulent emotions inside her. They glanced at each other and wiped hastily at tears, wondering how much she had heard. Her next words let them know she had heard enough.

"You mustn't follow my example . . . It is true, I have been a wife, and I have lived a life of scrupulous respectability. But I was put into a box just as surely as your mother was." She came forward slowly, groping for words to express things she had scarcely allowed herself to think.

"Like you, my girl, I was married and bedded and left . . . after only one night."

Gabrielle rose, seeing the eyes that were so much like Pierce's, now dark and luminous with pain. Behind that slip in composure, she glimpsed for the first time the person inside Lady Beatrice: a complex woman, controlling and opinionated, fiercely committed to a set of standards and a way of life. But there was something more . . . a deeper feeling, a sense of having struggled, of having won and lost.

"I was a green young girl when I married . . . fresh from my first season, dazzled by Royce St. James's good looks and charm. But I never had a chance at his heart." Lady Beatrice took a tight breath. "After one night, he was gone.

"I was tucked away respectably in the country for much of the year. At first, I tried to be exactly what he expected—demure, proper, respectable, accommodating. I saw to his household and made his life comfortable. I was the perfect wife. But I was only a wife. I never had any claim on my husband except his name. Pierce was born soon after, and the succession was secure. Royce never shared my bed again. I wanted more children, but . . ." She glanced at Rosalind, seeming both troubled and relieved by her recognition of what they shared. "So you see, I, too, was put into a box . . . a tidy, respectable, suffocating box."

Her eyes filled with moisture. "I love Pierce from the depths of my being. But he is his father's son, my girl. For your sake and for his, don't let him do to you what his father did to me. Don't let him lock you away . . . out of his life."

Gabrielle stood rooted to the floor, stunned, staring at her mother and her mother-in-law. They were women from entirely different worlds—one the perfect wife and the other the perfect mistress—the very embodiments of the two paths a woman could choose. The thing that separated them was passion. The thing that joined them was regret.

"I've always believed there were two choices for a woman: being a mistress or being a wife," Gabrielle whispered. "But, the duke decreed I could not be a mistress, and Pierce has made it clear he wants nothing to do with a wife." The ache in her heart was spreading through her entire body. "All I wanted was the chance to choose for myself."

"What would you choose, Gabby?" Rosalind asked. "What do you *want*?"

Gabrielle turned to the window and stared at the sun-drenched lawn, wishing some of the sun's light and warmth could dispel the chill in her. What *did* she want?

A month ago she could have answered easily: marriage, respectability, a bit of personal freedom. A month ago, she had believed that marriage would protect her. She had wanted to forever separate herself from the hurts and disappointments that love and intimacy and caring would inevitably cause. But marriage to Pierce had stripped her of that defense and plunged her headlong into the very joys and agonies she had struggled to avoid. Now there was no safe haven, no protection for her against the pleasures and the pain that love would work in her life. For good or for ill, she now had to face them . . . to survive and somehow surmount them.

She closed her eyes, and Pierce's face, his smile, and his warm laughter rose in her mind and filled her heart, warming, brightening it. She thought of shoes and roses, of vows and kisses, of all the sweet possibilities that had caused her to turn to him that afternoon at The Montmortaine.

"I want a husband . . . and a lover," she said softly, smiling through the prisms of her tears. "And I want both of them to be Pierce. I want to sleep in the same bed with him and eat at the same table. I want to talk with him and laugh with him and to see him smile at me the way he did before. I want to be a part of—no, a *partner* in his life. And I want him to be a partner in mine.

"I want to ride horses with him, to play chess with him and win. I want to plant roses with him and play the piano with him and read bedtime stories . . ." She paused and looked up, thinking of that rocking horse on the third floor. "I want to fill the nursery upstairs with our children, and with music and laughter. I want to grow old with him. I want to look at him when I'm sixty and say that I'm glad he's still my"—she caught her breath as the word unfolded in her mind and in her heart—"my *friend.*"

As Beatrice listened, that outpouring of longing went straight to her heart. It was difficult to imagine her worldly, licentious, and cynical offspring being friends with any woman. There were precious few *men* he would grace with that distinction. But there was no doubt in her mind Gabrielle was telling the truth.

"Pierce St. James," Beatrice declared, "is spoiled and stubborn and jaded. He cannot bear being confined or restricted in any way. He is much too bright and far too handsome for his own good, and he's positively enjoyed the libertine reputation he has made for himself. I'm not certain if he has a scrap of conscience left in him." Her rounded face softened just enough to reveal the lines that her worries about her son had etched in it. "Are you certain you want him, my girl?"

Gabrielle seized on the hope she sensed underlying her mother-in-law's words.

"Yes, I want him," she said, feeling those words claiming her, somehow setting her course.

"Then, if you want him, you'll have to be strong enough to stand up to him, to make him accept you into his life. You cannot allow him to stuff you away in the country and drag you out of mothballs once a year to parade about under society's nose."

"I could never abide the smell of mothballs."

"You would have to go to London . . . meet him on his own ground . . . take him on, toe to toe. It is only fair to warn you, London society can be quite difficult."

"No more difficult than living a solitary life . . . married to the man I want and need, and yet separated from him."

At that, Beatrice's smile dimmed. Gabrielle could see her struggling with something. A doubt? A decision?

"It has long been a goal of mine to see Pierce decently wedded and settled in a sensible and proper life . . . both for his sake and for the sake of the grandchildren I have wanted for so many years." A moment later, Beatrice banished the mist in her eyes. "You will need entrance and introductions and advice. People will be eager for scandal. Lord knows, my son has always provided the club hounds of St. James with more than enough grist for their gossip mill." She set her chin in a way that made her look startlingly like Pierce. "I'll do it. I'll help you."

Gabrielle was speechless for a moment, trying to take it in. Lady Beatrice was offering to help her make a life with Pierce?

"Why?" She searched Beatrice's face. "Why would you help me?"

Beatrice paused, sorting both her emotions and her words. "I held the boy too tightly for too long, and he has never forgiven me for that. The die is cast between us. But if I never have his forgiveness or his respect, at least I may have the satisfaction of helping to set his feet on a higher path . . . and helping him to have the home and family life I was never able to give him."

She squeezed Gabrielle's hand. "Be a good wife to him, my girl. And make him give you the care and respect a good wife deserves."

Gratitude shone through Gabrielle's tears.

"And I'll help too, my Gabby," Rosalind declared, her eyes glowing with maternal devotion.

"You?" Beatrice raised her chin and peered down her nose at Rosalind. "What do you know about London society?"

"Mercifully, not a thing," Rosalind said, tartly, drawing herself up straight. "On the other hand, I know a great deal about men and about seduction. And seduction is precisely what Gabby must engage in if she has her heart set on your libidinous beast of a son." She turned to Gabrielle with a knowing smile. "There is no quicker way to get past a man's defenses than to rouse his passions. If you want him, you'll have to be in his mind and under his skin constantly . . . until the day he turns around and you're really there, making wild and passionate love to him."

"That is appalling," Beatrice declared, looking genuinely disturbed.

"No, that is *passion*." Rosalind smiled with the sensual aplomb of one of the demimonde's great aristocrats. "Something that is very much a part of your son's life and a part of his desire for my daughter." She looked deep into Gabrielle's eyes. "If you want to live with that man, then you must use his passion to soften his heart and his head. And there is no one more able to tutor you in the arts of love than I."

It was true, Gabrielle realized. Pierce had wanted her and had loved her tenderly on their one night together, despite his anger and his distrust of her. She had to rouse that desire for her again and use it to claim a foothold in his world.

Then it struck her: *if she wanted Pierce for a husband and a lover, she would have to be both a wife and a mistress.*

It felt as if her feet had touched solid ground for the first time in weeks, and she was able to straighten above the bewildering flow of her life to glimpse things from a stunning new perspective. Who said women had to choose between just two paths? Who said a woman had to forfeit passion to be a good and respectable wife? Who said a woman who enjoyed a man's loving must be immoral and depraved? Just who decided these wretched things, anyway?

For the first time in her life, *she* decided.

She looked at her two tutors—one a pillar of society and the other the pinnacle of the demimonde—and understood that out of their mistakes and difficulties, out of their pain and disappointments, new possibilities were being born for her.

It was as if the sun came out in her face. Her cheeks flushed and her eyes sparkled with jewel-like intensity. With the pair of them helping her, Pierce didn't stand a chance.

18

D usk was falling as Pierce walked along the streets of
Mayfair three days later. He had just spent an
interminable afternoon in Conservative party meetings at
the Carlton Club, listening to choleric lords and potbellied
landowners rail against the depredations of Gladstonian
liberalism, and growing increasingly annoyed. When a
speaker launched a virulent personal attack on Gladstone's
sanity and integrity, the rebuttals that formed in his mind
sounded disturbingly like Gabrielle's voice: *These men are
much too eager to judge based on appearances.*

Even after he purged her voice from his mind, its
influence lingered. As every strident argument was put
forth, he found himself thinking about his party's fierce

opposition to Gladstone's "liberal" measures. For just a moment he let himself think seriously about what facts might lie behind the "appearances" or outside "the obvious" that formed the core of his party's positions. The resulting stream of unanswered questions left him feeling on edge and sent him for the door.

By the time Pierce reached his house on Park Lane and strode up the carriage turn, he was bone weary and looking forward to a double jigger of brandy, a good long soak, and a fat cigar. But the instant Parnell opened the door and Pierce caught sight of the pile of baggage and crates sitting around a piano in the middle of the entry hall, he felt a prickling on the back of his neck and sensed that lightning was about to strike . . . again.

"What the hell is all this?"

"I tried to reach you, your lordship," Parnell said, looking more frazzled than Pierce had ever see him. "They arrived this afternoon, with no warning—"

"They?" He gave the valises and trunks a cursory look, then settled his attention on the half-crated piano, which seemed ominously familiar.

"Your mother and Lady Sandbourne. They arrived just this afternoon, with that other woman. They insisted I put Lady Sandbourne's things in *your* chambers. But not knowing your wishes, your lordship, I left them here for the present."

Halfway through a groan, he realized that Parnell had made a distinction between his mother and Lady Sandbourne. The sense of it burst over him. "Lady Sandbourne? Gabrielle?"

Parnell motioned toward the drawing room. With each step Pierce took in that direction, the tension in his middle wrenched tighter. *Gabrielle. Here.* He found his mother in her usual chair, at her ever-present needlework, and across from her sat none other than Rosalind LeCoeur, reading a pamphlet of some sort. The sight of his priggish mother and his scandalous mother-in-law together in the same room—in his house—rendered him momentarily speechless.

"Good God," he finally uttered, causing them to look up.

"Well, if that isn't just like you." Beatrice set her knitting aside and rose regally. "Not a single word of welcome for your family."

"Family?" he choked out. He focused briefly on Rosalind, then looked at Beatrice in confusion.

"I've left that wretch, Carlisle," Rosalind explained. "And I simply could not bear staying in that awful house just now. Your wife and your mother were gracious enough to invite me to stay with them while I decide what to do with myself."

Pierce blinked, scarcely able to take it in. Rosalind had split with the duke? His mother and his wife had invited her to—

His wife. Scanning the room, he found Gabrielle rising from the window seat on the far end.

She was clad in a periwinkle blue moiré with a fitted bodice, and her hair was caught up in a loose twist. The stark simplicity of her dress emphasized her memorable curves, and its color heightened the intense blue of her eyes. She might have stepped straight out of one of his fevered dreams.

"Why aren't you at Thorndike?" he demanded irritably.

She glanced at the women, who now stood not far away. "I . . . we . . . have some *shopping* to do."

"Shopping?" He fairly choked on the word—a euphemism, he knew, for all sorts of nefarious and underhanded female doings. He wasn't a complete idiot. He knew a plot when he saw it. He looked from Gabrielle to Beatrice to Rosalind, watching their silent and inscrutable exchange of "feminese." They had taken over his house, and now intended to trap him, to control him . . . to . . . He had to make a stand, exert husbandly authority, or he was doomed.

He turned back to the door and thundered for Parnell, who arrived at a run. He ordered his carriage brought around immediately, then turned back to Gabrielle.

"Perhaps I didn't make myself clear when I told you Thorndike was to be your home. I shall certainly be more emphatic this time. Get your gloves and your wrap," he ordered, summoning every bit of masculine prerogative he possessed. "You're going back. Tonight." When she hesitated, he narrowed his eyes and seized her by the wrist. "Very well, if you insist on doing things the hard way . . ."

"I am not going back," Gabrielle said quietly, digging her heels into the thick pile of the rug.

"Oh, yes you are."

"I most certainly am not. At least, not until you go too."

"Fine. I'll take you. Right now." He tried to pull her along, but she strained against his iron grip. He shot a look at the two mothers, warning them not to interfere. "Dammit, Gabrielle, I shall carry you if I have to."

"Very well." She sank abruptly onto her knees, surprising him and defeating his belated attempt to keep her on her feet. "Carry me if you must." She primly rearranged her bustle to one side, then sat back on the floor.

"Fine!" he ground out. The next minute he was on one knee beside her, seizing her around the waist and sinking an arm beneath her knees. Her sputters of surprise were gratifying—she clearly hadn't expected him to carry through with his threat. But that first pulse of satisfaction quickly gave way to sobering reality as he strained to lift her. As he swayed and rose, she gave a cry and both of her arms flew around his neck. Steadying himself and trying to better his grip on her, he found himself panting, inhaling her scent. Roses—why the hell did she always have to smell like roses?

He strode for the front doors, trying not to breathe any more than necessary and getting nothing but red-faced for the effort. By the time he reached the front door, he was realizing that he'd made a major tactical mistake in picking her up so quickly and stalking out. Now he had to stand and wait for Parnell to return to open the heavy doors for him. Then he would have to stand and wait for Jack to bring the carriage around.

She was treacherously soft; he could feel his body growing hot and responsive where her curves were pressed against him. As he glanced anxiously back along the stairs, watching for Parnell, her arms tightened slightly around his neck, wreathing his head in her warmth and her bedeviling scent.

"This isn't fair, you know," she said quietly, her breath teasing the side of his face. "I've done nothing wrong. And banishing me to the country won't settle anything between us."

"There is nothing to settle," he declared grimly. Where the hell was Parnell?

"I beg to differ," she said. He could feel her staring at him but refused to meet her gaze. "But then, we'll have several hours to discuss it, in the carriage, on the way to Thorndike."

The silky insinuation in her voice sent a shaft of heat straight to his loins. His tensed muscles began to quiver with a new sort of strain as he struggled to keep from responding to her erotic suggestion.

At last, Parnell returned from summoning the carriage, spotted them, and rushed to open the doors. Relieved, Pierce carried her out onto the darkened steps to wait for the carriage. But a moment later, she began melting in his arms, pressing her breast against him and settling closer to him. Through her fitted bodice, he could feel the hard boning that contained her waist, and through the layers of her silk and muslin skirts he could feel the firmness of her thighs.

Suddenly he was remembering the sight of her bare breasts . . . creamy mounds, tight, velvety nipples . . . jutting, inviting, beckoning. A whisper of phantom sensation along his flanks recalled the feel of her bare thighs —strong, sleek, and silky—pressed intimately against him, parting for him, cradling his own. His skin grew hot and his breathing became labored. Trickles of excitation were wending slowly down the inner walls of his body, collecting and pooling in this loins.

Hours alone with her . . . in a darkened carriage . . . on moonlit roads. The deliberate yielding of her body against him promised a lush response . . . her softness at his fingertips . . . her mouth yielding beneath his, tasting, teasing, tempting him . . . her moist heat absorbing his fire and softly extinguishing it, then clinging to his skin, clinging to his senses . . .

In the dim light he looked down into her luminous jewel eyes, and cold panic seized him as he felt his desires rising, slipping slowly out of his control.

"I see your game," he declared, abruptly carrying her back inside and depositing her on the top of a trunk with a plop. "And it's not going to work. Go ahead . . . take over the bloody house. Hang chintz everywhere—get half a dozen cats—plaster crocheted antimacassars all over the place. Paint the damned shutters pink, for all I care!" Turning on his heel, he made straight for the front doors.

He spoke to Parnell, but loudly enough for her to hear: "I shall be at the Clarendon from now on. Have Peters bring my clothes and kit first thing tomorrow." Then the front doors rattled from the force of his exit.

She sat on the trunk, staring after him, feeling aroused and deprived and roundly frustrated . . . until the thought occurred that he was undoubtedly suffering similar complaints. She had touched him, she was sure of it. Desire had been palpable in his every breath, every fiber, every pulse of his being. When he looked deep into her eyes, she had felt him responding with an intimate caress of recognition. And in the darkness she had seen the answering glimmer of need in him.

She had been so close . . . in his arms . . . in his desires . . .

Footsteps caused her to look up, and she found Lady Beatrice and Rosalind hurrying toward her. "What happened?" Beatrice demanded breathlessly.

"He told me to hang chintz everywhere and to paint the shutters pink," she said with a small, triumphant smile.

"Chintz? Shutters?" Rosalind scowled. "With you in his arms, all he could think of was painting the house? He is more his mother's son than I thought."

Beatrice pointedly ignored Rosalind's nettling to focus on the nuances of Pierce's caustic remarks in retreat. "He's ceded you the house. Excellent. Then the next step must be to establish your place as his wife in the eyes of society. We have to get you out and about."

"That's absurd," Rosalind declared with a dismissive wave. "The next step must be to establish her hold on his passions. With them engaged, the rest will follow."

"She first needs to secure her place in his *world*." Beatrice bristled.

"She first needs to secure her place in his *bed*." Rosalind glowered.

In a blink they were nose to nose, the truce they had

tacitly observed since that afternoon at Thorndike unraveling before Gabrielle's eyes.

"Mother! Lady Beatrice!" She insinuated herself between them, calling them back to the challenge at hand. "I see no reason why we cannot work on *both*."

Rosalind straightened, a determined glint in her eye.

Beatrice raised her chin to a haughty angle.

"I'll have her in his bed within a week," Rosalind declared, tossing down a gauntlet.

"I'll have her at his side in public before week's end," Beatrice countered.

After a long, charged moment, the mothers withdrew, each to her chambers—one plotting to make her a wife, the other scheming to make her a lover.

Thus was born a potent, two-pronged attack on Pierce's aversion to marital bliss. Rosalind and Beatrice were both determined to see the recalcitrant bridegroom brought to heel within the week, and both spent the rest of the evening charting a strategy to achieve that end. The next morning, Beatrice seized the initiative by whisking Gabrielle away, first thing, to an appointment at a dressmaker's salon in the heart of Regent Street's exclusive shops. Gabrielle had protested that she needed no new clothes, but Beatrice rolled her eyes in forbearance.

"Don't be ridiculous, my dear . . . of course you do. Your wardrobe is woefully inadequate for a married woman in society. But, more than clothes, you need social contacts. And there is no better way to gain introductions and entrance to the first circles, than at the proper modiste."

They spent three hours in an elegant salon that was arranged more like a drawing room than a dressmaker's shop. Measurements were taken, then refreshments were served as they perused model dresses and sketches and fabrics . . . in the company of two prominent hostesses who were also at the task of acquiring new dresses. Lady Cecilly Morton and Olivia Tyler-Benninghoff were intensely curious about Gabrielle. The earl's sudden marriage announcement and speculation about the bride's origins had been a topic at every society event for the past ten days. They were surprised to see the formidable Lady Beatrice in public with her questionable daughter-in-law and were nothing short of amazed that she introduced Gabrielle with a blend of candor and delicacy that left no doubt that she was pleased by the match her worrisome scapegrace of a son had made.

As the appointment and the acquaintance progressed, Lady Morton mentioned that she had received Pierce's acceptance of an invitation to her annual charity gala and commented that she was looking forward to introducing Gabrielle to her guests.

"As am I," Beatrice declared, sending Gabrielle a speaking smile. "Your charity gala is always one of the highlights of the season. However, I must confess, I was bemoaning the timing of it to dear Gabrielle. We have been so occupied with settling in, we have scarcely had a moment to plan what to wear . . ."

Gabrielle watched her mother-in-law responding as if the gala had been at the very top of their social calendar all along and marveled at the woman's consummate aplomb.

"Are we going to her party?" she asked as they settled into the carriage.

"We certainly are. The timing is a stroke of pure fortune. There is no better place for you to make your debut in society at Pierce's side."

Gabrielle frowned. "But how can you be certain Pierce will be there?"

"Trust me, my girl, he'll be there. If there is anything Pierce cares about in this world, it's his blessed politics. And Cecilly's annual charity 'do' is a must for aspiring

politicians"—Beatrice gave her a gloriously devious smile—
"*and their wives.*"

When they arrived home, they found the drawing room
filled with brilliant silks, feather boas, and the scent of
expensive Parisian perfume. Gabrielle halted in the
doorway, surprised by the sight of three familiar faces.

"Who are these people?" Lady Beatrice demanded,
sailing into their midst, primed to defend her household.
The women were dressed to the nines, but one look at their
artificially enhanced beauty and knowledgeable eyes was all
that was required to know what sort of women they were.

"These, are my 'amorous experts.'" Rosalind gestured
proudly to her friends. "They have been retired for some
time now. But between them, they have a combined total of
sixty-two years of amorous experience."

Beatrice steadied herself on the back of a nearby chair.
The tension in the room was palpable as Rosalind made
introductions . . . and one by one, Genevieve, Ariadne,
and Clementine tactfully announced that they had never,
ever made the acquaintance of the old Lord Sandbourne.
Though her unspoken concern that she might be greeting
one of her late husband's dalliances in her own drawing
room was quickly put to rest, Beatrice was still clearly
appalled by their presence. It was a relief to all when she
excused herself and sailed out the door, leaving Gabrielle in
their hands.

"Gabby!" "Gabrielle!" and "*Chérie!*" The trio of retired
courtesans crowded around Gabrielle as soon as Beatrice
was out of sight and gave her enthusiastic hugs.

"Your *maman* has told us of your . . . how do you
say . . . predicament," Genevieve declared with a "*tsk*" of
dismay.

"A bloody outrage, it is," Clementine put in, giving
Gabrielle's cheek a pat.

"But not to worry," Ariadne assured her. "By the time we're finished, he'll be eating out of your hand."

The foursome bundled her straight upstairs and into Pierce's chambers, intent on seeing his most intimate environs in order to glean clues that might help in a seduction.

He was a man's man, they concluded from the massive, heavily carved furnishings. From the fine satin wall coverings, artful layering of bed drapes, and the breathtaking carpets, they deduced that he appreciated the ornate and intricate, the lush and the complex . . . most definitely a sensual and complicated man. And from the paintings and "Egyptian" artifacts here and there, they concluded that he had a taste for the exotic.

With their survey completed, they sat Gabrielle on the bench at the foot of the bed and began to expound.

"Walking, talking, laughing, nearly anything a woman does—short of blowing her nose—can be made into a seductive act." Rosalind began the tutorial.

"The old French saying 'Looks breed love'—it is very true, *oui?*" Genevieve took over. "The eyes speak but one language, everywhere. *Alors,* the best start for the seduction, is to catch the gentleman's eye and hold it. For a long moment. He must know this look is meant for him and him alone. And while you look at him, you say in your mind so that it shows in your eyes: '*Come and love me.*' And then you look away."

They stood her before a mirror and told her to imagine Pierce and to make her eyes say "come and love me." She blushed and shrank, but was finally coaxed to try it. Her expression looked more like a myopic squint than come-hither glance. Genevieve cleared her throat and offered to demonstrate. Gabrielle watched in wonder as the petite woman was transformed into a smoldering temptress, by just a look. Once, twice, three more times, Gabrielle tried, feeling awkward and self-conscious. The foursome exchanged covert glances of dismay and quickly moved on.

"Once ye got a gentleman's eye"—Clementine introduced the next part with a demonstration—"you make each movement just for him. Make 'im think they're created just for 'im . . . offered up for 'is pleasure." She dropped a handkerchief and stooped to pick it up in a graceful glide that fairly heated the air around her. Then she walked across the floor, swaying slightly, silk swishing in a way that suggested movement beneath her skirts. For a middle-aged woman a full two stones over what she had been in her active days as a *haute courtisane,* she radiated a sultry confidence that any man would recognize as sexual accomplishment. When she demonstrated sitting, turning, and the simple act of taking a hand, Gabrielle was amazed by the change in her.

Next, they had Gabrielle try walking, sitting, curtsying. After a strained silence, the women nodded to each other, agreeing that she still had time to practice and that a small waist and a well-fitted dress could make up for many deficits in sensual grace.

Then Ariadne took the floor. "Words, conversation must take on new meaning. Every comment must be spoken as if it contains a hidden message just for him. And glances will help punctuate each sentence. Like this: 'Most people don't like the *wet,* but I find rain marvelously *stimulating,* your lordship.' Or: 'I adore asparagus . . . when it is *hot* and *tender* and *well prepared.*' " The inflection she gave each example and the accompanying dip of her lashes made both statements seem the most suggestive comments in the world.

"Part of it is choosing the right thing to say, part of it is saying it properly. If you can work in the mention of sensory things—textures or colors with vivid description, scents and aromas that are alluring, or the mention of 'warm' or 'wet' or 'slow' or 'sleek,' things that evoke the senses—then you're halfway to a seduction."

They had her try it. "What a nice, *wet* rain," she said. Ariadne coughed and she tried again. "*Ummm . . .* Do I smell a *tender, juicy* leg of lamb?" Clementine choked back a giggle. Gabrielle's face flushed with color. This wasn't her wretched idea in the first place! "My, I can never resist a lovely"—she couldn't think of an appropriately seductive description and seized—"*plump* strawberry." The women broke out in laughter.

Rosalind dabbed her moist face with a handkerchief. "You see, Gabrielle, there is nothing more irresistible to a man than the fact that a woman wants him enough to let him know it. But if you let him know you want him too much, there will be no challenge in it. So you have to be careful to avoid the obvious."

"A man like your Sandbourne, he knows well the game," Genevieve asserted. "But with you, he cannot resist playing, eh?"

"Ye mus' keep him off balance," Clementine added. "Never sure whether yer beckonin' or just smilin' . . . whether yer ready to struggle or surrender."

They moved on to "touches." Incidental and purposeful. And they identified places for more explicit erotic contact: window nooks, behind doors, beneath dinner tables, and—Clementine's favorite—carriages.

"Carriage love's a whole study in itself," she declared. "There's somethin' about a dark carriage that brings out th' beast in a man. Ye start by sittin' close, without lookin' at 'im. Then ye remove yer gloves an' let yer fingers stray a bit . . . up 'is thigh, over 'is loins, an' inside the buttons of 'is shirt. Next thing ye know, yer skirts is up and yer riding postilion!"

The sense of what she meant sank in, and Gabrielle blushed violently.

"Yes, well . . . I think I need a breath of air," she said. "And I'm certain we could all use a bit of tea. I'll have Parnell bring some."

When she had darted out the door, Rosalind sighed as she led her fellow tutors downstairs to the drawing room. "It was so much easier for all of us. We always had someone to practice on."

After refreshments, during which Lady Beatrice tactfully stayed in her rooms to work on a bit of correspondence, the women whisked Gabrielle up to Pierce's chambers and tried again to help her walk, talk, and move seductively. The more they scrutinized and offered advice, the worse her performance became.

"Please," Gabrielle finally said, halting in the midst of an exercise that soon had her nerves in knots. "I know you all mean well, but I'm not sure I can do this."

"Don't be silly, Gabrielle," Rosalind said emphatically. "You have just as many juices as anyone in this room."

"That's not what I meant. Lord knows when I'll have the chance to tease and lure Pierce across crowded rooms. Who knows if he'll even *look* at me?"

Rosalind tapped her chin, scowling, thinking. "She has a point. Perhaps we need something more direct . . . something that can command his attention and rouse his passions quickly."

"This may be true, *non?*" Genevieve nodded to the others. "Perhaps she needs just to plunge into the middle of his life . . . his world . . . his heart."

"What? A grand gesture?" Clementine warmed to the idea with a broadening grin. "A great romantic boot to 'is stubborn backside."

"It would have to be something stunning." Ariadne threw herself into the contemplation of it. "Something unique. Something boldly provocative. Wait! There is one gambit I always meant to try. I never got around to it before my Gerald died. It is a bit exotic, but"—she glanced around at the paintings and the objets d'art in the chamber—"his lordship obviously has a weakness for the exotic. All right. Here it is."

Gabrielle braced for something outrageous. She wasn't disappointed.

"Cleopatra and Caesar."

There was a moment of bewildered silence. Ariadne expelled a disgusted breath. "Philistines! You know the story, surely. Cleopatra—that would be your part, Gabrielle —had herself rolled up in a fine carpet and carried to Julius Caesar—his lordship, of course—as a gift. Clever woman, Cleopatra, bypassing all those messy and tiresome diplomatic channels, going straight for the man himself. The rest, of course, is history. They fell madly in love. It was one of the great romantic gambits of all times. And it's perfect for Gabrielle." She enumerated the advantages on her fingers. "She would have surprise, seduction, and the piquancy of the clandestine, all in one."

"It's brilliant," Rosalind said, catching fire. "He's removed himself to that wretched hotel and Gabby needs a way to get in to see him. What better way than to be carried there in disguise and unrolled at his feet?"

"Think of it, *mes chéries*—" Genevieve painted the picture for them with her elegant hands. "The rug unrolls. Reclining there, in delectable dishabille, are the sultry eyes, the soft shoulders, the shapely limbs he has dreamt of seeing again."

" 'E'd be on 'er like wool on a sheep's back!" Clementine crowed.

Gabrielle was trying to work it out in her mind. They were proposing she dress up in some costume, roll herself up in a rug, and have herself carried to him at his hotel suite? "But once I was there, what would I do? I mean . . . is there more?"

Chuckling, they looked at each other, then at her.

"You'll talk with him, of course. Say what is on your mind," Rosalind said, watching her indulgently. "Tell him how you feel and what you want."

" 'Specially what ye *want*, love."

"And things will happen as they will happen, *oui?*"

"Whatever happens afterward," Ariadne observed with a wisdom born of experience, "he will know you want him. And he will have one more memory of searing passion to deal with in the long nights ahead."

It was a perfectly ingenious plan, Gabrielle had to admit. Once she was there, in his suite, she could make it quite difficult indeed for him to get rid of her. He would have to listen to her, to look at her, to deal with her as a person and a woman. It shouldn't be too difficult to get him to put his hands on her again, and when he did, she wouldn't allow him to take them away until they had given her exactly what she wanted. Afterward, with passions sated and pride barriers melted between them, she would talk to him, tell him about his mother's plan to introduce her to society, persuade him to come back to his house and give their marriage a chance. It would be an opportunity to let passion work for her instead of against her, for a change.

"All right," she said with a determined look. "I'll do it."

19

Charity was the farthest thing from Pierce's mood as he arrived at Lord and Lady Morton's gala that Saturday evening. He dreaded encountering the dragons of society and the power brokers of politics under one roof. Of late his reputation had taken a drubbing in both circles. But, this was the one major social event of the season that promoted humanitarian concerns. It was the place where members of the upper crust mingled with the mavens of charity and demonstrated their depth of character by their largesse. Putting in an appearance was critical if he was to counter some of the speculation attached to his name.

He stepped down out of his carriage onto the paved walk and mounted the steps to the fashionable Georgian brick mansion on Grosvenor Square. As he presented his card to the liveried houseman and waited to be announced, he surveyed the spacious, marble-floored entry and the lively crowd of guests. In short order, he spotted Lord Calvert, Dr. Richard Epperly, Sir William Hartshorn, and the staid but influential old marchioness of Queensberry—persons whose goodwill might prove helpful in salvaging his political reputation. By the time he was greeted by his hostess, Lady Morton, his mind was so set on mapping out a strategy of contacts that it took a moment for him to catch her unexpected question.

"Is she not with you?" She glanced past his shoulder. "We met, you know. Three days ago, at the dressmaker's." With a twinkle in her eye, she gave his hand a squeeze. "I can scarcely wait to introduce her—she'll be a sensation."

Pierce stared blankly at her for a moment. She had met —Gabrielle? Expected Gabrielle to arrive with him? He forced a smile, scrambling for a noncommittal reply.

"I . . . I came directly from another engagement."

"Ah." She inserted her arm through his, smiling. "Well, until she arrives, I shall have the pleasure of your company myself. I'm sure you know many of my guests, but there are several people I especially want you to meet . . ."

In roiling confusion, he escorted his hostess around the great hall and into the drawing room, greeting with distraction the very people that only a minute before he had been intent on impressing.

Gabrielle. Here. As they progressed through the gathering, dread of a different sort began creeping up his spine. Each and every one of London's philanthropic and political elite seemed to know that he was newly wedded and expressed interest in meeting his bride. Clearly, they had heard the gossip about him and his ill-gotten marriage and were eager to verify it firsthand. And he couldn't begin to imagine what sort of debacle lay in store for him if—*when*—Gabrielle arrived.

At length, Lady Morton was forced to relinquish him in order to return to her duties. Relieved, he made the circuit from drawing room to family parlor to conservatory to music room to dining room, drawing both murmurs of congratulations and silent stares. Periodically he raised his head above the crowd to watch the doors, but when he heard her announced, it took a moment to register that the Countess of Sandbourne was indeed Gabrielle. Hurrying back to the hall, he spotted her with their hostess, smiling and exchanging pleasantries under the vigilant eye of his mother.

As they turned to greet another middle-aged lady, he caught a full glimpse of Gabrielle, and for a moment was struck motionless. She wore a gown of lush emerald moiré. The low-scooped bodice was rimmed with velvet and a silk chiffon overskirt was swept back with a second overskirt into an elaborate bustle trimmed with a cascade of white silk camellias. At her shoulder, several real camellias vied for the eye with her creamy skin, and her upswept hair was accented by those same fragrant blossoms. With her deep green gown, pale breast, and golden hair, she looked like an exotic flower just coming into bloom. He caught himself inhaling, anticipating her scent, and furiously stanched that response.

Groaning inwardly he headed for her. It was going to be a very long night.

It was a tribute to Madame Marchand's instruction that Gabrielle appeared gracious, even glowing, as she greeted her hostess. Her mouth was dry, and inside her long kid gloves, her hands were icy. When Lady Morton mentioned that Pierce had already arrived, Gabrielle smiled with what she hoped would pass for wifely pleasure.

Then, through the swirl of bright silk gowns, sparkling champagne, and animated faces, she saw him coming across the drawing room, and her heart lost a beat. In his fitted black tailcoat and vest, and pristine collar and pearl white tie, he was without a doubt the most handsome man present. Heads turned and both fans and lashes fluttered as he passed. But in his eyes, fixed on her alone, there was a heated glint that sent a shiver through her.

He used the hand she extended to him to draw her closer to his side, while chatting with their hostess and giving his mother a nod of acknowledgment. Then murmuring an excuse, he spirited her through the adjoining parlor and into the conservatory, where he found a relatively empty area among some giant ferns.

"What the devil are you doing here?"

"Making new acquaintances . . . enjoying a gala party, I believe—"

"The hell you are," he said. "You've just come down with an agonizing headache. And I shall have to take you straight home." His hand tightened on her arm as if he was ready to drag her from the house.

"I have no such headache," she declared in a furious whisper. "And the only place I am going is in to dinner with the rest of the guests." Wresting her wrist from him, she gave her train a furious kick and headed for the doors.

The dinner bell kept him from going after her. As he followed the crowd toward the dining room, he prepared himself to minimize whatever damage she might inflict on his already battered reputation.

Lady Morton was gliding about the rooms, pairing gentlemen and ladies according to some cannily prearranged plan. Pierce quickly made his way through the other guests, intending to partner his bride himself. But before he could reach Gabrielle, Lady Morton had seized her hand and placed it in gruff old Sir William Hartshorn's, sending them off to the dining room together. When the hostess turned and saw his bereft look, she laughed.

"Poor Lord Sandborne—I've just given your bride away." She took his arm. "I have other plans for you, sir. I have reserved you for *myself*."

He smiled as genially as he could, telling himself that considering the stories circulating about him, it was a stroke of good fortune to be singled out as a dinner partner by the toast of London society.

In the dining room two long ranks of tables had been erected to accommodate the large number of guests. When their hostess was seated, the ladies followed suit, then the host and the gentlemen took their seats and the conversation quickly began all along the tables.

Pierce located Gabrielle several chairs down on the opposite side of the table. The sight of his unpredictable wife engaged in conversation with old Sir William, who was known to be as insufferably narrow-minded as he was influential in the Treasury, sent a wave of horror through him. He strained to catch bits of what they were saying.

"How long were you in Venice, Sir William?" Gabrielle was smiling.

Travels. A fairly safe topic, Pierce told himself.

"A week, thank God," the old fellow responded. "Blamedest climate. Foggy as old Blighty. Might just as well have stayed home. Endless rain. Wet everywhere."

"Then you must have been there in late autumn or winter." She looked up and caught Pierce staring at her. She looked directly into his eyes. "Most people don't like the *wet*. But I find rain marvelously *stimulating*." A smile curled her mouth into a womanly bow, and her posture softened with subtle allure. "After a time, you learn to accommodate the climate . . . move more slowly and dress for comfort. Heavy silks are quite out of the question. Cottons are so much better against the skin."

Something in the way she let her tongue linger over the words "wet" and "stimulating" sent a guilty shiver of excitement through Pierce. He had a brief, vivid vision of cotton underthings drawing back to expose soft, silky skin . . . then shook it off, appalled.

"Venice is a favorite of mine," he heard her say, with a voice warm enough to melt polar ice. He glanced their way. Old Sir William was being reduced to puddles. Pierce's throat tightened; he knew that feeling. "I spent nearly two months there and left feeling there was still so much more to explore. Tell me, did you have the chance to attend an opera at Teatro La Fenice?"

Pierce suddenly realized that the eyes of his own dining partners were trained on him, as if awaiting his comment or answer. Coloring, he smiled as winningly as possible. "Sorry, I didn't quite catch that . . ."

Moments later, his attention stole back to Gabrielle as Lady Chilton and Lord Rosebery, seated across from Gabrielle, began to ask her questions. He held his breath as they tossed out what they knew of Venice and she responded with lively comments on each cathedral, historical site, and restaurant they named.

"So much water everywhere made me quite nervous," Lady Chilton opined.

"To make peace with the water you must understand its gifts," she responded. "The riches and the pleasures it brings. But, I confess . . ." Pierce could see her audience leaning forward to catch whatever such a charming creature might have to confess, and found himself leaning her direction as well. "My favorite part is the way it laps at the feet of the beautiful old houses, splashes against the docks, and washes against the boats that glide through the moonlit waters, creating an enchanting night music for the city."

Her voice had taken on a seductive music of its own. He found himself thinking of the darkness, of the sound of water lapping, of enfolding her like that night music . . . gliding . . . rhythmic . . .

The sound of Lady Morton's voice brought him crashing back to reality, and he realized that she and everyone else along the table between them and Gabrielle had ceased talking to listen to Gabrielle.

"What a lovely way to put it, Lady Gabrielle," Lady Morton said with a sidelong glance at Pierce. "Since you love it so, I am surprised you are not there now . . . on your wedding trip."

A bolt of anxiety shot through Pierce as the others turned to look at him. Gabrielle gave him a blatantly adoring smile that, combined with her words, contained a wealth of private meaning.

"Oh, Pierce let me know from the evening we met that he does not travel when Parliament is in session. He is utterly devoted to his public duties and responsibilities." The warmth of her gaze suggested that she was equally devoted . . . to him. "I am quite content to postpone our wedding trip for a while. You see, I went to school in France and have been home only a short while. To me, *London* is new and fascinating. I am looking forward to exploring"—another warm glance his direction—"my new home."

That unleashed a storm of questions, comments, and suggestions that left Pierce gripping the arms of his chair with whitened hands. It seemed everyone had a view or a monument or a restaurant to recommend. And everyone had a question for her about her background or her surprisingly broad travels.

The expressive shadings of her voice, the enchanting motion of her slender hands, and the luscious sight of her all-too-bare shoulders slowly tightened the coil of tension in Pierce's stomach. His face felt hot, his collar grew tight, and his fingertips began to tingle. Her extravagant education and experiences in travel were being put to stunning use. It annoyed him beyond all bounds that she was so perfectly at ease while he was balancing on a razor's edge.

Gabrielle felt his gaze on her and read his thoughts in his face. But there was no doubt that she was holding her own among London's elite, and she knew that fact couldn't have entirely escaped his notice. Glancing around the table, she began to see that the discussion she had begun was so lively that Lady Morton's wonderful meal was in danger of being neglected. Adroitly, she recalled the others' attention to the marvelous cuisine at their fingertips by savoring and complimenting the delicate cold vichyssoise . . . thereby securing her hostess's goodwill, once and for all.

Pierce's goodwill, however, continued to elude her. She caught him staring fixedly at her between the fish and fowl courses, as she spooned the minted ice intended to cleanse her palate into her mouth. His continuing vigilance, as if he expected disaster to come crashing down on her at any moment, meant that he wasn't seeing her at all, but some commodity labeled "wife" that had to be stuffed back into its proper box. The thought rankled. Let him stare, she thought irritably. Let him worry.

She licked her lips, slowly, with luxuriant defiance . . . just for him. Instantly, his face reddened, and she had a delicious new game.

With each drink from her wine goblet, she surreptitiously licked the rim of her glass. With each comment by Sir William, she leaned in Pierce's direction, making the most of her low, tight bodice. By the time the glazed fruit and almonds and cheese were served, she had Pierce on the edge of his seat, roused and frantic that she was about to do something outrageous. Instead, she licked the sugary glaze from a grape and began to peel the skin from it with her teeth, strip by delicate strip, letting the juice bathe her lips in glistening sweetness. His nostrils flared as he jerked his face away and shifted in his chair. She smiled and popped the fruit into her mouth.

By the time Lady Morton finally rose and led the ladies out, Pierce was roiling, molten inside. All through the brandy and cigars in the dining room, he kept glancing at the doors. How was it that in the midst of London's political and social elite, with him desperate to repair the damage she had done to his reputation, she still managed to reduce him to a heaving, mindless tangle of desires? Peeling grapes with her teeth . . . tracing the rim of her glass with her tongue . . . all while charming the socks off the likes of old Hartshorn and Lord Rosebery . . .

And she did charm them. He had to admit that. By the end of the meal, old Sir William was all wine-warmed smiles and bluff good humor. Lord Rosebery was waxing poetic about the plight of the poor and various children's charities, glowing with delight at having found a kindred spirit in Gabrielle. And she had Lady Chilton openly regretting that she had never taken advantage of her seaside holidays to learn to swim.

When the two groups merged later in the drawing room for music and conversation, Pierce felt once again in control and determined not to let Gabrielle interfere further with his own plans for the evening. He managed to catch the eye of the speaker of the House of Commons and to have a moment with him before the dowager marchioness of Queensberry and the current earl of Devonshire descended on him to lobby for a "Charities" bill that would soon come before the House of Lords. Then, just as they were parting, Lord Rosebery, a notorious Liberal and a close friend of Gladstone's, loomed up before Pierce to exchange pleasantries and to inquire whether or not he had selected a favorite charity among those represented. When he said he had not, Rosebery proposed his own favorites, both children's institutions, for Pierce's consideration, and indicated that Lady Sandbourne seemed most enthusiastic about them.

Through it all, Pierce kept an eye on Gabrielle and gradually worked his way about the room toward her. In the company of his mother and their host and hostess, she was leaving a wide swath of admiration in her wake as she made her way through the jovial crowd. As he approached, his mother was saying: ". . . is really quite a pianist, you know."

"How lovely," Lady Morton responded, turning to Gabrielle. "Perhaps you would favor us with a sample of your music, Lady Gabrielle."

To Pierce's dismay his mother and their hostess bundled Gabrielle toward the piano in the adjoining parlor. Pierce went after them, intent on keeping Gabrielle from embarrassing herself.

"Really, Gabrielle . . ." He threaded his way through the group collecting about the piano. "I think it is time we were going."

"Surely not, Lord Sandbourne," Lady Morton said, putting her arm through his. "The night is young. You cannot deprive us of her company just yet, nor of the chance to hear her play."

Captive in his hostess's grasp, Pierce could only watch with ill-disguised tension as Gabrielle adjusted her distance from the keyboard, removed her long gloves, and began to play.

A melody began to build and thread around and through accompaniment, and soon Tchaikovsky rose like candle smoke, filling the great room. The music lapped around and through him, sweet and majestic, but with a hint of melancholy that resonated in his blood. He had heard her play and knew she was a capable pianist, but he also knew that in such an elite gathering, merely "capable" would be woefully inadequate. He hadn't guessed she possessed such skill at the keyboard. Suddenly his fears of being embarrassed by her performance were replaced by his private embarrassment at his ignorance of her.

She finished with Tchaikovsky and went on to selections by Liszt and Schumann, playing with increasing joy and intensity. Glancing around him at the admiring faces, Pierce realized that they were coming to share his appreciation of just how unique and talented his Gabrielle was. A possessive impulse surged through him as he mentally claimed those agile fingers, those lips drawn into a pout of concentration, that curvaceous form tensed and overflowing with artistic passion. When she finished, Pierce joined in the enthusiastic applause, perversely feeling quite pleased.

Lady Morton coaxed Gabrielle into playing just one more selection. She considered it a moment, then with demure smiles at Lady Beatrice's beaming face and at Pierce's unreadable one, she complied.

Beginning with a burst of elaborate fingerings that built to a dramatic flourish, she settled into a sonatalike piece built around a surprisingly infectious motif. The notes of that theme ran around and around in Pierce's head, familiar, teasing his recall but eluding recognition . . . until she looked up at him, her eyes bright with what he would have sworn was mischief. She was playing as if every note was meant for him and him alone. He remembered that look . . . Suddenly he recalled that melody and knew the words that accompanied it.

Whoops, Alice! . . . the ladder is bending . . .

Good God—she was playing "Whoops, Alice!" in front of London's most elite society! He looked around frantically at her audience but, thankfully, no one seemed to recognize the beer hall drinking song.

She played determinedly on, adding runs and soaring

crescendos that turned an indecent ditty into a veritable work of art. Her gaze drew his, holding it, speaking to him as surely as the music did. What it said, he was stunned to realize, was that she wanted him to recognize it, to remember.

In spite of himself, he did remember. Quiet confidences. Shared laughter. Sweet rebellion. Suddenly there was a fullness in his chest and a constriction in his throat. Deep within him, her overwhelming allure and her enduring passion for him began curling through him, invading his will, softening his resistance, capturing his—

Invading? Capturing?

Damn and double damn. Even knowing she had come here tonight to force her way into his life, to claim his name and status as her own, he found himself strangely unable to resist her. With a story and a laugh and a bone-melting, smile she had conquered society's skeptics and established herself as his lovely and gracious bride. And with a sultry look, the bite of a grape, and a beer hall song, she was perilously close to conquering his soul as well.

As applause and admiration swirled around Gabrielle, he stepped back, meaning to withdraw and work his way to the door. But Lady Morton seized his hand and put Gabrielle's in it, ushering the pair of them into the drawing room. He was trapped.

Gabrielle looked up at him and found him watching her with conflicting traces of annoyance and pleasure. She responded with a warm smile and felt his arm tighten beneath her hand.

Side by side, they weathered the accolades of well-wishers, the pointed questions of curiosity seekers, and the cold stares of society's propriety-mongers. She sensed his tension as questions and comments tested both her background and her composure. When the influential old marchioness of Queensberry cackled at one of her observations and patted her on the arm, an unmistakable gesture of acceptance, Pierce's eyes were full of relief and pride.

Thus, she was dismayed, moments later, when he turned to their hostess and offered his excuses, preparing to depart. "Oh, but you cannot leave so early . . . just when we were getting to know dear Gabrielle," Lady Morton declared.

He turned and met Gabrielle's gaze. "I wouldn't dream of depriving you of her company. By all means, she must stay and enjoy the party." Before she could object, he gave her hand a brief kiss and was gone.

"Where is Pierce?" Lady Beatrice asked a short while later, as Gabrielle joined her in the dining room for refreshments.

"He left," she answered, looking crestfallen. "He made excuses about a lot of wretched paperwork to do before tomorrow's session of the Lords. I had no chance to go with him . . . He insisted that I stay and enjoy the party."

"He did?" Absorbing the implications of that, Beatrice leaned close and patted Gabrielle's hand. "Don't fret, my girl. Don't you see what that means?" She looked like the cat that had gotten the cream. "It's a clear victory."

"It is?"

"But of course. You've faced him down, demanded your place as his wife, *and he ceded it to you.* Our evening has been a brilliant success! As far as both he and society are concerned, you are indisputably the new Lady Sandbourne."

Gabrielle's smile dawned as she realized that Lady Beatrice was right. It was indeed a victory. Thanks to her mother-in-law's cleverness, the generosity of her hostess, and her own much-practiced graces, she was now Pierce's wife in public. Lifting her chin and squaring her shoulders, she turned back to the rest of the guests, wondering how long it would be before she would be his wife in private as well.

Rosalind was waiting for them in the drawing room when they arrived home. She hurried out into the hall and paused to give Gabrielle a thorough looking over.

"Well, I see he wasn't of an amorous mood," she said as she approached, noting her daughter's pristine condition.

"He was, however, impressed with the way she enchanted the lot of them," Beatrice said, giving Rosalind a superior look. "She is totally accepted as his wife. Apparently I didn't need a full week, after all."

Rosalind bristled. "Nor, it seems, will I." She turned back to Gabrielle with a devious glint in her eye and squeezed her daughter's hands. "Tomorrow, my dearest, you will spend the night in your Sandbourne's arms . . . or my name isn't Rosalind LeCoeur."

By the next afternoon, it was clear that Rosalind indeed intended to make good on her promise. The Clarendon, one of the more fashionable hotels on New Bond Street, had a well-deserved reputation for service and discretion, but a bit of coin, judiciously placed, could still buy any bit of information in the place. By discreetly silvering a few palms, Rosalind had managed to learn that for the last several nights, Lord Sandbourne had come from his club at about ten, had a drink in the bar below, and then retired to his suite by eleven.

His schedule the next evening followed that same predictable pattern. He discreetly took dinner at Brooks's, spent a while in the Subscription Room, and then walked down the street to the Clarendon as night was falling. When Gunther returned to Sandbourne House with that information, the plan Rosalind had taken several days to assemble was set into motion.

• • •

In the bar of his hotel, Pierce had a drink at a table in the corner and read one of the late papers. He was just about to go upstairs to his rooms, when into the bar stepped three of his fellow Conservatives, including young Lord Catton, who was a rather decent fellow when not under the influence of the less-than-scrupulous Arundale. Before Pierce could slip away, the group hailed him and called him over for a drink. It proved to be an amicable encounter, the most enjoyable he had had in days. He was loath to see it end and suggested a friendly game of cards in a room upstairs. Being gambling men and without wives or families to put constraints on their time, they accepted.

On the way up, Pierce arranged with the head porter for food, chips, and fresh decks of cards to be delivered. Once in the small suite, the gentlemen shared a drink and news of the recent developments in governmental postings and preferments. In a short time, the cards and food arrived and they sat down to play a few gentlemanly rounds.

"And how is that bride of yours faring, Sandbourne?" Sir John Messing, KG, asked with a smile. "I say . . . is she a stunner? When do we get a look at her?"

Pierce stilled and gave the ruddy-faced old knight a dangerously calm look. But it seemed to be an innocent enough question. "She is quite well, thank you."

"And quite a stunner," Catton said, beaming with good-natured mischief. "I've met the lady, you know. At the Savoy one night. Dashed inconsiderate of you, Sandbourne, snapping her up before any of the rest of us got the chance."

Pierce took a quiet breath and tried to deflect their interest from the subject of his wife. "I had no idea you were so matrimonially minded, Catton. We shall have to see what we can do about finding you a wife of your own . . . to honor and obey."

"Three cards. I'll have three," Bennett England, MP, declared, surfacing from an immersion in the intricacies of the cards in his hands. "Now, what was that about Catton getting hitched up? Ye gods—am I the last to know everything?"

Pierce laughed and felt himself truly relaxing for the first time in days. "Three weeks from Saturday, at St. Paul's. The invitation is in the mail."

Catton sputtered for a moment, then laughed. "Curse you, Sandbourne . . . Do you want cards, or do you stand?"

The rug was new and full of the scent of dyes and the superfluous lint common to new pile. The smell and the tickling in Gabrielle's nose tormented her, and her wretched costume—harem pants and a silk chiffon blouse —was so thin that she was itching all over. Compounding her misery were the erratic thumps and bumps, as she was hoisted out of the lorry and carried through the side door of the hotel. Then she was propped at an angle on some stairs; she could feel the ridges of the steps digging into her side, while the sounds of muffled voices in contention swirled around her. She suffered a moment of panic when the rug was lifted once more and tilted, and she began to slide inside it. But after a moment, she managed to catch and brace herself, and she realized with relief that they were carrying her upstairs.

In the darkness of the rolled rug, fighting a sneeze and wishing with all her heart she could have a good scratch, she tried to comfort herself with thoughts of Pierce and to concentrate on what she was supposed to do when she was unrolled. She was supposed to sit up and shake out her long, dark hair, an "Egyptian" wig, and smile at him. The smile was the key—her overture, her peace offering. From there, she would have to get as physically close to him as possible and take her cue from his reaction.

Sit up, shake, and smile . . . She repeated it over and over as Gunther and Traxall, her mother's coachman, huffed and puffed their way up several flights of stairs, bouncing and jostling her all the way. At last she was level again—presumably on the proper floor. Her heart was thumping wildly as she heard the muffled sound of a knock at a door. When there was no immediate response, she held her breath, wondering if Pierce had unexpectedly gone out for the evening.

Then a faint creak of hinges and the sound of voices, one of which might have been Pierce's, reassured her. She was moving again, then shifted, probably being lowered. Battling back frantic second thoughts, she set her mind on Pierce.

"A gift for your lordship," she heard Gunther say.

"What the— A *rug*?" Pierce's voice was now perfectly clear. "Wait a minute—I know you," he declared as Gunther began to unroll the carpet. "Good God, it's—"

Suddenly everything was spinning as the carpet unrolled across the floor . . . Then air and light burst over her. For an instant she lay catching her breath and her balance. Then she sat up, flipped her long, exotic wig back over her shoulder, and promptly sneezed . . . straight into four incredulous male faces.

20

She froze, taking in the sight of the sitting room: the table with Pierce and three other men seated around it in shirtsleeves . . . the cards in their hands . . . the haze of cigar smoke and the redolence of aged whisky . . . and the horror dawning on Pierce's face.

"What in the hell?" He shot to his feet, toppling his chair back onto the floor.

He blinked, staring down at her, taking in her revealing garments and long dark hair. It looked like Gabrielle's face . . . Gabrielle's tempting body beneath those layers of sheer white chiffon and falling out of that corsetlike velvet vest . . . It was Gabrielle!

He grabbed his coat and rushed to throw it over her,

wondering wildly, desperately, what to do. His first impulse was to shove her straight out the door. But how could he with her in *those* clothes? Inserting himself between Gabrielle and his friends, he saw Catton rising with widened eyes and realized he had to get rid of *them!* "This is obviously someone's pathetic idea of a joke, gentlemen," he declared furiously. "I'm afraid I shall have to ask that we continue this game at another time."

They were on their feet in a flash, donning their coats and reaching for their hats. If any of them were tempted to comment on the delectable charms or the desirability of his "gift," the heat in his face stopped them. As they stumbled over each other in their eagerness to get out the door, only Catton dared to pause and look back at Gabrielle . . . with a grin of recognition spreading from ear to ear.

Pierce stood staring at the door after it closed. When he turned, he found Gabrielle had thrown his coat aside and sat once again in that shocking garb that somehow made her seem more naked than if she were wearing no clothes at all.

"Have you taken complete leave of your senses? What in God's name do you think you're doing . . . coming here . . . . like *that*?"

He raked his gaze down the veiled taper of her arms and the tantalizingly explicit curve of her hip. The diaphanous silk of her blouse was fitted to a tight jeweled collar at her throat, gathered onto pearl and sequin cuffs at her wrists and ankles. Her midsection was bounded by a velvet vestlike garment that pushed her breasts up, making it seem as if she were barely being contained in her garments. Around her hips, the legs of the trousers were gathered onto a tight-fitting yoke that was covered with the same gold braid, jeweled sequins, and pearls. She looked shamefully sleek and exotic, like something out of an erotic Arabian night.

"I'm sorry if I embarrassed you," she was saying when he managed to jerk his gaze from her voluptuously displayed body. "But—"

"Embarrassed me?" he roared. "Now why would you think that? My wife dons clothes fit only for a damned brothel . . . rolls up in a rug . . . and unrolls in my hotel room, in full view of a group of men . . ."

"They might not know I'm your wife. I'm wearing a dark wig."

"One of those men was Edward Dimsdell, Lord Catton —who has seen you before and only tonight was commenting on—" On how stunning and memorable she was. He paced away with two volcanic steps, then jerked back to stand over her. "Even if he didn't recognize you, it will be noised about that exotic tarts have been sending themselves to me rolled up in rugs! Dammit, Gabrielle!"— he punched a finger at her—"This is the last straw. I'll not be made a laughingstock by my wife, do you hear?"

He snatched up his coat, shoved his arms into it, and looked around for something to cover her with. "Stand up and put this on," he ordered, holding up his caped evening cloak. "I'm taking you straight back to Thorndike. Now."

"I will not." With desperate determination filling every particle of her body, she stretched out on the rug, on her back, and looked up at him with hot defiance.

"That won't work this time, sweetheart." When she just looked away, he snarled something unintelligible and knelt on one knee to pick her up.

She went limp. He found it impossible to insert his arms beneath her with her body so slack. Dropping to both knees, he worked one arm beneath her maddeningly pliant shoulders. She was soft and fragrant. Her breasts jutted above the edge of the vest as he lifted her . . . the silky fabric snared his hands . . . but he willed himself to ignore those erotic perceptions. Determinedly, he hauled her up to something of a sitting position, only to have her sink again when he bent in the other direction to seize her knees.

"Dammit, Gabrielle—" When he turned back to her, with fire in his eyes, she raised her head so that her face was within inches of his.

"Hypocrite," she charged softly, causing him to freeze in place. "You cannot bear the thought of being forced to abide by other people's rules, and here you are . . . making up a whole book of rules for me."

"You're my wife—my countess. And as such—" Stung by her charge and dismayed by the unexpected desire tightening his throat, he jerked his gaze from hers. "You cannot go about behaving like this in public."

"We're not in public," she responded, quietly, firmly.

He was achingly aware of just how private they were at the moment.

"You cannot go about doing such things in public *or* private. I won't have it, do you hear. Married ladies bear themselves with propriety, dignity, and decorum at all times. They do not have themselves rolled up in rugs and delivered to men in hotel rooms in the middle of the night! Nor do they play beer hall tunes in public, or lick their wineglasses, or peel grapes with their teeth—" He halted, realizing that he had just revealed how closely he had watched her the previous evening.

"Well *this* married lady does," she said softly. Too softly. He couldn't help looking at her. Her liberally exposed skin seemed to glow in the darkness. "And just who says what married ladies can and cannot do, anyway? Who says I can't peel a grape with my teeth . . . or take off my shoes under the table . . . or go without all-in-ones beneath my dresses." She narrowed her eyes and sat up to face him.

"I think it's about time I had a look at that rule book

you're always quoting me. Where is it? You're always so quick with your blessed regulations, you must carry it with you at all times." She held out her hand, palm up. "Hand it over."

He looked at her as if she'd lost her mind and jerked his hands from her. "Don't be absurd, Gabrielle."

Her smile should have warned him. "Is it in here?" She leaned toward him, and he abruptly sat back on his heels, watching in horror as she ran her hand down his chest and into the outer breast pocket of his coat. After a thorough exploration, she declared in sultry tones, "Not here. Then it must be inside."

Before he could prevent it, her fingers dispatched the single button of his coat, pulled the coat open, and quickly ran up and down the lining, riffling through his inside breast pockets.

"What the—" He grabbed her wrists and held them, arching back to escape her. "What in heaven has gotten into you, Gabrielle?"

"I want the rule book, Sandbourne." Her voice was low and compelling in a way that set his fingertips vibrating. "And I warn you . . . you won't leave this room until I have it."

He studied her face in the dim light, watching the play of light in her luminous eyes, smelling the sweet, complex scent of her perfume, feeling the impact of her nearness curling through his blood. His hands slowly relaxed but remained on her wrists and were carried along with them to his chest.

"Perhaps it's in one of these—" She dragged her hands down the front of his shirt and vest, splaying her fingers, tracing the contours of his ribs ever so slowly. When her fingers reached the edges of his vest pockets, she slid them inside and felt his stomach tighten as she stroked his waist, searching for that hypothetical book.

"Ummm." She was leaning against him now, making him feel her warmth, making him deal with her desire for him. "Clever man," she whispered. "You've hidden it well. Are you going to surrender it, or do I have to continue searching?"

By all means, continue searching, his body groaned.

"What do you want with my rule book?" he managed, through the haze of arousal rising in him.

"I'm going to burn it." She withdrew from his pockets and ran her hands down the sides of his waist to his hips, exploring. His breath caught as her fingers caressed their way down his loins to rest intimately on his thighs. "I don't want any more rules between us . . . except the ones we make together."

No more rules.

A moment later, his tie hung limp, his collar was undone, and his shirt was half open. She raked her breasts against his bared chest, wanting more, inviting the pressure of his body against hers.

"Do you want me, Pierce?"

That invitation to pleasure was irresistible.

"Gabrielle . . . yes . . ." He claimed her lips and, with the force of his kiss, gradually pressed her back onto the rug.

Sinking over her was like plunging into a bath of warm oil. Sensation engulfed him, soft and unguent, conforming and clinging to every part of him, saturating his parched senses. She was soft beneath him as he stretched out over her body, her curves yielding to the hard planes of his tautly flexed frame. Bracing on his elbows, he raked her mouth with his, relishing the velvety resistance that set his lips tingling, savoring the salty sweetness of her mouth. He stroked her skin, adoring the shadings of texture and the subtle variations of warmth across her face and breasts. He inhaled the rose scent of her skin, the faint musk of the cleft between her breasts, and the hint of cloves that clung to her garments. Every perception was familiar, but contained unexplored elements that beckoned to his hands, his mouth, and his eyes.

Suddenly he couldn't get enough of her. His hands flew over her face, her shoulders, and her breasts, seeking her inside those exotic trappings. Through the haze in his senses, he felt her tug at his vest and heard her throaty command: "Take it off."

In an instant, he was pushing up and sitting back on his knees, fumbling with his buttons, ripping off his vest. "All of it," she urged. "Take it off. Then mine too."

Mesmerized by the husky command in her voice, he jerked off his tie and collar and soon pulled his shirt from his trousers and shrugged it from his shoulders. For a moment, he stared at her as she lay between his knees . . . wrapped in diaphanous silk, her lips reddened from his kisses, her breasts straining against that jeweled bodice. She awaited his desires like an exotic houri, smoldering with passion that could be released only by his touch.

But something wasn't quite right. He sank his hands into her dark tresses and pulled that tangled cap away, baring her own tightly wrapped hair. Her fingers flew to search out the hairpins and send them flying. Soon her own hair was spilling out over the carpet in a luxurious golden torrent. He braced above her to comb his fingers through it, spreading it around her like rays of sunlight.

For a long moment, he absorbed the sight of her, radiant with desire. Then, getting to his feet, he scooped her up and carried her into the bedchamber. He let her slide slowly down his body so that she stood on her feet beside the bed. Then he sat down and drew her between his knees, running his hands over her provocatively displayed breasts and around her tightly bound waist and hips.

"Where on earth," he whispered as he laid soft tonguing kisses along the sensitive skin bulging above the rim of her vest, "did you get such clothes?"

"From . . . a friend," she murmured huskily, running her fingers through his hair and reeling him tighter against her. "You know who I am tonight, don't you?"

"Who?" He pulled the golden cord that laced her vest together, groaning with approval at the way it loosened at the top, relaxing its hold on her breasts.

"Cleopatra, Queen of the Nile." She halted for a moment, closing her eyes as he nuzzled aside the fabric and found her. "And you're Julius Caesar."

"Caesar and Cleopatra," he murmured, teasing her intimately with his tongue, making her stiffen and gasp softly as he nipped and kissed her. "Where ever did you get such a harebrained idea as rolling up in a rug like Cleopatra?" he said, sliding his hands down her buttocks, pressing her tight against his swollen loins.

"Well, I . . . *ohhh*, do that again . . . *that . . . there. Ummm.*" She undulated against him and stiffened with pleasure as his mouth tugged at her. When that breathtaking surge of heat cleared, she tried frantically to scrape together enough words for an explanation. Just now, he probably didn't need to hear that her sensual gambit was a ploy developed by her advisory committee. "From . . . a dream."

"A dream?" He found the hooks at the side of her harem pants and began to unfasten them. "You dreamed about me?"

"I have lots of dreams about you."

"Wicked dreams, I hope." He slid his hand inside the open placket.

"Delicious dreams." She gasped as he lay back on the bed abruptly, carrying her with him. She floundered as he swung his legs onto the bed and drew her over and astride him. Righting herself, she propped herself up on her arms, shocked by her position . . . which approximated the meeting of their bodies in passion.

"Tell me about these dreams of yours, sweetheart." He loosened the top of her vest and tucked it out of the way so that it framed a tantalizing display of creamy mounds and taut velvety nipples. "What did I do to you in your dreams, Cleopatra?"

"You unrolled me, then joined me on the rug," she whispered, feeling her body tightening intimately, rousing to the erotic potential of her own words. "Then you made glorious, naked love to me."

"Tell me how," he murmured, nuzzling his way up her neck.

"Perhaps I should show you, instead." Some remnant of her lessons in seduction popped into her mind. "Long, languid kisses . . . your sleek tongue stroking mine . . . wet, hungry kisses . . ." She demonstrated, boldly exploring his mouth, dragging her teeth along his lips and laving them with her tongue. He groaned and cradled her head in his hands to do the same to her.

"And?" His eyes were like burning coals.

"You stripped my clothes from me, piece by piece." She directed his hand to her half-opened vest. "You peeled the fabric back . . . kissed me . . . caressed me . . ."

Her stream of thought was lost in a torrent of sensation as he pulled her vest from her and tantalized the sensitive tips of her breasts. She squirmed, closed her eyes, and leaned harder against his hands, entreating more, willing him not to stop. But a moment later, he pulled her down so that he could kiss her again and slid his hands breathtakingly down her sides to stroke her thighs through the silky fabric of her costume.

"Then what?" he demanded, between thick, ravishing

kisses and masterful caresses. She could scarcely speak. Her whole body was one hot tremor of desire.

"Then you stripped off my bottoms and made me . . ."

"Made you what?" In a single powerful movement, he lifted her to her knees and began working the bottom half of her costume down her hips. She sank to the side and in a heartbeat, her bottom half was bare. "What did I make you do?"

He slid over her, rolling her onto her back and dragging his chest across her tingling nipples. As he kissed her, she forgot everything except the heavenly feel of his body sliding onto hers, the rasp of his trousers against her bare legs, the way he filled her arms, her senses, her heart.

"I . . . forget."

"Then, perhaps I can refresh your memory," he whispered against her lips. His body stiffened and withdrew for a moment, and when it came back, there was only skin against her skin. "I made you feel hot and feverish." He slid his knee between hers and soon was pressed intimately against her burning core. "And I made your thighs part." Then he flexed and slid his swollen shaft along the hot, sensitive groove of her sex. "And I made you squirm and shudder and sigh with pleasure."

His body arched again and again, and each motion did indeed cause her to shiver and gasp softly. Soon she was tilting her pelvis to meet his thrusts, pressing closer, directing that divine pressure with the subtle movements of her thighs and hips. Wrapping his ribs with her arms and his hips and buttocks with her legs, she strained against him, searching, seeking those sensations that fired her senses so that the boundaries of her body melted into his.

Tighter, harder, faster . . . They moved together with powerful strokes that sent quivers of response radiating through her.

Then her arousal exploded, bursting in her senses, shattering their limits, and for a time spreading her consciousness to the very edges of reality. She clung to him, letting wave after wave of sensation expand outward until it halted and began to contract, returning her to her scorched awareness. She lay sheltered by his body, smoldering with unmet hunger, her appetite only piqued by that taste of pleasure.

"Now," she said urgently, seeking his body with hers, coaxing his hips with her hands. He paused to stare down at her with hunger raging like a fire in his eyes.

"I think you remember this part."

He sank his arm beneath her shoulders, clasping her tightly against him, and began the slow, rhythmic joining of their bodies. Sensation surged with each thrust . . . hot and ravishing, stretching and filling her, changing her. When he lay fully imbedded in her glowing heat, he slowed and shifted his weight to one elbow. With his free hand, he traced her face, her breasts, her lips, her hair. She looked up at him, her eyes now silvery rings surrounding pools of black that bared the workings of her heart to him.

He felt the pull of her gaze and closed his eyes. But as he began to move within her, he felt her liquid heat lapping over him, absorbing him, dissolving his reserve. Even on the backs of his closed eyelids he could see her longing . . . her call that he meet her there, in that intimacy, in that ultimate giving. She seemed to move both beneath him and within him, like a tide, eroding the granite walls of his self-protection, melting his defenses . . . calling him, claiming him. The pleasure was too keen, the need too great. When she said his name, he opened his eyes and found himself looking straight into hers.

Now with every movement, every rush of pleasure, he both saw and felt the response deep within her. He felt himself being drawn into the very landscape of her soul, where he mingled with her hopes and dreams. And the last, desperate stronghold of isolation within him was finally breached.

She saw the wall around his heart tumbling down, saw the last barriers to his emotions succumbing to the tide rising in him . . . and felt a surge of exultation as she glimpsed in him the care and tenderness that he guarded so jealously. In that moment, in that sharing, she felt and understood in the language of the heart things that would take much time and thought, later, to distill into mere words. And though it wasn't necessary, though it was barely possible for her to speak, she said it anyway.

"I love you . . . too."

The smile on his face was enthralling to behold—part pleasure, part longing. He stilled and tensed. For that moment, as they looked at each other, they loved with all the tenderness they possessed . . . each honoring the strength and the vulnerability of the other.

Then they began to move again, each seeking fulfillment for the other and finding fulfillment in the giving. They touched and kissed and caressed, exploring the richness of their loving, until their passions crested and broke in joyful release. Pierce clasped her to him, groaning her name from deep within him.

Together they drifted, replete, luxuriating in the closeness they shared. They touched freely, fully, loving each other without reserve. When at last they settled back into their senses, each was reluctant to break the spell between them. Finally, he shifted to lie beside her, carrying her gaze with him.

"Shocking dreams you have, Lady Sandbourne," he teased softly, stroking her cheek. He had never seen her so unashamedly bare, so elementally feminine and alluring. Her eyes were that summer-sky blue again, so clear and untroubled that he felt he was seeing into her innermost being. And at the calm center of her, he glimpsed the satisfaction, the sense of accomplishment that permeated her.

"Not nearly as shocking as my experiences while awake, Lord Sandbourne," she said with a knowing smile, running a finger down the ridge of his nose. "You're quite the most scandalous and exciting thing that has ever happened to me. Wicked man . . . whatever will I tell my husband about you?"

"Tell him the truth." He grinned. "That we are collaborating on a book."

"A book?"

"Of rules."

As the sense of it dawned, she laughed softly, and he added: "And be sure to mention that I made love to you . . . all night long."

Waking in a strange bed was a disorienting experience that Gabrielle had had all too frequently of late. She started up in the middle of rumpled bedclothes the next morning, clutching the sheet to her and blinking as she tried to make sense of her surroundings. Remembering, she sank back onto one elbow and gazed with unabashed pleasure at the dented pillow beside hers. After a few moments, she rose and stretched languidly, feeling the impact of her night of passion in every tender and overworked part of her body.

She located her garments on the floor, donned them, and then padded into the sitting room, hoping to find Pierce there. The sight of him, seated at the table in his shirtsleeves, allowed her to release the breath she had been holding.

"Good morning," she said warmly.

He took one last sip of coffee and put his cup down on the tray, then rose and searched her with a look that avoided her face.

"You're dressed. That will save time." He reached for his coat and shoved his arms into it, then picked up his evening cloak and held it open for her.

She looked at the cloak, then at the tray on the table in confusion. "Without a bit of breakfast?"

"I'm certain you will be much more comfortable breakfasting at home." When she hesitated, he settled the cloak on her shoulders himself and, with a hand at her back, ushered her toward the door.

As they descended the steps to the side door of the hotel, she slowed and looked up at him, trying to catch his eye and read what was happening in him. But he kept his gaze averted and his jaw set. After abandoning himself totally in their loving last night, he was once again in supreme control of both himself and his circumstances.

The carriage was waiting by the door. He waved Jack to keep his seat and seized her arm to help her up the step. Frantic at the thought of being parted from him without a word of explanation or understanding, she halted on the step and turned, catching his gaze in hers and refusing to let it go.

His dark eyes, so often a window on his soul, seemed alarmingly empty. No, not quite empty, she realized as she continued to search them. There were traces of regret. "Pierce, please . . ." she said softly, placing her hand over his on her arm. At her touch, another emotion stirred deep in the center of him. A feeling she recognized. Fear.

An inexplicable surge of desperation filled her as he jerked his gaze from hers and abruptly handed her up into the carriage.

As the door closed and the carriage lurched, she struggled with her chaotic emotions. He had loved her all night long, taking her again and again to heights of passion, introducing her to all the delicious new sensations her senses could hold, and cradling her against him afterward as if she were something rare and precious. She had fallen asleep to the low, sweet rhythm of his heartbeat beneath her cheek, feeling that at last everything in her world was right and complete. And she had once again awakened to an empty bed and a strained parting.

When she stepped through the entry of Sandbourne House, Rosalind heard her and hurried out of the dining room, straightaway. Sweeping a critical eye over her disheveled hair and still kiss-reddened mouth, her mother gave a crow of delight.

"Well, there's no need to ask what happened. It's written all over you!" Rosalind rushed forward with compressed excitement and seized Gabrielle's shoulders. "Did he make you see rainbows or shooting stars or fireworks? I want every living detail—"

"Don't be insufferably common, Rosalind," Lady Beatrice insisted, coming up behind them. "It is enough to know that she was with him the entire night."

"Enough for whom?" Rosalind said, with an arch look over her shoulder.

Lady Beatrice glanced up to see one of the parlor maids stopped on her way up the stairs, watching, and she bundled Gabrielle and Rosalind into the drawing room and closed the great doors. Only then did the pair notice that the spark of triumph was missing from Gabrielle's eyes.

"What's happened, dearest? What is wrong?" Rosalind asked, pulling her to the sofa and settling beside her.

"I don't know," Gabrielle said, looking at her hands, captive in her mother's. "We had a wonderful night together. He was so tender and loving. But this morning he said scarcely a word to me—just put me into his carriage and sent me off."

Rosalind scowled, looked thoughtful for a moment. "Morning-after nerves," she announced with an air of confidence. "He's been a bachelor for a long time. It's only reasonable that he might have a few second thoughts on the morning after." She patted Gabrielle's tightly clasped hands. "Nothing to worry about, trust me. Last night he made you his lover, dearest, and nothing can change that."

Shortly, Gabrielle was ushered upstairs and into a steaming tub of scented water that gradually soaked away her aches. As she rested on her bed afterward, she went over and over the events of the previous evening, analyzing them in every conceivable light. The more she thought on it, the less certain she was that her grand romantic gambit had secured for her the sort of victory she sought.

It was true that she had overcome his outrage and embarrassment and had coaxed him to surrender his passion for her and make her his lover. But his curt and distant manner this morning made it clear that passion was all that he had surrendered.

Surrender. She sat up on the bed with her heart pounding. If there was anything in the world that Pierce loathed, it was the thought of surrendering to a woman . . . to his iron-willed mother or to her. Last night, it had been so easy to dismiss his misgivings, to concentrate on the pleasures and count on them to set the rest right. She had been so certain that a night of loving intimacy would dissolve whatever differences remained between them. But how quickly, after the closeness they had shared, his fears had risen between them again. How could he possibly be afraid of—

Afraid of loving.

The insight, so clear and unmistakable, startled her. How could she not have recognized the traces of anxiety in the depths of his eyes, when it was the very same fear she herself had suffered? He believed that to love was to give until you had nothing left. He was afraid of loving her, for he believed that loving her meant surrendering all that he was . . . turning over control of his very life to her.

Was there no way to reach through his suspicion and hurt to touch him, to convince him she didn't want to take anything from him? Was there no way to make him understand that in every bit of loving there is risk, but that there is also possibility?

She saw it all with dismal clarity. In seeking her rightful place in his heart, she had barreled into his life, stormed into his passions, and demanded his response. But, however good and loving her motives, he could only see her actions through his own fears and expectations. Every demand she made was a reason for him to withdraw.

He simply was not a man who could be grabbed by the passions and pulled into love. He had to be approached forthrightly, honestly, and ever so gently. Instead of grand gestures and overwhelming seduction, she would have to *invite* him into her life and let him choose whether or not to come.

A choice. Wasn't that what she had wanted for herself? And wasn't that what he had once given her? He had broken through her fears, overcome her defenses and reluctance. He had won her love . . . not with his title and his power and his status . . . not with his mesmerizing kisses or his masterful sensuality . . . but with his warmth and humor and decency . . . with his help. He had been her friend when she needed one most. And in so doing, he had proved what sort of man he truly was.

She had tried Lady Beatrice's way and Rosalind's way. Now she had to try her own way. Schemes could make her his wife and even his mistress. But in order to have his loving, willing presence in her life, she would have to deal earnestly and openly with him. She had to once again become his friend.

How on earth did she go about that?

21

The next evening, Pierce stood looking at the rain coming down in sheets in the darkened street outside the entrance to Brooks's and, with a quiet oath of disgust, repaired to the bar to wait for the downpour to end. After an interminable afternoon of weathering judgmental stares in the Lords, he made for the sanctuary of his club and had the misfortune to come face to face with Arundale and Shively. Shively tipped his hat and commented that Pierce was fortunate indeed that his accommodations at the Clarendon were so comfortable and so "well supplied." It was all Pierce could do to contain himself when Arundale added that he had heard that Lady Sandbourne was redecorating his house in his absence . . . in a rather unique "Egyptian" motif.

Obviously they had heard of his encounter with "Cleopatra" the night before. His worst fears were confirmed: Catton had recognized Gabrielle. Now, in addition to his notorious forced vows, he would have a notorious wife to deal with. And there was nothing that made a man look more a fool in society than an unconventional wife.

But just as galling as the impending infamy of his marriage and his wife was the embarrassment he felt about it. He had never cared a whit for society's opinion, never ever bowed the knee to the proprietymongers of the upper ten. He had worn his licentious reputation as something of a badge of honor—insisting that he was no different from the rest of upper-class males and feeling righteous for the candor with which he took his pleasures. Now here he was, skulking around amongst his peers, resenting and blaming his wife's behavior, when his own left more than a bit of room for censure.

He strode into the bar, his shoulders squared and his jaw set with aristocratic arrogance. His gaze fell on a lone figure who sat with his back to the rest of the members in the bar. The other tables were filled with faces he wished to avoid, so he ordered a brandy and headed for the far table, thinking that a strange face would prove a mercy in his current state. But as he approached, the table's occupant roused, and Pierce found himself staring into a pair of gray eyes that were alarmingly familiar.

The duke straightened and looked a bit disconcerted. "You," he said irritably, then after a moment, made a motion toward the chair across the table. Aware of the several pairs of eyes attending their meeting, Pierce acknowledged him with "Your Grace," then settled into a seat.

As Pierce sat down, he was taken aback by the duke's appearance. His robust face was noticeably gray beneath his fading suntan, and there were dark rings beneath his eyes. Though his coat and collar and tie were in impeccable order, his graying hair was uncharacteristically ruffled.

Carlisle lifted his glass, downed his drink in two swallows, and sank back into his foul mood. "Infernal women," he said morosely. Pierce knew instantly the source of his troubled state. "There's no pleasing them. A man hasn't got a chance in hell. I gave her every damned thing she ever wanted . . . a house, an income, clothes, jewels . . . luxury, travel, pleasure . . ." He leaned forward and continued in a furious whisper: "I've even been *faithful* to her! What the hell more does she expect?"

He waved to the barman to bring another glass.

"Respect." With his forehead propped in his hand, he fixed a bewildered gaze on Pierce. "That's what she wants now. Wrote me a letter. Says I never played chess with her. Goes on and on about how she never got to ride horses or smoke a cigar or to wear pink dresses, for God's sake. I think she's gone mad—that's what I think. Gone completely off."

With some of the turmoil purged from his system, he tugged his vest down and shifted his attention to his son-in-law. "Is my daughter well?" he asked, sticking out his chin as if expecting an argument. "She *is* my daughter, you know. I always knew that, no matter what her mother says."

"She is well enough," Pierce said, thinking *poor bastard* and struggling to keep his thoughts out of his expression.

"Take a lesson, Sandbourne." The duke pounded a finger on the tabletop to punctuate his advice. "If your wife starts prattling on about chess and 'respect' and smoking cigars . . . take a firm hand to her, straightaway. Don't stand for any of this 'respect' nonsense, or next thing you know, she'll be calling you a damned 'hypocrite,' kicking you out, and changing the locks on the doors!"

Pierce finished his drink as quickly as decency allowed, excused himself, and headed for the door. Rain or no rain, he had to get out of there. Mercifully, the head porter was able to secure him an umbrella for the walk back to the Clarendon. In the dark and wet of the street, Pierce exhaled and set his jaw grimly. The duke's words of wisdom had come about a month too late.

The success of Gabrielle's Cleopatra gambit was a source of great pride to Gabrielle's advisory committee on passion, who gathered the next afternoon in Gabrielle's chambers, for tea and details. They managed to drag a summary from a red-faced Gabrielle, who, to their disappointment, stubbornly refused to provide particulars. And when asked to give their opinion of his disappearance the next morning, they unanimously agreed it was probably "morning-after nerves." Men, they declared, were prone to pigheaded independence and were deathly afraid of admitting to needing a woman too much. And according to her committee, that fear was most pronounced on the morning after a long, salty bout of loving.

To Gabrielle's relief, Parnell knocked on her chamber door with a request that she join Lady Beatrice in the drawing room to receive a caller—the duke of Carlisle. Rosalind shot to her feet with widened eyes and insisted on accompanying her.

When they arrived in the drawing room, the duke was planted before the cold hearth with his feet spread, his hands gripping his lapels, and his chin set at a determined angle . . . that loosened at the sight of Rosalind. "What the devil are you doing here?" he demanded of his former paramour.

"I have come to stay with my daughter awhile,"

Rosalind declared, putting a protective arm around Gabrielle's shoulders and refusing to be intimidated.

"I might have known that you would be involved somehow," he said irritably.

"Involved with what? What am I accused of doing now? Corrupting the government? Bringing down the Church of England?"

The duke reddened, and his neck veins swelled. "I prefer to speak with my daughter alone."

"You may speak freely, Your Grace," Gabrielle said, glancing at Lady Beatrice and Rosalind. "I have nothing to hide from my mother or my mother-in-law."

The duke shifted a critical gaze from one woman to the other, then drew himself up straighter. "Very well. Are you aware, young woman, that as we speak, your husband is being vilified all over London?"

"What?" Gabrielle's knees weakened.

"Sandbourne is being made the subject of gossip and unsavory jest throughout the city. Your forced vows are not only common knowledge, they have become an excuse for the worst sort of invention and defamation. Fabrications about Sandbourne's activities are cropping up all over the place. Just last night I heard it being told about my club that a naked tart had herself rolled up in a rug and delivered to him!"

"Why that is . . . preposterous!" Gabrielle turned beet red and cast a look of alarm at her mother. "Pierce is an honest, decent, and upstanding man."

"Well, that is not the way society sees it, my girl." The duke stalked over to stare down at her. "He's not a randy young blade anymore, he's a married man. And as such, he is required to keep both his baser urges and his household in check." He glared at Gabrielle in a way that made it clear that he regarded her as belonging somewhere between "household" and "baser urges." "If a man cannot manage his private life and his household, how can he possibly be expected to manage the public trust?"

Gabrielle was speechless. The details of their marriage and of a romantic gesture gone awry had been parlayed by malicious tongues into a ruinous combination. He was slowly being ostracized because he had chosen to pursue his pass—

His *passion* for her. Her eyes widened. The idea that passion could prove dangerous for Pierce was nothing short of astonishing to her. She hadn't imagined that his desire for her could possibly have such dire consequences on his life and career. Always in her thinking, it was women who paid the price of passion. She hadn't imagined that men could be held to account for their passions as well . . . or that the rules of conduct for a married man and for an unmarried man in public life were different.

"Whatever your differences with your husband, you'd better set them aside, my girl . . . and soon," the duke declared.

Gabrielle looked from her father's glower to Lady Beatrice's distress, and her heart filled with a jumble of emotion. She headed abruptly for the door. Lady Beatrice followed and caught up with her in the upstairs hall, just outside the master chambers.

"Gabrielle—"

"I'm partly to blame for all of this," she said, facing her mother-in-law. "I have to do something to help." She paced a few steps away, then back. "What can I do?"

Lady Beatrice frowned and grew thoughtful. "The only way to deal with malicious gossip is to hold your head up and supplant it with something positive . . . to make new stories for people to remember instead of whispered gossip."

Gabrielle's mind started to race. It was time she began

behaving like a real friend—seeing to Pierce's welfare, helping him. She considered Lady Beatrice's words.

"Then I need something that will show his better side —his decency, his compassion . . . his generosity . . ." Her eyes lighted. "I think I know just the thing!"

Below, in the drawing room, Rosalind faced the duke through a charged and deepening silence. The sight of his drawn face and eyes ringed from sleeplessness had jarred her numbed feelings. Feeling a treacherous softening toward him, she tried to resurrect her anger and sense of betrayal.

"A bit late to take an interest in our daughter, don't you think?"

"Better late than never." He sighed tightly. "I cannot do anything about what is past, Rosalind. I can only try to do something about the present."

She tried not to look directly at him, but felt her gaze drawn inescapably toward his. Those gray eyes that she had seen change through every conceivable shade of passion, sent a crushing wave of longing through her chest.

"Can you do something to help them?"

"I can contact a few men I know in government, make it known that Sandbourne has my support . . . noise it about at Brooks's and at the Carlton that the rumors are nothing short of slander." He ran his hands down his face, trying to think what else was within his power. "I don't know how much good it will do, but I suppose . . . I might arrange to be seen with them in public."

That was a major concession, Rosalind knew.

"Thank you, Augustus," she whispered, her eyes misting. "It means a great deal to me that you would try to help our daughter."

For a long moment they stood, their gazes locked, their faces reddening. Details—a curve, a scent, a certain dip of lashes, a subtle shift in stance—crept into their awareness, reminding them both that the powerful attraction Rosalind had so carefully cultivated through the years was still there. She searched his beloved face and experienced a sensual warming that was always a prelude to pleasure. He searched her lightning blue eyes and felt a hot clutch of need constricting his chest.

"Get your things, Rosalind," he said, his voice husky and commanding. "I'm taking you home."

It was a moment before his response chilled her half-melted senses. "What?"

"I said, get your things. You've made your point. I'll give you your blessed 'respect.' Now, get your hat . . . I'm taking you back to Maison LeCoeur."

Her eyes slowly widened, as his orders sank in.

"I'm not going anywhere."

"Don't be stubborn, Rosalind. I'll give you what you want . . . I'll play chess and ride horses . . . You can wear pink every damned day if you want. It's time you quit this meddling in the girl's life and came home where you belong."

She stared at him, incredulous. He offered not a single word of love or understanding or reconciliation. "I cannot believe I was with you all those years . . . that I slept with you and loved you . . . and all that time, I scarcely knew you."

"Dammit, Rosalind, you're talking in riddles again," he fumed. "Of course you knew me—every way it was possible for a woman to *know* a man."

She gasped. "I've heard all I intend to hear." She started for the door, but he caught her by the elbow. "Unhand me." Wrenching free, she scalded him with a look. "You are without a doubt the most pompous, selfish, insensitive lout I have ever met. You don't want *me*, Augustus . . . You want a whore, a housekeeper, and a nanny. Well, go hire them and leave me be!"

While he sputtered, she turned on her heel and strode for the stairs in the center hall. He watched her go, with her head up and her bustle swaying, and had an irrational urge to seize her and carry her off—like some Sabine woman!

"Pigheaded woman," he rumbled, starting for the doors.

"Pigheaded man," came an unexpected response. Lady Beatrice stepped into the doorway, her eyes glowing and her expression set with a uniquely feminine disdain. She had been returning to the drawing room to retrieve her knitting when she realized it was still occupied and paused, within hearing of all that transpired.

"I beg your pardon," he said, backing a step.

"You're behaving like a fool, Carlisle." Beatrice advanced, sending him back another step. "You haven't the foggiest notion what she is about, do you?"

"This is none of your concern, Lady Sandbourne—" He drew himself up to his most formidable posture, only to find his display bettered by Beatrice's presence.

"You used her for your pleasure and convenience, without a single thought for what she wanted or needed."

"That's not true. I gave her everything she wanted: a house, a carriage, a—"

"Oh, she was highly paid. But a highly paid *what*? To you she always was, and still is, more whore than woman. You bark orders at her, demand that she obey as if she were a servant or child. And you're positively scandalized by the notion that she might want something in her life *besides you*.

"Well, this may come as a nasty surprise to you, Carlisle, but she does have ideas and yearnings that have nothing to do with your precious male hide. She is clever and witty, and she has a good—if regrettably reckless—

heart. She thought you loved her and was willing to live with you outside the bonds of wedlock."

"She is my mistress, for God's sake!" he declared, trembling with thwarted possession. "Mine. God knows I paid enough for the privilege. After all I gave her . . ."

"*Yours,* you say—as if you owned her—like an expensive painting or a cellar of vintage wines. She was a possession you bought and paid for, not a woman who agreed to live with you and love you. You *do* think she's a harlot, Carlisle."

His own words, reflected and interpreted for him, stopped him cold. For the first time, he realized that he had thought of Rosalind as his, body and soul. She *belonged* to him. The thought disturbed him, even as he clung to it. How dared she want more than he had given her? How dared she be more than he had known?

"I am shocked by your bluntness, Lady Sandbourne," he declared.

"Age has its rewards," she said with a perceptive smile. "Chief among them is the right to speak one's mind when one sees pride, arrogance, and stupidity ruining people's lives."

Stung, the duke stormed out of the drawing room and out of the house. Beatrice watched him go and felt a rush of memories . . . another argument, another man stalking out. But after a moment, that old tension faded, and she smiled ruefully.

"If only I had been so blunt years ago, with a different man . . ."

Two days later, Pierce found himself sitting in the restaurant at the Clarendon, staring out the leaded window at the morning sunshine on the pavement but somehow seeing into a darkened bedchamber . . . seeing Gabrielle's provocative mouth, her jewel-clear eyes lighted with internal fire, her luscious curves bared just for him . . . When someone paused on the walkway outside, blocking his view, he roused and shook off those plaguing images, only to find himself wondering what she was doing with her days and how she had managed to both put up with his mother and even win her over, and trying not to wonder whether or not she had cried after he left her at his house the other morning.

Moments later another dark shadow intervened in his line of sight; this time at a much closer range. "Sandbourne! I thought it was you. Saw you through the window . . ." Pierce looked up with a start to find Colonel Tottenham standing across the table from him.

"Gathering wool are you? Shearing season's long past." The colonel laughed at his own witticism and reached for the chair closest Pierce. "Mind if I join you?"

Pierce felt his gut tighten as he waved permission. "By all means."

"How are things . . . on the domestic front?" The senior MP was known for coming straight to the point.

"Fine," Pierce said with a forced smile. "How are things . . . on the political front?"

"No news is good news. Haven't heard your name taken in vain for a day or two now . . . though, you're still on a bit of thin ice where some of the party leadership is concerned. They're touchy about scandals in the private sphere, especially now that we're so close to bringing down the Liberals on moral grounds. Cannot afford to have *our* private peccadilloes made a public issue. Getting harder all the time to keep a spotless name. With all this damnable reform nonsense about, you never know when you'll run up against some 'shrieking sister,' radical socialist worker, or 'do-good' reformer and find yourself caught in a crack." He made a face of disgust. "It's got so that a bit of muslin on the side is hardly safe for a man in public life anymore."

Pierce steeled himself, purging his thoughts from his expression as he watched Tottenham. In his mind, he heard a voice saying: *hypocrite*. And this time it wasn't Gabrielle's voice; it was his. Do your dirty little deeds in private—whatever the traffic will bear—as long as no one finds out. Never mind integrity, decency, or morality . . . The party's sole concern was whether or not a man got "caught." Why hadn't it bothered him before? If he was so dedicated to honesty, so insistent on judging the opposition, why hadn't he held his own party to those same standards? What made a Liberal hypocrite any more dangerous or loathsome than a Conservative one?

"Another thing . . ." Tottenham beckoned him closer with a jerk of his head, then leaned closer and dropped his voice. "Thought you'd want to know. This Saturday night, midnight . . . Gladstone will have his last debauch. He'll have a drink at his club and wake up in a bevy of naked females at the Pavilion." His mouth twisted into a smirk. "Pity you can't be there. You'd enjoy seeing the old bugger's ruin."

Pierce made a grimace that passed for a smile and nodded. When Tottenham left, he sat for a time, feeling strangely conflicted by the news that Gladstone was about to receive his comeuppance. The old man had wrecked his life, humiliated him, and damn near ruined his political career. Then why was he sitting here feeling overheated and prickly, as if he ought to scrub his hands to rid himself of the contamination of knowing what was in store for the old hypocrite?

He left the restaurant, his mind set on the day's dismal readings in Parliament. He had just donned his gloves and was retrieving his hat from the rack when the desk clerk spotted him and hurried over. "I'm glad I caught you, your lordship." He held out an envelope to Pierce. "This came for you a short while ago . . . marked urgent."

His name was written in exquisite script on the vellum envelope. He secured a letter opener from the porter and opened it on the spot. It was a handsomely inscribed note which read:

> *Lord Sandbourne is hereby invited*
> *to a reception in his honor*
> *at the London Foundling Hospital*
> *on Guilford Street*
> *June third, at one o'clock in the afternoon.*

He read it a second time. London Foundling Hospital? Today? What the hell were they doing, giving a reception in his honor? He had no connection with . . . Dimly, he recalled having spoken to someone recently regarding something . . . At the Mortons' charity bash, old Rosebery had yammered on about some children's charities and said that Gabri—

Gabrielle. His whole frame stiffened at the thought of her. His heart began to hammer, and a feeling of expectation collected in his gut. She had done charity work at a foundling hospital and orphanage, near her school in France, and the children there had meant a great deal to her. The thought caused that unwelcome tightness in his gut to migrate into his chest. She had something to do with this, he was certain of it.

Dammit, he had no desire to play hide-and-seek all over London with her. He would have to go of course. He began girding himself mentally for the encounter. He would have to arrive and be gracious and pretend to know what the hell was going on . . . then take her home and give her a sound talking to before something else disastrous happened.

22

London Foundling Hospital had been established more than a century before. From a modest start it had grown to a facility that housed more than five hundred abandoned children in a large complex of reddish brown Georgian buildings set on a large greensward in Bloomsbury. As his cab drew up to the address on Guilford Street and turned into the gravel drive, he glimpsed a wide, grassy expanse of lawn, dotted here and there with mature trees. Groups of children in somber uniforms were milling about.

He paid the driver, tipped him generously, and told him to return in half an hour and to wait for him, however long it might be. Pierce entered the front door of the hospital. The starched-looking matron at the desk in the receiving room knew nothing about a "reception." While he waited for the matron to check and return, he became aware of two worn-looking younger women sitting on a bench across the way, one carrying a tiny bundle, the other with an infant in her arms and two small toddlers clinging to her threadbare skirts. The older children were whining they were hungry and climbing over their mother's lap, but she simply stared straight ahead with a deadened expression, ignoring their attempts to get her attention. Pierce averted his eyes, but not in time to avoid a tug of concern in the middle of his chest.

At last, a man in an austere gray suit and a tall woman in a dark blue uniform entered the receiving room and introduced themselves as the administrator and the head matron of the hospital. They welcomed him warmly and informed him that the reception was actually scheduled for five o'clock. They had asked him to come early for a tour and a chance to meet some of the children who would be helped by his generous contribution of the "Sandbourne Endowment." The reverent tone with which the administrator spoke those fateful words hinted at the size of Pierce's supposed generosity. He nodded and accompanied the administrator down the halls of one wing, past offices and classrooms, listening to a litany of improvements his donation would enable them to make.

They passed through a dormitory crowded with iron beds. The place smelled of vinegar and ammonia and the smell of warm, sweaty little bodies. He found himself trying not to inhale and averting his eyes from those beds and what they represented. He was relieved when they paused at an open door facing a small, paved court lined with flower beds and wooden benches. Taking a deep breath of the fresh air, he halted in the middle of it.

Seated on one of those benches was Gabrielle, dressed

in a fashionable blue skirt, white tucked blouse with a standing collar, and a simple cameo for decoration. Crowded onto the bench on either side of her and seated in a tight circle at her feet were a dozen little girls, all aged four or five, dressed in worn serge dresses and cotton aprons in varying shades of white. She was reading them a story, making the words come alive with her mimicry of voices. Their eyes were huge, their faces adoring.

The administrator excused himself, and Pierce nodded absently as the fellow left. He was intent on watching Gabrielle, feeling drawn to the scene and yet resisting it. This was what he had been lured here to see—the very picture of compassion and selflessness, the essence of all that was good and decent and desirable. Apparently he was supposed to be impressed and hand his life over to her . . .

Stepping out into the sunny court, he waited for her to notice him. But when she looked up, she merely smiled and returned to her work, asking if the girls had heard the story of the little gingerbread man. They answered with a chorus of no's. "Well, you will now." She reached into a canvas bag at her feet and pulled out another storybook that was filled with scraps of paper marking stories.

Irritation set in as Pierce leaned a shoulder against the wall and listened to the way a gingerbread man outwitted the farmer's wife, then the farmer, then the farmer's son, then a peddler along the road. Here, art—if it could be called *art*—imitated life, and it didn't take a genius to decipher who was really trying to outwit whom. Unlike her rapt audience, however, he knew how the story came out. He intended to take the part of the fox, not the farmer, and they would soon see who outfoxed whom.

When the story was over, her audience clapped with glee and begged for more. "Girls, there is someone here I want you to meet. He is a very important man. His name is

Lord Sandbourne, and he has just made a gift to the hospital that will enable you to have new books, a proper teacher, and new shoes when you outgrow those. I think he deserves a curtsy. Do you know how to curtsy?" She set her book aside and rose to demonstrate. One by one, she held their hands and had them say "thank you" and curtsy. They thought it splendid fun and insisted on doing it a second time . . . dissolving into a bedlam of giggles.

It took patience and tenacity, not to mention the bribe of another story, for her to collect them all and make them sit down once again. Then she pulled out another book and opened it to the story of the fox and the grapes.

Pierce stalked about the court with his arms folded, refusing to let any of this affect him. Children and stories and fables. It was a cheap, sentimental ploy. But, as she was explaining the moral of that tale, he realized that he had heard the story and its explanation before . . . recently. In fact, she had read it to him, not so long ago, in the privacy of her boudoir. The same story: "The Fox and the Grapes."

Gabrielle watched him pacing near the door to the courtyard. "Lord Sandbourne?" she called, bringing him up short. "Would you read one last story to the girls?"

"Me?" he snapped, then immediately checked his irritable reaction. "I am afraid not. I've only come to escort you home—as soon as possible."

"But that is not possible until I've read a few more stories. Girls, wouldn't you like to hear Lord Sandbourne read a story?"

She had done the unforgivable; she had set the children on him. In an instant, a dozen little girls were all over him, pulling on his coat and sleeves, patting and thumping him. One wrapped herself bodily around his leg. He was in danger of being entreated to death when he finally held up his hands in surrender. "All right! I'll do it."

It was as quiet as a church as he read the story of the

fox and the crow and then tried valiantly to explain the moral: the dangers of flattery. It was hard to put it in five-year-old terms—that people could say pretty things to you and about you when all they want is to take advantage of you. But then, the story was only partly for them, he realized. Its main target was himself. It was another of the stories she had read to him in her boudoir.

In spite of himself, he began to remember . . . the stories and limericks, the feeling of being in league with someone—with her. Trusting someone . . . as she had trusted him . . . and as he had begun to trust her. When the story ended, he rose quickly and handed Gabrielle back her book.

She had the children form a double line at the door, holding hands with their partners, as was their habit. One bright little face, at the head of the line, looked up at her and said, "Where is your partner? You have to have a partner."

The girls set up a clamor, insisting that "partners" was a strict rule. Gabrielle had to swallow the lump in her throat before she could force a smile and reach for Pierce's hand. "Very well. Will you be my partner, Lord Sandbourne?"

There were at least a dozen pairs of eyes fixed hopefully on him. Pierce knew when he was beaten. He took Gabrielle's hand and together they led the children out to the front lawn, where a stout older lady stood waiting to take them out for an airing.

Pierce stopped dead when his mother turned and spotted him, at the head of that line of little girls, holding Gabrielle's hand. "What are *you* doing here?" he sputtered.

"Helping," she responded calmly, then inserted herself between the pair at the head of the line. "Come girls." Taking their hands, she led them off.

"Helping what?" he murmured as he watched her go.

"Helping the children learn and grow," Gabrielle answered as they proceeded inside. "She comes here one day a week, when she's in London. She used to come more than that, but . . . she gets tired now. She reads stories—of course she calls it 'improving literature'—to the children. And she teaches the older girls sewing and helps them learn their reading and writing and ciphering." She smiled mischievously. "Around here, they still talk about the way she used to play football with the boys."

His face went blank. "She comes here to help? *She* played football?"

Gabrielle squared her shoulders, deciding he should hear it. "You didn't know, did you? She loves children. Your father wouldn't give her more than one child . . . abandoned her bed altogether, after you were born. So, for years, she has supported children's charities and donated sizable sums as well as many hours to help the children here." She led him back down the hall as they talked. "When she said she was 'off to see the children' the other day, I asked what she meant. And I asked if I could come with her. When I saw the children, I thought it would be good for both them and your ailing reputation if we made the hospital a sizable donation."

She paused and faced him. "I think you should know that I intend to come here regularly, with her." Taking a deep breath, she glanced at him and smiled. "I've another group that's waiting for stories. And I may need some help."

Some help? he thought, when he saw what awaited them. She needed a bloody regiment! The court was crawling with a dozen boys of nine or ten years, jumping, bouncing, balancing, and walking across the benches while trying to shove each other off—all while a harried matron barked orders and tried to corral them one by one. At the sight of Gabrielle, their eyes lighted and they became a bit more subdued. When she called for their attention and introduced Pierce as Lord Sandbourne, they frowned and glowered at him and mumbled their names, one by one. And while the matron got them seated and settled, Gabrielle turned aside to Pierce. "Actually, I had an ulterior motive in asking you here—"

"Ready, yer ladyship," the matron called, folding her hands and looking impatient to get on with it.

Giving him a smile of apology, Gabrielle nodded and took her place on the bench among the boys. She soon had them absorbed in the "Song of Roland," the epic story of a Frankish boy who grew into a hero through brave and cunning deeds. Tales of sword fights and outwitting ogres and sailing a boat single-handedly kept them wide-eyed and attentive for half an hour.

For a moment after she closed the book, there was reverent silence. Pierce could see daydreams and admiration in their young eyes. And he could see generosity and compassion in hers. And he couldn't help wondering what it would have been like to have a lovely and understanding tutor like her when he was a boy. Or a mother like her. She wanted children . . . she deserved to have children of her own. He could almost see her with a baby in her arms and a loving glow in her eyes.

Against his will, he recalled what she had said about his mother. Could it be true? Beatrice had wanted more children and had come here to help because she couldn't have more of her own?

"I don't know. Perhaps if we ask him . . ." Gabrielle was saying when he came back to the present. The boys squirmed and fidgeted and eyed him speculatively. He realized Gabrielle was talking about him. "His mother told me he swung a wicked bat, as a boy. And he was always quick on his feet at football. Perhaps he wouldn't mind . . ." She stood and most of the boys scrambled up with her. "Please, Lord Sandbourne. They would be ever so grateful if you could show them how to pitch a cricket ball and swing a bat, or how to move a football with their feet."

"Oh, please," "Please, sir!" and *"Pleeease do."* A veritable avalanche of pleading inundated him.

She smiled.

He didn't stand a chance. He was soon stripped of his gentlemanly coat and given garters for his sleeves and a whistle to hang around his neck. The cricket bats were splintery and decrepit and the leather footballs were old and cracked. But he soon had the boys out on the grounds, in the sunshine—running and kicking and passing the balls back and forth with their feet. Gabrielle stood at the corner of the building, watching, her eyes brimming with pleasure as she watched him running himself ragged and yelling himself hoarse.

After a time, Beatrice joined her. When she spoke, her voice was thick with emotion. "I never thought I would see a sight like this."

"He's a good man," Gabrielle said, turning in time to catch her mother-in-law wiping away a tear. "He has a very good heart."

Beatrice watched her jaded and worldly son helping children learn to play, and a wistful, faintly bittersweet smile tugged at her mouth.

"He does, doesn't he?"

It was past five when Pierce led his tired but still excited crew back inside. He was sweaty and disheveled and feeling oddly invigorated by the exercise and the boyish high spirits of his charges. It had been a long time since he kicked a ball about a field, and he had thoroughly enjoyed watching the boys throw themselves into the game with unbridled enthusiasm, holding nothing back, playing with their whole hearts.

"Please, sir." One of the boys turned to him as a

long-suffering matron herded them into their line to take them away to do chores before supper. "Will you come again? Tomorrow?" The others stared at him with raw hope in their eyes.

Pierce halted in the middle of removing his whistle and rolling down his sleeves.

"I shall have to see. I am a very busy man. Parliament is in session and—"

"See there." One little skeptic gave him a savagely resentful look. "I told ye . . . He's jus' a looker." Then he stalked to the front of the line, where he promptly started a shoving match with the boy at the head of the row.

Pierce stiffened, watching the boy, seeing all too clearly the disappointment that fueled his misbehavior. "A 'looker'? What is that?" he demanded of the boys putting the balls in the battered wooden box just inside the door. None of them wanted to say, but one finally looked up at him with guarded eyes.

"Them what comes to *look* at us," he answered. "They stay a time an' sometimes give us somethin'. But then they go home and don't never come back."

"They jus' come to *look*," his friend put in, then they hurried to take places at the end of the line. As they started off to their chores, their soup supper, and their iron cots, they cast him looks of longing and resignation over their shoulders.

He watched them go, feeling somehow exposed and uncomfortable. They resented people like him, who came to help, got their hopes up, and then, having gotten a dose of conscience-balm, never bothered to return.

Gabrielle's words about the children in France came back to him. He remembered her hurt, her resentment, and her work to help abandoned children. And he felt a keen impulse to come back again, to spend time with those boys, and to prove to them and to himself that he wasn't a just a "looker."

As he strode down the front hallway, he saw Gabrielle standing in the front reception area, holding his coat. She had donned a jacket that matched her skirt and a stylish tailored hat. He was so focused on her and on the sweet turmoil the sight of her stirred in him that it took a moment to register that she was standing with the administrator, the head matron, and two others, a man and a woman. And the man was Lord Rosebery.

His step faltered. What the devil was he doing here?

"Rosebery." He nodded to the nobleman, then, after a moment's consternation, remembered the reception. "Pardon my informality." He extended his apology to the older woman with a glance and reached for his coat, donning it.

"Ahhh," Rosebery said with a hint of amusement. "I would bet a few guineas that they've had you chasing a ball around a field until you're ready to expire."

"As a matter of fact, they have."

"Beware, Sandbourne." The aging lord leaned toward him with a tone of mock confidentiality. "I had 'coaching' duties here for a time, myself. These women will run you ragged, if you give them a chance."

Pierce shot an accusing glance at Gabrielle and stiffly returned Rosebery's smile. "I believe I have just had that lesson from my wife, sir." Then he turned to the unknown lady beside him. "I do not believe we have met, madam."

"Not formally." The gray-haired woman extended her hand while Rosebery apologized for not introducing them. "No doubt they thought we were already acquainted . . . since I attended your wedding."

Pierce's mouth opened, but no sound came out.

"Pierce, this is Mrs. Gladstone," Gabrielle said, watching his reaction warily.

"So happy to make your full acquaintance at last," Catherine Gladstone said, clasping his hand. "You know, William used to come here with me. He was always snared into coaching the boys too. There are so few men to direct the boys' activities." She smiled fondly. "He'll be delighted to see you're carrying on the tradition. He feels very strongly about these boys having exemplary men to model themselves upon."

Exemplary men. Mrs. Gladstone was clearly unaware of her husband's dire opinion of him.

"Well, it is quite past five o'clock," the administrator said, consulting his watch. "The board has gathered in the parlor for the reception." He waved a hand to direct Pierce and the rest of the group toward a large set of double doors at the end of the main hall. "We must apologize for so small a turnout, your Lordship, but on such short notice . . . Our governing board meets only quarterly, and they were eager to extend their appreciation to you and Lady Sandbourne, firsthand, before another three months pass."

The large oak-paneled room already contained a number of handsomely dressed matrons and dignified gentlemen. One by one, they were introduced to Pierce and Gabrielle and extended their gratitude for the compassion and civic spirit behind his gift. With each bit of unearned praise, Pierce felt a bit more manipulated and a bit more annoyed. But he managed to maintain his composure until he looked up and discovered an appallingly familiar face bearing down on him across the parlor.

"Lord Sandbourne." William Gladstone drew up before him with a cool smile. "I must apologize for being late. The endless business of government, you know."

As Pierce straightened, Mrs. Gladstone came to her husband's side. "William has had to give up his 'coaching' duties, but he remains active on the board here." She turned to her husband with a genteel smile. "His lordship spent the better part of the afternoon directing football matches, William."

"Indeed?" The glint in Gladstone's dark eyes hinted at a private amusement that rankled Pierce. "Well, it would seem wedded life agrees with you, Lord Sandbourne." He glanced at Gabrielle, standing nearby. "Marriage does have a way of altering one's priorities and changing one's perspective on things."

"First endowments, then charity work," Rosebery put in, with a teasing grin. "Next thing you know, he'll be coming over to our side of the house!" The comment drew discreet laughter from the other board members.

Red crept up out of Pierce's collar as he made a grimace of a smile, counterfeiting good humor, then buried his nose in his cup of tea.

Marriage has a way of altering . . . changing one . . . Those words, so lightly spoken, went straight to the core of him. As soon as the administrator finished his brief speech of appreciation on behalf of the board of governors, Pierce began to work his way to the door. Declaring that they had a pressing engagement that evening, he captured Gabrielle by the elbow, glanced at Gladstone, and ushered her out.

They managed to make it into the cab and out onto the street before Pierce erupted with a round "Dammit!" He turned on Gabrielle. "Gladstone and Rosebery—of all people! By tomorrow, word of my *reform* will be all over London!"

"I certainly hope so," Gabrielle said determinedly.

He stiffened. "You meant this to happen, didn't you? You planned the entire thing!"

"Don't be ridiculous, Pierce. I had no idea Mr. Gladstone and Lord Rosebery were on the board of governors. I certainly didn't expect, when I decided to make the donation in your name, that they would insist upon something like a reception. But, honestly, being seen doing a bit of charity work with abandoned children cannot possibly do you harm. If they do noise it about, it could only be to your credit."

"To my credit?" He stared at her with mounting outrage. "Running around like a madman . . . chasing a ball with a pack of snot-nosed orphans?"

"What better way to repair your reputation? This was a perfect opportunity for you to be seen as the charitable and generous man you are."

"*Charitable* and *generous?*" He stared at her, finally seeing the full scope of her maneuverings. "Damme, if you're not a piece of work," he snapped. "The vows are scarcely a month old, and already you're ordering and rearranging my life. Deliberately seeking out Liberal company, invading my hotel rooms, disposing of chunks of my fortune, and now roping me into charity work with penniless orphans . . . all under the guise of repairing my reputation. Well, it won't work. I am who I am. And no one who has spent time with me will put stock in such nonsense."

"Then, perhaps it is time to change whom you spend your time with," she responded hotly. "Perhaps you should begin spending time with people who see hope and decency in the world around them, instead of hypocrisy and intrigue on every hand. Perhaps you should spend some time with people who have faith in you and care about you. Perhaps it's time you made some real friends instead of just political allies who can turn on you with every change of wind."

Her words stopped him cold.

For the last week he had stumbled about in a haze, clinging to his anger so that he wouldn't have to face the sharp loneliness he felt without her. In truth, he had always been alone—he saw that now. He had always had companions in leisure, allies in politics, and connections in commerce; he had played cards and plotted elections and made financial deals with a number of men. But with all the time and experiences he had shared with them, there was scarcely one of them he could genuinely call a friend. And when his reputation began to suffer recently, there was not one person who came forward to defend him or even commiserate with him. Not one.

A pair of luminous blue eyes came into focus before him. No, there was one.

Her.

His heart began pounding and his chest felt crowded, his palms dampened. Against his better judgment, he looked into her eyes. He had never needed, never longed for friendship or love before his time with her. He hadn't even understood what they were. He might have gone on his whole life enmeshed deeper and deeper in empty pleasures and pointless political intrigues if he hadn't cynically accepted her proposition . . . if they hadn't "pretended to sin" . . . if he hadn't come to see her as a woman and a friend. If he hadn't come to love her.

The turmoil he had struggled all afternoon to contain, now burst its bonds, raging free. He was in love with Gabrielle. Thoroughly. Irrevocably. There was no escape and no compromise. It was there inside him, like a layer of bedrock newly exposed . . . part of the foundation of him, impossible to dislodge or to ignore.

He felt the control he had fought so hard to preserve slipping from his grasp.

She saw it all—the confusion, the anger, the fear—and knew something was happening in him. Impulsively, she reached for one of his hands. He tensed with resistance.

"Perhaps it's time you spent less time interfering with

my life," he declared, "and spent more time getting on with your own."

Even knowing that those words came out of his fear and turmoil, she felt their sting in her heart. Struggling with her hurt, she finally subdued it enough to make one last try.

"Pierce, I know I've upset and embarrassed you and invaded your house . . . and it probably seems as if I'm trying to take over your very life. That was never my intention. I only wanted to be a true and loving mate, a partner in your life." Moisture rose in her eyes. "I cannot change the fact that we are legally married. All I can do is try to give you back some of the choice that was taken from you." She searched his taut and troubled face.

"I am willing to be your wife, your lover, or your friend." Her voice was barely a whisper. "But you have to tell me what you want. The choice is yours."

He stared at her, emotion rising in him, then abruptly rapped on the window of the cab. The driver slowed and pulled to the side of the street, and Pierce bolted from the carriage as if the hounds of hell were after him.

As the cab lurched into motion, Gabrielle slid to the window and looked back at him through a stinging blur . . . watching his formidable figure growing smaller and more distant, until he was out of sight.

She had just gambled everything on the love he guarded so tenaciously. She had tried to resurrect the friendship between them by helping him repair the damage she had inflicted upon his reputation. And instead of recalling the bond of caring and respect that had once existed between them, her efforts had only driven a deeper wedge between them. His hurtful words repeated over and over in her head.

It's time she got on with her own life, he said.

A life without him.

. . .

For two weeks, Beatrice had assiduously courted the guardians of the guest list of the Albermarles' Derby Ball. There was, in fact, a whole round of dances planned for the night following the running of the immensely popular Derby at Epsom Downs, in late May. But it was the Albemarles' ball that ranked as one of the premier social events of the London season. All of London society aspired to it, but only four hundred of the "upper ten" were graced with invitations.

Beatrice had drawn upon every social debt, favor, and bit of goodwill owed her in the upper strata to see to it that they received invitations. Despite all of her work, she had been unable to secure an invitation until Gabrielle's and Pierce's successful appearance at the Mortons. The invitation had come by messenger, the morning after the dinner party. True to her nature and station, Lady Beatrice was weak-kneed with relief one moment and indignant the next at the idea of being invited so late to something of such magnitude. Unthinkable of them, she declared, to presume she wouldn't have another engagement elsewhere.

Fortunately, however, she had planned well ahead for the event. A suitable ball gown was the first thing she had ordered for Gabrielle on their very first shopping expedition. She had spent some time drilling Gabrielle on the order of precedence and the elaborate etiquette required at such an event. And she had even taken some of the family jewels out of the vault to be checked and cleaned by her jeweler.

The one thing Beatrice couldn't have anticipated, and was at a loss to cope with, was Gabrielle's deepening reluctance toward the ball. Beatrice and Rosalind were aware that Gabrielle and Pierce had had words when he brought her home from the foundling hospital. Gabrielle remained somewhat vague about the content of their exchange, but the impact of it was certainly clear. She behaved as if she might never see him again.

For the next two days, each time Parnell answered the door, she sprang to her feet . . . only to have her expectations dashed when it turned out to be a courier from the jeweler, an acquaintance of Lady Beatrice's, or one of her mother's three friends, who called each day to report on their efforts to call in a few discreet debts of honor to help counter the rumors about Pierce in the male preserve of St. James. But as each day passed without a message or a visit from Pierce, Gabrielle's spirits sank a bit lower.

By that Friday evening, both Rosalind and Beatrice were perfectly bewildered by the apparent failure of their campaign to bring Pierce into the matrimonial fold. They had done everything right, they told themselves. Gabrielle had charmed society and charmed Pierce. She had roused his passions and proved her prowess in a bed as well as a drawing room. And with her donation to the foundling home, she had gotten him to help both penniless orphans and himself. Validated by such respected philanthropists as Lord Rosebery, word of his patronage and involvement at the hospital was gradually spreading. Everything had gone splendidly.

And for all their successes, Gabrielle seemed no closer to being a part of Pierce's life than when they started.

Rosalind found Gabrielle sitting on a bench in the small, walled garden at the rear of the house, looking as if the weight of the world were on her shoulders. Rosalind sat down on the bench beside her daughter, and a moment later Gabrielle was sobbing in her arms.

"Why do men have to be so difficult?" Gabrielle said, later, resting her head on her mother's shoulder.

"I wish I knew," Rosalind murmured, stroking Gabrielle's hair.

After a few moments, Gabrielle drew a shuddering breath. "What if we never work things out? Do you suppose I'll ever quit missing him . . . wanting him?"

"I don't know, dearest. That's one aspect of loving a man I have little experience with." Above Gabrielle's head, Rosalind's eyes also filled with tears. "I'm afraid we'll just have to learn about it together."

23

The early June night was warm and alive with sound, and the sky was as clear as was ever seen in London's soot-laden environs. It was suitably grand finish for Derby Day, and the duke's home was suitably elegant for the most glittering event of that celebration. Albermarle Hall was a veritable palace . . . a huge, Palladian structure of gray limestone with dramatic arched windows, iron gates, and a full set of gardens, all set on the western edge of fashionable London.

When Beatrice and Gabrielle arrived, they had to wait in a line of carriages to disembark, and once they were through the stately front doors, they were directed up the sweeping center stairs to another line for introduction. As they were announced, they proceeded into the ballroom and straight to the receiving line to greet the duke and duchess and other dignitaries that included the lord mayor of London and the governor of the Derby.

Heads turned and eyes widened as they passed. A wave of recognition rippled out behind them, followed by whispers of surprise. The dowager and the current countess were nothing short of stunning together—so eye-catching, in fact, that most onlookers failed to mark the fact that the earl himself was not with them. It was an effect Lady Beatrice had counted on. They had sent the invitation on to Pierce, hoping he would accept, but there had been only ominous silence from the Clarendon.

Pierce's mother had purposefully chosen a gown of black moiré, trimmed with ecru white velvet, to serve as the perfect foil for Gabrielle's ecru white satin, trimmed with sinuous black embroidery set with beads. Gabrielle's bodice was cut lower than she was accustomed to wearing, and her shoulders were completely bare, except for the strands of jet bugle beads that draped across her shoulders. At her waist and in her hair she wore gardenias, which matched the color of her dress, and at her ears and around her throat she wore a stunning set of rubies surrounded by a tracery of diamonds—part of the Sandbourne family jewels.

As the strains of the orchestra floated out over the assembled guests, the two women gradually made their way around the ballroom, encountering Lady Morton, Olivia Tyler-Benninghoff, and the countess of Devonshire, along with a number of other new acquaintances. Though no one asked after Pierce, it was soon apparent from their comments that they assumed he must be somewhere else in the burgeoning crowd.

But, there were others who noted Pierce's absence and assigned an entirely different explanation to it.

"Well, well. What have we here?" Arundale's eyes

lighted as he spotted Gabrielle coming down the stairs from the ballroom, and he gave Shively a nudge with his elbow. "The incomparable Gabrielle." He nodded toward the gallery outside the ballroom above, then, from his vantage point near the drawing room doors, scanned the entry hall and the grand salon. "*Sans* Sandbourne. Brazen minx . . . scarcely a month after her forced marriage, she is out and about in high society."

"And without the annoying encumbrance of a husband," Shively mused. "I say—it didn't take her long to put Sandbourne out on his ear."

"Clever little tart," Arundale said with appreciation of both her beauty and attributed ambition. "She's already on to fresh game." As he ran his gaze over her elegant gown and exposed shoulders, his handsome mouth twisted into a smirk. "And since we have nothing better to do . . . let's help her find it."

The doors between drawing room, salon, and dining room had all been thrown open to facilitate the flow of guests, and the music of a string quartet provided a luxurious cloud of sound on which guests floated from one room to another. The house was nothing short of spectacular: gilded ceiling friezes, imposing portraits and monumental landscapes, huge, ornate mirrors, pastel silks and tapestries covering ornate French furnishings.

But Gabrielle attended it all with half a thought, until two male forms loomed up before her, jolting her from her self-absorption. "Lord Arundale, Lord Shively . . . How splendid to see you," she responded to their approach with a genuine smile. Familiar faces were a welcome diversion from her anxiety, just now.

"Lady Sandbourne!" Arundale put his hand to his chest as if struck physically by her presence. "By the heavens, you're like an angel . . . a healing for the jaded eye, a balm for the world-weary soul." He gave her hand a kiss of exaggerated reverence, then did the same to Lady Beatrice.

Shively tried to outdo him, declaring over Gabrielle's hand: "You rival Springtime herself tonight . . . with your vibrant warmth and grace. Sandbourne is a fortunate man, indeed."

"And I will count myself most fortunate, as well"—Arundale put in—"if you will grant me the honor of leading you out for the first waltz." His handsome golden looks and stunning gray eyes were impossible to refuse. With a glance at Beatrice, who maintained her silence and her staunchly neutral expression, Gabrielle accepted.

"And what of me? Will you promise me the first waltz after the intermission?" Shively entreated. He glowed with boyish pleasure when she agreed and penciled both their names onto the dance card dangling from her wrist.

When they parted, Beatrice finally vented her disgust. "I wonder that the duke would allow those two into his house," she whispered irritably. "There must be a desperate shortage of single men this season. Pedigreed scoundrels, the both of them. No better than they have to be at any given moment."

"They have been nothing but charming to me," Gabrielle said, studying her mother-in-law's forbidding countenance.

"Wretches . . . the lot of them." Beatrice snapped her fan open and nodded to an acquaintance as they strolled through the dining room. "Reckless and high-living and full of the-devil-take-me. 'Trouble on the hoof,' as your mother would say."

Pierce stepped into Albermarle Hall, handed the footman his invitation, and took a deep breath to prepare himself for what lay ahead. He was elegantly turned out: attired in black evening dress, freshly shaved, with his dark hair shining with attention. But on closer scrutiny, he showed signs of wear, especially in the lines strain had etched at the corners of his eyes.

For the last four days he had been haunted by the anguish in Gabrielle's face as he left her in the carriage. And for the last four days he had struggled with the choice she had given him.

Wife, lover, or friend? The beleaguered cynic in him scoffed at that offer, casting it in the most manipulative light possible. Clever of her to offer him a choice when she knew she already owned his passions and was rapidly establishing herself as his counterpart in society. "Lover" and "wife" were thus easily explained; she risked nothing in offering those. It was the "friend" business that proved a sticking point in his thoughts. She could claim the right to a legal and social association and even engage his sexual passions, with or without his genuine agreement. But she could never be his friend, except by his free choice.

To make matters worse, yesterday he had found himself standing on Guilford Street, staring at a group of boys chasing an aged football around on the grounds of the Foundling Hospital. Something compelled him to take one step and then another down the drive toward those front doors. He had spent the rest of the afternoon in his shirtsleeves, with a whistle around his neck, yelling until he was hoarse and running to the point of exhaustion. And when he was through and led the boys back inside, one looked up at him with a pair of enormous blue eyes, shining with trust, and paid him the compliment of his life: "I knew ye weren't no 'looker.'"

Those huge blue eyes. Joyful. Trusting. Suddenly he had go to the Albermarles' Ball. He had to see her and somehow settle his relationship to her once and for all.

Now he stood at the entrance to the duke's ballroom watching Gabrielle executing the figures of the opening quadrille, on the arm of Sir William Hartshorn. Dressed in elegant white trimmed with sinuous black embroidery, she seemed to shimmer in the candlelight. For a time Pierce could see no one else on the dance floor. She was a vision . . . filled with energy and grace, moving like a wave in sunlight.

When the dance ended and the old knight returned her to Lady Beatrice's side, Pierce resettled his vest, squared his shoulders, and headed for them. But he was recognized and caught by Lady Morton, who hinted and cajoled until he asked to take the floor with her later. By the time he extricated himself, strains of the first waltz were already floating over the dance floor and he looked up to find Gabrielle being led out once again—by none other than Arundale.

The sight of her in the rake's arms sent a shock through him. She was smiling up at his erstwhile companion in debauch as if he were the worthiest of men. Both fair and blond, they made a stunning visual match as they spun in slow, mesmerizing circles around the floor. The sinuous embroidery of her swishing skirts merged with the black of Arundale's trousers, forging a sensual link between them that aroused Pierce's most possessive instincts.

By the time he came across Beatrice, he was roiling inside.

"No doubt, this is your fault," he said fiercely.

She turned with a start, then followed his gaze back to Gabrielle, before speaking. "I'm afraid this entire situation is your own doing. You pursued her and claimed her, and you got more than you bargained for. It serves you right."

The familiar annoyance he always felt with his mother was a welcome distraction from his misery. But before he could retort, Beatrice seized him by the arm and led him a few steps away, to a more secluded spot.

"I know you despise advice, but . . ." Quiet urgency

filled her voice. "Don't let your silence toward Gabrielle go on too long or grow too deep, or you will have the rest of your life to regret the damage that is done." She caught his gaze in hers and softened, allowing him to see some of the pain and longing she carried inside. "Don't let pride or resentment or misguided notions of freedom ruin your chance to have a good life with her. What good will your precious freedom be to you when you're sixty years old and utterly alone . . . with only your regrets to keep you company?"

Pierce stiffened, angry with her out of habit. But for the first time in his adult life, he also found himself listening to her, sensing a softening in her, a genuine concern in her words.

"I want you to know," she said quietly, searching his face, "I've arranged to have a good bit of my inheritance placed in your name. I decided not to wait on the first grandchild. I shall just have to hope that you won't be selfish in that regard . . . that you will give that adorable girl the children she wants."

Pierce felt his world again shifting under his feet. For thirteen years she had conducted an all-out assault upon his freedom. And now she was releasing her frantic grip on him, granting him the independence and recognition he had spent a decade of rebellion trying to achieve.

"But—why?"

"Because . . ." She sighed and glanced toward the dance floor. "I believe I can trust you to do what is right." With a bittersweet smile, she pulled him down and kissed his cheek, then walked away.

The motion and the music on the dance floor ended. Pierce scanned the dancers and located Arundale escorting Gabrielle to the far side of the ballroom. Above the crowd, he had a perfect view of his wife being steered into a pack of randy young blue bloods. From forty feet away he could see the speculation in their eyes and the indecent appreciation in their smiles and knew exactly what they were thinking. He knew, because little more than two months before he had been one of them . . . lustful, calculating, cynical, on the prowl for the slightest whiff of carnal opportunity. And the thought that they might consider Gabrielle an "opportunity" positively gored him.

He struck off furiously, intent on retrieving her.

"There you are," he called out, before he quite reached the group. Only Arundale held his ground—and Gabrielle's hand; the others discreetly melted away.

"Pierce," she said. "There you are."

At close range, her dress was even more provocative than he had realized; a narrow waist that came to a seductive point, embroidery that curled slyly over her breasts, and scarcely a scrap of cloth on her from her nipples up.

"Sandbourne, old man." Arundale smiled pleasantly under Pierce's scathing look. "Trust you to find not only the beauty of the year, but also one who dances like a goddess."

Pierce ignored Arundale and took Gabrielle by the elbow. "Come, Gabrielle."

"Until next time, Lady Sandbourne." Arundale gave her hand a gallant kiss.

"Until the next time, sir," she answered with a forced smile.

Pierce imprisoned her hand on his arm as they circled the ballroom, heading for Lady Beatrice. "May I have my hand, please?" she whispered tightly. "I need to check my dance card."

"No, you don't," he declared grimly. "I have the next dance."

The orchestra was striking up the next waltz, and he led her out to the edge of the floor. As they began to dance, he felt her moving gracefully under his hand at her waist, looked down, and found himself treated to a breathtaking view of her décolletage . . . the same view Arundale had undoubtedly enjoyed minutes earlier.

"That damnable dress," he growled. "Whatever possessed you to wear such a thing?"

Her face flamed. "Good Lord, Pierce, look around you. My gown is entirely proper—perfectly within keeping for a young married woman without children. Your *mother* helped me choose it, and heaven knows, there is no one more proper than she is."

"It's indecent. Arundale and his lot were salivating."

"They were not. They were charming and respectful," she protested.

"I know that group—hell, I used to *be* that group. They want only one thing from a woman. And they'll *not* have that from you."

Hurt washed through her, dissolving some of the starch from her, leaving her trembling. When they swirled near the ballroom doors, she summoned enough force to break from his grasp, and she headed straight for the doors. She didn't stop until she reached the terrace, hoping that the darkness would hide her tears and allow her to regain enough control to find Lady Beatrice and leave.

Pierce saw her disappear onto the dimly lit terrace and thought about going after her. But what would he say to her? He was churning inside; his emotions, his thoughts, his very soul, were in turmoil.

He stalked back along the gallery and into the parlor, so absorbed in his own thoughts that he didn't see Arundale and Shively at the far end of the gallery, watching him. They had kept the newlywed couple under close scrutiny.

"Well, well," Arundale's voice was heavy with sardonic pleasure. "Trouble in paradise, it would seem. Lady Sandbourne probably could use a 'friend' just now." He laid the back of a languid hand against Shively's lapel. "Give me ten minutes with her, then join us in the gardens. By then she will have forgotten all about her little tiff with Sandbourne and will be occupied with more pleasurable matters. And I would guess she will prove quite . . . entertaining."

With a conspiring wink, Shively strode off, and Arundale strolled toward the terrace doors with a carefully calibrated smile.

There wasn't a dry thread left on Gabrielle's handkerchief, and the tears were still burning down her cheeks. She sat on a stone bench at the side of the terrace, cloaked in shadows, staring out at the moonlit garden and struggling to recover her emotions.

"Gabrielle?"

She turned with a start to find Lord Arundale standing behind her, silhouetted in the golden light streaming from the gallery windows.

"I thought it was you," he said with surprise. "Are those tears? Heaven—what is wrong?" He sat on the bench beside her and gently turned her face toward his, scowling at the sight of her tears. Immediately, he offered her his handkerchief, and as she accepted it, a sob escaped her. "Come. You cannot stay here . . . someone may see you." He put an arm around her and urged her to her feet, cradling her gently against his chest as he led her down the terrace steps and along the garden path.

He found them a bench that was sheltered from the terrace by hedges and shrubbery and sat down with her, still holding her against his side. When she made to move away, he held her back, drawing her head down against his shoulder and stroking her hair. "There, there," he said, letting his hand glide down her back and linger warmly at her waist. "Tell me what happened. Was it Pierce?" When she didn't speak, he drew back and lifted her chin, dipping his head to look into her eyes. "What did the wretch do this time?"

She stared into his pale eyes, finding them luminous with concern. She was so confused, so hurt, and he was being so very kind . . .

"Well, it doesn't take a genius to know that he's not treating you right," he said, his voice so soft and sincere and reasonable. "Moving out of the house, abandoning you, refusing to accompany you into society . . . He's an idiot, pure and simple."

"I don't know what to do," she whispered. "He's always hated the very idea of marriage. And here he is, stuck in the middle of a marriage with me. One minute he wants me, the next he can't abide being in the same room with me."

"Then he's a bigger fool that I thought," he said with quiet vehemence. He raked his hand up her back in a way that sent a shiver up her spine with it. "If I had a beautiful and sensual wife like you, I would consider myself the luckiest man alive. I would honor and cherish you. And I would certainly never abandon you in my bed."

He ran his free hand along her cheek and let his fingertips linger along her lips.

"P-please, Lord Arundale," she said, feeling a rustle of uneasiness at those sensations, but not quite able to pull away from the comfort he offered.

"Oh, yes. *Please*, Gabrielle, let me offer you a strong shoulder to cry upon." Pulling her slowly, steadily into his arms, he ran a hand over her hair and urged her head toward his chest. "Let me offer you refuge. I will count my night complete, my passion fully requited, if you will but consider me . . . your special *friend*."

"What is it?" Catton said irritably as Shively dragged him by the sleeve toward the terrace doors. "I was just getting on famously with that scrumptious Miss Froelich. What's going on?"

Shively halted and leaned close with a smirk. "Arundale's got Sandbourne's hot little piece in the gardens. You've got to come and see—"

Catton thrust back, scowling. "Sandbourne's piece? You mean his wife?"

"The delectable Gabrielle herself." Shively's face glowed with the effects of both liquor and licentious delight. "Come on, this should be fun."

Catton scowled with comprehension. With a look back toward the drawing room, he followed Shively uneasily into the gardens and out toward one of the bowers that was shrouded in moon shadows. There he glimpsed two others of their rakish set lurking behind a hedge, peering at something beyond it. This was a wicked game indeed, he realized. It wasn't just a bit of seduction; it was a calculated bit of humiliation, played out before an audience.

"No. Truly, your lordship, I must be getting back— please—" Her words carried a frantic edge that the others behind the hedge seemed to find viciously amusing. Catton backed away. When Shively and the others were absorbed in what was happening beyond the hedge, he turned without a sound and headed back into the house at a run.

Pierce stood in the dining room, suffering the prattle of Lady Jane Montgomery and Maribel, the dowager duchess of Devonshire. They were so pleased, they told him, to meet his lovely wife and were so gratified to see him "settled" at last.

"How fortunate you are to have found a young woman of such generosity of spirit and such compassion," the duchess rattled on. "You never know what you're getting with these 'modern' girls. I've heard from several persons how your wife spurned the notion of a costly wedding trip to donate the funds to the London Foundling Hospital. Would that other wives showed such charity . . ."

He managed to squirm through that interminable encounter, only to walk straight into another. Lord Asbury, one of the Conservative leaders in the House of Lords, took him aside and with great aplomb announced: "Dashed clever of you, Sandbourne—that Foundling Hospital business. Always good to be seen as compassionate toward widows and orphans and the working classes. Keep it up until you're reestablished, then get out of it. No need to waste time on something the women can do."

Barely constraining himself, Pierce withdrew into the entry hall, where he glanced longingly at the front doors and was caught yet a third time. Lady Elsie Hartshorn, old Sir William's wife, was both old enough and crusty enough to actually say what was on the minds of half the matrons present: "That wife of yours seems to be doing you a world of good, Sandbourne. Always said that was what you needed . . . a good woman to make a good man out of you . . ."

He felt as if steam must be coming out of his every pore before he managed to get away. A good woman. He didn't need that pretentious lot to tell him Gabrielle was a pearl, nor that she had been cast before one of society's prime swine—and she had managed to make a better man out of him.

He stopped dead in the middle of the drawing room, feeling a wave of insight breaking over him. The changes he had so dreaded and fought had already taken place. She hadn't *made* him a better man; she had *made him want to be one.*

Then, what the hell was he so afraid of? What was he doing living in a hotel . . . isolating himself from her . . . spending sleepless nights trying to fight his own needs, denying himself something that was as necessary to him as air. It made about as much sense as holding his breath until he turned blue. And was just about as childish.

"Sandbourne!"

Through his kaleidoscopic thoughts, he caught sight of a frantic Catton bearing down on him. "Catton? You look like you've seen a—"

Catton seized him by the arm. "It's your wife," he murmured. "Arundale lured her into the garden." He waited for the first part to register and held Pierce's arm tightly, as if expecting a drastic reaction to the rest. "And they are not alone."

Catton's grim expression embroidered a wealth of meaning around those terse statements. Lured into a garden . . . with others looking on. It was Sutterfield's wife, all over again. A member of their group had lured the vain and licentious wife of an aging peer into darkened gardens during a society ball, for a quick, hot bit of pleasure, while a group of puerile profligates hid in the bushes and watched. Pierce had been one of those in the bushes. And so had Arundale. Now Arundale had lured *his* wife out . . .

Gabrielle. Pierce felt a surge of white hot fury rising through his gut, invading his chest, then erupting in his head. "Where?" he demanded, in a voice that scraped the bottom of its register and picked up brimstone.

"No, your lordship—*please*—don't—"

Gradually, in the last few minutes, words of comfort had turned to suggestive whispers, gentle touches to unwanted caresses, and solace to a frightening sensual demand. Gabrielle had finally shaken off her haze of grief and despair enough to realize the danger of her situation— locked in Arundale's embrace, held forcefully against his body in a dark, isolated garden.

"I insist you release me, immediately," she demanded, shoving at him.

He laughed coarsely, releasing her just enough to force her arms down her sides and trap them there. "Not yet— not when I am set to give you a taste of my—*esteem.*" He proceeded to give her a revolting taste of his liquor-soaked mouth instead.

"Let me go!" She wrestled with all her might, struggling to avoid his wet, avid lips and failing. A second time he forced his mouth down on hers, probing her clamped lips crudely with his tongue and trying to push her down onto the stone bench with the force of his weight.

"*Nooo!*" Frantic to stay upright, she managed to catch and brace herself with her hands. "Let me go," she choked out, feeling his body rubbing against hers, shuddering with revulsion as his wet mouth slid down the side of her neck. "I warn you, I'll scream—"

"Playing hard to get, Cleopatra?" he taunted, panting with both excitement and exertion, as he tried once more to pin her mouth beneath his. "That's not like you."

Sounds of scuffling and confusion erupted behind them. A cry rang out and a body came hurtling through the hedge behind them, just missing the bench, then sprawling on the gravel path before it. An instant later, a second body joined it, and both lay groaning in shock on the ground. Startled, Arundale straightened and loosened his grip on Gabrielle. Panicky with desperation, she wriggled her arms up between them, and, as a third form came crashing through the hedge, she shoved with all her might and broke free. Lurching from the bench, trembling so that she could scarcely stand, she staggered back with her arms clamped around her waist. And she discovered Pierce standing over the two on the ground with his fists clenched and his chest heaving.

"Pierce!"

He looked up and stared at her for a moment, taking in her crumpled gown, her swollen lips and the fear and shame visible in her eyes. Then he reached down and lifted one of the men partway by the front of his coat.

"S-Sandbourne—we didn't mean anything—I swear!" the wretch stammered. "W-we were just having a bit of a joke—we were just watching—it was all Arundale's idea!"

"Lying bastard," he snarled, giving the wretch a shake and dropping him back on the ground. "I ought to thrash you within an inch of your worthless lives." From the way the pair flinched, it was clear they thought him capable of it. "If I ever catch you even looking at my wife again, I'll have your guts for garters—do you understand?" When he nodded, Pierce backed a step, allowing him to get to his feet and back away. His ashen companion shrank back on the ground, then scrambled up, nodding.

It took a moment for the horrifying reality of it to assemble in Gabrielle's head. Those men had been in the bushes . . . watching . . . while Arundale tried to . . .

It had been some sort of plot to ruin her good name, to humiliate both her and Pierce. In her distress over Pierce she had fallen right into a vicious trap that could have destroyed both of them.

"Come now, Sandbourne . . . We were just having a bit of fun," Arundale declared nervously, rising and spreading his hands in a mocking gesture of conciliation.

"Fun, Arundale? Luring my wife into a darkened garden and forcing yourself upon her, while these fools look on, is your idea of *fun*?"

"It used to be *your* idea of fun—or have you forgotten?"

"Damn you!" Pierce lurched toward him, and Arundale fell back by the same amount.

"I hardly had to force myself on her, Sandbourne." Arundale's eyes darted to Gabrielle as he tried to redirect Pierce's fury. "It is a wise man, who knows his own wife.

Surely, by now you know yours—the way she teases and flirts, the way she leads men on. She insisted we have some privacy, begged me to stay with her, to hold her . . . said you didn't pay her proper attention. She offered to let me take your place in her bed, since you don't seem so inclined . . ."

"No!" Her voice sounded hoarse and desperate in her own ears. "It's not true."

"Take a bit of advice, Sandbourne," Arundale offered, taking Pierce's pause and the tumultuous look he was giving Gabrielle as signs that he was entertaining serious doubts about his wife's character and fidelity. "Keep her locked up, if you expect to have any confidence in your heir . . ."

"Dear God," she choked out.

Those words unleashed a surge of fury in Pierce. He pivoted, lunged, and drove one fist square into Arundale's midsection and the other into his face, sending him sprawling back onto the path. Then he stood over the rake's crumpled form, with his shoulders swollen and his fists still clenched.

"You filthy, lying bastard. I do know my wife—every aspect of her. And because I do, I know exactly who is to blame here, Arundale. There is not a more trustworthy woman on the face of the earth . . . nor a more honorable person. She is not capable of deceit."

Gabrielle felt dizzy and confused, and her knees wobbled beneath her. Her heart was pounding so loudly that she feared she had heard it wrong, somehow.

"You're the one who needs to be locked up, Arundale. You and the rest of these buffoons who follow you around like mindless fools. I swear to you, if you ever so much as look at Gabrielle again, I will take immense pleasure in tearing you limb from limb." He turned to the others. "And you—Pattersall, Grandley—if I hear a whisper of this anywhere, you may be certain I shall come looking for you. And you will wish the breath that uttered that gossip had been your last."

In shock, half-blinded by tears, and unable to speak for the constriction in her throat, she saw him coming for her. Her knees gave way when he touched her shoulders, and she sagged against him, grabbing the side of his coat. A moment later, he had lifted her up in his arms and was striding through the darkened gardens.

24

He located the gate at the side of the garden and carried her into the stable yard, which was filled with rows of stylish coaches and carriages. After a brief search, he spotted his own vehicle and carried her directly to it. Depositing her on the seat, he climbed onto the hub of one wheel and called for Jack. The driver came at a run and informed him that it would take a while to get the carriage out, since several coaches had to be moved before they could reach the street.

"Do what you can. Take us straight to the house." Pierce ducked inside the carriage with her, closed the door, and sat for a minute, letting his eyes adjust to the darkness.

The only light was that which came from the torches and carriage lamps outside.

After a time, she looked up at him with eyes that glistened in the dimness. "I'm sorry, Pierce. I just went out onto the terrace to collect myself, and suddenly he was there, lending me his handkerchief and telling me he wanted to be my friend. I suppose I should have known better, but I was so upset, and he seemed so sympathetic."

"Hasn't anyone ever told you that appearances can be deceiving?"

She wrapped her arms around her waist. "I suppose I deserve that. You said he was a vile, miserable wretch who only wanted one thing from a woman." She took a shuddering breath. "And you were right."

"Appearances are often deceiving." He gave her a pained smile. "But, sometimes, what appears to be a rat really is a rat." He reached up to stroke her cheek and found it damp. He handed her his handkerchief, and she wiped away the remnants of her tears. "I told you, sweetheart, I know that group. I used to be a part of it." He caught her chin on his finger and tilted it up to him. "And it's taken me a while to come to terms with the idea that I'm not the man I used to be, and that you are responsible."

"I am?"

There was a shout, followed by the jerk of the carriage, and he released her chin and reached for her hand.

"Until you came along, I hadn't heard from my conscience in years. Now, it seems, I hear from it at the drop of a hat. I cannot listen to my party's propaganda without wondering about their motives and thinking of alternative proposals . . . a rather inconvenient habit for a politician. I find myself looking at women in the streets and worrying whether they have a place to sleep at night. I see ragged children and I think of your foundling hospitals. I read the newspaper and wonder what details *didn't* get printed. And, strangely enough, I don't seem as eager to judge people for being human and fallible."

She felt the comforting warmth of his big hand around hers and remembered what he had said to Arundale. "Pierce, did you mean what you said in the garden?" she asked, hope rising anew. "About me?"

He nodded, searching the tension in her features. "Every word."

"That you trust me? And you believe I am honorable?"

"That, and more." At that moment in the garden, when he saw her standing there, with tears running down her face and her heart in her eyes, he had known her utterly. He knew the depth of her heart and the earnestness of her passions. He knew she would never betray him, not even out of hurt or anger.

"How much more?" She held her breath.

"A great deal more. You're generous to a fault, honest, softhearted, a little devious, and more than a little determined. And you're passionate about the things you believe in, like helping children . . . and like me. You believed in me, sweetheart. And, because you believed in me, I have to believe in you. And in your love."

"I do love you," she said softly. "With all my heart."

"I know." From the softening of his powerful face, she could see what that knowledge meant to him. "I was running, Gabrielle. From you. From being changed. From being controlled. Then, tonight, I realized that no matter how long or how far or how fast I ran, no matter where I went . . . you would still be there. Because you're here"— he put his hand to his chest—"inside me."

"And?" she insisted with a beaming smile.

"That isn't enough?" He gave her a look of disbelief, then it dawned on him what she wanted. "You're going to make me say it, aren't you?" When she nodded, he took a deep breath and braced. "You women and your words," he muttered. "All right." He took both her hands in his. "I love you, Gabrielle St. James. With all my heart. And I miss you."

Her face was radiant, dazzling as she made her final demand.

"*And?*"

He broke into a bewildered grin. "You want still more?"

"There is the little matter of a *choice* you had to make." She focused fiercely on him, coiled with expectation, sensing what his answer would be, but aching to hear it.

"Oh, yes. My choice." He wagged a finger at her. "Very clever of you to offer me one, Gabrielle. A master stroke, in fact. But, I've decided I'm not especially keen on the particulars of your offer. I mean . . . who says I have to have you for my wife *or* my lover *or* my friend?"

Her smile dimmed. "What?"

"What if I decide I want all three?" There was a devastating twinkle in his eyes as he leaned closer and seized her other hand. "What if I want to help you at the foundling hospital, like a friend . . . then escort you to a dinner party, like a husband . . . and afterward make wild love to you in the carriage, like a lover?"

"Oh, I see." Her heart soared as she looked into the depths of his dark eyes, that were like the night sky, littered with stars. "You expect to get a wife and a mistress and a friend in the same bargain . . . three for the price of one. I always said you were a shrewd one, Lord Sandbourne."

"I'm afraid 'shrewd' has nothing to do with it. You see, the time we spent in your boudoir, *pretending to sin,* was far and away the most fun I've ever had. And I can't help wondering if it might prove to be just as much fun to *pretend to be respectable* with you."

She laughed, bubbles of mirth rising from the depths of her soul. "Pretending to be respectable? I think I'd like that. It sounds like us. But . . ." She gave him a teasing scowl that couldn't quite make her smile disappear. "If we pretend to be respectable, will I still be able to do this?"

Sliding against him, she pulled his head down and gave him a wildly hungry kiss in which she tugged at his tongue and gave his passions the spur. His answer sounded a bit short of breath.

"I believe . . . we would have to make allowances for that."

"And this? What about this?" she murmured against his lips, pulling his tie and unbuttoning his collar. Kissing her way down his chin and down his throat, she gave the base of his neck a rake with her teeth. In a heartbeat she was popping the studs on his shirtfront ripping open the button placket of his undershirt . . . and pressing lush, tonguing kisses down one side of his breast. Then, prying his shirt back inside his coat, she found his nipple and began to flick it with her tongue and give it soft nips with her teeth.

"Yes—" he groaned. "*Ohhh,* yes. We'll definitely allow that."

"And this?" she asked, having difficulty getting her breath as she sat up on her knees on the seat by him, and pulled down the bodice of her gown, just enough to bare two taut, velvety nipples.

"*Ummm* . . . I'm afraid I would have to insist on this" —he dipped his burning face to rub his cheek against one tightly contracted tip—"*regularly.*" He kissed and caressed her breasts, licked and teased and nibbled . . . until he couldn't bear it anymore. Wrapping her waist with his arms, he hauled her across his lap and buried his face in the rose-scented valley between those erotic mounds.

She wriggled seductively on his lap, knowing exactly where to direct her weight as she rubbed and writhed against his swollen shaft. They kissed and pressed and caressed until their passions threatened to explode out of control. It was only when she made to hike her skirts and sit astride his lap—postilion style—that they moved apart long enough to realize the carriage had stopped.

"We're here," he said hoarsely, leaning ahead to peer out the window. She sagged against him, boneless with need. "And I don't think you gave me an answer."

"Answer?" She said, breathing hard. "What was the question again?"

He grinned. "Do I get three for the price of one?"

She bit her lip, eyeing him seductively. "How about an even trade? Husband, lover, and friend . . . for wife, mistress, and friend."

He leaned back against the seat, looking at her, thinking he'd never seen a more erotic sight in his life than her, sitting there with her breasts peeking above her bodice, her hair coming undone, her eyes black with roused passions. For all the hunger in his body, there was a poignant fullness in his chest, in his heart. With a soft, desirous smile, he extended his hand to her. "Agreed."

"Agreed." She shook his hand. "But, I think a bargain as unique as this should be sealed with something a bit more memorable than a handshake." Mischief played at the corners of her mouth. "Come to bed with me, and I'll give you a night you'll never forget."

With a triumphant laugh, he lurched for the door, but she held him back. "Really, Lord Sandbourne. You cannot be seen emerging from a carriage in such a condition. There are standards to maintain."

He glanced down to find his shirt and his trousers both standing open.

When they had righted their clothes, they descended from the carriage and entered the house. It seemed like an eternity before Pierce was lighting the candles in the bedchamber and then taking her into his arms.

When he surfaced from one of her absorbing kisses, he ran his hands over her satin and her jet bugle beads. "I've been dying of curiosity," he murmured against her hair, recalling his curiosity earlier in the evening. "Are you or are you not wearing all-in-ones under your dress?"

She shivered as he traced her ear with his tongue. "There is one sure way to find out."

"Yes?"

"Take it off."

His whole body was on fire, trembling so that he could scarcely make his hands function at her hooks and laces. Piece by piece, he peeled her garments away until she stood in camisole, garters, and stockings . . . and a smile. There were no all-in-ones on the floor. Then she insisted on returning the favor. His coat, his vest, his shirt and undershirt fell to the floor, followed closely by his trousers. As she knelt to remove his stockings, she paused on her knees before him, looking up his long, angular body. One by one, she removed her hairpins and her flowers. And when her hair was free, she combed it with her fingers and then began to rub it over his swollen and aching loins.

"Merciful—" He closed his eyes and held his breath. "Where did you learn such a thing, Gabrielle?" After a moment the sensation stopped, and he opened his eyes to find her standing before him with desire flickering like a flame through her entire countenance.

"I've been taking lessons." She smiled and took him by the hand, leading him to the bed, turning the covers back. Absorbed in watching her shapely bottom sway, he could barely recall what he had asked, much less make sense of her answer.

"Lessons?" He shook his head and blinked as she slid across the sheets and held out her arms to him.

"Mistress lessons." The sultry demand in her eyes spilled over into her voice. "I intend to be the perfect mistress."

"The perfect mistress?" None of his mental faculties

were functioning as he slid into the bed and into her cool, silken arms.

"*Ummm.*" She wrapped his neck with her arms as he settled between her thighs. "Want to see what I learned in lesson one?"

They lay together afterward, exhausted, glowing, stuffed to overflowing with satisfaction. For a while, he luxuriated in the feel of her against him. She fit perfectly . . . in his arms . . . in his heart. She was like a piece of him that he hadn't even known was missing until he found her. With her in his arms, feeling her pressed warmly against him, he felt strangely full and complete. He had found the perfect mistress. And the perfect mistress was his wife.

"I missed you," she said softly, turning her head on his arm to gaze fondly at him.

He sat up, looking intently at her, then slid from the bed to rummage around in the bottom drawer of the highboy across the room. When he came back, he placed in her hands a shoe . . . once pristine white brocade and lush satin rosettes, now bedraggled and water-stained. She stared at it, feeling a crush of tenderness in her chest, then looked up to find his eyes luminous.

"I missed you too," he said. And there in her hands was the proof. He had gone back to retrieve her lost shoe and he had kept it safe, all this time. "I missed your laugh and your loving and your honesty. I missed my best friend."

She sat up and threw her arms around his neck—still holding that shoe—and kissed him with all the joy and passion in her heart. When she was too breathless to continue, she halted and pressed her forehead to his, looking into his eyes, reveling in both the intimacy and the title he had just bestowed on her. "Best friend. That has a wonderful sound. Who would have guessed that two months ago we would be here, like this . . . married and loving . . . and best friends."

She grinned. "You know what we should do? Send Mr. Gladstone a thank-you note. Or, if you'd prefer, we could just name our firstborn after him." The arrested look on his face made her laugh. "Wait—I had forgotten. I promised to name my firstborn after *you*. I'm afraid Mr. Gladstone will have to settle for the second-born. Or the third . . ." She paused and leaned back. "We will have a third, won't we?"

The sudden tension in his face and frame puzzled her. She laid her hand on his face. "What is it? Is something wrong?"

He sat up. "This is Saturday night. What time is it?" Bolting from the bed, he rummaged about in his discarded clothes for his pocket watch. "Almost half past eleven! Damn, damn, and double damn!"

"Pierce? What is it?" She had never heard him be so profane. Grabbing a sheet and rolling up onto her knees on the bed, she watched him pacing and running his hands through his hair. Then he stopped and stood staring at her.

There she sat, in the bed they now shared, rosy with the effects of his loving, her eyes shining with trust and belief in him. Suddenly his conscience was in massive revolt.

"Tell me again . . . how appearances are deceiving . . . how Gladstone really did just try to rescue you . . . how good and decent his intentions toward those street women are."

"What?" She slid to the edge of the bed.

"Tell me again that I'm a different man . . . a better man," he demanded, his countenance catching fire as he came to her and took her by the shoulders, searching her face. "Tell me what *you* would do if you knew someone else was doing something questionable and perhaps even underhanded—supposedly with the highest of purposes.

Do two wrongs ever make a right? What would you do, Gabrielle, if you knew someone you disagreed with and disliked was going to be hurt very badly?"

"What are you talking about, Pierce? What's happening? I want to help—but you'll have to tell me what is going on."

He stared down at her bewilderment and spoke to himself as much as to her.

"A miscarriage of justice . . . that's what's happening," he declared, realizing it was true. "As we speak, Gladstone is being drugged and dumped in a bed full of women, in a brothel. And just after midnight, several leading men will burst through the door and discover him there with a group of prostitutes who will swear he's been their regular patron."

"But that would"—her eyes darted over the scene being conjured in her mind—"humiliate him, ruin him."

"That, I believe, is the idea," he said grimly. "When the news is carried to the palace and reaches the newspapers, both his career and his government will be finished."

"But that's vile. He's a decent man. I'm convinced of it. Perhaps he doesn't show the best judgment where prostitutes are concerned. But, in that regard, he has the company of at least half of the men of London!" She looked up at him. "Pierce, two wrongs never make a right. It is only when you do the right thing for the right reasons that things are truly *good*."

He could feel those words echoing through his heart, calling him to do what was good and right despite his personal feelings toward the man. The trust in her face, collected into his heart, became a moral imperative. He pressed a quick, hard kiss on her lips, then released her and rushed for his clothes.

"Life was a hell of a lot easier when I was a hedonistic,

amoral wretch," he muttered, shoving his feet into his stockings and his legs into his trousers.

"What are you going to do?" She slid from the bed, watching him dress.

"I have to try to stop it."

In a heartbeat, she was in the dressing room, pulling out a dark blue serge skirt here and a white cotton school blouse there. He found her wrestling into her petticoat and fumbling with her blouse buttons.

"And just what do you think you're doing?"

"I'm coming with you," she declared, drawing her skirt on over her head and settling it around her waist. He seized her arm as she reached for her jacket.

"The hell you are! The Pavilion is a brothel . . . a fancy one, perhaps, but a pleasure pit all the same. And I'll not have my wife setting foot inside such a place."

"And I won't have my husband setting foot inside one without me," she declared defiantly. "If something goes wrong and disaster strikes, at least we'll be in it together. Besides, you might need a witness of some sort. And who better to vouch for you than your wife?"

There were times, Pierce realized, as he bounded into the carriage after her minutes later, that being a tyrant had definite appeal. Then he felt her hand insinuating itself into his and looked over at her. Her eyes glowed with pride and determination. On the other hand, being a reasonable and indulgent husband had its good points as well.

The Pavilion was housed in a large brick building situated squarely between clubmen's row and the theater district of the Haymarket. Outside, it was singularly undistinguished and to the untrained eye might even have passed for a warehouse or shop of some sort, with apartments making up the top floors. Inside, however, it was arrayed in lavish style and was widely considered to be the poshest brothel in all of London. It admitted only the most select clientele to its drawing and gaming rooms and bar on the first floor. And only those with plenty of coin to pave the way were provided for in the twenty or so private rooms upstairs.

When the carriage pulled up by the rear door in the alley, Pierce checked his watch—eleven fifty!—and ordered Gabrielle to stay in the carriage. She promptly joined him on the pavement, resetting her prim bonnet and refusing to be left behind. Grumbling to her to keep behind him, he approached the heavy door and knocked. Gabrielle was glad for his presence between her and the gargantuan figure who answered that summons. To her surprise, that man-mountain seemed to recognize Pierce. A bit of haggling ensued, and Pierce made up a story about wanting the use of one of the more exotic rooms for a bit of "private sport."

"Madam won' like it," the huge fellow declared, eyeing Gabrielle darkly. "You bringin' in yer own piece. She'll 'ave my ears if she finds out." But in the end, the money was too good and he relented. "As long as yer in an' out in an hour."

He led them up an unpretentious set of back stairs to the top floor and bade them wait by the door while he checked the corridor and located a suitable room. He returned shortly and beckoned to them. They followed him down a luxuriously appointed hallway filled with exotic odors of perfumes and incense and an even more potent musklike scent that a seasoned voluptuary would have recognized at first breath.

They heard someone coming. The hulking fellow quickly pushed them into a mirrored chamber constructed around a huge silk-clad bed covered with pillows. Palms and gilded screens and Moorish arches set along the mirrored walls were meant to suggest a Persian harem, with all its fleshy delights.

While Pierce put his ear to the door, listening, Gabrielle examined the room in amazement. "Is the entire place like this?" she whispered, touching an ornate lattice arch and quickly drawing her hand back. "Look at all these mirrors. They must have cost a fortune."

"They don't stint on setting the right mood," he said with a wry whisper. "That is part of the attraction here. Each of the rooms on this floor is done in a different decor. This is the Arabian room. There's a room modeled after the hall of mirrors at Versailles, one after a pharaoh's pleasure barge, another after a Viking longship—liberally supplied with furs. For more exotic tastes, there's a slave market in the Casbah and a monk's cell, rather unusually equipped. There is even an exact duplicate of the queen's bedchamber at Osborne House . . . complete with the wreath and memorial to Albert pinned to the headboard."

"Really?" Then her eyes narrowed. "Just how do you know so much about this place?"

He blinked. "Some . . . shameless and depraved acquaintances of mine told me all about it." He turned quickly back to the door, listening, and she turned back to the mirrors, fascinated by the way they reflected into each other, casting multiple images of her through the walls themselves.

"Say, wouldn't it be interesting to actually . . . someday . . . come here and—"

"Gabrielle!" he whispered. "We don't have any time to lose. I would guess Gladstone is on this floor, in one of the more exotic rooms." He opened the door, peering out into the vacant hallway, and took her by the wrist. "Stay close. We'll just have to try the doors and see which has been left open to invite 'visitors.' "

They crept along the hall, trying doors, finding several locked, with shocking noises coming from inside. They finally found one open and empty—a room made like an Egyptian pleasure barge with oddly shaped golden chairs and huge fans made of feathers. "Have you ever seen anything like that in your life?" she whispered, her eyes as big as saucers. Pierce declined to answer, dragging her away from the door. Voices in the hallway, around the corner sent them scrambling back into a doorway, pressed against the panels with their hearts pounding. But whoever was in the hall soon disappeared down the stairs.

Taking a deep breath, he pulled her around the corner and into another long corridor. A large, ornate staircase descended from the middle of the passage, and the sounds of music and laughter wafted up from the floors below. They tried two more doors before discovering one at the end of the hall . . . unlocked . . . and occupied.

Pierce spotted four striking young women clothed only in camisoles, drawers, and striped stockings, lounging around on a huge bed and on the sofa at the foot of it. Unaware of his presence, they seemed faintly bored. He heard one ask if the old boy had "come to" yet, and another checked and answered that he was beginning to waken. Pierce pulled back and nodded to Gabrielle.

"The bastards have a warped sense of humor," he said irritably. "Knowing how Queen Victoria despises his politics, they've put him in the replica of her bedchamber."

25

Taking a deep breath, he barged inside and pulled Gabrielle into the room after him. They found themselves in a bedchamber nearly filled by a massive mahogany bed with a stately wooden half canopy hung with floral bed draperies. Along one wall was a huge painting of a reclining nude, and there was a low-backed sofa at the foot of the bed. The prostitutes lounging on the sofa and chairs flew into action at the first sign of motion by the door. Climbing onto the bed, they laughed and made ribald comments and frolicked around a half-clad form that lay prostrate on the covers.

Gabrielle was stunned, but Pierce hurried to the bed

and began pulling the women from Gladstone. "Get off him, for God's sake—the old man's half comatose!"

"*Now* he is," one of the tarts said with a wicked smile, snatching up the camisole she'd discarded only a minute before. "But you should have seen him an hour ago."

"Save the act," Pierce declared irritably. "I know what you've been paid to do, but the plan's off—every bit of it."

"The hell, ye say!" One hard-eyed professional inserted herself on the bed between him and Gladstone. "We was promised a fine bonus for this little piece of work. And we ain't goin' nowhere 'til we get it."

At the sound of their raised voices, Gabrielle rushed to the bed. "Pierce—we don't have time to argue. They'll be here any moment." She turned to Gladstone and began patting his leathery cheek and calling his name. His eyelids fluttered and his slack mouth moved with a low groan. "He's coming awake." She pulled the prime minister's arm and tried to lift him to a sitting position. "Mr. Gladstone, wake up! We have to get you out of here—you're in grave danger!"

"Help us get him dressed and out of here without being seen," Pierce told the women as he hurried to help Gabrielle, "and I'll *double* your bonus."

The women glanced at each other, then fell to their aid. Gladstone was limp and heavy, but with one person under each arm and another holding him up by the back of his trousers, they managed to put his arms in his coat and button his vest. They were halfway to the door with him when they heard the sound of male voices outside, growing louder, coming their way.

"It's them," Pierce said with a groan. "Lock the door!" One of the women sprang to the door and turned the key while Pierce looked frantically around the room. "Is there no other way out?" When the courtesans shook their heads,

Pierce looked to Gabrielle, who looked desperately to the bed.

"We'll have to hide him," she declared, abandoning the prime minister to Pierce's and the others' grasps while she hurried to the bed and lifted the bed skirt. "This is the only place big enough to hold him. Quick—put him under the bed!"

"If they search, that's the first place they'll look," Pierce protested.

"Not if we find a way to distract them." She looked at their four accomplices. "That will be *your* job." They balked at the idea, until she declared: "For *three* times your bonus."

Gladstone chose the moment they began stuffing him under the bed, to come to life. "Oh, no! Somebody will have to keep him quiet," Gabrielle insisted, tugging on Pierce's arm, indicating he must go under the bed with Gladstone. When he protested, she gave him a wicked glare. "I'm not strong enough to hold him . . . and I doubt your reputation could stand the strain of being caught in a brothel with five women. They won't know me from Eve, so—"

"Why do you always have to be so damned logical?" He knelt and slid under the bed with the prime minister.

She turned to the women, who regarded her and her demure bonnet and proper serge skirt and jacket with expressions ranging from sly smiles to blatant contempt. What did she do now? What was a plausible excuse for a respectable woman being caught with four prostitutes—on a bed, in a brothel, in the dead of night? Pounding on the door and raised voices demanding entry shook an idea free in her head.

"A book!" she declared, looking frantically around the room at the heavy mahogany furnishings. "Is there any sort of book in here?"

"Oh . . . yeah," one of the women said, turning to rummage about in the bedside cabinet.

"Onto the bed, all of you. And if they come near it, do something—anything—to distract them." The women complied, frowning at one another and shrugging. Gabrielle accepted the book and settled on the foot of the bed facing the four of them. "Now, try to look a bit repentant. I want them to think I've come to read to you and to try to get you to change your ways."

That was how Gabrielle came to be sitting in a fancy brothel, on the foot of a facsimile of Queen Victoria's personal bed, holding an ornate edition of illegal French lithographs, and pretending to read a sermon from it on the evils of the flesh . . . to four scantily clad and rather bemused prostitutes.

The door crashed open moments later, and four gentlemen, accompanied by two uniformed constables, burst into the room. Gabrielle turned with a start and a look of great indignation.

"How dare you break in on us—like . . . this?" She found herself looking straight into a face she recognized . . . a face that set her blood draining from her head.

The duke of Carlisle had been approached on a matter of great national urgency that evening as he sat in his club. A crime against order and decency was being carried out at that very moment, the conservative guardians of Britain declared, and they called upon the duke to do his duty to queen and country. William Gladstone, they informed him, was at that very moment embroiled in a revolting debauch in the city's foremost brothel, and several men of unimpeachable standing were needed to serve as witnesses.

In just such a fashion, the earl of Westover and the renowned jurist and justice of the Queen's Bench Sir Henry Maynard had also been recruited for the task of standing witness to the prime minister's depravity. They had arrived at the notorious Pavilion, with Colonel Tottenham and two uniformed constables, bent on carrying out their grim duty as nobles and leading men of the realm. But, instead of witnessing Gladstone engaged in hideous debauch, the group discovered an eloquently outraged young woman, primly dressed and bonneted, sitting on a bed facing four half-naked ladies of the evening.

The duke's eyes widened as he found himself staring into his daughter's face. For a moment he was struck perfectly dumb, unable to comprehend the sight of her, there in the most fashionable brothel in all England.

"What the hell are *you* doing here?" he roared above the confusion and consternation breaking out among the others.

Gabrielle panicked for a moment, unable to make sense of the fact that her father was there, staring at her in growing horror. Once again she was caught up in a scandal, and once again he was the one doing the catching. Her heart pounded, her mind raced. This time there was more at stake than just a bit of personal humiliation. Reputations, whole lives, hung in the balance. She was literally *sitting* on two political careers!

"I might ask the very same of you, sir!" she came to life, springing to her feet, clutching the book to her bosom. "Who are *you* and what do you think you are doing . . . breaking into this room?" For a long moment, she entreated her father with widened eyes, beseeching him not to expose her. His hesitation gave her the time and the courage to seize the initiative. Flinging a hand toward the women on the bed behind her, she took a stand before the group of men. "Heaven knows, these poor women have little enough privacy and time to call their own. I will thank you to please leave. And close the door after you!"

"Time to call their own? What *is* going on here?" one of the other gentlemen demanded.

"Can't you recognize a bit of rescue work when you see it?" she rejoined.

She had to be half mad, facing the pack of them—facing her own father and behaving as if he were a total stranger. She could see him teetering on the brink of speaking and prayed he wouldn't give her away.

"Where the hell is he—Gladstone? I know he's here somewhere—what have you done with him?" A tall, pinch-faced fellow in military style dress paced about the room in mounting frustration, then rushed to the bed drapes hanging from the half canopy and tore them from their ties, searching behind them. He turned a suspicious eye on the bed, but one of the prostitutes slid to the side of it, crossed her arms under her breasts.

"*Ohhh*, no ye don't," she said, sticking her chin up at him. "Ye don't climb in this bed unless yer willin' to pay for it."

"Pay for it?" Tottenham fairly choked on the words. He could scarcely insist that he had every right to be there . . . on the grounds that he had *already* paid for it.

"She come to read to us," one of the other women spoke up with a hostile look.

"Yeah. Paid to give us a bit o' time away from the gents . . . to 'rescue' us."

The duke's confusion was being overwhelmed by the general consternation. Gabrielle could see his mind working, could almost read his thoughts in his face. If he identified her, he would, by association, bring an avalanche of humiliation down on his own head. Whatever she was really doing here, he could not afford to have her identity exposed.

Gabrielle's knees weakened under her father's furious regard. With as much dignity as she could summon, she sat down on the side of the bed. "This healing time, in these poor women's lives is very precious, gentlemen. If you insist on staying, then you are welcome to pull up a chair and listen." She gave them an accusing stare. "In fact, I think it might do you a world of good to hear a few words on the subjects of purity and decency." Turning back to the women, she lowered the book, opened it, and glanced for the first time at one of the pages. Blushing scarlet at the picture that greeted her, she looked up with widened eyes. The professionals simply smiled.

"A-as the writer of Ecclesiastes says . . ." She improvised desperately, hoping it would sound convincing, employing some of the rescue talk old William had given her. "What good is it to toil upon the earth? What does it avail? What good are riches, or fame, or beauty, or even pleasure . . . if you have no purpose, if you wander lost in a wilderness, estranged from all that is good and honest and decent?" She looked up from the book with the colored image of two bodies lasciviously entwined burned into her vision. Her throat tightened so that she had to force out the words. "You need not be a slave to men's desires. You can make your lives pure again . . . make your bodies once more into the vessels of the eternal that they were meant to be. You can choose. You can reclaim your dignity, virtue, and personhood . . ."

"He's not here, Tottenham," the duke said, turning on the colonel.

"What sort of ridiculous game is this?" the earl demanded in high dudgeon.

"He must have finished early . . . or been warned that we were coming," Tottenham protested, feeling thwarted and foolish. When the others turned on their heels and stalked from the room, he could only shake a finger at Gabrielle demanding, "Don't you move, young woman—you've a great deal to answer for!" Then he hurried after his witnesses, apologizing profusely and framing excuses for his faulty intelligence, all the way to the street.

For a moment they sat in tense silence, listening to the voices fading in the hall. Then a thump under the bed set them scurrying to lift the bedclothes and help Pierce and the prime minister out into the air and light. The effects of the drug were quickly wearing off, and Gladstone was regaining consciousness, if not mobility.

"Where am I?" He blinked, trying to focus his vision.

"You're safe, Mr. Gladstone," Gabrielle said, putting her arm through his and motioning Pierce to help him as well. "And we're going to get you out of here."

With the help of the four professionals, who stood watch and secreted them down the back stairs, they managed to get Gladstone out the door and down the alley to their waiting carriage. But when they arrived at the coach, a form stepped out of the shadows, and they found themselves facing an irate duke of Carlisle.

The sight of them, bearing the sagging prime minister of Britain between them, was the duke's second nasty shock of the evening. Upon leaving the bordello, he had used his indignation with Tottenham to insist upon taking a cab home by himself. Then he quickly retraced his path to the brothel, located the rear entrance to the place, and spotted a carriage waiting a short distance away in the alley. The coach bore a crest, which he guessed would prove to be Sandbourne's, so he stationed himself in the shadows to confront his wayward daughter. Now he discovered his scandal-prone offspring in league with her scapegrace husband, spiriting the head of the British government away from an orgy in a brothel!

"What the hell is this?" he demanded when he could use his tongue again.

"Don't just stand there," Pierce ordered, "open the door and help us get him inside."

Taken aback by their disregard for his righteous ire, the duke hesitated a moment. Then, sensing the urgency of getting Gladstone out of sight, he did as Pierce commanded. When he had helped hoist Gladstone into the carriage, he boldly climbed in after them, glaring at them in the dim light as the carriage began to move.

"We did it!" Gabrielle said, sagging with relief and smiling at Pierce.

"What's happened to me?" the old man buried his face in his hands and rubbed his eyes. "My head hurts . . . and I cannot seem to s-stand on my own . . ."

"You've just been rescued from the queen's bed, Mr. Gladstone," Gabrielle said, tidying his crumpled collar and disheveled coat and giving Pierce a saucy look. "By a woman you once rescued, a gentleman you once ruined . . . and four rather expensive ladies of the evening."

The prime minister was understandably confused. The duke was understandably bewildered and outraged. And as they proceeded to 10 Downing Street, the story of how they came to learn of Gladstone's plight came tumbling out. Certain elements—Pierce made certain they remained anonymous, since he had no ironclad proof of their connection to Disraeli—had set out to catch Gladstone in a sexual indiscretion with the prostitutes he was wont to try to "rescue." Failing that, they had decided to entrap him instead—drug him and install him in a bed in a brothel, where he would be "discovered" by unimpeachable witnesses. Pierce had learned of the plot and told Gabrielle. Together they decided to rescue the prime minister.

When Gladstone had been safely delivered into his wife's hands—via the back door and the kitchen Gabrielle remembered so vividly—they climbed back into their carriage and sat in deepening silence, enduring the duke's censuring stare.

"Mr. Gladstone is not a debauchee. You know how he watched over me. He really does try to rescue the women he talks to on the streets," Gabrielle explained. "It was nothing short of criminal that they tried to make a man of his stature and accomplishments into a figure of public ridicule. We simply couldn't allow that to happen."

"All right—I'll grant that something had to be done," the duke said grudgingly. "But whatever possessed you, Sandbourne, to take your wife on such a dangerous venture?"

"Take her?" Pierce looked at Gabrielle, glowing in the light of the streetlamps they passed, and laughed. "I couldn't stop her." Feeling her hand stealing into his on the seat, beneath her skirts, he squeezed it and grinned at her.

When they delivered the duke to his house, he paused in the carriage door and gave his unconventional daughter one last disapproving look. "Take a word of advice, Sandbourne. If you have any sense at all, you'll take that wife of yours in hand and keep a firm grip on her at all times. If you don't—mark my words—you'll live to regret it."

As they headed home in the darkened carriage, Pierce pulled Gabrielle into his arms and she curled contentedly against his chest.

"He's right, you know," she said softly.

"Your father?" He set her back enough to look at her. She had that mischievous look.

"If you have any sense, you *will* take me in hand." She seized his hand and slid it to her breast. "Frequently."

He chuckled. "What am I going to do with you?"

"I have a few suggestions," she said, rubbing her cheek against his shirt front. "One of which I saw in a book tonight—I had no idea they put such things in books. And another I've had in mind for some time."

"Plotting again?"

"I have never *plotted*," she objected. "Well, not very much. What I have in mind is more in the way of a *proposition*."

"Another one?" He groaned. "The last one you made me resulted in my being imprisoned in your boudoir and forced to romance you and seduce you . . . then to marry you. I was forced out of my bed, my house, and very nearly out of my mind—not to mention nearly being drummed out of society and the Conservative party . . ."

"Well, the worst that could happen to you in this one is that you would become a father." She gave him a glowing smile. "You've made me a mistress, a wife, and a friend. I'd like to propose that in the next year or so, you do your best to make me a mother."

He pulled her hard against him and kissed her until she was dizzy.

"I accept."

Epilogue

Late April, 1886

Sandbourne House was awash in lights and merriment that cool spring evening. A gala party was underway, celebrating Pierce's appointment to the cabinet in the newly formed Liberal Government, headed by none other than William Gladstone. For the better part of the last year the Conservatives had held office, but their government had finally collapsed in disarray. Now, for an unprecedented third time, the Grand Old Man had been asked to form a government, and he was quick to select a rising young Liberal, the earl of Sandbourne, for the cabinet.

Gabrielle stood midway on the stairs, dressed in a champagne white silk gown with a teal satin bodice decorated with elaborate white cutwork embroidery that distracted the eye from the fact that her middle was starting to expand again. Gazing out over the festive crowd, she felt a glow of warmth at the sight of the friends and acquaintances she and Pierce had made over the last three years enjoying their hospitality. Through the drawing room doors she could see Pierce greeting friends and accepting congratulations on his appointment, and she smiled and set a course for him.

But as she reached the bottom of the stairs, Parnell announced the duke of Carlisle, and she looked up to find her father bearing down on her with a frazzled expression. He grazed her cheek with a kiss, then swung an agitated gaze about the center hall. "Where is she?"

There was no need to ask who was meant.

"Mother arrived some time ago," Gabrielle said, looking around for her mother. "Come, I'll help you find her. It will soon be time to put William to bed."

Slipping her arm through his, she accompanied him through the throng of guests, searching each room until at last, they heard Rosalind's throaty laugh coming from the half-opened library door . . . carried on a pungent curl of smoke.

"I might have known," the duke growled, pushing open the door to discover Rosalind ensconced on Pierce's mahogany desk in a circle of gentlemen. She was gowned in her now customary navy silk dress with an elegant lace collar and her hair was done in the simple style she wore every day in her work at the Magdalen Society Home. And she was smoking a small black cigar.

"Why, there he is now," Rosalind said with an indecently flirtatious smile. "Augustus, darling, we were just talking about you. I'm afraid I can't recall the length of that horrid crocodile you killed on the Congo River."

"If so, it will be the only damned thing you've forgotten in the last twenty years," the duke said gruffly.

The laughter that greeted his remark was a recognition of his predicament as the central figure in a sizzling roman à clef penned by Rosalind . . . a thinly disguised and highly publicized account of her twenty years as a woman of pleasure. In the first two years after her abrupt retirement from the demimonde, Rosalind had taken Beatrice's advice and thrown both herself and her considerable financial resources into all manner of public and charitable causes. She possessed a perfect genius for parting men from their money—a skill she had perfected at the expense of the duke—and organizations that served the charitable trust were quick to embrace her fund-raising skills and provide her with almost instant acceptance. Then in the last year, feeling ever more stifled by her mounting respectability, she produced a flaming novel that had sent ripples of shock through London's elite and chagrin through the duke of Carlisle.

"I would have a word with you, Rosalind," he declared, looking very much like a man with something urgent on his mind. "Now . . . if you please."

He had to wait for her to put out her cigar and watch as the gentlemen around her vied for the privilege of lifting her down from her perch on Pierce's desk. But in a short while, he was escorting her up the main stairs toward the nursery.

Gabrielle sighed as she stood at the bottom of the main stairs, watching them go, then she headed for the drawing room, where she found Pierce engaged in conversation with Lord Rosebery and Lady Devonshire. Putting an arm through Pierce's, she pried him gently from their company and urged him toward the stairs.

"I believe you promised to say good night to your son."

"So I did." He smiled down at her, warmed by the sight of her jewel-bright eyes and sumptuously displayed charms.

"Father arrived a few minutes ago," she said.

"I thought I heard a crack of thunder." He chuckled. "Poor man, your mother has been driving him mad." The duke's heated pursuit of Gabrielle's mother, after an affair of more than twenty years' duration, never failed to amuse Pierce. But it also tantalized him. The three years of his marriage to Gabrielle hadn't dimmed her attraction for him in the least, and he couldn't help but wonder if his passion for her would be as fervent as the duke's for Rosalind after two decades of loving. "I hope she says 'yes' and puts him out of his misery."

"Yes?" Gabrielle gave him a puzzled look. "To what?"

"He has asked her to marry him." When she halted on the stairs, looking stunned, he urged her to continue up the steps. "He spoke to me last week . . . said he was about to propose and asked what I thought."

"My parents . . . married?" She stopped again.

"Impetuous and impossible of him, I know." His smile filled with mischief. "But being the impetuous and impossible sort myself, I couldn't think of a single good reason to object to my father-in-law marrying my mother-in-law . . . titles be hanged. In keeping with family loyalties, I promised to lend him my support if he runs afoul of the gossipmongers of St. James."

"My parents . . . married," she said with wonderment, thinking for a moment of her own wedding three years before, of the strange courtship that preceded it and the determined seduction that followed it—of rosebushes and shoes and harem pants and orphans playing football . . . She came back to the present with a smile. "I must have a talk with her, straightaway . . . give her a few bits of advice on being a wife . . . on handling a husband."

He groaned, leading her on up the steps. "If you do, then it's only fair that I give the duke a few bits of advice about marriage with a LeCoeur female. LeCoeur women make perfect mistresses, but as wives—"

"Yes?" She raised one eyebrow.

"They far surpass perfection," he murmured smoothly.

"First-rate diplomacy, your lordship." She squeezed his arm and glowed with pleasure. "It is no wonder the prime minister insisted on having you for the Foreign Office."

The nursery was awash in soft evening light and in the giggles of a dark-haired toddler being swung aloft by the ruddy-faced duke, while Rosalind, Lady Beatrice, and the child's nurse looked on anxiously. The women turned to Gabrielle instantly.

"Talk to the man . . . He's impossible!" Rosalind insisted, pointing at the duke.

"He's getting the child all wrought up," Beatrice declared with crossed arms and a knitted brow. "It will take hours to get him to sleep after such excitement."

"Don't be old sourpusses," the duke declared, lowering the boy and then giving him up to Gabrielle when she reached for him. "A boy has to have a bit of fun now and again. Right, Wills?" His buoyant mood was a fair hint of Rosalind's answer to his proposal.

"Are we to understand that you said yes to the duke," Gabrielle said to her mother as she cuddled her apple-cheeked son.

When Rosalind looked to the duke with her heart in her eyes and nodded, Beatrice realized what had transpired and gasped. After a moment, she settled into a beaming smile. "Well, it's about time the pair of you came to your senses!"

There were hugs and congratulations all around. Then at the nurse's discreet reminder, they passed little William around for good-night hugs. When Rosalind took too long with her turn, Beatrice complained, "Come, come, Rosalind. Don't be greedy," and reached for the boy.

"Greedy? Who is being greedy?" Rosalind said, turning so that Beatrice couldn't reach him. "You have him every night."

Gabrielle looked to Pierce and nodded. He cleared his throat for attention.

"No need to argue," he announced. "In another six months, there will be two grandchildren—one for each of you to spoil."

They looked to Gabrielle, who colored with pleasure, and Rosalind abruptly surrendered little William to Beatrice so she could hug her daughter instead.

"Another grandchild. How wonderful!" she crooned, glowing with excitement. "I know just what we'll call him: *Lochinvar.*"

"Lochinvar?" Beatrice was scandalized. "We'll do no such thing. He'll be called *Horace* . . . after my great uncle, who acquired the family fortune." Rosalind drew herself up with a daunting look of hauteur.

"Horace is a perfect name—*for a mule.* Gabrielle's child is born of a great love, a burning passion. He deserves a noble, glorious, romantic name—like Lochinvar."

"He deserves a dignified and stately name, not something taken straight from a theater playbill," Beatrice insisted. "Horace."

"Lochinvar!"

"Horace!"

The grandmothers were nose to nose as Pierce and

Gabrielle slipped out and closed the door behind them. She paused, looking up at Pierce, her eyes sparkling.

"What *will* we call the baby?"

Pierce pulled her into his arms, feeling a pulse of pure joy flooding his heart.

"Why don't you give it some thought." He gave a wicked laugh. "And then make me a proposition."

Author's Note

I hope you enjoyed *The Perfect Mistress*. Though Gabrielle and Pierce and the details of their romance are very much fiction, rest assured that the attitudes, events, and intrigues portrayed here are indeed based in historical fact.

In Victorian thinking, sexual relations between husband and wife, even those required to produce desired children, were considered morally suspect. But the urges for passion and romance remained, and for the upper class, a hidden world devoted to pleasure and passion—the *demi-monde*—became the accepted outlet for the urges of men. (It was the belief of the day that women were not troubled by such urges!) Children, property, and respectability were the province of the wife and marriage, while sex, romance, and love were the sphere of the mistress and liaison. The public line between the two was discreetly and irrevocably drawn.

A wide range of liaisons existed in the demimonde: from brief encounters to long-term partnerships resembling marriages, from impersonal sexual transactions to passionate and enduring relationships. The women of the demiworld, generally termed "courtesans" on the continent and "mistresses" in Britain, were adept at allurement and persuasion and sometimes wielded great influence through the men they loved. But they also endured tense vigils between their lovers' visits. And they were forced to do whatever was necessary to keep their attractions fresh and their lovers interested . . . even if that meant sacrificing other ties and relationships.

As sexuality became increasingly repressed, Victorian society came to focus more and more on the illicit expression of sexuality in the culture and on the women who had been marginalized enough to have to resort to it as a means of support. Debate over prostitution became astonishingly public and graphic—affording a repressed society the titillation of reading about and discussing sex at length, couched in the context of deploring the "great social ill" of prostitution. (The safe sex of the 1880s was to talk of prostitution!) People high and low became involved in the discussion and called on the leaders of society and the government to do something about it. Some leaders, like Prime Minister William Gladstone, took the plight of the "fallen woman" so seriously that they personally engaged in rescue work among them.

Shocking as it may sound to us, for most of his adult life—more than forty years—William Gladstone did indeed walk the streets of London and visit brothels and introducing houses, attempting to "rescue" women engaged in prostitution. A true product of his era, Gladstone was a complicated, sexually repressed, and frequently troubled man. From all accounts of his behavior, he seemed to genuinely care about the moral and spiritual redemption of the prostitutes he engaged in conversation. But he also acknowledged in his private writings that his higher motives were tainted by the vicarious sexual thrill he received from his encounters with them. Just as surprising was the extreme patience with which his good wife, Catherine, bore his peculiar avocation. On numerous occasions, he brought young prostitutes home to her to bathe and feed and lodge under their roof. Only as he aged did she seriously object to his "night walks" and then primarily out of concern for his physical health.

Gladstone's fascination with prostitutes was a public secret that more than once teetered on the edge of becoming a public scandal. In the early 1880s a group of Conservative politicians, led by a Conservative MP named Colonel Tottenham, did indeed set spies on Gladstone, hoping to glean evidence of his having committed sexual indiscretions with prostitutes. To their grave disappointment, they were unable to produce conclusive proof of anything more than poor judgment on the prime minister's part.

Thus . . . Gabrielle's and Pierce's story could have really happened! Driven into the street by an argument with her mother, a courtesan's daughter truly might have been picked up by the prime minister, then intercepted afterward by one of Tottenham's spies, a nobleman with a well-developed sense of the absurd and a weakness for the smell of biscuits . . .

I'd like to think that *The Perfect Mistress* may make readers stop to think about our human tendency to judge people and events by their appearance, about the roles society assigns us as men and women, and about the possibilities that could exist if men and women were to become friends as well as marriage partners and lovers.

About the Author

BETINA KRAHN lives in Minnesota, with her physicist husband, her two sons, and a feisty salt-and-pepper schnauzer. With a degree in biology and a graduate degree in counseling, she has worked in teaching, personnel management, and mental health. She had a mercifully brief stint as a boys' soccer coach, makes terrific lasagna, routinely kills houseplants, and is incurably optimistic about the human race. She believes the world needs a bit more truth, a lot more justice, and a whole lot more love and laughter. And she attributes her outlook to having married an unflinching optimist and to two great-grandmothers actually named "Polyanna."

WIN A TRIP TO VERONA, ITALY
and many other great prizes

and
The Perfect Mistress
SWEEPSTAKES

ONE GRAND PRIZE: A trip for two to Verona, Italy, includes round-trip airfare via **Lufthansa**, one-week accommodations and an autographed copy of both Leonard Slatkin's new album, ***Romeo & Juliet***, and Betina Krahn's new romance novel, ***The Perfect Mistress***.

One First Prize: A **Kenwood** CD home stereo unit with a collection of five different recordings of ***Romeo and Juliet*** conducted by such great maestros as Toscanini, Koussevitzky and Slatkin.

Five Second Prizes: An autographed copy of both Leonard Slatkin's new recording, ***Romeo & Juliet***, and Betina Krahn's new romance novel, ***The Perfect Mistress***.

500 Third Prizes: A ***Romeo & Juliet*** CD or a copy of Betina Krahn's ***The Perfect Mistress***.

Prizes provided by:

VERONA, ITALY...A MYTHICAL DESTINATION

Leonard Slatkin's new recording of **Romeo & Juliet** and Betina Krahn's latest romance novel, **The Perfect Mistress**, take you to Verona, Italy. Enter the sweepstakes and you may have the opportunity to visit and experience the beautiful Italian town in which the Shakespeare play *Romeo and Juliet* takes place.

ROMEO & JULIET... THE MUSIC

Following the unprecedented international success of the magical *Carmina Burana*, Leonard Slatkin and the Saint Louis Symphony Orchestra bring us an extraordinary interpretation of one of Tchaikovsky's greatest scores, **Romeo and Juliet.**

Based on Shakespeare's legendary play, the Tchaikovsky score depicts, with the most exquisite musical language, the passion and drama of the most beloved story of all times, that of Romeo and Juliet. This stunning new recording is available on CD and cassette at your favorite record store.

MAIL TO: R&J/Perfect Mistress Sweepstakes
c/o RCA Victor Red Seal
1540 Broadway - 40th Floor
New York, NY 10036-4098

Name _____

Address _____

City/State/Zip _____

Phone(day) _____**Phone(night)** _____

See next page for official rules.

Romeo & Juliet and The Perfect Mistress Sweepstakes

No Purchase Necessary

OFFICIAL RULES

1) **To Enter:** Complete the official entry form (also available at participating retailers while supplies last). Or you may enter by hand printing on a 3"x5" postcard your name, address (including zip code), daytime and evening phone numbers and the words "Romeo & Juliet/Perfect Mistress." Mail entries to: R&J Sweepstakes, c/o BMG Classics, RCA Victor Red Seal, 1540 Broadway, 40th Floor, New York, NY 10036-4098. Entries must be received by December 1, 1995. Limit one entry per person. No mechanically reproduced or illegible entries accepted. Not responsible for lost, misdirected, mutilated entries or entries not received by the deadline date.

2) **Random Drawing:** Winners will be determined in a random drawing on or about December 4, 1995, from among all eligible entries received. Odds of winning depend on the number of eligible entries received. Potential winners of the Grand and First Prizes will be notified by mail on or about December 30, 1995, and will be asked to execute and return an Affidavit of Eligibility/Release of Eligibility/Prize Acceptance Form within fourteen (14) days of attempted notification. Noncompliance within this time may result in disqualification and the selection of an alternate winner. Return of any prize/prize notification as undeliverable will result in disqualification and an alternate winner will be selected. Travel companions will also be required to execute a liability release.

3) **Prizes and Approximate Retail Values:** Grand Prize winner will receive a trip for two (2) to Verona, Italy. Trip consists of round-trip economy class air transportation on **Lufthansa** from **Lufthansa** gateway city closest to winner's home to Verona, Italy, six nights, double-occupancy hotel accommodation, an autographed copy of Leonard Slatkin's recording of Romeo & Juliet, and Betina Krahn's novel, "The Perfect Mistress" ($3,640.00). One (1) First Prize winner will receive a **Kenwood** CD stereo unit and a collection of five (5) different recordings of Tchaikovsky's Romeo & Juliet ($658.00). Five (5) Second Prize winners will receive an autographed copy of Leonard Slatkin's recording of Romeo & Juliet and Betina Krahn's "The Perfect Mistress" ($21.98 each). Five Hundred (500) Third Prizes of a Romeo & Juliet CD with Leonard Slatkin conducting the Saint Louis Symphony Orchestra ($15.99) or a copy of Betina Krahn's new romance novel "The Perfect Mistress" ($5.99USA/$7.99C each). Any additional cost and expenses incurred and not specifically included in Grand Prize, including transportation to **Lufthansa** gateway city, meals, transfers, taxes, gratuities and incidental expenses, are the sole responsibility of winner. Travel must be taken on dates specified by sponsor and is subject to availability. Other restrictions may apply.

4) **Eligibility:** Open to U.S. and Canadian residents (excluding residents of the province of Quebec) who are 18 at the time of entry. Employees of BMG Music, Bertelsmann Inc. and Bantam Doubleday Dell Publishing Group Inc., their parent, affiliates, subsidiaries, directors, officers and agents, and their immediate families or those living in the same household, are ineligible to enter. Potential Canadian winners will be required to correctly answer a time-limited arithmetic skill question by mail. Void where prohibited by law. Sweepstakes subject to federal, state and local laws.

5) **General Conditions:** Winners are responsible for all federal, state and local taxes. No substitution or cash redemption of prizes permitted by winners. Prizes are not transferable. Sponsor reserves the right to substitute prize of equal or greater value if prize is unavailable. Acceptance of prizes constitutes permission to use winners' names, photographs and likenesses, for purposes of advertising and promotion without additional compensation, unless prohibited by law. Travel companion must be over the age of 18 on date prize is awarded.

6) All entries become the property of sponsor and will not be returned. Winners agree that the sponsor, its subsidiaries, affiliates, agents and promotion agencies shall not be liable for injuries or losses of any kind resulting from the acceptance or use of prize. By participating in this sweepstakes, entrants agree to be bound by these official rules and the decision of the judges, which are final in all respects.

7) For the name of major prize winners available after January 1, 1996, send a stamped, self-addressed envelope to: Romeo & Juliet/Perfect Mistress Sweepstakes WinBMG Classics, RCA Victor Red Seal, 1540 Broadway, 40th Floor, New York, NY 10036-4098.

If you loved

THE PERFECT MISTRESS

*Look for Betina Krahn's next
enchanting historical romance*

THE ANGEL AND
THE CYNIC

*to be published by Bantam
in the spring of 1996*

DON'T MISS THESE FABULOUS
BANTAM WOMEN'S FICTION TITLES